DANGER AND DOMINANCE

BLACK FOX SECURITY DOMS
BOOK 1

GOLDEN ANGEL

For all the Gingers

1

———

DAVID

Looking at the report in front of him, David couldn't help but frown. He didn't want to complain about the assignment his boss, Lincoln Black, the owner of Black Fox Security, was giving him and his team, but...

"This is outside our usual wheelhouse," he said finally, putting down the file on Cassidy Simone. She was a pretty woman with long dark brown hair, hazel eyes, and very girl-next-door features in the picture that came with the file. She was smiling in the picture, eyes bright and sparkling with joy, bow-shaped lips spread wide to show off her grin.

"It is," Lincoln agreed amiably from where he was seated behind his desk, watching David's reaction. About fifteen years older than David, Lincoln's salt and pepper hair was mostly salt, and he'd lost some of the muscle tone he'd once had from sitting behind the desk. He was still fit, though, and kept his skills sharp.

Black Fox Security provided a variety of services, from short-term contracts for visiting, high-profile clients, to advising large corporations on their security, to training, and sometimes taking on government contracts that made use of the team's special forces backgrounds... but this was the first time that they would be protecting a woman from her ex-boyfriend.

Lincoln didn't even usually take these cases when the people involved were celebrities, though he was always happy to give recommendations to fulfill their needs.

"Why are you making an exception for her?" David asked when Lincoln didn't seem inclined to elaborate further. David didn't usually question him. Lincoln had been his commander in the field and had literally held David's life in his hands. He'd been a damn good commander, too, which was why David and his entire team had been happy to come work for him after being discharged.

"Because Drew and Naomi asked me to." Lincoln raised his eyebrow when David just stared at him. Drew was another member of his team and Naomi was his wife, who worked for a non-profit that helped abused women.

"Why isn't Naomi helping her?" They all supported Naomi's work in various ways and had even provided protection for the shelter in the past when it had been warranted, but they'd never done one-on-one work like this before. Especially since there was no saying when it would end.

"There isn't room for her at the shelter while they're undergoing renovations. If this is still a problem when they're done, Cassidy can move there. In the meantime, Drew asked me for help." Lincoln studied him. "Is there a problem?"

"No." David managed to keep himself from shifting in his seat as Lincoln gave him a hard stare. Sometimes, his dark eyes took in a lot more than David would like. "I'm just confused as to why we're putting resources toward this, which is not our specialty, when we're already short-staffed."

He hated to bring that up, but it had to be said.

Black Fox Security was currently run by Lincoln and Harris Black, two brothers who had started the company with Lincoln's best friend, Marshall Devlin. Each partner had their own team they were in charge of. Unfortunately, last year, they'd discovered that Marshall was stealing money from the firm as well as sleeping with Lincoln's wife. They'd managed to cut him out of the firm, and Lincoln was now divorced, but Marshall's entire team had left with him.

There were still contracts to be upheld that had been put in place when they had three teams, and they were all still scrambling to play catch up.

"That's why she's going to live with Jensen for the time being. He has an extra room, top-of-the-line security, plus his brother lives there, so an extra guard of sorts." Lincoln was still studying him in a manner that was making David increasingly uncomfortable. "She's coming from Stronghold, that club Drew's cousin owns, and he feels personally responsible for ensuring she's protected."

David grunted. He'd seen that in the file as well. Cassidy and her ex, Don Reeve, had been members at the kink club in Washington, D.C., before Don ignored her safe word in the middle of a scene at the club, and he'd been immediately kicked out. Which was when it was discovered that his and Cassidy's relationship was abusive, and the club had come together to keep her safe over the past year.

Unfortunately, Don hadn't forgotten about his ex, and he'd started stalking her, showing signs of escalation. Recently, several club members had seen him near both Stronghold and Marquis, Stronghold's sister club, and the manager of Marquis' tires had been slashed. The general consensus was that Cassidy was in danger.

David didn't disagree with the general consensus; he just wasn't sure why they had her running to a different state to be hidden by an elite security firm rather than just facing the douchebag and putting him in jail. Then Cassidy would be safe, and so would any other woman who might make the mistake of dating the asshole.

Douchebag's picture was also in the file. David wasn't exactly the right person to ask about another man's attractiveness, but he had a younger sister, so he had some idea of what women looked for. The guy was blond, with dark eyes and a fairly muscular body. He looked like an All-American boy. He was probably pretty good at faking it at first, too.

The desire to find the asshole and pound him into the ground until he promised to leave Cassidy alone was strong enough to have David flexing his fingers, but he also had to think about his team. They were already working overtime, keeping up with all the contracts. Adding something else to their plates could end up being dangerous.

They needed rest. They needed sleep.

If they didn't get those things, reflexes were affected. Attention was affected. Someone could get hurt.

There were places better able to deal with Cassidy's situation than they were—Naomi's shelter being one of them.

But he also knew that Drew would do what his cousin asked of him. Unlike David, Drew was close to his family. A family member had asked him for help with Cassidy, and for some reason, they'd come to Lincoln instead of the shelter.

He still didn't know why Lincoln had agreed, though.

"Why didn't they go to the police? Get the asshole up on charges?"

"I don't know. You'll have to ask her." Lincoln seemed bemused. "I do know that they're hoping she won't need to be here for too long. Her ex is escalating, and they're hoping with her out of the picture, he'll either forget about her or he'll do something that allows them to bring charges against him without involving Cassidy."

That made David throw his hands in the air as he jumped to his feet and started pacing, trying to shake off some of the angry energy that was building up in his body. Losing his temper on a woman who had been abused was the last thing he wanted, but the whole situation was pissing him off.

"He was abusing her. Why didn't she file a report when they rescued her?" Instead, they'd used his assault on another club member to threaten him, telling him to stay away from Cassidy. But once the statute of limitations on filing charges was up, he'd come right back like a bad penny. "What happens if, instead of escalating when he can't find her, he just gets some other girlfriend who doesn't realize what she's getting into?"

Lincoln shot him a sympathetic look from where he was still sitting.

"This isn't the same situation as Tasha, David," he said gently.

Of course, he would remember.

"Not yet, but it could be." He could still remember the sight of his ex in the hospital bed, face battered blue and purple, lip split, bandages over the stitches in her stomach where she'd been stabbed. He'd been her ex, but she hadn't changed her emergency contact number. David rubbed his hands on his pants, trying to rub away the sweat that always immediately sprung to his palms at the memory. They'd broken up, but he'd still cared about her. He'd still gone running when he'd gotten the call from the hospital, then he'd been there for her through her recovery and the trial.

It was five years ago, and he could still remember every second of how helpless he'd felt. How enraged he'd felt. Especially when the bastard's ex-girlfriends had lined up to testify at the trial. Tasha's lawyer had found them and convinced them to testify, to show a pattern of abuse, and they had.

Not one of them had filed a report. If they had, Tasha never would have dated the man. She always ran her dates, doing her best to stay safe. She almost hadn't dated David because, as special forces, there had been a lot about his past that she couldn't look up.

She'd tried so hard.

The bastard was behind bars now, while Tasha had moved to California and was happily married with one kid and another on the way. He should have been past this reaction, but he wasn't. Abuse cases always made him edgy, which was why he normally stayed away from Naomi's shelter.

Tilting his head back and forth, he cracked his neck, then rolled his shoulders, pushing some of the tension from them. Lincoln was looking at him with sympathy.

"Are you going to be okay?" Lincoln asked. "I can have someone else run lead on this. Mason, perhaps." Their resident psychologist and profiler.

Temptation to hand it off to someone else beckoned for just a moment, but he knew his duty. Temptation passed, and David shook his head.

"I'm team captain. It's my responsibility." He made it a point never to ask his team to do something he wouldn't.

Lincoln nodded slowly. He might have said something more, but the phone on his desk rang. His gaze flicked to the phone, to the caller ID, and he leaned over to pick it up.

"Yes, Jennifer." He paused. "Okay, thank you. We'll be right there." He looked at David as he hung up the phone.

It was time to go meet their newest client.

———

CASSIDY

The drive up to Pittsburgh had been odd. Scary in its way because she was going into the unknown. New city, new people, new club... she'd made some friends while she was in Maryland, once she no longer had Don controlling her every move. She'd felt comfortable and safe at Stronghold, but she'd never felt safe when she was at home, school, or work because she knew Don was still out there.

Over the past few months, she'd felt less and less safe until she'd finally agreed that getting out of town was the best move. She didn't want to leave, but it wasn't just her own life at stake. Don had been messing with the people who had saved her. If he was going to hurt someone, she'd rather it be her than any of them.

Although she didn't want to be hurt, either.

Why can't he just leave me alone?

That was the thought running through her head over and over again, then she'd feel awful because if he was leaving her alone, that might mean he had moved on to someone else. That he might be hurting another woman.

She wished he would just get hit by a bus.

Sometimes, when she was thinking about what she would do if he ever showed up in front of her again, she pictured killing him. He would come at her, and she would stab him, right through the heart, over and over again. Running him over with a car. Getting a lucky shot in and breaking his nose, hitting him in the exact right way to send bone splinters into his brain—though she wasn't actually sure if that was a real thing or not, she'd read about it once. Or shooting him. She'd been taking shooting lessons. She didn't have a carry permit, which was why she only ever pictured that happening if he broke into her house.

Self-defense.

Maybe she'd end up in jail, maybe she wouldn't.

But she'd be safe because he would be gone.

Mistress Julie, who was also her therapist, had told her it was perfectly normal to fantasize about situations that would make her feel safe again. Though she hadn't told Mistress Julie exactly how often she had that particular fantasy. Constantly. Daily. Every time she stepped into a new space, she would end up with a new one—how he might appear, how he might attack her, how she would defend herself.

How she might be proactive.

She couldn't help it. Her brain just did it. Every time.

But coming to Pennsylvania, sneaking away so he didn't know where she was, maybe her brain would finally stop.

Maybe she'd finally be able to sleep.

"What do you think?" Kincaid—her current bodyguard, Dom from the club she went to, and friend—asked as they crossed over a huge bridge. Tall, dark-haired, and handsome, the former police detective was a big, broad-shouldered guy whose self-assurance made it easy to feel like he had everything under control. His very presence was calming.

Cassidy took in her first view of the city. Things were lower than she'd expected. Not a ton of skyscrapers. She'd been thinking it would be more like New York City, but it wasn't like D.C. either. The huge river through the center of the buildings, the hills and dips, and the darker colors of the buildings made it nothing like the place where she'd been living the past few years.

"It's pretty." Which was true enough.

"It is."

Kincaid let them lapse into silence again, driving through the streets as Cassidy studied her new home. The streets were narrower than she expected. More like Georgetown than downtown D.C. Lots of brick. There were some tall buildings, casting long shadows over the streets, but there were a lot that were only a few stories high as well.

A sense of calm settled over her. Everything was so unfamiliar, so foreign, she couldn't imagine Don here as easily as she did back home. The idea of him jumping out of one of the alleys, of him being in the car behind them—or somehow devious enough to be in the car in front of them—seemed impossible.

She sighed in pure relief.

Pulling up in front of a fairly nondescript brick building, Kincaid turned the car into a parking lot. There was a security guard in a little booth next to the entry gate. Cassidy watched in bemusement as Kincaid signed them in, handing over his driver's license. The guard's eyebrows rose, and he glanced at her, but when he scanned Kincaid's ID, he nodded and handed it back.

The barrier arm rose, and Kincaid pulled into the parking lot. The entire interaction had been conducted in total silence.

"Was I supposed to give him my license, too?" she asked nervously.

"If you were anyone else, yes, but we're trying to keep your license completely off the radar, remember?" Kincaid pulled smoothly into one of the open spots. "They're going to get an ID made for you that will get you in and out of this building that no one will be able to track."

A little chill went up and down her spine. Cassidy hated to think that this was necessary. That Don might find some way of tracking her through her driver's license, her credit card, or her social security number. She was going as off-grid as they could get her, and it was a constant reminder of how unsafe she was.

"Right," she muttered.

Kincaid reached over, putting his hand atop hers when she went to undo her seatbelt. His dark eyes bore into hers, firm but kind.

"It's going to be okay, Cassidy. It's to keep you safe, but it won't be for forever."

God, she hoped he was right.

2

———————

Walking into the main office of Black Fox Security, Cassidy took a good look around. She'd never been inside a security firm before. There hadn't been a sign on the outside of the building, but there was one above the receptionist's head as they walked in.

The receptionist was a very pretty, very young Black woman. Not that Cassidy was that old at twenty-eight, but she was pretty sure she was a few years older than the young woman behind the desk, which surprised her. She'd been expecting someone older, maybe a little hardened in personality. *Check your assumptions at the door.*

They'd had to come up to the second floor of the building to where the offices were. Kincaid explained that the first floor was dedicated to various training facilities and a locker room. The top floor was storage.

Cassidy clung to the bag she had over her shoulder because she didn't know what else to do with her hands. If Kincaid didn't have a boyfriend, she might have tried to cling to him, but she didn't want to be that person.

"Hello," the young woman chirped, smiling broadly. Her navy-blue suit dress was professional-looking, conservatively cut but also flattering. She had very straight black hair that brushed against the shoulders of her jacket. "How can I help you?"

Wait, shouldn't she know?

"Kincaid Cavill," Kincaid said, looking at the younger woman with curiosity. Apparently, he hadn't met her before, either. Was that usual? "I'm bringing in Cassidy Simone to meet Lincoln."

The young woman brightened and hopped to her feet, leaning forward to reach across the desk. Kincaid immediately stepped forward to take her hand and shake it.

"Oh, hi! I'm Jennifer Johnson. I just started last week. It's nice to meet you."

"Nice to meet you, too. Does this mean Mrs. Dartmouth is officially retired?" Kincaid let go of the younger woman's hand and stepped back again, glancing at Cassidy.

"Not yet, just on vacation this week to see if I can handle things on my own." Jennifer grinned, obviously not at all worried about her ability to do so. "She'll be back next week for her final week. There's going to be a retirement party if you want to come."

"Maybe." Kincaid smiled, but his tone was completely noncommittal. "I just met her pretty recently myself, and it's a bit of a drive."

Around three hours, give or take some for traffic. They'd had it lucky, coming up on a Saturday afternoon when there wasn't some kind of event.

"Makes sense." Jennifer turned to Cassidy, still smiling but appearing apologetic. "Sorry, not trying to ignore you. I'll let Mr. Black know you're here. He's expecting you."

"Thank you," Cassidy said softly.

"Come on, let's sit down," Kincaid said, gesturing. There were four chairs and a large couch across from the desk where Jennifer was sitting, to the right of the doors she and Kincaid had come in through. The news was playing on the television on the wall beside them, but all they were showing was a video clip of a waterskiing squirrel.

Cassidy couldn't help but smile. It was nice knowing that there was so little going on in the world that they were taking the time to show something so silly. The squirrel looked like it was having fun.

She'd barely had time to sit down before two men came striding down the hall to the right of Jennifer's desk. Their footsteps weren't very loud, but even with the television on, Cassidy was so attuned to her surroundings, she heard the padding of their shoes against the carpet and immediately turned to look to see who was there.

Kincaid jumped to his feet as the two men reached them. Both of them were tall and very handsome. The older one was wearing a suit. He was much older, with a deep laugh and frown lines, salt and pepper hair, and an air of authority that would have a lot of the submissives at Stronghold staring at him with stars in their eyes. If he wasn't a Daddy, he was definitely a Zaddy.

The other man made her more nervous. He was almost as tall as Kincaid, almost as broad-shouldered, but somehow seemed to take up more space. A redhead with a shortly cropped ginger beard that covered his jawline, his hard blue eyes met hers with an electric sizzle that had her dropping her gaze immediately.

Good grief, what was wrong with her?

She hadn't felt an actual attraction to a man in months. She'd stopped being attracted to Don long before their relationship had ended, and even though she'd scened at the club, she hadn't been attracted to any of the men she'd scened with. All the scenes had been purely platonic.

Why now?

He wasn't even her type. He was too big. Too muscular.

Too threatening.

And she was hyperaware of him and the way he was studying her, even though she wasn't looking at him.

"Kincaid, good to see you," the older man said, smiling widely before he turned his attention to Cassidy. When she peeked at him, she could see soft encouragement in his expression. "And this must be Cassidy."

"Hi," she said quietly, still avoiding the redhead's gaze, though she did her best to meet Lincoln Black's. "I'm sorry about this."

She didn't know what else to say. She was sorry because she couldn't help but feel like a lot of people were having to shift their lives around just because of her. And unlike the people back in D.C., no one in Black Fox had even met her before. It seemed like a lot to ask of complete strangers.

"It's not your fault," Lincoln reassured her, patting her hand. "And we're going to keep you safe. This is David. He's my team captain." He turned to gesture to the redhead, dropping her hand as he did so. "He's going to help you get settled."

"We've found a place for you to stay with some housemates, so your name won't be on the lease," David said briskly.

He was staring at her. She could feel it. But she couldn't make herself look at him. His voice was deeper than she'd expected, gruffer.

"You'll have to find a job yourself, but Jennifer... you met Jennifer?" She nodded. "Okay, Jennifer has bookmarked a bunch of listings you might be interested in. The first three months of your rent have been paid for, so you have a bit of time before you have to look."

Wasn't she supposed to not be using her driver's license or social security number?

They must have some way around that. Kincaid had mentioned an ID...

She didn't ask because she didn't want to seem like she was questioning him. They were the professionals, after all. She was just the dumbass who got involved with the wrong guy, excused the red flags, and had to be rescued because of it.

So, she just nodded in response.

"Who is she going to be living with?" Kincaid asked, though there was a bit of an edge to his voice. She got the impression he was going to make sure he was satisfied with the arrangements before he left her there, which she appreciated.

"One of our team, the youngest, but he's solid, so don't worry about that," David replied. She wondered how old he was. Older than her, she was pretty sure, but she couldn't begin to try to figure out by how much. He had one of those ageless faces that meant he could be in his twenties or his forties or anywhere in between. "He has a housemate, and they had an empty room. The house has a solid security system, and Jensen knows that as long as she's there, he'll be spending every night there. If something comes up where he's unable to, another team member will take his place."

Cassidy wasn't sure how she felt about someone else always being around. She'd been scared of living alone the past year, but when Don had started harassing her again, someone was always with her, and that had been hard to deal with, too. She hated the idea that someone might get hurt because they were staying with her. It made her feel responsible, and all the darker daydreams she had—the ones where she didn't manage to fight off Don and she was killed or worse —all involved her friends also dying while trying to defend her. That was another reason she'd agreed to move.

She couldn't let her friends keep staying with her. She couldn't sleep while they were there, in the line of fire. When Kincaid was around, that had helped, because she trusted he knew how to defend himself.

Maybe the fact that it was security guys would help her relax.

"Good," Kincaid said. "If Don figures out where she is and follows her up here, you'll need to warn Jensen that he may become a target, too. Several members of our club had strange things happening to them, along with the escalation directed at Cassidy."

She could feel her shoulders bowing inward before Kincaid put his hand on the small of her back, and she deliberately straightened up. She didn't need another lecture about how this wasn't her fault. Of course, it was her fault. But everyone wanted to absolve her of the guilt she carried and for the burden she was placing on everyone, and she didn't like making them feel like they hadn't succeeded. Even though they hadn't.

Lincoln stepped forward.

"Okay, Cassidy, why don't I take you around to meet the rest of the team?" He offered his arm to her with a charming smile. She managed a small one back. "We'll let Kincaid and David talk through any further details, then Jensen will take you to the house to get settled in."

Taking his arm, Cassidy nodded. If she was disappointed that it wasn't going to be David showing her around, she definitely wasn't going to show it.

She felt oddly safe here. If Don somehow followed her in here, there was a wall of highly trained muscle between him and her. People who could take care of themselves.

She wondered if any of them were armed.

Part of her, the part that she was the most ashamed of, really hoped they were.

***

DAVID

Cassidy Simone didn't look anything like the smiling young woman in the picture. She looked like that woman's frightened, exhausted, anxious sister. Her smile was barely there, and it disappeared quickly. Even when it did make an appearance, there were bags under her eyes and shadows within them, and even her hair seemed duller. The light that had burned inside her hadn't just been dimmed; it had been snuffed out.

That made him want to simultaneously pull her into his arms and reassure her she was safe and that everything would be all right and also go hunt down her douchebag of an ex and make sure he never bothered her again. By whatever means necessary.

Keep him from hurting anyone else, too. From snuffing out another woman's light. Or even her life.

It didn't help that the moment their eyes met, he'd felt a spark of something other than anger. He was attracted to her. Immediately. Unexpectedly. Which was entirely unwelcome, given the circumstances. A complication on top of an already complicated situation was the very last fucking thing he needed.

Watching Lincoln escort Cassidy down the hall, he frowned. He was supposed to be giving her the tour. What further details was he supposed to go over with Kincaid?

"What the hell is your problem?" Kincaid asked as soon as Lincoln and Cassidy had turned down the hall, jerking David out of his reverie.

"Excuse me?" For a moment, he thought Kincaid might have caught him staring at Cassidy's ass, which was the least professional thing he could be fucking doing right now. He glared at Kincaid, trying to hide his inner flailing.

Fuck, he really hoped the other man hadn't noticed him staring at Cassidy's ass.

We do not get emotionally or physically involved with the clients.

"What. Is. Your. Problem." Kincaid repeated, enunciating each word and biting it off at the end. "Don't act like there isn't one. Even Lincoln noticed your shitty attitude. I bet you were supposed to give Cassidy the tour and take her to the house. Otherwise, there was no point in you being here to meet her."

Relief at realizing Kincaid had *not* noticed him staring at Cassidy's ass warred with his indignation. He was doing his damn job; that's why he was here, and if Kincaid was that concerned, then maybe he should be doing more about it himself instead of passing the buck to David.

"There was no point in me being here, anyway. First of all, what's the likelihood of her ex following her up here?" he asked. Especially with all the precautions they were taking to keep her hidden. "And secondly, if it was that high, why the hell didn't she report him to the police?"

"You know why. I put all of that in the report unless, of course, you didn't read the report."

"Of course, I read the report," David snapped, losing his temper. Tasha's face floated through his mind. She deserved to be safe, and so did Cassidy, yet a kink club thought they could handle abusers themselves instead of doing what they were *supposed to do.* "I read all about how your little club tried to handle everything themselves instead of filing a report, just so she could save some face and not have to admit that she was at a BDSM club when the incident happened. Did any of you think about what happens after that? What if he had left her alone and gone to do exactly the same thing to someone else, all because she didn't file an actual report, and he faced no real consequences?"

Kincaid's face was getting redder and redder, but David didn't care. It felt good to finally be able to vent to someone about this. He couldn't exactly do it to his own team or his boss. Kincaid was part of the firm now, but he wasn't on David's team, and he wasn't going to be working here in Pittsburgh. He was going to be in his own office, down in D.C., with his own team.

"And you think he would have faced real consequences if she'd filed a report?" Kincaid snapped back, which surprised David. "There's a fifty percent chance—hell, probably even more—that if she tried to file a report, the officer would hear BDSM club and immediately write her off. Or tell her that there's no point because, obviously, she invited that kind of treatment. If she got lucky and got someone who takes her seriously and takes the report, all those things will come up in court and worse. Any attorney would go through her entire sexual history to make her out to be some sort of slut, on record, then he'd walk away scot-free."

Well... fuck... if a former police detective was saying that... While he'd realized Kincaid was personally involved since Cassidy was a friend and part of his club, he'd expected Kincaid to agree with him a little more. Still, now that he'd taken up the point, David felt compelled to defend his position.

"But at least there would be a record for future women. That way, if they look him up, they'll know."

It could save another woman like Tasha.

"He's blackballed from every BDSM club in a four-state radius. Any submissive who tries to go to a club with him will immediately find out, and most of the people who choose to throw house parties rather than go to the clubs have some kind of connection to those in the know, so they've been warned, too. Not to mention, several of our submissives had taken it upon themselves to watch the dating apps and FetLife in case he pops up there."

The anger that had buoyed David was quickly leaking out. He knew the world didn't work the way it *should* work. The way it was supposed to work. The cops sure as hell weren't perfect. He knew that.

Kincaid kept going, kept lecturing.

"We can't protect everyone, but we did our best, and as a former police officer, I can tell you that we did far more than they would have. And we protected Cassidy, which is now your job, and if you'd rather throw her to the wolves, if you don't care what reporting and a trial would have put her through as a person, and you only care about some hypothetical future women—which, by the way, would have still had to look him up and then believe what they found—then I'll ask Lincoln to assign her to someone else.

"She already feels guilty as hell for what he's been putting her friends through, on top of her fear for herself. She doesn't need your self-righteous bullshit over a situation that you would never, ever find yourself in and therefore could never fully empathize with or know what you would do if it did happen to you."

Applause sounded from behind David, making him jump. He spun around to stare at Jennifer, who was now standing behind her desk, hands high in the air as she clapped. Her fierce gaze was focused on the redheaded team leader, whose shoulders sagged even further.

"You tell him, Kincaid."

"Oh, come on, Jennifer, what if you or one of your friends dated him or someone like him after?" David's tone turned almost whining as he pleaded with the younger woman to see his side. "I know you all research your dates like you're the FBI. You'd turn up the fact that he'd been taken to court, and you'd be forewarned." She had a lot in common with Tasha.

"We'd find it, but a lot of these guys are good at explaining things away. Oh, it was a vindictive ex. Oh, she was lying because she didn't truly understand kink. Oh, it was a false accusation. And people believe that shit." Jennifer put her hands on her hips, narrowing her eyes at him. "Not only that, but because I'm a woman, I have friends who have tried to get restraining orders. I've had friends who have been dismissed by the police for 'lack of evidence' or because it was his word against theirs.

"Have you ever had to stand by a woman's side while the cops rip apart her 'story' while she's still shaking from the trauma? No? Okay, then. You're so obsessed with what the 'right' thing to do is, sometimes you forget that what's right for one person might not be what *you* deem is right for society. And that's why you're wrong."

Shit, and now Jennifer was looking at him like he was a bad person. He didn't do well with verbal arguments. Fast decisions under pressure were his specialty, unless it was with words when he couldn't quite find his tongue. Especially because bringing up Tasha now would just look like an excuse. That is why he tried not to get into arguments.

"I'm not a bad person."

Good, David. Great argument. Stellar. You're knocking it out of the park, buddy.

Jennifer raised her eyebrow at him.

"I didn't say you're a bad person, but you are an uncompromising and often judgmental one who needs to work on their empathy. Especially when it comes to situations that you, as a white, straight man, will never understand because you will never have that lived experience."

David threw his hands in the air in defeat. It was easier than arguing, and he knew they were right. He wasn't really pissed at them; he was pissed because Cassidy *should* be able to go to the police and have them take her seriously. She *shouldn't* be judged because she was in a kink club when the assault happened.

It offended every single one of his sensibilities that women trying to get away from abusers had so much of the system working against them instead of for them. He didn't like it, but he also didn't have to live in it personally.

"You're right. No, I know. I see it sometimes, but I am always on the outside." He sighed, rubbing his forehead. "I'll try to be nicer to Cassidy."

"Glad to hear it," Kincaid said. "She deserves a break."

With that, Kincaid spun on his heel and stomped down the hall Lincoln and Cassidy had gone down. David should, too, but he wasn't ready yet.

This morning was hell, and he'd been completely thrown not only by the case but by his reaction to Cassidy in person. And he had the unhappy feeling that both Kincaid and Jennifer now thought a lot less of him because he wanted to be able to do the right thing and have the goddamn system, which he'd fought and bled to protect, do the right thing, too.

So, he stood there in the lobby, trying to gather his thoughts and remember that wanting justice wasn't a bad thing in and of itself.

"You okay there, Ginger?" Jennifer asked, using his call name, her voice full of false sympathy. Little brat. A rush of affection went through him. One of the reasons she'd been hired was because, despite her youth, she didn't take shit from any of them. Which they all needed.

"Yeah, I'm good." He glanced at Jennifer. She beamed at him.

"That's what I like about you, Ginger. You handle criticism well." She was completely sincere, which helped soothe some of his ire.

"Thanks," he said dryly. "I aim to please." With a sigh, he straightened up.

Time to get his game face on.

Be nice to the client. But not too nice.

Do not get emotionally or physically involved with the client.

3

Cassidy

Lincoln escorted her through what he called 'his' side of the building to introduce her to the rest of the team. She was both relieved and reluctant to be walking away from David. A one-sided attraction to one of the men guarding her did not seem like a serendipitous start. Part of her was happy to know that she could still feel attraction, so maybe Don hadn't totally broken her, but another part of her was incredibly uncomfortable.

They stopped briefly in Lincoln's office, and he gave her a panic button, taking a few minutes to show her how to use it. It would alert him, David, and whoever was at the front desk if she pushed it.

There were office spaces for the whole team, but no one was in them. They were in the breakroom. It was a beige and grey break-room, just like any other, but all the tables and chairs had been pushed to the side to make more floor space. There was a fridge, a bunch of cabinets, and a few baskets with snacks on the counters, though she couldn't see what was in them because she and Lincoln had to stand in the doorway.

Two of the men were in the middle of the open space, hands pressed flat against the floor, bodies moving up and down in unison with a fluidness that was beautiful to watch. Cassidy stared at all the rippling muscles, her mouth slightly dropping open.

One of them was Black, with long dreads that had been pulled up into a bun on his head. He was shirtless and wearing sweatpants on his lower half. The other was brown-skinned, but she didn't think he was Black—though she couldn't see his face, his hair made her think he was either South Asian or Latino or possibly mixed. He was wearing jeans and a white wife-beater tank top.

In front of them, near their heads, another man was standing. Like Lincoln, he was wearing a jacket and button-down shirt with dress pants, but he didn't have on a tie and the top button of his shirt was unbuttoned. His head was bent down, his focus on the watch he was holding up in front of him, making it impossible to see his face, though she could see that he was wearing thin, wire-frame glasses. She'd been around Kincaid long enough to know that he was probably just as well muscled as the men doing the push-ups, just from the way his jacket hung from his broad shoulders.

The only other woman in the room was perched on the countertop next to the fridge, which was behind and a little to the left of the man in the suit. She had long dark hair that had been pulled back into a ponytail and was eating from a small bag of popcorn as she watched the show with gleaming dark eyes. She was wearing black leggings and a red tank top with a black sports bra underneath, which showed off her own muscles. Cassidy couldn't help but stare with envy.

The whole scene helped her feel a little better. If Don suddenly burst through the door, every single person in there looked like they could wipe the floor with him without even breathing hard.

It also made her feel like she needed to work out more. She wanted muscles. She wanted to be able to wipe the floor with Don— or anyone who threatened her—without breathing hard.

"Come on, Jensen, you've got this!" The woman cheered, popping a piece of popcorn in her mouth. She was the only one who seemed to have noticed Lincoln and Cassidy's appearance in the doorway, and she winked at them as she spoke.

One of the men doing push-ups, Cassidy couldn't tell which one, grunted.

"I hate to interrupt," Lincoln drawled, "but our new client is here to meet you."

Sudden groans echoed through the room as the two men stopped their push-ups and rolled into sitting positions. Sweat glistened on both of them, and they were panting for breath. Still, neither of them took her attention. Nope, her full attention went to the man in the suit, who had been timing them, as he looked up.

He looked almost identical to Master Asad from Stronghold. Other than the glasses and a slight difference in the way he held himself, she would have sworn they were twins. Well, that and she'd never seen Master Asad wearing a suit.

"We knew you were there. Jensen and Drew just wanted to see if they could finish their competition first," he said, grinning as he stepped between the bodies of his tired friends, holding out his hand. Seeing Cassidy's expression, he winked at her. "Don't tell me, Asad didn't mention that he had an older, better-looking cousin."

"Um, he did not," Cassidy answered truthfully, and literally, because Master Asad would never describe anyone as better-looking than him. It seemed that he and his cousin had a similar sense of humor.

"I'm Mason Bahrami, at your service."

"Mason is our profiler and psychologist, and he also sometimes serves as Claudia's spotter," Lincoln said, gesturing to the woman who had hopped down from the counter and come to say hello. She had a wide smile as she held out her hand.

Cassidy had no idea what a spotter was, but she nodded. She could look it up later.

The other woman nudged Mason out of the way with her shoulder, and he smoothly stepped to the side, unperturbed by her literally barging through him. She was petite, several inches shorter than Cassidy, yet she walked with an assurance that Cassidy was used to seeing from the club dominatrixes.

"Claudia Delgado, sniper and wrangler of these twits," she said cheerfully, taking Cassidy's hand to shake. "I told them they didn't have time to finish this before you came back to meet us. Jensen's been practicing, and he's lasting a lot longer than he used to. In more ways than one."

"Claudia!" Shaking his head, the man in the tank top got to his feet as he complained. He flashed a brilliant smile at Cassidy. Now that she could see his face, she was pretty sure he was Filipino. He was very handsome in a boyish way. She would guess he was about her age or maybe a year or two older. "Jensen Reyes, nice to meet you. Please ignore everything they say about me."

He winked at her as he held out his hand, and Cassidy found herself smiling back, even though her body didn't light up the way it had for David.

"And Drew is the last member of my team," Lincoln said, gesturing at the last man as he was getting to his feet. "He is Patrick's cousin, so I'm not sure if you've met before."

Cassidy shook her head. They had not, but she could see the similarities between the two. Drew towered over her, easily the tallest person in the room, even without his hair adding to his height. He also had a similar, easy smile as he shook her hand.

"It's nice to finally meet you, Cassidy," he said in a deep voice that very much reminded her of Patrick.

Huh.

She glanced back and forth between Drew and Asad.

"You both have cousins at Stronghold." She shook her head in amazement.

"It's a really small world, sometimes," Lincoln said, chuckling. "We were surprised when we realized it. Did Patrick or Kincaid explain that we're all also members of the local club, the Outlands?"

"Yes." It had been a relief to hear because it lessened the chance of anyone judging her for being kinky. That had been part of the reason she'd felt comfortable coming here.

Of course, Patrick hadn't said whether they were dominants, submissives, switches, or anything in between, but if there was a single submissive in this room other than her, Cassidy would be shocked. The whole room fairly sizzled with protective dominant energy, all of it focused on her. A feeling that was familiar, yet this also felt like more because the people in this room had the training to back it up, and she didn't have to worry as much about them getting hurt.

Although she still would worry some. She already, immediately, liked all of them, and therefore, she didn't want any of them to get hurt, but they also seemed a lot less likely to be.

"Any time you want to go, someone from the team will go with you," Lincoln told her. "Someone is there most of the open nights, anyway. Bunch of perverts." He said it affectionally, obviously including himself in the grouping.

"Thanks, Head Pervert," Jensen joked, saluting him and making the others laugh. Cassidy giggled.

"Baby pervert there is who you'll be staying with," Lincoln continued, ignoring Jensen's indignant 'hey!' and talking over him. Claudia and Drew both snickered. "Just ignore the flirting and the posturing. Underneath that, he's a solid guard."

As if reminded of the seriousness of the situation, Jensen sobered, the smile immediately wiped from his face.

"We'll take care of you, Cassidy, don't worry." The corners of his mouth turned up. "But I'm sure we can find a way to make it fun while we do it."

"Of course you are," Mason murmured, giving him a look of fond resignation. Personally, Cassidy wasn't so sure, but she had to admit it seemed like it might be an actual possibility. If she wasn't so emotionally drained, she might have cried right then and there from relief.

Which, thankfully, she didn't because Kincaid joined them a moment later, and she was pretty sure he'd be upset if he'd let her out of his sight only to find her crying a few minutes later.

DAVID

Jensen's house was in Regent Square, about fifteen minutes

outside of downtown. The houses were big and drafty, the yards were small, and there were still little bakeries, shops, and a park within walking distance. A lot of young families lived there because of its location. Drew and Naomi lived about a mile away, easily within walking distance.

When Jensen had moved in, he and his brother had started doing a lot of work on their house, fixing it up. The house was historical, originally built in the 1920s, and had a lot of beautiful carved wooden detailing on the wainscotting that went throughout the house and on the staircase banister. There were also several original stained-glass windows.

They hadn't taken any of it out; instead, they'd been refinishing and enhancing what was already there. The front porch had needed some shoring up and repainting, as had the back. As security went, they'd installed an alarm system on every single one of the doors and windows up all three stories. The closeness of the neighbors also meant that people noticed when someone new was around. Several were out on their front porch watching with interest as Jensen parked his car, followed by Kincaid and Cassidy, and finally David.

He waved at old Mrs. Tulieman when he got out of the car, and she waved back, grinning. He gave it twenty minutes before she was knocking on Jensen's door, pie in hand, wanting to find out what was going on. Thirty at the most. He swore she kept a freezer stock full of them to excuse her nosiness.

Nosiness they were counting on, along with several of the other neighbors. If Cassidy's shitty ex somehow found out where she was and started hanging around the neighborhood, these were the kinds of neighbors who would notice. Unlike the condo building where David lived—half of the condos were rented out to tourists regularly. No one paid attention to each other, much less to who belonged there and who didn't.

He'd liked the anonymity, but it made for a less secure place.

Something that he hadn't minded up until now.

Though he had to admit, it wasn't like his sterile, millennial gray décor was going to get the same reaction from Cassidy as Jensen and

Mick's house did. Even before they went inside, he could see her wide-eyed reaction to the gigantic house, staring up at it from the street.

"Damn." Even Kincaid was impressed. "This place is huge."

"Just wait till you get inside," Jensen said, grinning as he came up beside them where Kincaid was opening the trunk. David got there before him, though, pulling the large suitcase from the interior. It had wheels, but he held it by the handle. While it wasn't exactly light, he could bench a hell of a lot more than its weight. Jensen grabbed the smaller duffel bag instead, leaving Kincaid to take the slightly larger duffel.

They trooped up to the front porch, which had a table and benches on the right-hand side and a porch swing on the left. David saw Cassidy looking at the swing wistfully, like she wanted to try it out immediately.

Not advisable, considering it was on the front porch, in full view of anyone driving by on the street. On the other hand, as long as her ex wasn't driving around the suburbs of Pittsburgh, and why would he be...

No. Stop it. She needs to start as she means to go on. And why do I care whether she wants to sit on a front porch swing?

Yeah, he did not want to examine the answer to that question too closely.

"Let's get inside and off the street," he said gruffly, gesturing as he moved. Jensen opened the door, and David was the first one through, taking a moment to look around and make sure the area was clear, even though Jensen had a top-notch security system.

It was just habit.

It also meant he got to see Cassidy's face when she walked inside and saw the interior for the first time. The way she lit up, her mouth dropping open as she took in the chandelier hanging from the copper ceiling over the foyer, the ornate staircase coming from the back of the house, and the colorful wallpaper lining the walls, made something in his gut stir.

She looked more like her picture and less like the frightened little mouse who had shown up at Black Fox Security's door.

"Oh my God..." Slowly spinning in a circle, she took in the entire foyer and the rooms beside it. Jensen had a home office off to the right, and the living room was on the left. He and his brother had chosen to furnish the first floor with heavy antiques, adding to the overall atmosphere. "This is incredible."

Pure joy had lit up her face, and she walked forward as if in a trance, going straight for the staircase and placing her hand on the end of the banister, tracing her fingers over the carved decoration on the top of the column.

"I've never seen anything like this outside of a movie," she said. "It's *beautiful*. And you just live here?"

"Yup. My brother and I like old stuff." Jensen grinned.

"Me, too." She turned and beamed at Jensen.

Yeah, she would not have liked his apartment at all. Not that it mattered, and it should definitely not make him feel jealous of her reaction to Jensen's house. Jensen's house was amazing. Everyone always agreed on that.

"Then you'll definitely love this place." Jensen chuckled. "So, you have your choice of where to sleep. My brother and I are both on the second floor, and there is a third bedroom there, but we also have the third floor, which is set up for guests. We figured you can pick wherever you feel most comfortable."

David set down the suitcase when Cassidy hesitated.

"Why don't we have a look around," he said, walking toward her, gesturing to the stairs. "I can show you around and show you all the security, and you can make your decision once you've seen the house."

Immediately, Cassidy nodded, looking up at him with not just relief but trust brimming in her hazel eyes. Trust that he knew what he was doing. Trust that he would keep her safe.

Something squeezed inside his chest.

He was so fucked.

4

———————

CASSIDY

The house was stunning. When she pictured a safehouse, she'd been picturing living inside a safe or something. A lot fewer windows. Less furniture. Definitely not somewhere that was beautiful, inside and out. Or somewhere that felt more temporary. Like a rental.

The second-floor room David showed her was nice, but the third floor was even better. It was obviously set up for guests, with two smaller rooms furnished with beds, a bathroom, and a huge rec-type room complete with a kitchenette. It was almost like an apartment unto itself; the only thing it was missing was a stove and oven, though there was a toaster oven and a microwave. If she wanted to, she could stay up here and be completely private, though if she wanted to actually cook, she would need to go down to the first floor.

"I think I'd like to stay up here," she said, standing in the middle of the rec room. The house beside this one was close enough that she could see their windows, though their shades were drawn. Somehow, she liked the closeness. When she looked down, she saw nothing but yard on both sides. The bushes that divided them were too low for anyone to hide behind.

Unless Don could scale brick walls, he wasn't getting up here. For a moment, she considered the idea of a grappling hook or something like that, but then he would have to break the window, and Jensen had already explained that the glass was incredibly difficult to break through. It wasn't bulletproof, and firefighters weren't going to have any difficulty getting in with their axes, but a regular hammer would bounce right off. He'd even offered to demonstrate, though Cassidy had reassured him that she trusted him.

"Absolutely," Jensen said. "I guess if David's done showing you my house, we can go get your bags." He snickered when David shot him a look.

"You can go get her bags, Baby," David said, making Cassidy and Kincaid blink. It didn't sound like he was using 'baby' as an endearment, yet she couldn't think of another reason why.

"Yes, Sir, Ginger, Sir," Jensen said with a salute, clicking his heels together, though they didn't actually click since he was wearing tennis shoes. David rolled his eyes, though the corners of his lips tipped up in amusement. Since he didn't smile much, Cassidy was intrigued by the small change in expression.

"Ginger for the red hair?" she asked.

David turned back to her, one hand rising to slide his fingers through the red hair in question.

"It's my call sign... *was* my call sign when we were active duty. We still use the same ones when we're on a mission now, though we try to call each other by our real names for the most part when we're not. Otherwise, Baby gets snippy." The little smile on his face widened into an honest-to-goodness grin, and Cassidy couldn't help but stare.

As hot as he was when he was brooding, he was even more attractive when he smiled. Especially when he was smiling at her. Her body was coming to life in a way she found utterly disturbing, mostly because it was so unexpected. His gaze met hers, and she felt a little zing go through the room... though she couldn't tell if she was the only one feeling it.

"Is he 'Baby' because he's the youngest?" she asked, dragging her gaze away from David's and returning to look around the room.

"Yes."

"Aren't you all called the Spice Doms at the club?" Kincaid asked, not bothering to hide the laughter in his voice. Cassidy spun around again to look at David, whose grin had dropped into a look of resignation.

"Also, yes. The subs were kind of responsible for our call signs after seeing us together at the club. They came up with their own names for us, and they kind of stuck." He shrugged ruefully, though he was still watching Cassidy rather than looking at Kincaid. She wasn't sure what kind of reaction he was hoping to get from her, but she couldn't help but giggle as he explained. "I'm Ginger, Mason is Posh, Drew is Sporty, Claudia is Scary, and Jensen..."

"Aw, poor Baby," she said, outright laughing this time, though she quickly tried to stifle it when she heard Jensen coming up the stairs. His footfalls were very heavy, though he was moving fast. They all went out into the hall to meet him and saw that he had both duffles slung over his shoulders, the straps crossing across his chest, and her roller case in his hand.

Yet he hadn't even broken a sweat coming up two flights of stairs with all of that on him.

"Luggage delivery," he said with a grin, coming to a halt on the landing. "Which room did you want to take?"

Cassidy immediately pointed to the one closest to him. Both rooms were nice, but she wanted the one closer to the staircase. Just in case there was an emergency at night; that way, she'd be right next to the stairs. Also, there was a window that was right over the porch roof, so that if danger came up the stairs, she could go out that window and not have to drop down as far. If she could hang from the windowsill, she'd only fall about a floor before hitting the porch roof, which was gently sloped, so she could roll over to the edge of it and then drop down onto the flowerbeds below.

The other bedroom looked out over the side and the back, and she didn't want to have to jump out a third-story window straight to the ground if she had another option.

"Perfect," Jensen said cheerfully, heading into her chosen room.

She was starting to think he was never anything *but* cheerful, which was nice since they were going to be living together. Don had rarely been cheerful, even in the beginning of their relationship. She'd taken his seriousness to mean that he was a serious guy and that he would be serious about her. Now, cheerful sounded good.

Which made it hard to explain why she was so drawn to David.

Maybe her internal 'picker' was broken.

Or maybe she just felt safe with him, even if he was serious and broody.

"I've got to get back to the office," David said, glancing at his watch before looking up at her and Kincaid. "If you think you'd be up for it, I could gather everyone together to come over here for dinner. Let you get to know the team a little better right off the bat and give Kincaid a chance to hang out with us a little more before he goes back to D.C."

"Sure, Ginger," Jensen called from the bedroom, a series of thuds emitting at the same time as he put down her bags. "Just give them a tour of my house and then invite everyone over to dinner."

"Well, we could do it at someone else's, but I thought Cassidy might be tired of traveling for today," David retorted.

Jensen appeared in the doorway, grinning widely.

"I'm just joshing ya," he said. "Dinner here sounds great. You're buying. Kincaid can take the other guest bedroom if he wants."

"Noted," David said dryly, raising his eyebrow in question at her and Kincaid.

Kincaid looked at her.

"I love the idea, but don't feel like you have to stay if you don't want to…" Her voice trailed off because part of her was sad to see him go. In some ways, he was her last tie to Stronghold and D.C. Once he left, it was just her in this new place, with new people and a whole new life.

As usual, Kincaid seemed to read her thoughts rather than listening to what she was saying. He was unnervingly good at that.

"I'll stay." He smiled reassuringly at her before turning to David.

Something altered in his expression, making it seem like the two men were facing off. Measuring each other up. "It'll be good to hang out with the team a bit. Plus, not having to drive three hours home on the same day sounds nice."

"What about Zach?" she asked. Zach was his boyfriend, a really super sweet guy who also happened to be a sadist. She didn't want to put them out if Zach was expecting Kincaid to come home, and she had the sneaking suspicion that Kincaid was only staying because he thought she'd be more comfortable if he did.

"I'll give him a call. I have an overnight bag in the car with me. Zach knew I might not feel like driving home tonight. And this is better than grabbing a hotel room." Kincaid flashed a grin at her. "As David said, I could use some time hanging out with the team, too."

It made her feel a little better that he wasn't putting himself out just for her.

<u>David</u>

The dinner idea had been an impromptu one, but it was one of his better ones. No emotional or physical entanglements with the client, but also, this wasn't their usual kind of case, and he wanted Cassidy to know and trust the rest of the team. Since she didn't have a single bodyguard assigned to her or even a pair, they needed her to respond quickly to all of them.

Mrs. Tulieman also ended up being invited by Jensen when she brought her pie over, which she was very pleased about and which meant she would be even more invested in keeping an eye on Cassidy. The friendly older lady was sharp as a whistle and kept up with all the neighborhood gossip. If someone came around looking for Cassidy, she would be one of the first to know, and now she knew to tell Jensen, his brother Mick, or one of the other team members immediately.

"You should come to game night," Claudia was telling Cassidy.

Dinner was long since over, and the groups had spread out a bit around the first floor. Mason and Mick were in the kitchen cleaning up while Jensen and Kincaid kept them company, chatting. Kincaid had finally relaxed enough to take his eyes off Cassidy, which was a good sign.

Claudia, Naomi, and Cassidy had taken over one of the couches in the living room, their backs to the dining room where David was standing next to the table, sipping the beer he'd been nursing all evening. Lincoln and his wife Ashley had come for dinner but left as soon as it was over. She'd just recently gotten over the flu and still tired easily, which made Lincoln hover. Mrs. Tulieman left at the same time, giving Cassidy a hug and welcoming her to the neighborhood.

David could have gone to join the other guys in the kitchen, but he found himself reluctant to do so. He was also smart enough not to infringe on lady time. So, he just stayed put and listened. There was no harm in learning more about their new client. It would help him make sure that they protected her better.

As team leader, with everything else that was going on, making sure she didn't fall through any cracks was important. Plus, he needed to get a gauge of her personality, make sure she wasn't the type to try to dodge her protection and put more work on him and his team. If she was, they'd still protect her, but it would mean taking different measures.

Yup. That was why he was standing here listening to Cassidy's conversation rather than in the kitchen having his own. No other reason.

"Game night?" Cassidy asked hesitantly.

"Yeah, it's ladies only, Thursday nights at my house," Claudia said, glancing over her shoulder at David. He wasn't surprised she'd realized he was there. "You don't have to come every week. Whoever can come is welcome. There's usually a bit of a rotation. There are a couple other subs from the club who come. Ashley comes sometimes, and we have a good time."

"What kind of games do you play?"

"Depends on how many people show up," Naomi replied. "Claudia has shelves full of games. If only one person shows up to play with her, she has a selection to choose from. If ten people show up, she has a selection to choose from. If six people show up, you're probably playing Seven Wonders."

"It is my favorite," Claudia confessed, grinning.

"It's a lot of fun. You should definitely try to make it. Even if you're not into playing games, it's nice to hang out," Jennifer put in.

Cassidy twisted around from where she was sitting to look at David, giving him a bit of a start. He hadn't realized she knew he was there. If he had…

Well, no, he probably still wouldn't have retreated to the kitchen if he was being honest with himself. His reasons for listening in were good, and it wasn't like he was hiding it. He was just trying to be discreet.

"Is it okay if I go to game night?" she asked him.

Fuck. He recognized the thrill that went through him as she asked permission, his control freak of a Dom trying to surge up in recognition of a pretty submissive who he was more attracted to than he wanted to admit, ceding any kind of control to him. He pushed back against that instinct because she was not his submissive, and she was not asking in that capacity.

She was asking because she was under their protection—his protection—in a way that had nothing to do with kink.

"Yes," he said, doing his best to keep his voice even, especially with Claudia watching. She read him a little too well sometimes. "Claudia's place is secure. If at any point we're worried your ex might actually know where you are, we may move game night here for a bit, but obviously, right now, that isn't a concern."

"Great, thank you!" Cassidy was a lot more relaxed now, and David was happy to see it. She should be able to relax because she was as safe as she could be.

Going from D.C. to Pennsylvania, Kincaid would have noticed and mentioned a tail. Plus, the second he'd shown up, the guard at the booth had taken note of all cars going by the building during the next half hour. They had cameras on the building, too, of course, and part of David's afternoon had been spent looking at the tape for the hour after Kincaid and Cassidy arrived. Every single car that had passed by had Pennsylvania license plates, and no pedestrians had walked by during that time.

If someone had followed them from the office, he would have noticed because he'd been looking the entire time, even knowing it was unnecessary.

He took another sip of his beer, leaning against the wooden frame that outlined the large opening separating the dining room from the living room. Listening. Observing.

Ignoring how damn attractive Cassidy was when she relaxed enough to smile and laugh.

Don

Staring at the computer screen, Don cursed.

What the hell was Cassidy doing in Pittsburgh? And where in Pittsburgh was she? The trackers he'd inserted into her shoes were spread out. A couple pairs here, a couple pairs there...

His jaw clenched as anger rippled through him.

Bad enough that those assholes at Stronghold had broken them up, manipulating her into thinking that the way they expressed their love and devotion to each other was wrong, but now they'd actually moved her to another state? And yes, he knew it was them.

Fucking interfering, snobby ass, think they know everything kinksters. They preached about there being no one true way, but then they thought they could dictate everyone's relationships, anyway. They still thought there was a wrong way.

Cassidy had been a good girl before that night.

She hadn't been perfect—if she had, she would never have tried to use something so stupid as a safe word, and she'd have just trusted him to take care of her, the way he always had—but she'd been close.

Then they'd ruined everything. Convinced her that he was a bad guy. Convinced her that she should stay away from him.

They couldn't keep them apart forever.

Cassidy was his.

No matter where they moved her to. He'd find her.

And Pittsburgh wasn't very far away at all.

5

DAVID

The evening was winding down, and David was finding himself reluctant to actually leave, even though he had an early morning tomorrow. Once the dishes were done, everyone ended up in the living room, taking turns talking to Cassidy and getting to know her a little better. At one point, Mick stepped outside and came back in, smelling vaguely of pot.

David shot Jensen a glance. Grimacing, Jensen reassured him that the only reason Mick was indulging in his vape was because there were so many of them there. Mick had some social anxiety about large groups and tended to keep pot around, but he didn't smoke it all the time, and he definitely never would if it was just him and Jensen in the house with Cassidy. He understood the stakes.

Only slightly reassured, David knew he'd be keeping an eye on that situation, though he had no reason not to just accept Jensen's assessment. And Mick wasn't supposed to be a line of defense, not really, just an extra set of eyes. This first night, his eyes were not something they needed.

Even if her ex had been watching her, David felt sure he *hadn't* followed her. With all the precautions they'd taken, as far as her ex knew, she had just disappeared. She'd even left her phone behind and had a new burner phone, which only Kincaid and a couple people at Stronghold had the number for.

It sucked to cut her off from her friends there, but hopefully, it wouldn't be forever. If the incidents down in D.C. against the club members stopped, they'd be able to reassess the situation. He did hope that her disappearance from the area would mean that her ex lost interest, but considering the man had waited a whole freaking year already, he didn't have high hopes.

Obsession and that kind of patience was never a good sign.

But it was always possible. And he couldn't worry too much about the Stronghold and Marquis clubs and their members and possible escalation down there once Cassidy's ex realized she was gone. They weren't his responsibility. It always felt wrong to compartmentalize like that, but he'd found during his time in the military that it was necessary. They would have to take care of themselves. He and his team would focus on Cassidy, even though she was now out of the danger zone.

His phone rang, and he pulled it out of his pocket, checking the caller ID, then grinned widely, his heart jumping up a bit in his chest. Turning away from everyone, he headed to the kitchen to get away from the general noise as he answered.

"Hello."

"Hey, big brother, how are you?" Audrey's warm voice filled his ear, an extra bounce in her tone which he was happy to hear. She'd been out of sorts the last few times they'd talked.

"I'm good, how are you?"

"I'm *fantastic.*"

"That's really good to hear. Any particular reason why?"

"I'm moving to Pittsburgh!" She sounded oddly triumphant.

"What?" He leaned against the counter in the kitchen, blinking in surprise. Of all the things he'd expected her to say, that had to be toward the bottom of the list. "Why? I mean, not that I'm not happy to hear it, but I thought you were solidly set on staying in Philly." With their parents. That was the part he left unsaid. He and

Audrey had an unspoken agreement about not talking about their parents.

"I was." Now, there was a slight hint of hesitation in her voice, which meant that, yes, this decision did have something to do with getting away from their parents. Something she'd been loathe to do after David had cut contact with them and "ruined" all their dreams, according to them. "But I decided it was time. And I bought a bakery. I found one for sale in Pittsburgh, and I bought it."

"Congratulations!" David hesitated because he knew that was what Audrey had always wanted to do. He wondered how their parents had reacted, but he didn't want to ask.

"It's actually on the same street as your office."

Immediately, David's brain flashed through the street. There was only one empty storefront, formerly a café. They'd occasionally gotten lunches there, but the food had gone downhill after the owner retired and new management took over, and it had ended up closing.

"Where Joe's Café used to be?"

"That's the spot!"

"That's a great spot."

"Right? I'm not moving quite yet. I need to find a place to live, and there's some work that needs to be done to turn the café into a bakery, but I have the lease, and I've started figuring out what I want to renovate and everything." She sounded so gleefully happy, David hated to put a damper on her mood, but he couldn't help but ask.

"So... do Mom and Dad know?" Silence. Crap. He felt like a jerk. "Sorry, I shouldn't have asked."

"No, it's fine. I mean... you know. They're not thrilled. I'm pretty sure they think I'm gonna fail and come crawling back to them." The cheerfulness in her voice was more forced now. "They didn't try to forbid me or anything, though."

"I guess they learned their lesson with me," David said with a dark chuckle; being cut off from his family hadn't really been funny at all.

"I think they might be coming around with that, too," she said.

"They weren't at all upset that I was moving to Pittsburgh. They even said they might come visit for the holidays once I'm settled. I think they're hoping to see you."

"So, they've stopped thinking I'm an abusive, perverted horror because I'm kinky?" he asked dryly.

"Well... Mom's been reading some books..."

Yikes. Okay, he did not want to know more about that. Though if it helped his parents better understand the lifestyle, he was all for it. He just didn't want to hear about it.

But as much as part of him wanted to see his parents again, wanted their approval again, there was one more sticking point.

"Good to know, but if we're doing the holidays, they're going to have to see Grandma, too, because I'm not leaving her out." Their only living grandparent wasn't actually blood-related to them. She was their mom's stepmother. She'd married their grandfather when David was two, so neither he nor Audrey remembered life without her, and she'd always been a good grandparent to them. His mom didn't feel the same ties, and when her father had died and her step-mother had gotten sick, her attitude had been 'let her family take care of her'.

As far as David was concerned, she was his family. So, taking care of his grandmother was exactly what he'd done. Just another disap-pointment for his parents to add to the list of ways in which he'd disappointed them.

They'd disappointed him first.

"Well, we'll cross that bridge when we come to it," Audrey said, that forced cheerfulness back in her voice. She couldn't help but try to play peacemaker, which put her in an awkward position. One that David tried not to exacerbate. It was hard being the only person who talked to everyone. "I'm looking forward to living closer to Grandma so I can see her more often."

"She'll be thrilled to see you," he said honestly. "And I'll do what-ever I can to help you with the bakery and the move."

"What bakery?" Jensen asked as he came into the kitchen, dropping his beer bottle into the recycling bin and going to the cupboard to get a glass. David watched approvingly as he switched over to water.

"Audrey's. She's opening one in Pittsburgh." All of his team knew of Audrey, and a few of them had met her, though it had been years since they'd actually gotten to see her. Jensen was one of the ones who had not had the pleasure yet.

"Hey, Audrey!" Jensen said loudly. "Congratulations on the bakery!"

"Bakery?" Mason popped through the kitchen door as if he'd been summoned, which wasn't too surprising. He had a carb addiction and a sweet tooth a mile long, which was why he worked out more than any of them. He had to counteract all the sugar and carbs he put into his body if he wanted to maintain his physique—and he did want to maintain his physique. "What bakery?"

"Audrey is opening a bakery in Pittsburgh. On our street."

Mason's eyes lit up with interest. He was another one of the ones who hadn't met Audrey before since he'd had his own family things going on when she'd been in town to see David.

"Do you think she'd be open to making baklava?"

On the other end of the phone, David could hear Audrey laughing.

"Tell whoever that is that I'm happy to make baklava and whatever other requests they want to put in," she said.

"It was Mason," he replied. He looked at Mason. "Audrey says she's happy to make baklava." He did not pass on the rest of her message because he had no doubt that Mason would take her up on it, and Audrey was too nice to say no, even if the requests got overwhelming. And Mason would have a lot of requests if he knew he could be indulged.

Cassidy

Only being able to hear snippets of what was going on in the kitchen was slightly maddening. She'd noticed the moment David had left the room, even though she'd been in the middle of talking to Drew and Naomi about the women's shelter where Naomi worked. Although Peggy's House technically took in whoever needed help, the majority of their clients were women.

Cassidy had donated some of the clothing, shoes, and jewelry she didn't expect to wear. Part of her had wanted to donate everything to them and go shopping for a brand-new start, but she couldn't afford that, and she wasn't allowed to use her credit cards or apply for new ones. It left too much of a trail for right now.

Hopefully, once she got a job, she could get rid of more and go shopping for new things. Jennifer had reassured her that everyone on the list could be contacted by Black Fox and the situation would be explained to them so that they could figure out how to pay her. It was not a long list, but at least it was something.

"Who's Audrey?" she asked. Whoever she was, David had wanted to talk to her so badly, he'd left the room, despite the fact he'd been hovering literally the entire evening until now. If he had a girlfriend, maybe she'd been completely misreading the zings of attraction she'd thought she felt between them. Maybe it was all one-sided.

Jennifer shrugged and shook her head—she didn't know.

"Audrey?" Drew lifted his head from where he'd been looking at something on his phone. "That's David's sister. Why?"

"Audrey is opening a bakery," Mason said, coming back into the room to join them. "She's moving to Pittsburgh and opening a bakery on the same street as the firm." He ran his hand over his stomach, smoothing the fabric of his shirt down, but the gleam in his eye said he wasn't thinking about his six-pack but about the baked goods he was going to fill it with.

Claudia clapped her hands together.

"Great! I love Audrey! Maybe she'll want to come to game night, too."

Sister. Audrey was his sister.

The relief she felt made Cassidy want to kick herself. Just because she was attracted to him did not mean he was attracted to her, so being relieved he was talking to his sister and not a girlfriend didn't matter. Especially since he'd been the least welcoming of the entire group.

Yes, he'd been watching her. Yes, he'd been civil. But he hadn't exactly been encouraging or trying to make friends with her the way the others had. She wasn't taking it too personally, though; he seemed to hold himself apart from everyone. Maybe because he was the team leader and not just part of the team.

Everyone seemed excited about the prospect of the bakery and of getting to see Audrey again—well, those who already knew her. Jennifer, Naomi, and Drew were delighted they were finally going to get to meet David's sister. Mason was looking forward to both, although more the bakery than meeting David's sister. The four of them had apparently only seen her in pictures so far.

It was a nice way to end the evening.

Once Drew and Naomi decided to head out, it was like the signal for a mass exodus. They'd already cleaned up from dinner, so there wasn't anything to do except say goodbye. David was the last to go after making sure she had the phone number for everyone on the team in her new phone. She'd gotten Naomi's and Jennifer's, too. It was nice having multiple numbers to add to the three she'd started with—Kincaid's, Patrick's, and Law's, her last connections to Strong-hold and Marquis.

She'd been reassured that, eventually, she'd be able to call some of her friends, too, but right now, they wanted as few people with a way to contact her as possible. Her old phone and her old emails were being monitored. If her ex stole someone's phone or managed to hack it, he wouldn't find anything. Even Kincaid, Patrick, and Law didn't have her number saved anywhere electronically.

Sometimes, she wondered if it was overkill, but it did make her feel better. She was scared of Don. Scared of the fact he'd come back. Scared of the way he hadn't let her go. She knew the statistics. She was lucky she had people who were willing to help her, so she was going to do exactly what they told her to.

"Tomorrow, stay home," David directed her. "Look over the job sheet Jennifer gave you. Just try to relax, okay?"

Cassidy nodded. Relax... now that was something she hadn't been able to do in a long, long time, but she would like to try. She might even succeed. Being in a totally different city, a totally different state, knowing all the steps they'd taken to erase her trail and keep her location secret...

She could finally breathe a little easier.

Which was the whole point of the move, after all. That and protecting the Stronghold members, who had stepped up to help her even though they didn't have to. She really hoped Don just let the whole thing go now.

David's gaze moved over her face, as if he was searching for something in her expression. Her breath caught in her throat, suddenly aware that he was standing closer to her than he had all day, looking down at her with her head tipped back up to meet his gaze. Almost like they were about to kiss.

Which was crazy, of course, and all in her head, but her body didn't know that and was reacting like he really was about to.

A noise off to the side made her jump, and they both looked over. Kincaid had just come out of the kitchen and was staring at them.

"Have a safe trip home," David said to him, giving him a nod.

"Thanks."

Without looking at her again, David turned and walked out the front door.

Which was not at all disappointing. Definitely.

It was safe.

"I'm gonna go get ready for bed. Do you need anything?" Kincaid asked her, walking forward, dropping his arms from where they'd been crossed over his chest. His dark eyes were full of concern for her.

"No, I'm good. I'll get ready for bed, too." She was suddenly aware of how exhausted she was.

"Good. You look like you need some sleep." Kincaid slung his arm around her shoulders, maneuvering her toward the stairs with him.

"I haven't been sleeping well," she admitted.

"Of course not. That's about to change, though." He gave her shoulders a little squeeze. "It'll be a lot easier to sleep here, I bet."

Cassidy had a feeling he was right.

6

DAVID

On Sunday mornings, David took his grandmother to church. It was not his favorite thing to do, but she liked to go in person and be part of the community. It made her happy to have him with her, and she at least went to a church he liked. The pastor and her wife were members of the Outlands, and so were several of the congregation. They did a lot of good in the community, with a food pantry, a clothing collection, and all sorts of other kinds of outreach. Sometimes, he even volunteered to support the services they were offering those in need.

But he could have done that without attending. That was in service to his grandmother. Plus, it was a good excuse to see her each week. They would go out to lunch afterward to talk and catch up.

As always, his mind wandered during the service. Normally, it wandered to work.

This week, it wandered to Cassidy.

Which was still work, he temporized.

But his mind wasn't on how to protect her. They had all her protections in place.

He kept thinking about *her*.

How was she spending her day? Was she feeling better after a night at Jensen's? Was she scared when Kincaid left? If he'd left already. They hadn't discussed what time he would be leaving.

Kincaid wasn't too happy with him right now, so they hadn't talked much. Kincaid would have to suck it up, though, because he might be right, but David had still made some good points. He wasn't going to apologize for wanting things to work the way they were supposed to. Or for worrying about what would happen if Cassidy's ex started dating someone else.

Were they just going to watch him for the rest of his life, trying to interfere with any relationship he had?

That didn't sound feasible. He and Kincaid had both been right, in their way, whether Kincaid wanted to admit it or not.

They might be able to keep Don out of the clubs, but that didn't mean keeping him out of the dating pool. There was only so much they could do about an adult woman deciding that she wanted to date him. And now that he was banned from the clubs, if he was even dumb enough to try going back to one after his last ex had been rescued from one, he would just keep his activities to himself. The next woman would have even fewer avenues for help than Cassidy had.

Not my circus, not my monkeys.

Which was easier said than done.

He took in a deep breath and let it out slowly, ignoring the little look his grandmother shot him.

That he was worrying about Stronghold and Don's possible future girlfriends was a measure of how safe he felt Cassidy was now. Which was good. She deserved to be safe. To live a little—within the parameters they'd set up until they were sure her ex had moved on and wasn't looking for her.

She was a submissive, so she'd probably want to visit the Outlands, eventually. It would probably be best if David screened any Doms that she scened with. Or maybe she wouldn't be interested in scening at first. Had Kincaid mentioned if she'd kept going to Stronghold after her rescue?

Even if she hadn't, if she felt safe enough up here, she'd probably want to go. David would make sure he was familiar with her limits so he could keep an eye on her there. Just in case she panicked or had a flashback or needed anything.

Maybe he should scene with her first. That was probably a good idea. He'd be able to get a handle on her needs, her triggers, then he could watch out for them even when she was scening with other Doms. That way, he could make sure she chose Doms who would match well with her. Doms who would understand what she'd been through and not push her too hard.

Yes, that was a good idea.

Not exactly his purview as her security, but what kind of Dom would he be if he didn't make sure a submissive under his protection in one way was protected in all ways? It wasn't outlined in his responsibilities, but he wasn't the kind of man who only took partial responsibility. All or nothing was more his speed—and 'nothing' tended to be a challenge, if he was being honest. He was far more comfortable taking on all responsibility.

A sharp elbow in his side made him flinch, and he looked down at his grandmother, frowning.

Her head only came up to his shoulder when they were sitting down. She was dressed in one of her "Sunday suits," as she called them—today's was powder blue—and a matching blue hat perched on top of her flossy white hair. The wrinkles around her laugh lines deepened as she grinned up at him unrepentantly.

"The church service is over, David." Her voice, high and light, had a distinctive crackle to it that made it instantly recognizable in a crowd.

He blinked and looked around. Sure enough, the swelling music wasn't another hymn or the choir; it was the recessional. All around them, people were gathering their things and starting to stand up... and he hadn't even noticed.

Way to be aware of your surroundings, David.

But he couldn't kick himself too hard. He always relaxed his guard during service. Normally, he wasn't so lost in thought that he missed the end of it, though. In large part because he was usually eagerly awaiting the end so they could get to the part of their Sunday tradition that he liked the best—after church lunch with his grandmother.

"Right, sorry." He got to his feet, holding out his hand to help her to hers. Her hazel eyes were still sharp, and she was eyeing him suspiciously.

"What were you thinking so hard about?" she asked.

"Work."

It was technically the truth. Not one that she wholly bought, though, because she continued to eye him suspiciously as they made their way out of the sanctuary and through the greeting line to say hello to Pastor Nikeisha. David smiled, said the right things, and made sure he was focused on what was in front of him and not veering off to think about Cassidy.

Not that it helped his grandmother forget. She held her peace all through the car ride to the House of Starrett, their preferred Sunday lunch place, and until they were seated with their menus and had their drink orders in. Once he was lulled into complacency, that was when she struck.

"What are you working on right now?" The innocence in her voice didn't fool him any more than his answer of 'work' earlier had apparently fooled her.

Sighing inwardly, David looked up from the menu. It wasn't like he really needed it; he already knew he was going to get a salmon salad. The menu was just a prop to help him hide from this exact conversation.

"Well, there's a fundraiser coming up to kick off Senator Marlin's campaign for governor. We're coordinating with OHS to provide security for the event." High profile because not everyone was happy that an Indian woman was running for governor. Governor Williams had been exceptionally popular during his time in office, but he was ready to retire, as was his lieutenant governor, so the field was wide open.

Since Governor Williams and Senator Marlin were from the same party, everyone assumed she was the natural successor, but there were already rumblings from some areas about both her race and her gender.

"That's good. I like the senator," his grandmother said cheerfully. She eyed him. "Anything else?"

"That's the biggest thing going on this week. We have a lot of other smaller jobs, though." He went through the full list, which was a bit overwhelming. He'd already told his grandmother about how the firm had lost a team and the two remaining ones had needed to split their jobs, so she didn't need an update on that. As her eyes glazed over, he slipped in that there was a bodyguarding job right in the middle of all the other ones he was listing.

She didn't even notice.

By the time he was done, the server had returned. Once they'd put in their orders and returned their menus, his grandmother was looking at him suspiciously.

"And that's it?"

"That's it. There's a lot going on, so I guess that's why I'm so distracted."

"Hmph."

Some sixth sense was telling her that she wasn't catching everything, but obviously, she couldn't quite figure out what she was missing. David picked up his water glass to hide his smile as she made another little noise, this one of resignation, indicating that she was giving up.

"Are you doing anything this afternoon?" she asked.

"I was going to work out and look at some of the schedule for this week. Why?"

"Would you have time to take me to book club? I can probably get a ride home from one of the other ladies."

Now it was David's turn to give his grandmother what she called 'the hairy eyeball.'

"Why can't Laura take you?"

Laura being the 'companion' they'd hired for her just three weeks ago. His grandmother didn't need full-time care, and her wits were sharp, but she needed help around the house, someone to keep her company, and she couldn't drive anymore because her eyesight had gotten so bad. So, she needed a daytime companion to get her around and keep her occupied.

So far, they'd been through nine in one year. Either they quit, or his grandmother took it upon herself to fire them.

Grandma waved her hand.

"Oh, you know."

"No, I don't know, that's why I'm asking. What happened to Laura, Grandma?"

She made that hmphing noise again, and David glared at her.

"Fine. I had to fire her."

A headache was starting to form between his eyebrows.

"Why did you *have* to fire her?" He did his best to keep his tone patient and understanding, even though he didn't understand. Laura had been perfect. She hadn't had a traffic violation since her first year of college, she'd taken some nurses classes before deciding it wasn't for her but was still certified in CPR and first aid, and she was in night school, so she was available all day.

"Because she wanted to quit but was too stubborn to." Grandma jerked her chin upward defiantly. "I was doing us both a favor."

"Why did she want to quit?" Aka—what did his grandma do?

"She didn't like my soaps. Or the books I was reading. She got all prissy about it. And she said I cursed too much. But I'll curse as much as I fucking want."

David's lips twitched, though he did his best to suppress it because his grandmother didn't need any kind of encouragement. Good freaking grief.

"What's the book for this week?" he asked, resigned.

"Milking His Lass."

He pinched the bridge of his nose, closing his eyes against the images that were brought to his head.

"It's about hucows," his grandmother said gleefully.

"Stop. I've heard enough."

"You and Laura, apparently."

Even though it put him in a bind, he had a lot of sympathy for

Laura. Unfortunately, that meant finding another companion for his grandmother. This time he would make sure that they understood exactly the kind of books her book club liked to read. And he'd send Laura a bonus check to make up for being fired.

"When did you fire her?"

"Friday. I told her I'd tell you today." Totally unrepentant, that's what she was.

David sighed. Back to the drawing board.

"Okay, I'll have people stop in to check on you this week, and we'll set up a round of interviews for next Saturday." Just one more thing to add to his to-do list.

"I'm sorry, David, but she really wasn't right for me. Maybe this time you can let me choose who to hire?" She actually sounded sincere and a little pleading.

"You didn't say no to Laura."

"I wasn't excited about her, either. I wanted that nice young man."

"You only wanted Marcus because you thought he was cute. He was completely unqualified." David had looked into the guy when his grandmother had stated her preference. Marcus might look good in a pair of shorts, but he'd had three speeding tickets in the last year alone, an outstanding parking ticket, didn't know how to cook, and hadn't held any kind of job for more than six months.

"Let me choose this time, no matter what their qualifications are, and I promise I won't fire them." Widening her eyes, somehow, his seventy-two-year-old grandmother managed to look like a puppy dog begging for a treat. David groaned. He was going to regret this, he could feel it already, but maybe letting her choose one time would mean she wouldn't chase the person off.

He only needed someone to last for longer than a month, so he could get through some of his work. And he could just do a deep dive on everyone coming in for an interview ahead of time instead of afterward the way he usually did. It would take more time, doing a deep dive on all applicants instead of an initial screen, then deep diving on the ones they were actually considering, but in this case, it might save him time in the long run.

Because if his grandmother kept needing replacement companions, he was going to lose time he didn't have over the next few months.

"Fine." And if it didn't work out, then *he* could fire them. "You can choose your next companion, and I won't argue with your choice."

"Good. Thank you, David." She beamed at him.

Yeah, he was going to dive deep every single applicant *very* carefully before the interview.

$$7$$

<u>*Cassidy*</u>

For the first time in years, Cassidy slept in. Not only that, but she slept *hard*. From the moment her head hit the pillow until Kincaid came in to gently shake her awake because he didn't want to leave without saying goodbye, but he had to go, she was so deeply asleep, she didn't even dream. And, for the first time in years, she actually felt rested when she woke up.

She was no longer worrying that she was going to piss Don off, no longer waking up with a start in the mornings because she was afraid she was going to sleep past him. He'd hated it when she was 'lazy.'

In D.C., every night, she'd lay down then get up again, just to make sure she'd locked everything and set the home alarm.

She'd close her eyes, then open them again at every tiny noise she heard, every creak of the house, every dog that barked outside, every car that came to a stop on the street.

Her head would spin with all the ways she was vulnerable. Wondering if Don might come that night and find a way in, climbing up the fire escape. Convincing someone to let him into the apartment building, then ending up at her door. Breaking the lock. Breaking in the door.

On the worst nights, her brain would offer up horrific images of him burning the whole building down just to get to her. Who would escape. Who wouldn't. And then, even if she got outside, he'd be waiting for her... and he'd either drag her off screaming while everyone fought the blaze, or he'd stab her or shoot her and leave her to bleed out in the parking lot of her burning building.

It didn't matter how unlikely she, logically, knew such a scenario was. How out there. Her brain never let her rest.

But not last night.

Last night, she'd felt wholly, truly safe in a way that had let her anxiety take a breather.

Waking up to that feeling made her tear up, though she did her best to hide it because Kincaid was already acting reluctant to leave her there, and if she cried, he might not go. She'd interrupted his weekend, and his life, enough. So, she sucked it up, kept the tears at bay, and got up to walk him to the front door, where she gave him a huge hug, waving as he left.

It felt so strange to be left behind.

A noise behind her made her turn, though not out of fear that Don might be behind her, and the lack of fear felt almost strange.

"We saved some breakfast for you," Jensen said, coming down the hallway. Today, he was wearing another tank top and a pair of black sweatpants, looking slightly sweaty, as if he'd been working out. "It's on the stove. Kincaid said you aren't picky."

"I'm not. Thank you so much." She beamed at him, touched that they'd cooked for her. For a while, she'd been living with other people, other club members, in their guest rooms, but it had been too much. She'd been too worried about whether or not they'd be able to defend themselves if Don came calling.

Here, she felt like she didn't even need to worry about that because he didn't know where she was.

Freedom.

That's what this feeling was. True freedom she hadn't been able to feel back in D.C. because she'd known he was always somewhere nearby, that he was in the same city. That he knew where her club was, her favorite spots to go, her friends... Granted, he still knew where all of those places were, but everyone was on high alert, and she didn't think he was crazy enough to try to hurt someone else to get to her.

Not that they would know anything about how to contact her. Which was a measure of safety for them. The only people who did know could take care of themselves.

Unless Don had a gun.

Was he obsessed enough with her to threaten someone with a gun to try to find her?

She didn't think so.

She really hoped not.

"You all right, Cassidy?" Jensen asked, sounding concerned and making her startle.

Her brain had been so busy coming up with reasons to be worried over the people she'd left behind, she hadn't realized she was standing in the middle of the kitchen, staring into space or that Jensen had joined her. She really needed to get it together.

"Yeah, just... worried about what might happen to my friends back home when Don realizes I'm gone," she admitted because she felt like she could. Jensen didn't know them, so she wasn't going to be making him worry about them, and she could tell him because he wasn't one of the people she was worried about.

Even better, he didn't immediately tell her not to worry, the way her friends always had. They were all so confident they could take care of themselves... which was what everyone thought until something happened to them they couldn't take care of. She'd always thought she could take care of herself, too.

Jensen seemed to be thinking about what she'd said while she went to the stove to get her breakfast. There was a plate on the counter, and eggs, bacon, and pancakes were in a pan on the stove with a lid over it. The burner was off, so it wouldn't burn, but the lid had kept everything fairly warm.

For a moment, she just stared, touched by the thoughtfulness.

Don would never have...

Which was why Don was a crappy boyfriend even before he'd become straight-up abusive. He was good at being generous and sweet in big ways, especially when he was apologizing, but 'thoughtful' was out of his wheelhouse. The little day-to-day tiny moments of thoughtfulness, like making extra breakfast and then keeping it covered and warm for her because she hadn't come down to breakfast yet.

In fact, other than when he was apologizing, then bringing her breakfast in bed—which she hated because sitting in bed eating wasn't comfortable; she'd much rather have a chair—he'd never made breakfast for her.

"I suppose he could go after your friends, but there wouldn't be much point," Jensen said thoughtfully as Cassidy picked up the plate and started to put food on it. "None of them know exactly where you are, right? The best they can tell him is that you left, and no one knows where you are."

"Three of them do," she said. "I wouldn't be surprised if they told their partners, too."

"Okay, so six people total. Out of a lot." Jensen shrugged. "Abusers don't get away with what they do if they start showing their true colors to the world. They're smart enough, savvy enough, to put on a good front to everyone."

"Yeah, but Don already showed his true colors to the Stronghold members." Cassidy sat down at the buffet part of the counter on one of the high barstools. As she did so, Jensen started putting away the food she'd left in the pan in glass containers and cleaning up. "Oh, I can take care of that when I'm done."

"Nah, I've got it. You're supposed to be relaxing on your first day here. We can institute a chore schedule tomorrow." His dark eyes sparkled as he grinned at her. "If you're hungry, feel free to grab whatever you want from what we have. Mick has a couple things labeled as just his, but otherwise, everything is communal."

"Thank you." She felt bad just sitting there eating while he cleaned up the food he'd made for her, but she couldn't exactly stop him.

"No problem. Anyway, Don might have let the mask slip in front of them, but that doesn't mean he's going to want to get caught doing something that could send him to jail, right?" Jensen took the pan over to the sink and started cleaning it. "That means he's extremely limited in anything he can do."

That was true. The way they'd been able to keep him away from her for the past year was by threatening jail.

The night that he'd been kicked out of Stronghold, the night that she'd been rescued, he'd rammed his car into Master Law's on his way out of the parking lot. And then he'd fled the scene. Master Law had threatened to bring him up on charges if Don came anywhere near her.

Which had worked for a whole year until the time ran out for Master Law to be able to charge Don. A whole year where he'd left her alone, where he hadn't bothered anyone else.

Instead of losing interest in her, he must have gone and looked up how long Master Law had to make good on his threat, then waited it out. That's what she'd assumed. It had made her feel relieved that he wasn't out there hurting some other woman while simultaneously terrified he was so focused on her.

He'd also protected himself by not going after Master Law or anyone else from the club again. Even when he'd come back, he wasn't doing anything that actually hurt anyone. The closest he'd come to doing something that he could be in real trouble for was slashing Mistress Olivia's tires, but they couldn't prove that was him.

"So, you don't think he'll bother them?" she asked, desperately wanting it to be true.

Jensen hesitated.

"I don't think he'll be dumb enough to do anything that could get him jailed." He gave her a sidelong look. "As you know, there's still a lot he can do that won't put him in jail, but at the very least, I don't think you have to worry about him deliberately hurting anyone."

That made her feel better. As much as she didn't want him bothering anyone at all, Jensen's frank assessment of the threat level was a relief. He didn't try to give her false platitudes or empty reassurances that Don would leave everyone alone... but he truly believed Don wouldn't hurt anyone.

There was that.

If he hurt someone because of her... she'd been in therapy long enough to know that logically, he was making the decision, and it was because of him and not because of her, but that wouldn't stop the guilt she felt. She'd already tried to pay for Mistress Olivia's new tires and been roundly rejected. No one blamed her for Don's actions... but she still felt the guilt.

If she hadn't gotten involved with him in the first place...

If she'd seen the red flags at some point...

If she'd gotten away sooner...

If she'd just kept her mouth shut at Stronghold instead of trying to safe word.

It had been a call for help, but she'd done it without thinking through the consequences for other people. She'd done it without thinking about how everyone else might be affected. She felt incredibly selfish when she thought too much about it.

All she'd been thinking about at that moment was herself, how much Don was hurting her, and hoping someone would make it stop. Hoping someone would come rescue her. Iris, Master Law, and the rest of the Stronghold members had, at a cost to themselves.

"Cassidy. Eat."

For the first time, Jensen's Dom side showed through, and Cassidy's fork was halfway to her mouth before she realized what she was doing. She'd heard the command, and her hand had moved of its own accord.

Shoving the forkful of pancake into her mouth, she stared at Jensen. He might have a boyish face, he might be the youngest of David's team, and his nickname might be 'Baby,' but he was definitely a Dom. Meeting her gaze, seeing her taking a bite, he nodded approvingly and went back to drying off the pan he'd just washed.

Well, damn.

Even knowing that appearances could be deceiving, she hadn't entirely expected that of him. He was so happy-go-lucky. Especially compared to some of his team. Like David.

She wanted to ask Jensen about David, but she couldn't think of a question that wouldn't sound like she was fishing for information. Because, of course, that's exactly what she would be doing. Maybe if she asked about the team as a group?

"How long have you been with Black Fox Security?" she asked. That was safe, right?

"Since it started." Jensen hung the pan up in its place on the potholder hanging from the wall before turning to face her, wiping off his hands. "Lincoln was our commander in the field, and when he left, we went with him. It took a bit of time since we weren't all able to leave at once, but we all knew we wanted to join him."

"Kincaid said you each have your own specialties?"

"We do. We're all pretty well-rounded, but we have our things. Like Mason with psychology and profiling. Claudia's our sniper, and we all take turns being her spotter, but Drew is the best at it. He's also the muscle when we need it."

"What about you?"

"I'm the sneaky one. Like a ninja." Jensen winked at her.

That made her laugh. But he'd still left out the person she really wanted to hear about. Why was she so interested in David? She couldn't really say, other than her instant attraction to him. Which was not a good reason to be trying to find out more about him. It would be a good reason to stay away.

Her 'picker' when it came to men sucked, as evidenced by Don.

On the other hand, if she was going to be protected by a team of people, she wanted to know more about them. That was reasonable.

"Does David have a specialty?" Since she'd asked about Jensen specifically, it couldn't hurt to ask about the final team member. Nothing suspicious at all.

"Nope, he's our ginger of all trades." Jensen grinned. "He knows a little about everything. I think he feels like he has to since he's technically in charge of our missions. He doesn't like it when he doesn't understand something or has to ask us to do something he knows nothing about."

"That makes sense." It also made a good leader, she would imagine. Not that she'd ever been in a place to know.

"What are your plans for today?" Jensen asked. "Did you want to go anywhere?"

"What? Oh, no," she said as she realized he was thinking about whether he would need to accompany her anywhere. "I don't need to go anywhere. I was thinking I would look over the job listings Jennifer gave me yesterday and see what's available, then just... try to decompress."

"Cool. What were you doing before?"

"Um..." Cassidy hesitated, feeling her cheeks heat with shame because she knew how what she was about to say was going to sound. "Well, Don didn't want me working, so I was going to nursing school, but I dropped out."

Red flag. She knew that. At the time, it had sounded good, though. Why work if she didn't have to? Why not stay at home and do whatever she wanted to do and keep up the housework so they could save some money instead of having someone come in to clean? And if she decided she really did want to be a nurse, she could always go back.

But somehow, they'd never had the money when she wanted to go back, even though he'd 'saved' money by getting rid of the cleaning service he'd had. Somehow, it had never been the right time for her to go back. According to him.

"Ah. Gotcha." The expression on Jensen's face was sympathetic, not judgmental, but it didn't matter.

She was judging herself.

"Well, I don't know if there will be anything in there that correlates to that. I think it's mostly admin-type stuff, but who knows."

"Admin-type stuff sounds great." That's what she'd been doing at the temp agency where she'd gotten a job. Master Adam from Stronghold had helped her out with that. Now, she was getting help with this job.

At some point, she was going to have to stand on her own two feet. Even if it meant Don finding her.

But not yet.

Not right now.

Maybe when she was ready to do that, she'd move somewhere far, far away. Europe might be nice. She'd always wanted to visit Ireland.

"Well, good luck. Let me know if you need anything."

Jensen shot her a smile and ambled out of the kitchen, leaving her alone to think about what she was going to do with this temporary stopover between the life she was escaping and the life she wanted.

8

———————

DAVID

As soon as the elevator doors opened on Monday morning, an unwelcome sight greeted David's eyes. He could see straight into the Black Fox Security lobby where Jennifer was standing behind her desk—not sitting—with an unhappy expression on her face as she faced down a blond man David recognized immediately and who definitely did not belong there.

Scowling, David stalked out of the elevator.

His movement must have caught Jennifer's attention because she turned her head, and relief flashed across her face. Seeing her change in expression, Marshall turned around. Unlike her, he scowled as soon as he saw David.

Pulling the glass door open, David raised his eyebrow, keeping his anger off his face as he faced off against the former third owner of Black Fox. Everything about Marshall offended his sensibilities, from the fact he'd been embezzling from the firm to knowing the man had been sleeping with Lincoln's first wife before their divorce. Even though he'd supposedly been Lincoln's best friend.

Jennifer slowly sank back down onto her chair, watching both of them warily but no longer so on edge now that David was there.

"How did you get in here?" he asked before Marshall could say anything. "I thought your access was revoked." He was going to have to have a word with Samuel and the other gate guards.

Marshall smiled. Maybe David was biased, but it was a smarmy smile. And it didn't reach his eyes, which remained coldly blue as he met David's gaze.

"Hello, David, good to see you, too."

"I wish I could say the same, but I'm pretty sure I'm not supposed to be seeing you in here anymore."

Lifting his shoulder in a shrug, Marshall looked smug, and he didn't bother answering David's question.

"I'm here to offer you and your team a job."

"No thanks." David didn't even have to think about it.

"Well, don't be so hasty, David." Marshall's smile grew and seemed more sincere. Whatever he was up to, he was genuinely happy about it, which made David even more suspicious. "You don't know how much money I'm offering to come join my team."

David snorted.

"There is not enough money in the world." Seriously. Even if Lincoln fired him, David would rather be on the street than work for someone like Marshall. He didn't trust him, he didn't like him, and he didn't think the man had an ethical bone in his body.

Something in Marshall's eyes flashed. He didn't like being told 'no'.

"Well, I'll just stay here and put my proposal to the rest of the team. You don't speak for all of them."

Another snort of derision.

"Trust me, when it comes to you, yes, I do."

He heard the sound of the elevator doors opening behind him and conversation drifting out into the hall that was abruptly cut off.

Speak of the devils. Turning his head, he saw that it was a full elevator. Not just Claudia and Drew, but two of Harris' team as well, Seth Loving and Miguel Gomez. That made two snipers and two of the muscle. Both Drew and Miguel were built like mini tanks. None of whom had any love for Marshall, either.

David felt fairly certain he could drag Marshall out by the neck of his suit jacket if he needed to, but Marshall had a few tricks up his sleeve. Faced with an overwhelming force, there probably wouldn't be a need for a forcible exit.

They came in, Claudia leading the way. Her dark eyes were cold, flat, and hard the way they went when she was in her sniper head-space. There was a reason her call sign had been Scary. Lesser men ran when they got that look from her. Even David had to steel himself, and he could see Marshall doing the same as her snake-like gaze rested on him.

"What's Shit Stain doing here?" she asked, directing the question at David even as she continued to stare down Marshall. Behind her, Seth and Drew snickered.

The other man bristled at her nickname for him but pasted on his smile again, acting as if he hadn't heard it.

"I'm here to offer you all three times what you make at Black Fox to come work for me on a very important job... top secret at the moment, so I can't tell you the details until you come join me." He made the offer in a coaxing tone, hinting at big things, teasing them with the secret.

It didn't work—to no one's surprise except Marshall.

"No." Claudia didn't bother to listen anymore. She just started walking again, straight toward Marshall, who jumped out of her way rather than allow her to run into him as she headed toward the back. She paused at the desk. "You okay, Jen?"

"I'm great." Jennifer gave her a thumbs-up and a weak smile. "No job offers for me, apparently. Not that I would take it."

"Yeah, we're good," Seth said, snorting in a manner that was very reminiscent of the way David had done. He'd started walking, too, though he didn't try to walk through Marshall like Claudia had. "I like making less money. I wouldn't know what to do with more."

"Three times is a lot and yet still not enough," Miguel joked, keeping up with Seth.

They acted as if they didn't see Marshall as they walked around him, heading for their side of the office. Drew didn't say a word, he just walked over to the front desk and leaned on the edge of it, arms crossed over his chest. It was clear he was hovering protectively around Jennifer and also effectively stated his preference without a single word.

Marshall's face had turned bright red, a little vein throbbing in the middle of his forehead.

"You're all going to regret this." He spat the words out. "You have no idea what you're turning down, what you could be—"

"Doesn't matter," David told him. "We'd rather have our souls than your money. You can take the answers you've already gotten as representative of the entire firm. Your team might have followed you, poor bastards, but the rest of us see you for what you are, and we want nothing to do with you. Get out. Don't come back. And I will be figuring out how you got into here in the first place, and that way will be closed to you from now on."

Marshall's upper lip curled in a sneer.

"You do that." The words were a challenge. "You'll be sorry for not taking my offer, though. Black Fox is dying. You can't keep up the workload without me. Lincoln and Harris don't know shit about running a business. That's why they had me in the first place. And there's nothing any of you are going to be able to do about it."

Stalking out, he hit the glass door like he was trying to shatter it—not that he could, not without a storm of bullets, but damned if he didn't try, anyway.

David watched him go with a frown.

It didn't matter that he'd been entirely in the wrong. He was obviously carrying a grudge.

"Did he really think we were going to go work for him?" Drew asked incredulously.

"He can be bought, so he assumes everyone else has a price as well." David shook his head. "I'm not sure he understands the meaning of the word loyalty." He turned to face Jennifer. "What was he saying to you before I got here?"

"I asked if he had an appointment, of course, even though no one had anything on the calendar." She looked anxious. "Just in case someone forgot to put one on. I didn't know who he was, and he wouldn't give me his name. He said he needed to talk to Lincoln and that he knew his way back there. I told him he needed to wait out here, and we were arguing about that when you got here. He was only here a few minutes before you, thank goodness. I was about to call Mason. He was the only one in already. I take it that's Marshall?"

While she hadn't met the man before, she'd heard about him.

"That was Marshall," David confirmed grimly. "If he shows up again, call whoever is in the office. Immediately. We're going to have to figure out how he got in, though. Samuel should have known better than to let him into the parking lot, and if he came from the sidewalk... Shit. He probably came from the sidewalk."

Before the building officially opened, they could get in using their key cards. Marshall had either stolen someone's or found a way to clone one. There was someone at the front door during office hours, but not twenty-four-seven. The parking lot booth had a guard arrive earlier and leave later than the walk-up. That might need to change if Marshall was sneaking around. He would have to talk to Lincoln.

So, David started his day reviewing the security footage and confirming that Marshall had arrived by way of the front door, using a key card, before anyone was on duty downstairs. Then he'd had to go ask Jaxon, Harris' computer guy, to find out whose keycard Marshall had used and shut it down. It turned out to be an unregistered one, so he set Jaxon on the task of setting up new key cards for everyone and shutting down access for all but the new cards.

He still didn't know exactly what Marshall was up to because he doubted this was the end of it, but the man was already proving to be a massive fucking headache.

Then, when David was done with all of that, he had to get started on everything for the senator's upcoming fundraiser.

Despite being a hell of a lot busier than he wanted to be on a Monday morning, he did remember to stop by to check in with Jensen that Cassidy had settled in okay. He'd been tempted to text her, but...

He needed to keep his head in the game, and she was a distraction. A very pretty distraction but a distraction, nonetheless. Jensen responded that she was hanging around the house and looking at the job options, and David had to be happy with that. No point in going to check on her himself, after all. No matter how much he wanted to.

His team was relying on him.

<u>*CASSIDY*</u>

The days seemed to simultaneously rush and trickle by. The days felt like they were taking forever as she got through them, yet, somehow, she blinked, and it was Thursday. Game night with the ladies. Which she was very grateful for as something to break up the tedium.

She had gotten out of the house a few times with Jensen, going out to run errands and just see a little more of the city when he did so. The lack of memories with Don helped her anxiety a lot. She was sleeping better than ever, she wasn't jumpy at the stores, and she didn't imagine him around every corner.

Compared to how she'd been before, this was practically blissful.

She'd forgotten what it felt like to just *live* instead of feeling hunted all the time. Afraid all the time.

The colors seemed brighter. People were no longer so threatening. New places were interesting instead of nerve-wracking. And she was hungrier. She felt like she could actually eat.

Which meant she'd spent most of the week cooking for Jensen and Mick, who had thrown themselves on the food like hungry wolves. Both of them told her they enjoyed cooking, too, but they were happy to get a little break. And it made her feel better about living with them rent-free. Like she was giving back a little bit.

She still felt guilty because one of them was always home, or someone from the team stopped by to cover for them when they couldn't. One time, it had been Mason; another time Claudia. Mason had talked to her the whole time, and Cassidy considered it an impromptu therapy session. Claudia had decided Cassidy needed a workout and to learn some self-defense moves. She had not been wrong, and she'd agreed to start coming over at least once a week to keep that up with Cassidy.

Despite all that, Cassidy still felt restless. Like she was supposed to be doing something, and instead, she was sitting around slacking. At any minute, Jensen and Mick were going to start resenting her cramping their style. She was sure they didn't want to have to be home all the time taking care of her.

Especially when there was no reason to think that she was in any danger up here. It wasn't like back at home where Don knew where her friends were and where Stronghold and Marquis were. Kincaid, Patrick, and Law had all texted her this week to let her know that there had been no more sightings of Don and no more harassment since she'd left. It had all stopped, as though he'd lost interest because she wasn't there.

Which was such a relief and helped assuage some of the guilt she'd been feeling about leaving. But now, she felt guilty about the fact that if she'd left earlier, maybe he wouldn't have harassed her friends at all...

I can only control myself.

She let out a deep sigh as Jensen pulled up in front of a pretty stone house. It looked almost like a cottage out of a fairytale, complete with a little turret on the left side. Not at all what she'd pictured for Claudia, but somehow, now that she saw it, it fit.

"Everything okay?" Jensen asked, looking at her with concern.

"Yeah, just a little tired." It was an easier explanation than everything going through her head. Perhaps not the most believable one since she was finally getting enough sleep every night. She was actually feeling better than ever, but she was still emotionally tired. Depleted, really.

"Don't worry, you're going to have fun. You've already met Claudia, Naomi, and Jennifer, and everyone else is really nice. Actually, speaking of..." He twisted around in his seat and pulled a paper bag out from behind her seat, handing it to her. "Would you mind giving this to Jennifer?"

"Sure." She peeked inside. "Are these the pickled veggies you bought the other day?" He'd bought five different kinds of pickled vegetables—asparagus, Brussel sprouts, carrots, onions, and a jar of mixed vegetables.

"We bought."

"Your money."

"You helped pick them."

Fair enough. She hadn't known they were for Jennifer, though; she'd thought they were for him and Mick. She didn't like pickles, but she hadn't had the heart to tell him that when he'd been so intent on picking out a good selection.

"Why didn't you give them to her at work?"

He shrugged casually, avoiding her gaze. "Feels a little weird to be giving someone a gift at work. You can pass them on to her tonight without it being weird."

Cassidy narrowed her eyes, studying him.

"Jensen, do you have a crush on Jennifer?"

"What? No!" Now, he looked at her with an affronted expression, but she wasn't buying it. The Baby doth protest too much. "She's way too young for me. I just know she likes pickled vegetables and thought we could pick some up for her. But I don't want her to feel weird about accepting them from me or thinking that I'm trying to hit on her or make her uncomfortable at work or anything."

Well, if Jennifer didn't return Jensen's interest, Cassidy could see how that might make work awkward. She could see his point about Jennifer being young, though the age difference between them couldn't be more than ten years. The same as Master Law and Iris back at Stronghold, and she'd definitely heard of bigger ones. But Jennifer was just out of college.

At any rate, Jensen looked so defensive, she just smiled. She didn't call him out on the fact that he was practically stumbling over his words to reassure her that he didn't have a thing for Jennifer. Which meant he probably did.

"Got it," she said. "I'll make sure she gets them and that she knows we picked them out together."

Sheer relief replaced the anxiety in his expression. Yup, he totally didn't like her.

"Great. Thanks." He smiled weakly. "I'll be back to pick you up later. I'm only five minutes away at David's."

David lived only five minutes away?

Immediately, Cassidy bit her lip against asking the question. There was no reason to. It didn't matter. She knew Jensen had checked in daily with David about what she was doing because Jensen had told her, but it wasn't like David was interested in her beyond that.

Unfortunately, it seemed Jensen wasn't the only one with a crush.

She hoped that his was more attainable than hers.

9

____

DAVID

Every time someone opened his door, David's head snapped around to see if it was Jensen. He was dropping Cassidy off on his way over to David's. Not that David expected anything to happen to them on the way, but he was still anxiously awaiting Jensen's arrival.

During game nights, Claudia got the ladies together to play games, and the guys gathered at David's to watch movies. Usually, the kind their significant others weren't interested in. Quite often, they were pretty bad. Tonight, they were watching Wrestlers vs. Zombies. David did not anticipate it becoming anyone's new favorite.

Unfortunately, Drew arrived first. Then Mason. Then, finally, Jensen. Normally, Lincoln joined them as well, especially when Ashley went to game night, but they had decided to go to the Outlands tonight. Lincoln had not been happy about Marshall appearing at Black Fox earlier that week, even though they hadn't heard from him since. He had some extra energy to work off, and Ashley was only too happy to assist.

With everyone around, David couldn't exactly pounce on Jensen and demand to know how Cassidy was doing, even though he kind of wanted to.

He'd spent the past few days with everything under his control, everything running smoothly, and the only pie he didn't have his fingers in was Cassidy. Even with the daily updates from Jensen, he didn't feel like he knew what was going on. Was she still anxious? Had she picked out a job? Did she feel comfortable leaving the house?

Jensen's daily 'she's doing fine' texts should have been enough, but they weren't. The amount of information was incomplete. And if he didn't know what was going on, he couldn't anticipate problems or figure out how to help.

"Baby Bodyguard! How's the easy life?" Drew asked, joking, when Jensen walked in.

"Easy," Jensen joked back, sauntering in. "Seriously, we should take up bodyguarding from home more often. It's the easiest gig I've ever done. I get to work and train from home while eating amazing home-cooked food for every meal."

David scowled at him.

"You'd better not have her cooking for you all the time just because she's there."

Putting his hands up in a gesture of surrender, Jensen was already shaking his head before David finished speaking.

"We told her she didn't have to and that we were happy to start a rotation. She said it gave her something to do and that she'd let us start taking turns once she got a job." He grinned. "You know I don't mind cooking. Though, I'm happy to eat her food. She's a damn good cook."

Somewhat mollified, David nodded, trying to figure out how to get more information out of Jensen without being obvious.

"How's she doing?" Mason asked, looking up from his phone. He'd already taken over his favorite corner of the couch and likely would not budge until forced to.

David tried not to appear too eager to hear the answer, moving into the kitchen to get the popcorn started now that Jensen was here. He grabbed the bag of kernels, a bottle of oil, and the pot he used while Jensen moved to the armchair he favored. There was a thoughtful expression on his face, as though he was trying to decide how to answer, which was not reassuring.

"I think she's good. She came out with me a few times this week to the store. Claudia has been training her in self-defense, and I told her I'd help out with that if she wanted. She was timid but motivated. But..." His voice trailed off.

"But what?" David asked from the kitchen before Mason did with the prompt, too impatient to pretend otherwise.

"But she listens to a *lot* of true crime. And watches it." Jensen shook his head in bewilderment. "Every time she's alone, that's what she has on. Sometimes, it's just in the background. A lot of it is downright disturbing, man. There are cold cases, solved cases where the asshole who did it got away, missing persons, and way too many dead women. I don't want to tell her what to watch or listen to, but I'm starting to get concerned."

"Do you think she's afraid we're going to let something like that happen to her?" David asked, frowning. He didn't like that idea at all.

Drew chuckled darkly, leaning back in the armchair opposite of Jensen, making it rock slightly under his body weight. Reaching up, he brushed one of his dreads out of his face.

"It might be something like that, but Naomi said there are some women at the shelter who also really enjoy true crime. Some of them like hearing about the survivors, some of them feel relief from the acknowledgment of 'at least I didn't end up like that', some of them are trying to understand what makes people do the terrible things they do...and some of them just like to solve the mystery. I'm sure there's a ton of other reasons, too." Drew shrugged. "I don't think we need to worry. Unless she seems really anxious?"

"No, that's what's disturbing; it's almost like it calms her." Jensen shook his head. "Mick and I are the ones getting anxious hearing about all the things that could happen to her. Like, not that I didn't know, but it's different hearing all the graphic details and the after statements and shit. I'm getting jittery. I checked the locks and the security system five times last night. Mick had to go take a pot break when I got home because he was getting so wigged out."

Looking over at Mason, feeling a bit concerned himself, David was slightly reassured that Mason didn't seem bothered at all.

"It's totally normal. It might be her way of coping, but it might just be what she's naturally drawn to," Mason reassured Jensen. "Nothing to worry about. Try to ignore it if you can."

"Easier said than done," Jensen muttered, rubbing his hand over his face. "At least she's Claudia's problem tonight."

The first popcorn kernel popping in the pan meant David could focus on that rather than the conversation, which was a relief. He wasn't sure what to make of Cassidy's entertainment habits. Not that it was any of his business.

Once the first kernel popped, it only took a few minutes for the rest of them to go, quickly filling up the pot. David quickly heated some butter in another pan, melting it while the kernels finished. Talk had already moved onto the upcoming fundraiser and the smaller jobs everyone was doing, whether or not Jensen should challenge Drew to another push-up match or wait a little longer, and whether Lincoln might be hiring someone for their team soon. Especially with Marshall getting into the building when he shouldn't have.

Abigail, their IT/hacker, had decided to stay active duty with the NSA rather than moving to the private sector with the rest of them. No one blamed her, she was happy with her job and was doing good work, but it had left an open spot on their team, which was why David had had to go to Jaxon for help. Before everything went down with Marshall, Jaxon and Marshall's guy Zeus had split the duties, but now it was all on Jaxon.

They needed a replacement for Abi, but it wasn't exactly easy, and Lincoln was busy with a lot of other things as well.

"Popcorn's ready," David said, causing a mass invasion of the kitchen as everyone came to collect their bowl and add the toppings they wanted.

Everyone steered clear of Jensen as he pulled out his own personal favorite, which David refused to store. He didn't want the

Trinidad scorpion powder anywhere near his food. He liked a bit of spicy as much as the next person, but that shit was lethal.

"Hey, careful," Mason said, turning and hunching around his bowl protectively as Jensen carefully sprinkled a tiny amount of powder over his own bowl straight from the bag.

"Pussies," Jensen said cheerfully, closing the bag, then putting it back in the Tupperware he carried it in. Both of which were necessary precautions because if that shit got in your face, you were going to be a seriously unhappy camper.

"If you won't touch it with your bare hands, you can't call me a pussy for not wanting it on my popcorn," Mason retorted. Considering he also had a higher spice tolerance than the rest of them, his caution made the rest of them even more adamant about keeping it away from them. He'd been the only one to try it the first time Jensen had brought it around, and after his hacking reaction, complete with running nose and red eyes, no one else had been willing to try.

"That's what she said," Drew cracked, making them all laugh.

David grinned. As much as he wanted to know how Cassidy was doing and what she was feeling, he was happy to be hanging out with his guys tonight.

He'd ask Claudia how things went tomorrow.

⁂

Cassidy

A ladies' game night. Not something she was used to doing. She'd had a few nights hanging out with some of the other Stronghold girls after being rescued, but there had always been at least one man in the house, too. And they'd never been like this.

Everyone had always tiptoed around her, avoiding certain topics, avoiding talking about their own happiness. Movies were up for discussion, and books, but any relationship news was stated with an apologetic look at her. The people who had seen her at the club hadn't known how to treat her.

Cassidy wasn't sure what they could have done differently. Nothing, probably. Especially when Don had started stalking her. She'd stopped going anywhere that she didn't have to and stopped hanging out with her friends, always too worried about what might happen to them if she was with them.

She didn't have to worry now, though.

Don had no idea where she was.

Plus, something about Claudia made her feel extremely safe, as though she could take care of anything that might come through her front door... or back... or window... Especially since, out of the whole team, she was the 'scary' one.

It also helped that everyone was laughing and joking freely, no one watching what they said, no unspoken reminders of her ex. They were all too busy teasing Jennifer over the pickles Cassidy had brought her. Not a single person seemed to believe they were from both Jensen and Cassidy. Jensen had neglected to mention that this was not the first time he'd given Jennifer pickles, though considering the way Jennifer was being teased, she could understand why he'd tried to include Cassidy in the gift. He was in for it the next time he saw any of these ladies.

"No, no," Naomi said reassuringly, patting Jennifer's hand in a manner that had Jennifer narrowing her eyes at the older woman. "I think it's really sweet that he wants to give you his pickle."

"*Pickles*," Jennifer said, emphasizing the plural.

"Little weird that he has more than one, but you do you." Claudia snickered.

"Argh!" Jennifer covered her face with her hands, shaking her head, though she was laughing at the same time. "Ya'll are the worst! There is *nothing* going on with us! He just wanted to give me... pickles."

"Yeah, I don't know why everyone is making such a big dill out of it."

Dead silence as they all turned their heads to stare at Yasmine, then the entire room cracked up. Puns were honestly the last thing Cassidy would have expected from her, though they'd just met. Yasmine was, for lack of a better word, elegant. Built like a model, tall and lithe, she had thick, long black hair, tanned skin, and eyes so dark brown, they were nearly black. She was striking in every way.

Everyone was wearing some kind of yoga pants or pajamas to be comfortable, but only Yasmine looked like she'd just come from a photo shoot.

If she wasn't so nice, Cassidy would find her wildly intimidating.

Scratch that. She did find Yasmine wildly intimidating, but she was so nice that some of it was rubbing off. The pun helped. Yasmine was now grinning widely as she took a sip of the dirty martini she'd made. Claudia had a full bar set up, along with a small fridge of bottled and canned drinks.

Cassidy hadn't had a drink in a really long time. She'd been too worried about what would happen if Don showed up and she was tipsy or, worse, drunk. So, she'd opted for a cider rather than going for the hard liquor. She was halfway through the bottle and already feeling looser, gigglier.

Relaxed.

"Okay, enough about Jensen's pickle," Claudia announced, causing another wave of giggles through the room as Jennifer groaned and flopped back on the couch. "We need to figure out what we're going to play. Seven Wonders?"

"No, no, I told you, I've got a new game," Naomi said, jumping up from her seat, drink in hand, as she hurried over to her bag by the door. "There's only five of us, which is perfect."

"What is it?" Jennifer asked, calling after her, obviously desperate to keep the change of topic going. Naomi was bent over, rummaging through her bag, while everyone looked on curiously. Claudia was pouting a little at not getting her way but seemed intrigued by the idea of a new game.

"It's called Deadly Dowagers." Naomi straightened up, holding up a small box. "We're going to kill off our husbands to increase our fortunes."

"Son of a bitch, I'm in!" Claudia jumped to her feet, and Cassidy burst into another bout of giggles.

This was the best night she'd had in a long time.

10

———

Learning Deadly Dowagers was fun, and thankfully, the game was fairly easy. Although, of course, that did mean that a lot of non-game talk happened.

"How's the job hunt going?" Jennifer asked Cassidy. "Have you picked something?"

Cassidy hesitated before answering, and not just because she was trying to decide whether to kill her current husband or if she should wait another round. She didn't want Jennifer to feel bad.

"I've been looking at them," she said. "I called a couple of the places." She should be grateful for any job, and she knew that, but part of her wished there was a way to do what she wanted to. So many other things were going her way, why not that one?

"I've got another job to add to the list if you want," Jennifer said, looking up from her cards. "It's not a guarantee, but she's doing interviews on Saturday. An older woman who needs someone to help her out—driving her around, keeping her company, helping with meals and stuff like that. I don't know if you'd be interested—"

"I am!" Cassidy said quickly. Was it nursing? No, but it sounded a lot more like what she wanted to be doing than any of the other options that had been on the list.

"Great. I'll set up the interview for you and send Jensen the information, okay?" Jennifer beamed at her.

"Thank you so much."

"Awesome, glad you got that worked out... so, whose husband gets to live through this round?" Claudia asked.

Cassidy couldn't help but laugh. Claudia was an absolutely ruthless game player. It was good because she kept things on track; otherwise, it would take them forever to get through a game. They were on their second round of Deadly Dowagers after a first play-through of learning how to do it, and Cassidy was pretty sure that they'd still be barely halfway through the first round if Claudia wasn't there.

"I'm killing mine," Naomi said, flipping the card for her current husband over to show his grave. "What are the options for the seventy-dollar husbands?" Claudia slid the cards her way so she could peruse them.

"I'm going to let mine live," Cassidy decided. She wanted to grow her estate a little more before she took him out, so she got a better payout.

This game was brutal and hilarious.

"I'm going to kill mine, too..." Yasmine said. "Can you hand me the fifty-dollar husbands?"

Cassidy giggled. Claudia handed them over but muttered something under her breath, apparently unhappy with how her game was going in comparison to the others. Cassidy already knew she wasn't going to win, but she was thoroughly enjoying just playing and hanging out with everyone.

"Anyone going to the Outlands tomorrow night?" Yasmine asked, picking out her new husband and handing over the money needed to secure him.

"Me," Claudia said.

"Drew and I are going."

"Not me," Jennifer said immediately. Cassidy glanced at her, a little surprised because there was something in her tone, and Jennifer smiled reassuringly at her. "No judgment. I would very much like to get my freak on, but my parents are members there, and I would rather die than run into them at a kink club. Especially if they're... doing something. And even if they aren't there, their best friends are my honorary aunts and uncles, and they aren't just members, but one of them owns it."

"Plus, your dad would probably have an aneurism," Claudia pointed out, snickering.

Jennifer rolled her eyes.

"Not just him. I'm pretty sure Uncle Gavin and Uncle Aiden would stare down anyone who even tried to talk to me. I'm pretty sure my aunts would be cooler about it, but who knows." She shrugged. "Eventually, maybe I'll get out there, but in the meantime, I just read and fantasize."

"That sucks, I'm sorry," Cassidy said, completely honestly. She'd never thought about multi-generational kink. She had no idea if her parents had been kinky or not.

"It is what it is." Jennifer took another sip of her drink. "You should definitely go through."

"I... guess I could." Cassidy wanted to but, at the same time, couldn't help but feel nervous. Yes, sometimes everyone knowing who she was and what she had been through meant they treated her like fragile glass. But in the club, everyone knowing who she was had meant never having to explain her past. If she scened with someone new, that would mean talking about everything with them.

Doms needed to know that kind of thing before a scene, especially for any triggers she might have.

She did want to go, but 'tomorrow' seemed so soon.

On the other hand, left to her own devices, she was honest enough to admit that she would probably put it off and put it off and put it off...

"Yeah, I will." She managed to say it with a bit of confidence. "I don't know if I'll scene though."

"There's absolutely no pressure to," Claudia said. "If you decide you want to, I can point you in the right direction and make introductions. I think it would be a good idea to get out and meet the local people, though. Most, if not all, of the team will be there in addition to us, so you won't be totally alone."

Most, if not all?

Did that mean David would be there, too? Cassidy shifted uneasily in her seat. She wasn't sure how she felt about watching him with someone else. On the other hand, maybe that would help her get over her crush.

"We can introduce you to more of the game night players, too." Yasmine smiled at her. "And you can tell us the difference between the Outlands and Stronghold and Marquis."

"Sounds good." It really did. Other than maybe having to watch David with someone else. But that would probably be good *for* her, even if it didn't sound like fun.

***

*D*AVID

Eyeing Jensen, David frowned. The night was wrapping up, though it wasn't quite time to leave yet, but even so, he wasn't sure he should let Jensen take Cassidy home.

"Are you sure you're going to be okay to drive?"

Even as the words came out of his mouth, he knew the likely reaction of everyone, and he was not wrong. Drew and Mason both looked at him with pure confusion while Jensen raised his eyebrow with bemusement.

"I've had two beers. I think I'm good, although I can have another glass of water if it will make you feel better." Jensen snickered. "Why, is there a reason you're extra worried about me tonight, Ginger?"

David scowled at him.

"There's nothing wrong with being worried when you're on guard duty. I'm just making sure."

"Uh-huh."

"Speaking of, Naomi just texted me," Drew said, making both Jensen and David turn to look at him. He was staring down at the phone in his hand. "She says Cassidy is going to the Outlands tomorrow."

Immediately, David frowned, digging in his pocket for his own phone.

"Why didn't Claudia text me?"

"I'm sure she will. Or Cassidy will tell Jensen when he picks her up." Drew smirked, his fingers moving over the screen of his phone, texting something back to his wife. "Naomi is telling me because she wanted to let me know that she wants to spend some time with Cassidy tomorrow."

Which meant Drew needed a heads-up so that he knew he wouldn't have his wife entirely to himself all evening and could adjust his plans accordingly. He and Naomi were in tune like that.

"Who wants guard duty tomorrow?" Mason asked. "I don't mind taking it if you all want to go scene."

David eyed him suspiciously. He'd expected everyone to try to 'not it' the duty. Why was Mason volunteering? Did he want to spend more time with Cassidy? Maybe see if *she* would scene with him? That would make it pretty easy to guard her.

Don't get emotionally or physically involved with the client.

Mason knew the rule as well as David did... but sometimes, rules got broken. Did Mason have an interest in Cassidy that went beyond duty?

"Not me, obviously, although I can do it while she's talking to Naomi, but we have plans for tomorrow night," Drew replied, shifting where he was sitting on the couch so he could shove his phone back into his pocket.

"I'd like a break from guard duty, even if I don't scene," Jensen admitted. "Cassidy is great, but I was hoping to totally relax tomorrow night."

"You don't want to scene?" David asked Mason, doing his best to sound noncommittal rather than suspicious.

"I don't *not* want to, but..." Mason shrugged. "I don't know. I haven't really been feeling it lately."

"That's not like you," Drew said, frowning and twisting to take a closer look at him. David couldn't help but frown, too. Mason was responsible for keeping the rest of them on an even keel, and he had his own therapist, but if he was struggling, David wanted to know about it. "What's going on?"

"I don't know." Mason leaned his head back against the couch. "My mom's been bugging me about finding someone and settling down again lately."

"That's not anything new," David pointed out. Mason's mom was much more hands-on than any of their mothers. Not that his parents were a good example, but Drew and Jensen both had moms who were involved in their lives. Mason's mom put them to shame, though, from the stories Mason told.

"Yeah, she suggested doing an arranged marriage since I'm having so much trouble finding a life partner."

Point in case.

"Holy shit," Jensen breathed out the words. "You aren't actually considering that, are you?"

Silence. David sat up, staring at Mason, who was avoiding all of their gazes. Drew looked horrified. Jensen actually had his hand on his chest. If he'd been wearing pearls, he would have been clutching them.

"There is some appeal to it," Mason admitted. "It's also not that unheard of. My parents were introduced to each other by their parents, and they worked out great. There's something to having someone who has known you since birth picking out someone they think would be good for you."

"But what about the parts of you that they don't know?" Drew asked.

"Yeah, what if they choose someone vanilla?" Not that vanilla was the worst thing to be, David supposed, but he also couldn't imagine stopping being kinky just because his parents had chosen someone for him who wasn't. And his parents definitely would. They'd insist on it, probably, since they'd been so horrified by him being kinky.

"Well, you don't just meet at the altar; this isn't *Married at First*

Sight or whatever." Mason chuckled. "We'd meet ahead of time. Get to know each other over a few dates and decide if we suit."

"So, more like *90 Day Fiancé*. Sorta." Drew shrugged when they all looked at him. He stretched his arms out and brought them down to rest on the back of the couch. "What? Naomi likes bad reality TV, and it's hard to tune it out. Some of it's actually fun to watch."

"I'm not sure since I've never seen it, but that sounds closer," Mason said dryly. "If we're completely incompatible, we don't get married. But if we seem compatible, we do, then we make it work. Might even fall in love. It happens more often than you think."

Or maybe people were fooling themselves into thinking they were in love because they were stuck. Not that it was any of David's business why people did what they did. It wasn't like he was some paragon of successful relationships. He also would never let his parents arrange his marriage. He'd rather die alone.

Maybe he'd let his sister...

"Anyway, I don't mind keeping an eye on Cassidy. I'm not really in the mood to scene, and it'll give me an excuse not to."

"I'll hang out with you just to keep an eye on things. If she does want to scene, I want to have a word with the Dom first. And I want to keep an eye on her for her first time in the club."

Mason nodded in understanding. "Sounds good. We can both keep an eye on her."

Great. And tomorrow, he'd make sure that he and Mason were on the same page about how to handle the Doms at the club in relation to Cassidy. The others didn't need to hear about that for now.

11

____

CASSIDY

All dressed up and totally not freaking out. Cassidy hoped. She was really trying not to. She hadn't realized how much more comfortable she'd felt returning to Stronghold rather than going to a new club.

New club meant new people, new Doms... and some of them might be like Don. It was possible. He had felt like he could go to Stronghold, after all. He hadn't thought anyone would intervene on her behalf. Abusers didn't announce themselves. If something happened up here, it would be her word against someone who was established in the club, someone with friends and connections.

She could end up with another Don. Someone who acted like they cared, who pretended they could give her everything she wanted and needed, then eventually changed.

Stop it. Breathe. You have friends, too.

Claudia had already said she'd look out for her. Plus, she didn't think Naomi or Yasmine would let her get in over her head, either.

Sometimes, it was hard to stop the spiral of her thoughts, the immediate jump to worst-case scenario.

She couldn't help but think about how this could be a trap. She'd show up at the club, and Don would be there, waiting. He'd maneuvered to get her there, away from Stronghold, and everyone at the Outlands believed him and not her, and they'd drag her to him, kicking and screaming. They'd watch as he whipped her bloody, then cheerfully send her home with him, collared and chained and no longer able to fight back.

Common sense reasserted itself.

Logically, she knew Black Fox Security could be trusted. That Kincaid wouldn't work for them, much less hand her over to them, if he didn't trust them. That two of them were related to her friends back in D.C. That her friends would check in on her. That absolutely nothing had been said or done to think that her guards were anything other than dedicated to protecting her.

But her head still went through the whole scenario, a fucked-up little movie on anxiety.

The good thing was that it was so outlandish, so far removed from what could possibly be real, it was very easy for her to dismiss the fear... eventually. After she played it out in her head. After her heart was pounding in her chest. After the metallic taste of terror coated her tongue.

But that was a lot better than back home, where the fear went with her everywhere. Back there, even though her fears were unlikely, they were not impossible. Especially with the way Don had been popping up around her. Knowing that things could get so much worse.

Here, her fears were a lot more easily dismissed because she knew she was safe.

Grabbing her favorite pair of club heels, the only ones she'd kept rather than donating to Naomi's shelter, she headed out of her room and down the stairs. Even though she was very practiced in walking in the four-inch heels, that didn't mean she wanted to walk down two flights of staircases in them when she didn't have to.

"Damn, girl, looking good!" Mick said, coming out of the kitchen as she neared the bottom of the staircase. He let out a low whistle. "Maybe I should start going to this club, too."

"Absolutely not," Jensen said dryly, following his brother out of the kitchen. "You'd find yourself tied up and your balls at the mercy of some dominatrix, screaming for me to help you and ruining my night."

"It was only that one time!"

"One time was more than enough." Jensen shook his head, glancing at Cassidy. "She hadn't even touched him. He just didn't listen when I told him what he was getting into. He told her he was willing to try anything once. That ended up not being true, though he didn't realize it at the time."

"She said she wanted to play with my nads, but really, she just wanted to crush them," Mick said mournfully. He looked at Cassidy. "You wouldn't crush my nads, would you?"

"Um... no?" She couldn't help but laugh. Mick was hilarious. A total himbo in some ways, incredibly smart in others, and always a sweetheart. She could see him as a submissive, though she imagined he would drive his top crazy.

"I told you I would find you a dominatrix who won't want to crush anything if you wanted me to," Jensen scolded in exasperation. "You weren't interested."

"What can I say? I like a bit of danger." Mick shrugged again and winked at Cassidy when Jensen made a noise like steam was escaping his mouth.

Pressing her lips together, Cassidy hid her smile as she sat down on the bottom of the steps to put on her shoes. Sometimes, it was hard to tell when Mick was truly clueless and when he was just trying to get under his brother's skin, but in this case, he was clearly enjoying winding his big brother up.

"Just not so much danger my balls *actually* get crushed. Anyway, it's fine. I'm baking tonight to test out some recipes, anyway."

"Can we taste test them?" Cassidy asked. She'd already found out that Mick was a phenomenal baker. While he worked a regular nine-to-five in the office, he had a side hustle on the weekends with a farmer's market.

"Absolutely. I'll leave them out on the counter when I go to bed," Mick replied cheerfully. "Have fun, y'all."

With that, he trotted up the stairs. Whatever he was working on tonight, he obviously hadn't started it yet. Well, no matter how tonight went, there would be baked goods to look forward to, so at least there was that.

"You do look good," Jensen said, giving her an admiring once over. Cassidy smiled at him as she tied the ribbons on her shoes. He held out his hand for her to take, helping her to her feet. The platform heels made her several inches taller than him, but he didn't seem bothered at all by the height difference. "Do you know if you want to scene tonight?"

"I haven't really thought about it... I figured I would go and see how I felt once I got there," she confessed. "I feel a little nervous about scening with someone I don't know."

Such an understatement, but admitting out loud that she was terrified of choosing another abusive Dom was too much. She hadn't even said it out loud to her friends, though she'd hinted around it. All of them had reassured her that, of course, that wouldn't happen.

But there were no guarantees. She never thought she would get into an abusive relationship in the first place.

That wasn't her.

Until it was.

"Gotcha. Mason and David are going to be keeping an eye on you, so if you do decide to scene, you can just let them know. They can make recommendations on who you scene with," Jensen said carefully.

David was going to be keeping an eye on her? A little tingle rippled through her body. *And Mason.*

But Mason didn't make her tingle.

"Um, great," she said.

Yeah, she didn't know if she was going to be able to scene tonight if she knew David was watching her. But at least she could go and meet people.

<u>*David*</u>

Watching the front door of the Outlands, waiting for Cassidy, was making David antsy enough that Master Gavin took notice. The club owner was behind the bar tonight, serving drinks and keeping an eye on things with the help of his wife, Leah. Wearing nothing but a kilt and boots, the Dom was in incredible shape for a man in his fifties. David hoped that he would look as good in twenty years. Even the salt and pepper of his hair and beard looked good on Master Gavin, making him appear distinguished.

"Everything all right?" Gavin asked, coming to a halt on the other side of the bar from David, frowning. He spoke with a light Scottish brogue that had a tendency to thicken when he was emotional. "Should I be expecting trouble of some kind?"

"No, sorry." David took a deep breath, turning toward the bar, though he positioned himself so he could still keep half an eye on the door. He forced his shoulders to relax. If he was wound up enough to disturb Gavin, he was wound up enough to disturb others as well. "Did Patrick tell you about the guest Jensen is bringing tonight?"

Understanding flashed in Gavin's eyes.

"Yes, he mentioned she's fled from a bit of trouble at home," Gavin said carefully, wiping down the counter in front of him. "My understanding is that it's highly unlikely to follow her here. Is that not the case?"

"No, it is..." David's voice trailed off as he tried to find a way to reassure Gavin without making it sound like he was a schoolboy with a crush. "As far as we can tell, she hasn't been followed, and her ex should still have no idea where she is. I'm on guard duty tonight, though, just in case, especially since this is her first time here. It's not my usual kind of job, and I'm feeling a bit antsy."

"Mm-hm. And she's submissive?"

"Yeah." David's head turned back toward the entrance as the door opened. His senses went on alert and then relaxed again as Mistresses Terrin and Amara walked in together, laughing.

"Pretty?"

"Beautiful."

"And you're attracted to her."

"Yeah— I mean, what? Wait, no." David shook his head, as if he could shake off his answer that easily. He glared at Gavin. The older man smirked at him. "I wasn't paying attention to your questions. That wasn't... I'm not..."

"Sure, son. Whatever you need to tell yourself." Still smirking, Gavin moved away as Terrin and Amara approached the bar, ostensibly to take their drink order. Really, probably, so he could have the last word.

David scowled after him, but there really wasn't anything he could do. Calling Gavin back to emphatically tell him that David was *not* attracted to Cassidy would only be confirmation that he definitely was.

And he couldn't even say truthfully that he wasn't. It was best just to let it go and hope Gavin didn't talk about it with anyone else. Because nothing was going to happen between him and Cassidy, anyway.

Still scowling, David spun on his barstool, defiantly facing the door, as if he didn't care what Gavin thought.

Which was why he saw the moment Cassidy came in. She walked through the door with her chin held high, though he could see the nervousness in every line of her body. She was walking in despite her nerves.

Her long brown hair had been pulled back into a high ponytail, which meant her hair couldn't be used for cover, showing off her stunning features and long neck. She wore nothing around her neck, which made it look like it was begging for a collar. The dark purple and black corset she was wearing pushed her breasts into deep cleavage, nipping her waist in to be almost impossibly small and making her hips appear extra curvy against the black PVC skirt tightly wrapped around them. She made the pear shape look damn good. Long legs ending in high heels with ribbons that tied around her ankles completed the look.

It was a lot of bare skin showing, and David couldn't help but drink in the sight of her. She'd been beautiful in her regular clothing, with her hair constantly swinging down to hide her face.

This outfit, though? The expanse of creamy skin against the dark colors of her clothing, face exposed to the world, looking like submissive sex on a stick... His groin tightened as he sucked in a quick intake of breath.

He was so caught up in looking at her that he barely noticed Jensen coming in behind her until the man moved to her side, and she turned to say something to him. Her gaze flitted around the room, taking in the main floor of the Outlands until her eyes reached him. They locked in on each other, and David could practically feel the air sizzle between them.

"Yeah, definitely not attracted to her." The soft Scottish burr on Gavin's last word was mocking.

David groaned inwardly.

Fuck.

12

CASSIDY

The Outlands weren't much like Stronghold or Marquis.

Like Marquis, the location was downtown rather than being completely off the beaten track like Stronghold. But, like Stronghold, there was no indication that this was a kink club. The windows were covered with heavy curtains and dark glass to keep anyone from being able to see in, and there was no sign.

As soon as she and Jensen stepped inside, there was a small space between the door they had just come through and a second door, which she assumed led into the club. Anyone walking in who didn't belong here would immediately be ejected by the big man standing at the other door.

"Hey, Gareth," Jensen greeted the man cheerfully. "This is Cassidy. She's not a member yet, but she probably will be soon. Tonight, she's hanging out with Claudia, and Mason and David will probably be hovering."

In some ways, Gareth reminded her of Jared, one of the Doms who guarded the foyer of Stronghold. He wasn't quite as tall, but he was close, with shoulders nearly as broad. But he was white with very pale blond hair and bright blue eyes, like a mountain-sized Targaryen.

"Collecting all the Spice Doms?" Gareth asked, and it took Cassidy a moment to realize he was talking to her and making a joke. "You're missing Sporty."

"I think Naomi's joining us, too," she said quietly, smiling up at him. "Gotta catch 'em all."

Gareth burst out laughing while Jensen sighed a very deep sigh. Poor Baby. Out of all of them, he probably had the hardest nickname to deal with, especially since he was a Dom.

"You'll do," Gareth said, grinning as he opened the door for them.

That door led into a foyer that was another cross between Marquis and Stronghold. Not as luxurious as Marquis, but not as bare-bones as Stronghold. There was carpet, and the walls were painted a rich dark green. The room was small but spacious enough to fit a small group of people. There was a desk with a small rack of coats behind it. A pretty black woman stood behind the desk, smiling as they walked in. She had shoulder-length hair that had been pressed straight, the ends brushing the tops of the spaghetti straps of the shimmering green dress she was wearing.

Jensen introduced her as Eben, and she welcomed Cassidy to the club before taking the lightweight jacket Cassidy was wearing to cover up the corset and tight skirt she was wearing underneath. The outfit wasn't totally inappropriate for an evening out at a regular dance club, but she still felt more comfortable with something over it until she got to the club.

Even in the club, even after Mick and Jensen's compliments, she was fighting the urge to cover up a little more. Another difference from Stronghold and Marquis. She hadn't felt quite as exposed, quite as vulnerable, walking into either of those places as she did tonight because tonight she was facing mostly strangers.

Or maybe you're feeling nervous because you know David is going to be watching over you.

Definitely another big difference between the clubs back home and the club here. Back home, there hadn't been any Dom she was attracted to. There were plenty she found attractive, but she hadn't felt a spark with any of them. Not like she had from the moment she met David.

So, it was no wonder she was feeling a bit like a nitwit.

Jensen held the door open to the club proper, and Cassidy stepped inside in front of him.

The club was full of people. Like Stronghold, it seemed that the main floor was dedicated to mingling and nonsexual activities. The majority of it was taken up by a bar. There were also tables and a small dance floor, much smaller than Stronghold had, and at the moment, no one was on it. The tables were half full. The wooden bar was more ornately carved than any she'd seen before, with dragon heads carved into it at various intervals.

It would not have looked out of place at a regular restaurant, other than the submissives kneeling beside the tables rather than sitting at them with their partners. Also, most bars didn't allow shirtless bartenders.

As she scanned the room, her gaze caught on David's, and her breath arrested in her throat. He was looking right at her, his expression carved from stone, his eyes blazing as they met hers. Suddenly, she could barely breathe, and it wasn't because of the corset.

Like Jensen, he was wearing leather pants. Unlike Jensen, he was also wearing a black button-down shirt that somehow made him appear even more intimidating than if he'd gone shirtless. It was also a little disappointing because part of her had been hoping to see a little more of him. She couldn't deny that it was a sexy-as-hell look, though.

"Oh, good, there's Ginger," Jensen said, coming up beside her. "I guess he's on duty first."

Right. Because he was here for her, just not in the fun way. Cassidy let out her breath with a long, silent sigh.

An older man stood behind David on the other side of the bar, watching her with interest as she came closer. He looked like he might be naked since his lower half was covered by the bar, showing off a muscular upper body that defied the grey of his hair and beard.

Amusement curled the edges of his lips as he watched her come closer.

With her height, she was able to see that he was *not* totally naked behind the bar, though she was a bit dumbfounded by the red plaid fabric she could see around his hips. What *was* he wearing?

And was she focusing on him as a way to help her not focus on David?

Yes. Yes, she was.

"Hey, man," Jensen said by way of greeting when they reached David. "Evening, Gavin."

"Evening, Jensen," Gavin said with a Scottish accent that had her staring at him, smiling easily at Jensen before transferring his gaze to her. "And this must be Cassidy."

Realizing he already knew her name gave her a jolt before she realized she recognized his, too. Master Gavin Craig, owner of the Outlands, father of her friend Mitch back at Stronghold. He knew her name because he was the owner, not because he was Mitch's dad, but it still gave a feeling of relief to know they were related. She hadn't met him before, but he was familiar by proxy.

"Hello, Master Gavin." She summoned a smile, trying to keep her focus on him and not on David, who was now standing close enough to her that all the little hairs on her arms were standing at attention, as if they could reach across the space to him. Her body's reactions to him were wildly embarrassing, considering he hadn't given any indication that he returned her interest. She really hoped no one else noticed them. "It's nice to meet you."

"A pleasure, love," Master Gavin said, reaching across the bar to shake her hand. Cassidy automatically put hers out to meet his, a little surprised by how firm and comforting just having him hold her hand was. He had that kind of aura, putting her immediately at ease and making her feel safe.

Beside her, David was glaring at the other man.

"Your accent is not normally that thick," he accused.

Chuckling, Master Gavin dropped her hand as a woman appeared beside him. Blonde-haired and blue-eyed, it was clear where Master Mitch got most of his looks from. He might have the same eyes as his dad—and maybe he'd look more like him with facial hair—but he resembled his mother more.

"He likes to use it to impress the ladies," the woman teased, smiling at Cassidy. Obviously secure in her relationship, she didn't seem at all bothered by her husband's mild flirting. She reached out her hand as well. "Hi, I'm Leah. I think you know our son Mitch?"

"I do. And Domi, of course," Cassidy said, shaking Leah's hand as well. Gavin put his arm around his wife, smiling down at her with pure love in his gaze. No wonder Leah didn't care if Gavin was charming to everyone; it was clear where his heart lay.

Now, that was the kind of relationship Cassidy had always wanted. Watching them, it was all she could do not to sigh wistfully. She wondered if Mitch knew how lucky he was that his parents were still so deeply in love.

As the two stepped back, she could finally see that Master Gavin was wearing a kilt on his lower half. Damn. Lucky Leah. *Tuck that under things I should definitely not ever say to Mitch unless I want to see his head explode.*

Not that she was going to be seeing Mitch any time soon to say it to him. Something that made her feel a little down, but she pushed the thought away. Maybe he'd come up here to visit his parents, and she could see him and Domi then. Though, then they'd know she was here, but she trusted them not to tell anyone. Her brain tried to push an image of Don somehow finding out that they knew where she was and torturing them to get the information, but she shoved that away, too.

There was no reason to think Don was that crazy just because he'd been abusive and occasionally violent and fixated on her for over a year and stalked both her and her friends. Plus, some vandalism that had been escalating.

Stop it.

David's hand touched her upper arm, the contact shocking her out of the spiraling thoughts and images flooding her brain and replacing them with sudden awareness of his nearness.

"Do you want a drink or anything?" he asked, his voice low and oddly intimate. Or maybe she was projecting, wishing it was.

"Water?"

He nodded, turning to Master Gavin to make sure the other man had caught that.

"Cassidy! There you are!" Yasmine's voice made her jump, and David's hand dropped away from her arm. Cassidy turned toward the other woman, who was smiling widely. She was holding out her hands, almost as if she wanted a hug, but instead of putting her arms around Cassidy, when Cassidy raised her hands, Yasmine caught them with hers and slid her hands up Cassidy's arms to rest in her elbows. Then she leaned forward to give Cassidy a kiss on each cheek.

Part of Cassidy felt like she should have known a hug wouldn't be Yasmine's style. Cheek kisses were much more in line with her elegance.

In her fetish clothing, she looked like she'd just stepped off the page of a kinky magazine. A high-end one.

Her PVC dress hugged her body, a huge cutout dipping low to show off her cleavage even though the fabric had a high neck and covered all of her shoulders. There were more cutouts at her waist, showing off triangles of her skin, and the short skirt didn't matter because her thigh-high boots nearly touched the hem of it. On her wrists, she wore black leather bracers that laced up the insides of her forearms. Her eye makeup was smoky, and her lipstick was bright red. Next to her, Cassidy felt plain in every way.

"You look wonderful," Yasmine said, not letting go of Cassidy's arms as she stepped back to look her up and down. "I love those shoes."

"Thanks, they're my favorite." And that was why she couldn't hate Yasmine.

It helped that David didn't give Yasmine more than a casual hello, obviously not interested in her. A moment later, Naomi and Drew walked in the door and joined them, then Claudia and Mason. The growing crowd attracted more people, and Cassidy found herself being introduced to one person after another and hoping they didn't expect her to remember all of their names.

Everyone's friendly warmth, the lack of knowledge about who she was and why she was there, showed in their curious interest and helped her relax inch by inch until the only piece of disquiet was her hyperawareness of the redheaded man watching her.

13

———————

David

A new guest to the club, outside of Newbie Night, always drew interest in large part because it was presumed they were there *with* someone. Nosiness in the club abounded. The fact that Cassidy appeared to be unattached—since the Dom who brought her immediately went off to flirt with other submissives—only created more interest. Especially from the other Doms.

David did his best to thwart them by taking up space near her, watching her intently, and glaring at anyone who looked like they might make her an offer. This was her first night here; they could all give her some damn breathing space. No need to circle her like a pack of wolves trying to decide who was going to get the first bite.

No one was biting her while he was around.

Yasmine wasn't helping either, pointing out various Doms and giving Cassidy a rundown of their preferences and her opinion on their skills. Though, at least she wasn't pushing Cassidy toward any particular Dom. She was just giving her a general overview of the club Doms—and including occasional bits of gossip.

"That's Master Lucas. He's fun, but you can't expect anything serious from him. He and Eben have this on-again, off-again thing.

They're terrible for each other, but they can't seem to stay away from each other." Yasmine shook her head sympathetically. "Oh, and that's Master Aiden. He's Mistress Cyana's submissive now, but we still call him Master Aiden."

"Oh... so he's a switch?"

"Only for her," Yasmine said cheerfully. "He used to be the club's biggest playboy. He was a really good Dom, too. Some of the subs were hoping they would start tag-teaming, but so far, they're staying fully monogamous and not even scening platonically with anyone else."

"It's been fun to watch," Claudia put in, grinning as she watched the unlikely pair across the room. "Put the fear of God into a lot of the Doms, wondering if the same thing could happen to them."

"Do you have a Dom you're interested in?" Cassidy asked Yasmine. "Like, someone I shouldn't play with?"

"Oh, no." Yasmine shook her head emphatically. "I have sworn off getting involved with anyone any time soon."

"Because she's the queen of bad dates," Naomi put in with amusement. "I have never met anyone with worse dating luck."

"It's true." Yasmine sighed. "Have you ever heard the saying 'always a bridesmaid, never the bride'? That's me in the club. If I start dating or agree to start scening more regularly with a Dom, he's pretty much guaranteed to find his perfect submissive before he and I can really get started. And if I try dating outside of the club..." She made a 'kaboom' noise, her hands moving in front of her to indicate an explosion. "I have been on the worst dates known to man."

"Like what?" Cassidy leaned forward with interest.

"Like that time her date brought his mom," David said before Yasmine could respond. It wasn't because he wanted Cassidy's attention on him for a moment. Not at all. It was just that the incident was burned into his brain because he happened to be at the same restaurant that evening on a pretty terrible date of his own. Though, at least she hadn't brought her dad. He and Yasmine had hung out at the bar afterward, comparing notes and comforting each other.

It had never gotten physical between them, they just didn't have that kind of spark, and that night had cemented their brotherly-sisterly relationship.

"No!" Cassidy gasped, turning to look at Yasmine, who nodded somberly.

"He did. David saw it, so I have a witness. Though, he wasn't as bad as the guy who spent the entire time talking about his ex. He ended up drunk, crying, and calling her while I patted his back and offered moral support. They're engaged now." Yasmine shook her head. "I'm invited to their wedding, but I'm not going, obviously."

Cassidy's mouth dropped open, and David's brain immediately went to a dirty place despite the conversation. It wasn't his fault that he saw her open lips and immediately wondered what his cock would look like between them—he wasn't trying to; it just happened.

"What about the guy who only matched with you because he thought you were a model, then was pissed you're actually in finance?" Claudia asked, snorting. "He was literally mad you had a brain."

"Oh, and he had the worst-smelling breath, too." Yasmine made a face. "Not that we kissed, but I could smell it across the table. He was taking garlic pills for hair loss for some reason. I didn't question it because I didn't really want to know."

"So, you never make it past the first date?" Cassidy sounded both appalled and sympathetic.

"Sometimes, I do, but it always goes downhill pretty fast." Yasmine sighed. "Best boyfriend I ever had lasted a year. It ended when I ran into him with his wife and two children at a grocery store."

"No!" Cassidy's hands actually flew to her mouth to cover it, much to David's simultaneous disappointment and relief.

"Yup." Yasmine smiled, but it was obvious to David that this one still hurt. It had only happened about two years ago, and that was when she'd sworn off men. David had tried to get her interested in one of the guys on his team, to no avail. Again—no spark. "The good news is, when he tried to come to the Outlands about six months after that when his wife left him, he saw me, turned beet red, and hightailed it out of here."

Mason sidled up to David's other side, drawing his attention away from the conversation.

"Hey, do you know if Cassidy is up for scening tonight?" Mason asked, causing David to immediately go on high alert.

"I don't know. Why?" He didn't mean to bark out the question, but that's how it came out. Mason eyed him with some curiosity and suspicion.

"Roger is interested in asking her to scene, but he noticed you watching over her and assumed she's under your protection."

Good. That was exactly the vibe David had been doing his best to give off. He pressed his lips together.

He couldn't answer for her unilaterally, as much as he wanted to. Roger was a good Dom, a steady one, who was one of the club sub's favorites. He was a deft hand at the whip, generous with aftercare, and a generally good guy.

Right now, David kind of hated him.

Clearing his throat, he nodded. "I'll check and see if she wants to scene."

God, he hoped she said no.

<u>*Cassidy*</u>

A flare of awareness tingled along her skin, sliding up the back of her neck, and she turned slightly to see David suddenly standing much closer to her. He'd been part of the group conversation but hanging back a bit and definitely not invading her personal space until this moment. She had almost been able to pretend like he didn't affect her.

Almost.

Now, he was standing so close to her that if she just leaned a little, they would touch.

Not leaning was suddenly an effort.

"Are you interested in scening tonight?" he asked gruffly.

Immediately, Cassidy straightened to attention.

"With you?" She didn't know why she asked because who else would he be asking for, but she needed a moment to get her brain back on track. That was the last thing she'd expected him to say. She sounded a lot more breathily hopeful than she would have liked, considering she wasn't sure what her answer should be.

David blinked, a little furrow appearing between his eyebrows. "Me?"

Oh. Maybe she hadn't been wrong to ask.

"Who else?" Flustered, she drew back from him slightly.

"Ah, well..."

"This should be interesting," Claudia said, softly laughing. "Yeah, David, who should Cassidy scene with?"

Looking over Cassidy's shoulder at Claudia, David scowled at her before returning his focus to Cassidy.

"Maybe we should step away from the table for a minute to talk."

"Sure," Cassidy said, despite the round of protests that rose up behind her. Everyone was nosy. Which she appreciated on one level, but she also wanted David to be comfortable, and stepping away would help with that. Plus, she wasn't sure she wanted everyone listening to him reject her.

They didn't go far, only a few steps away, which gave them enough space to talk privately as long as they stood closely together. Very closely. With his head bent toward her in a manner that made her whole body flush. She tried not to squirm under his focused attention.

"Let's start with... do you want to scene in general? Then we can move on to who you'd like to scene with," he said, which sounded eminently reasonable, but there was a problem.

"I won't know if I want to scene unless I know who I'd be scening with." She wasn't going to scene with just anyone. Especially when she was surrounded by strangers. "Claudia also said she'd give me the okay on whether or not she thought a Dom would be good for me to scene with."

"Claudia, Yasmine, *and* Naomi will probably all weigh in," David admitted, his mobile lips twitching in something reminiscent of a smile before it faded again. His expression went completely blank, so she couldn't tell what he was thinking at all as he studied her face. "Um. Did you want to scene with me?"

Yes.

But only if he wanted to scene with her.

"I don't want you to feel like you *have* to scene with me." Because how utterly humiliating would that be? She'd only been interested because she'd thought he was offering. She would never presume to ask.

"I know I don't have to, but did you want to? You seemed interested when you thought I was offering."

"Yeah, but then I found out that you weren't actually offering," she countered, crossing her arms over her chest. It wasn't defiance so much as wanting to feel like she had some kind of defense against him. Maybe a little bit of a self-hug.

"I wasn't *not* offering." His expression was still decidedly neutral, but he was examining her very closely, as if he was trying to read her mind.

If only she could read *his.*

"Well, if you're not offering, then you don't have to scene with me," she said, trying not to sound irritated, even though she kind of was. Well, not irritated, exactly. Feeling rejected. Like he'd gotten her hopes up, then it turned out to be false.

His stone-faced expression was slowly giving way to a frown.

"I just said I wasn't *not* offering!"

Cassidy blinked, trying to put together the double negative.

"So, that means you *are* offering?" She just wanted to make sure she understood what he was saying because right now, she was very confused about whether he actually wanted to scene with her.

"If you want to."

"You're the Dom, you're supposed to decide!" There was no way in hell she was going to admit she wanted to scene with him if he didn't want to scene with her.

Had he just growled?

Cassidy squeaked, starting to step back as he stepped forward, reaching for her. His hand caught her around the back of her neck, halting her retreat, and her breath caught in her throat. A heated flush went through her whole body, flaming her cheeks and making her sensitive parts tingle.

Behind her, she could hear a chorus of feminine "ooohs", proving the other women were definitely paying attention, even if they hadn't been able to hear the full conversation. Since none of them were jumping in to stop what was happening, she could only assume all three of them approved.

"Cassidy, I would like to scene with you, but we need to lay a few ground rules first."

Staring up at him, wide-eyed, she nodded her head. Well, nodded it as much as she could when he was holding her by the back of her neck. And why was that so freaking hot? She'd never liked being choked, but no one had ever held her by the back of her neck before.

It was intimate, but more than that, it made her feel safe. Protected.

Part of her wanted to melt against his grip, but the other part of her was on pins and needles, waiting for the rules.

His eyes were jade with little flecks of gold, his gaze boring into hers.

"Rule number one, this is a scene only. Since my team is guarding you, it would be a conflict of interest for me to be involved with you in any way outside of the club."

Did that mean that he would want to be if there wasn't a conflict of interest? Moot point. She felt a little flare of anger for yet another thing Don had stolen from her. If she and David had met in another way... and yet, they might not have met at all if it wasn't for Don.

Either way, what he was saying was the most sensible route for them. It wasn't like she was trying to jump into a new relationship. She was still trying to get rid of the old one.

"Rule number two..." He stopped for a moment, as if he'd forgotten rule number two, before he cleared his throat and kept going. "Rule number two, we are going to go over everything that might trigger you before we start, and rule number three is that if you feel uncomfortable or unsure at any point in the evening, you are to say your safe word. And rule number four is that nothing that happens inside the club affects us outside of the club. Agreed?"

Cassidy relaxed because none of that was unreasonable, and all of it made sense to her. She nodded.

"Agreed."

14

———————

*D*AVID

Get a fucking grip on yourself, man.

He'd started going over rules, but he'd only actually had one prepared and had to make up the most ridiculous additional rules on the spot and hope he didn't sound too ludicrous. If he'd been think-ing, he would have just told her his expectation without calling it rule number one out loud, but...

Well, fuck.

He'd been flustered.

He hadn't wanted to admit that he wanted very badly to scene with her and that he was going to have to rein himself in from flip-ping his shit if she scened with someone else. Having her agree to scene with him had felt like a sigh of relief, even though he knew he was going to have to put up with his team ribbing him for it.

Already, Claudia was smirking at him from her seat, like she'd guessed what was about to happen. Naomi was smiling slightly but with a warning in her eyes, silently sending the message—*don't fuck this up.* Yasmine gave him a little nod, but she was cautious, too.

Stepping to the side, keeping his grip on the back of Cassidy's neck, he at least got them facing the same way so he could lead her away from her little group. More privacy was better at this point. He could at least tell his team that he wanted to make sure she was okay scening in the club and that it didn't have anything to do with how badly he wanted to get his hands on her.

No one was going to think badly of him for making sure she was alright to scene or wanting to get a handle on what she liked so that he could make sure she found appropriate partner pairings.

"Over here," he said, leading her to the balcony that looked over the lower floor of the club. When the Outlands had first opened, that had been the only floor of the kink club, and this upper level had been a restaurant during the day and a dance club at night. Now, it still functioned as a restaurant in the evenings on this floor, but only for kinksters who wanted to come have a meal before the evening's festivities started—and they started earlier than they used to. Master Gavin had said he was too old for everything to start at nine o'clock at night now. The restaurant opened at four, and the downstairs opened at seven instead.

Cassidy's eyes widened as she got her first good look over the balcony rail, and David watched her watching the people below. Her lips parted as her gaze darted around. The overlook was very large, showing off most of the floor beneath them. Most of what couldn't be seen were the private rooms, so even once they headed down to the lower floor, they wouldn't be able to see what was going on in those, anyway.

From here, they could see the various St. Andrew's crosses and nooks around the walls of the Dungeon, as well as the tables, chaises, benches, and various other pieces of bondage equipment that were set up around the club. At one, a woman was bound to a doctor's examination table while another woman dripped hot wax onto her breasts, making her cry out and writhe against the straps holding her in place.

The spanking benches were occupied, but most of the attention was going to a male submissive who was getting caned. By the way he howled every time his body jerked, David suspected there were prob-ably weights or something else hanging from his balls, even though he couldn't see from this angle. Mistress Michelle looked like she was enjoying herself thoroughly.

The alcoves were half full of people in various stages of undress, either chained to the wall, clinging to a cross, or bound to a frame. Leather smacked against flesh. Moans, cries, whimpers, and gasps filled the air, punctuated by the barking orders of the tops and dominants, with the low hum of a violet wand strumming beneath it all.

Sex was in the air, and David found himself stroking the side of Cassidy's neck with his thumb without meaning to. He couldn't help it. Her skin was so soft. Plus, it seemed to soothe her, so as a good Dom, he couldn't stop in good conscience. She turned her head to look at him, her hazel eyes alight with eagerness and desire.

Despite what had happened to her, she didn't seem at all hesitant to be here in the club with him. She trusted him. And that was even more of an aphrodisiac than the outfit she was wearing.

"I've already read over your survey and limits," he said. It had been part of his preparation for watching over her tonight. Stronghold's survey wasn't exactly the same as the Outlands, but it was close enough, and Master Patrick had sent it along with her file as well as providing a copy to Gavin. "Is there anything you want to specifically stay away from this evening?"

She hesitated, and he could feel her tense slightly under his fingers. There was something, he could tell, but she didn't want to tell him.

Giving her a stern look, David tightened his grip on her a little.

"Cassidy, tell me."

"I don't want to be tied up," she blurted out. "Or cuffed to anything."

She didn't want to be helpless with a Dom she'd never scened with before, unable to get away. David nodded immediately and felt her relax again, her sigh of relief almost inaudible but noticeable. The fact that she'd been anxious about making such a reasonable request made him want to go find Douchebag Don and pound the asshole's face into the ground.

Fucking abuser masquerading as a Dom. He was the kind of shitbag who gave the lifestyle a bad name.

Now, it was David's turn to let out a slow breath as he pulled in his emotions. Cassidy's ex had no place here; he needed to focus on Cassidy herself. Not just because he wanted to but because she deserved it.

***

CASSIDY

One day, she would be able to tell her Dom a preference without feeling fear racing up her spine, but today was not that day. Even though, logically, she'd known that David would not be upset by her request. She didn't want him feeling like she didn't trust him—she did, or she wouldn't want to scene with him at all—but she hadn't been able to be secured in place without panicking ever since that scene with Don.

She'd been working on it at Stronghold, but always with her friends. Other submissives. Mistress Julie or Mistress Olivia. Never with a male Dom. Now was not the time to jump into trying that, especially during a real scene and not deliberate exposure therapy. Especially because the last thing she wanted to do in front of David was panic and embarrass herself.

They'd barely managed to get to the point of agreeing to scene together. The fact he'd mentioned possibly scening together in the future gave her hope that this wouldn't be the last time, but she had a feeling that hiding her stipulation, then panicking because she'd hidden it, would be a deal breaker for him. Don wouldn't have cared because he wouldn't have cared that she was panicking, but none of the dominants she'd made friends with at Stronghold would have tolerated that from their scene partners.

"Anything else?" David asked. "Implements that you want off the table? Are you okay with public scening, or would you prefer private?"

"I'm fine with any implements that aren't already on my no list."

Canes were a hard no for her, as were single tail whips, but she was completely open to floggers, paddles, crops, and others. There were a few kinds of nipple clamps that were hard noes for her as well, but it left plenty open. "Private if there's any sexual contact."

She didn't particularly want an audience for her first time having sex post-Don.

"No need to worry about that," David said, breaking eye contact to turn his attention back to the activities below them. "We're going to keep it completely platonic. It would be unethical of me to scene with you otherwise. If that changes how you feel about scening with me, I understand."

"It doesn't." She would rather scene with him without sex than scene with anyone else with.

Why she would be willing to jump into bed with him so soon after meeting him, when she hadn't found anyone back home that she felt interested in doing so with, she didn't know. Her unexpected attraction to him had locked on hard.

Though, she wished that he was maybe a little more unethical. Or that the circumstances didn't make him feel that sleeping with her would be unethical. But she kind of got it. She'd read bodyguard romances before. They definitely weren't supposed to sleep with their clients.

Too bad this wasn't a Lexi Blake novel. That security team always ended up sleeping with their clients.

David didn't seem the type to unbend, though. She was surprised he was even scening with her.

His thumb moved up and down the side of her neck as his gaze returned to hers, as if he was stroking her for giving the right answer. Caught by his eyes, Cassidy pressed her thighs together, trying not to whimper. Knowing that she was getting no sex, she didn't want him to know how turned-on she was.

Just a scene.

Platonically.

No biggie.

"We can still check to see if there's a private room available if you prefer."

Did he prefer a private room? Maybe that's what he was trying to say. He might not want his entire team watching them scene, especially since she was technically their client. Even though she knew he was trying to give her what she wanted, what she really wanted was to give him what *he* wanted.

However, she wasn't going to challenge him on how he was supposed to be the one making decisions right now. With his hand on her, their agreement to do a scene together, she did not want to 'learn a lesson' tonight.

"Whatever you prefer, Sir."

His green eyes warmed, the edges of his lips curling up. Yeah, she'd uno-reversed him. Successfully, this time.

"Okay, little spark. Let's go downstairs."

Little spark. Why that made her feel melty all over again, she wasn't sure. Maybe it was just because he'd given her a nickname at all, even though she didn't entirely understand it. And she wasn't going to ask and make him explain. It didn't matter.

She let him lead her around the edge of the balcony over to where the stairs down were. The door for an elevator was right beside them for anyone who needed it. Cassidy liked walking down the stairs, though, because more and more of the bottom floor slowly came into view, like a striptease of a club.

Though the far side that was under the balcony was mostly walls and doors, there were more alcoves set along the wall between the doors. There were also photographs similar to the ones in the lobby at Marquis. Striking images in black and white, the light and shadow on the people depicted within them made them appear especially dramatic. All of them were kink-based, adding to the eroticism in the room on what would have otherwise been a blank space.

The noise seemed to get louder as they descended, and she felt her excitement rise in response. It didn't matter that most of the scenes happening didn't directly involve more than two people.

There was a sense of community just walking into the space, even more so than there had been upstairs.

She and David garnered several curious looks, but no one approached the way they had upstairs. Cassidy got the impression that meeting someone new around the bar was one thing, but now that she and David were in the Dungeon, everyone was going to mind their own business. For now.

It was very much like at Stronghold.

It added to her sense of community and being in a place of friends. Just friends she hadn't met yet.

All of which paled compared to how it felt to walk through at David's side, his hand on her neck gently guiding her through the crowd. She knew it was likely her imagination, but she couldn't help but feel like he had a possessive hold on her. Probably because she wished it was a possessive hold. It was definitely protective, which made sense.

"I think that alcove is open," he said, bending to speak low in her ear, sending a little shiver up and down her spine. It took her a moment to realize which one he was talking about because all the ones she saw were occupied, but then she realized the one in the very far corner was empty. Its corner space in the back of the room made it more private and harder to see into.

The wallpaper in the alcove made it look like brick, and there was fake ivy hanging down from a few places. The whole little area was set up to be its own little mini torture den, depending on what the Dom wanted. D-rings and hooks were inset up and down the sides, waiting for rope or chains, as well as along the ceiling. There was space for a St. Andrew's cross if they wanted one.

Between the various D-rings and hooks were hanging implements and little handles on what looked like might be drawers. The brick pattern of the wallpaper made it harder to tell, but she was pretty sure they were drawers, reminding her of the way Stronghold and Marquis had spaces for toys.

Cassidy jumped when a submissive appeared beside David, a small bag in hand.

"Here, Master David, enjoy," the man said, grinning and winking at Cassidy. She smiled back.

"My club bag," David explained as the man walked away, setting the small bag down at his feet. "If I'm not planning on scening, I tend to leave my regular bag at home, but I like having some things here in case I change my mind."

Made sense to her. But that meant he hadn't been planning on scening?

Had he changed his mind because he wanted to scene with her?

Or had he decided to scene because he thought she wanted to scene with him?

How pathetic am I in this scenario?

Stop thinking about it. You're already in it. Just enjoy. It doesn't matter.

It did matter to her pride, but she could shove that aside for now. Even if he hadn't planned to, he seemed eager now, and that would have to be good enough for her.

Thankfully, he didn't seem to notice that she was all up in her head. He was staring at the alcove, frowning in focus. She recognized the look. A Dom who was thinking about what he was going to do for his scene, how he was going to torture his submissive.

Cassidy's pussy clenched, her insides fluttering in anticipation. She was also way more nervous than she had been at Stronghold. None of those scenes had felt like they mattered, other than to prove to herself that she still craved kink, that Don's abuse hadn't changed that.

This...

They weren't going to have sex.

David had been clear that everything was going to stay in the club.

But, somehow, it still felt like it mattered.

15

_____

From a hidden vertical slot in the alcove, Master David had produced a wooden bar that he set up across the top of the space. It went all the way across, above her head. About an inch in circumference, it made the alcove look a bit like a closet, which made her want to giggle.

"Okay, little spark." Master David patted the wooden bar with one hand as he turned to look at her, his other hand coming out as if to draw her forward. "Come hold on to the bar."

Ooh.

It didn't take a genius to figure out that he was going to use the bar to have her hold position since she'd requested not to be bound. It was low enough that she could easily hold on to it but high enough that she would be stretched out and at his mercy. There wouldn't be anything for her to lean on, like with a cross. It was more like an impromptu frame.

Stepping into the alcove, Cassidy started to reach for the bar.

"Face the other way," Master David said gently, his hands going to her hips and turning her in place.

She liked it a little too much when he touched her.

Reaching up, facing out toward the rest of the club—a lot of which she couldn't see thanks to being in the corner—Cassidy wrapped her fingers around the wooden bar. There was just enough space that Master David could circle around her, though he certainly wouldn't be able to flog her back while she was in this position.

Trying to guess what he might be planning, realizing that she didn't know him well enough to even have a clue, was exciting and nerve-wracking in equal measure. At Stronghold, she'd gotten to know the Doms well enough to know what to expect. The submissives tended to compare notes, so she hadn't needed to scene with one to know that he was an ass guy or a tits man or had a fondness for using his belt over any other implement.

With Master David, she had no idea.

Fear chased anticipation chased arousal chased nervousness.

Holding the bar tightly, her tongue darted out to wet her lips, which felt like they had suddenly gone dry. She tilted her head back slightly as Master David walked around behind her, studying her from every angle. His fingers trailed along the narrow band of skin that had been exposed between her corset and her skirt, thanks to how she was stretched upwards.

The little touch sent sparks fizzing up and down her body, her nipples feeling itchy as they tightened. She squirmed in place, which shifted the stiff fabric of the corset, rubbing her breasts against the interior, stimulating the little buds further. Her quick intake of breath wasn't just because he was touching her but because of the emotions careening around inside her.

Master David came around to her front, his head bent to look at her, to study her expression. She met his gaze, heart in her throat, as his fingers continued to move over her skin. Then he walked around behind her again. This time, he stopped behind her, and she had one moment to wonder what he was going to do—her senses ruffling in anticipation—when she felt the tug on her corset strings.

The constriction around her torso relaxed, and she let out a shuddering breath.

The cords tugged again, and the corset loosened further.

David came around in front of her, taking hold of the top edges of her corset where the clasps were. His fingers slid under the fabric, pressing into the soft flesh of her breasts, then his gaze clashed with hers. He looked her directly in the eye as he pushed the sides of the corset together and lifted the side with the top clasps, opening it.

Cool air slid over her body, hard nipples puckering further as the corset was dropped to the side of her, leaving her exposed from the waist up. David's gaze dropped admiringly, taking in her curves as he put his hands on her sides and slid them upward to cup her breasts.

"Very pretty breasts, little spark," he murmured, and she felt herself flush with approval. "How sensitive are they?"

"Um... in comparison to what, Sir?" she asked breathlessly, shivering as his hands cupped the soft mounds and squeezed. Heat and need surged inside her, and it was all she could do not to whimper as his thumbs brushed over the hard buds of her nipples.

He chuckled.

"Fair enough. Tell me when it hurts." His fingers closed around her nipples, his gaze locking onto hers again as he did so. Cassidy's lips parted in a gasp as he pinched the sensitive nubs hard. She started to lift up on her toes.

"It hurts, Sir."

"But you don't want me to stop, do you?"

Cassidy shook her head, feeling her ponytail swinging, hair brushing against her upper back with the movement. If he stopped now, she'd be disappointed.

His grip tightened, crushing the tender buds, and she went up on her tiptoes, her head falling back as her body arched, thrusting her breasts at him as if begging for more. It hurt, but it felt so good at the same time, assuaging the ache inside her, making her throb along.

Rolling her nipples between his fingers, he pinched them, tugging on them and testing her with each little bit of torture. Seeing how much she could take. Eyes closed, mouth open, she panted, moaning as he took his time playing with her. The bar she was holding onto creaked, her fingers flexing on its length.

Holding still was so much more difficult than being held in place, and she regretted that she wasn't ready to be bound. It would have been a lot easier than keeping her hands on the bar when all she wanted to do was reach down and hold on to his wrists.

"I think these pretty nipples need some jewelry."

"If it pleases you, Sir."

Whatever he wanted.

David

Fucking hell.

His cock was rock hard and aching to be released from his pants.

Why did I say no sex again?

Because I'm a dumbass.

No, because I'm professional.

A professional dumbass.

It was the right decision, and he knew it, but he didn't have to like it.

Already, he was pushing against the lines governing his behavior. It wasn't like he had to play with her breasts to give her a satisfying scene. He just hadn't been able to keep his hands off her, and right now, he had an excuse not to. Besides, she liked it. And he had planned to make sure he knew what her limits were so he could keep an eye on her... ascertaining them for himself made sense.

The stiff buds were now a darker pink, flushed from all his ministrations, than they had been when he'd first pulled her corset free of her body. The urge to bend down and suck one rosy nub into his mouth was almost overwhelming, but that felt like going over the lines he'd drawn in the sand for himself. So, clamps it was.

Cupping one breast with his hand, he closed the rubber-tipped clamp around it.

Cassidy moaned low in her throat, and he felt the sound of it all the way down his body to his dick, which throbbed against his pants. The clamps were at about mid-tightness because he wasn't sure how much she would be able to take. The other clamp hung from the chain connecting them, and he scooped it up, switching his hold to her other breast, hefting it so he could attach the clamp to that nipple as well.

"How does that feel, little spark?" he asked, watching her face closely for her reactions. She was like a banked fire, simmering low in the embers, tiny sparks floating off her, not quite ready to come roaring back to life. What would it take for her to fully catch fire and flare again?

Would he be the one to turn her spark into a flame?

"Good, Sir," she said breathlessly, her voice huskier than before.

"I think you can take a little more then, don't you?" The question was rhetorical. He was already reaching to hold the first clamp, his other hand grasping the tiny screw and turning it to tighten the grip.

"Oh!" She went up on her toes, her head falling back again as the clamp tightened around her nipple, squeezing it tighter with every turn of the screw. David gave it a good four turns before moving to her other nipple and repeating the process with that clamp.

By the time he was done, she was panting for breath, shuddering, and shifting the muscles of her arms and shoulders as they bunched together and relaxed. He bet that if he thrust his fingers into her underwear, he would find her soaking wet.

But I'm not going to do that because I'm a professional dumbass.

"There we go," he said with satisfaction, giving the chain hanging between her breasts a little tug. She squeaked as he released the chain, and it bounced, breasts jiggling from the motion. Wide eyes met his, filled with heat and need and pleading. "Let's get you turned around. I want to use the flogger."

That and he needed her to stop looking at him before he said fuck it and threw his ethics to the wind just because he wanted to get laid. He didn't know why she had such an effect on him, but he couldn't deny that she did.

Maybe because she was forbidden fruit. If he could have her, he wouldn't want her as much.

Or maybe I'm fooling myself.

Ignoring the insidious little voice in his head, David kept his hands on her hips as he spun her around. Once she was no longer facing him, once he couldn't see her big doe eyes peering up at him anymore, once her breasts were no longer begging him to touch them, he felt like he could breathe a little easier. As much as he'd enjoyed watching her expressions, the interplay of fear and excitement chasing across her face in equal measure, seeing them was also making everything harder. Especially his cock.

The ends of her hair brushed across her shoulder blades, and David carefully moved her ponytail so it hung down in front of her.

"Bend your head forward so the flogger doesn't catch your hair," he ordered. The last thing he wanted was the strands of leather getting tangled with the silky strands of her hair. Was it even possible? He wasn't sure, but he wasn't about to take the chance.

Cassidy's head bent just a touch, and David couldn't help but slide his finger down her spine, tracing the long length of her back until the waistband of her skirt cut him off. Her skirt was definitely staying on. He wasn't a fucking masochist, and he had already been torturing himself.

As his finger moved over her back, her shoulders rolled, then relaxed, and he saw her let out a long sigh. Good. That was exactly what he wanted for her. She should be able to relax. To feel safe. To know that she was protected.

"Good girl," he said, giving her butt a pat over the PVC skirt. Not hard enough to be a swat, but firm enough that she'd be able to feel it. "Stay right there."

"Yes, Sir," she murmured as he moved away, going to his bag to get the flogger he kept there. It wasn't his favorite flogger, which was in his regular toy bag, but he liked it well enough, and it was perfect for tonight. Light enough to be on the edge of stingy and thuddy while the knots on the end of it added a bit of extra weight and sensation.

Getting into place, he felt eyes on him, and he looked over to see Claudia watching him from about ten feet back. He raised his eyebrows at her, but she just nodded. She was watching over things, most likely so that she could reassure Cassidy that she had. If it were anyone else, David might have felt insulted at the lack of trust, but he knew this was about Cassidy, not him.

Besides, if Claudia caught something, some reaction, that he missed, he'd thank her for it.

Refocusing his attention on Cassidy, he flicked out the flogger, letting the leather fall over her bare shoulders in a pattern of sensation. She shuddered, rolling her shoulders again, her head moving back and forth.

Stepping forward, he ran his hand over the spot where he'd just landed the blow.

"How was that?" he asked. To him, it had been light, but this was their first time scening together, and he wanted to make sure he had a good understanding of her limits.

Cassidy turned her head slightly, enough so he could see her profile and that she was smiling as she sassed him.

"A little weak. Sir."

The way she said it was daring, as if she was testing him. Seeing what he would do. He wasn't sure if it was because she was bratty or because she was uncertain of how he would react to an insult. Though, she didn't tense when she said it, so he hoped she was just feeling comfortable enough to push him a little.

Very well.

Challenge accepted.

16

CASSIDY

Daring to brat at Master David should have felt more dangerous than it did. The fact that she was more excited than fearful meant she trusted him more than she'd realized. Part of her knew she was testing him, just a bit, to make sure that he was everything he seemed...

She hadn't needed to worry.

He didn't get upset. Or yell. Or immediately lash out at her.

Instead, he chuckled with clear amusement and gave her butt another little pat before stepping back.

A corner of her mind was braced for serious impact in case his initial reaction was to lull her into complacency.

The flogger fell again, harder this time, thudding against her skin, stinging her shoulders and upper back, but it was by no means a vicious strike. It was still meant for her enjoyment. Part of the reason Cassidy enjoyed the flogger was because it was almost like a massage.

David was very, very good at it.

Not too hard, not too soft; he'd found the place that was just right.

Her nipples and pussy throbbed in time with the flogging. The tight grip of the clamps had faded, the little buds numbed somewhat from being pinched so tightly. Sparks of the stinging pinch returned when she squirmed, and the chain bounced, gravity tugging at the clamps as the chain between them moved.

Swinging it over and over, the leather rain pattered against her skin, again making her wish that she didn't have to hold on to the bar. That she could truly let herself go, let herself be free…

But that required either a very different position or some kind of bondage to help her hold herself in place.

The flogger paused, and Master David came closer again. She sensed his movement even though she couldn't see it. Felt his hand before it touched the now-sensitized skin on her shoulders and upper back. Bit back a moan as he ran his callused fingers over the pinked spots he'd just flogged.

"What color are you, little spark?"

"Green, Sir."

The stoplight method of communicating the experience was what had saved her at Stronghold. It was a common way of keeping in touch between dominant and submissive, and everyone knew that 'red' meant stop.

Cassidy had only said it once.

She shuddered.

"Good girl," Master David said, running his hand down her back again, bringing her back to the present and pushing her memories of the past out of her head. "Now spread your legs a little more. I want your feet wider apart."

A widened stance meant her upper body was stretched out more, her breasts thrust out in front of her, and the tight fabric of her skirt inched upward. The little coverage she had over her butt threatened to give up entirely and show him and anyone who might be watching a nice view of her lacy thong. It stopped just short of rolling up over her curves as she settled into place.

"Good, right there."

Cassidy jumped, squealing, as the flogger hit the inside of her thighs. For some reason, even with the widened stance, she hadn't been expecting it. Her breasts bounced with her, far more heavily than when she'd been squirming. She squealed again as the chain tugged on her nipples, reigniting the sharp sting from being clamped.

The flogger itself hadn't actually hurt that much more than on her shoulder blades. The skin of her inner upper thighs was so much more sensitive than her shoulders, but he hadn't swung the flogger as hard. Mostly, it had surprised her.

"Back in position, Cassidy." The flogger snapped at the backs of her legs, the knots hitting her thighs just under the hem of her skirt.

Spreading her legs again, her pussy quivered with needy arousal.

This was supposed to be a platonic scene. The same kind of scene she'd had since leaving Don.

Sure, there had been times she'd gotten aroused during a scene before—she was human; it happened—but it hadn't felt like this. The need hadn't been so great. The desire hadn't been so overwhelming. She couldn't remember the last time she'd been this aroused. It was long before she'd been rescued from Don, if she'd ever even felt this way with him. And she wasn't sure she had.

The flogger flicked up between her legs again, some of the strands catching the plump edges of her pussy, barely protected by the scrap of fabric over them. She moaned, pushing her hips back as much as she could.

More.

She wanted—needed—more.

The leather snapped at her tender flesh, adding to the tumult of sensations, to the pain and the pleasure swirling inside her. Master David moved his aim back and forth between her legs and her shoulders, pausing occasionally to check in on her. A hand on the back of her shoulders. One sweeping up and down between her legs, checking the warmth emanating from her skin, but not touching her pussy. The tease was horrendous.

Then, the flogging began to slow. He was bringing her down from the high rather than pushing her over the edge. Letting her simmer. Letting her slow. Cassidy wanted to scream from frustration... but this was the deal.

This time, when he stepped forward to check on her, she didn't tell him 'green.'

"How are you feeling, little spark?"

"Sparky," she replied, which didn't really make sense, but somehow she had the feeling that he understood. She could hear the strain, the need in her voice, which made her wonder if he had heard it, too.

He laughed, but it was different this time. Not just amused. As if she'd made him think.

"Hold still, little spark," he murmured. This time, when he stepped away, the flogger didn't come down again. Instead, a moment later, he stepped up behind her, one arm wrapping around her torso, the other one going down between her legs, under her skirt.

Her thong was already soaked through, and she knew he had to feel it when he pressed his fingers over her mound.

But he wasn't trying to finger her. The moment he touched her, he must have pressed a button on the tiny vibrator that was now on his fingers. The vibrations against her clit were shocking, making her go up on her tiptoes as the sensations hit her hard and fast.

It was strong as hell, merciless against her sensitive flesh, and her thong did absolutely nothing to protect her.

She arched, crying out, pressing her ass back against him. The hard ridge of his erection nestled between her buttocks, his hot breath wafting over her neck. He wasn't panting, but he was breathing hard, and she could feel every one of his breaths as his chest moved against her sensitive back. The arm around her torso shifted, and then one of the clamps released her nipple.

Pain and pleasure pulsed through the tiny bud as blood flow surged, plumping the crushed nubbin. At the same time, Master David circled her clit with the vibrator. Then he took off the other clamp.

Her nipples pulsed.

Her pussy clenched.

Her senses were rioting, her body reacting, and she felt him moving against her as he cupped her ribs with the hand that was holding the clamps. She could feel them dangling from the chain where it was pressed against her side, the cool chain digging into her.

If only he'd touch her breasts again...

Not that it mattered.

The tumult of sensations coalesced into a single point of pure ecstasy, then burst over her as he pressed the vibrator firmly against her clit. She cried out, moving against the little toy, against his fingers, rubbing her ass across his cock, utterly wanton and utterly uncaring that they'd agreed to a platonic scene. It was all she could do to hold on to the bar and not let her hands drop as her climax peaked and fell, and she was left gasping and quivering for air.

"Good little spark," Master David murmured in her ear.

The vibrator turned off, and her knees went weak as she whimpered.

She felt... good.

So good.

And a little woozy.

This was the most intense scene she'd experienced in a long, long time. In a good way. A really good way.

Closing her eyes, she leaned back against Master David and let him take care of her. Trusting that he would.

DAVID

His dick hated him with the passion of a thousand suns, and he couldn't blame it.

His balls were so blue, they might as well be royalty.

He'd been about two seconds away from embarrassing the hell out of himself and cumming in his pants. The only thing that had saved him had been movement out of the corner of his eye, catching his attention, and when he turned his head, he'd seen Claudia still watching.

Still keeping an eye on things.

If it hadn't been for that, he really might have jizzed in his pants. Which he would have never lived down.

Already, he could hear Claudia's voice in his head.

Platonic, my ass.

At least he'd managed to keep from getting his dick wet. He was going to be clinging to that distinction. He hadn't penetrated her in any way, not even with his fingers.

But he couldn't worry about Claudia right now or what his team would think. He had walked all over the line tonight, but hopefully, he hadn't crossed it. He was going to need to step back and reassess the situation, but first, he had a submissive who needed aftercare.

Juggling Cassidy, his bag, and her corset wasn't easy, but thankfully, one of the club submissives saw his struggle and came over to help. Veronica carried his bag and Cassidy's corset while he scooped up Cassidy into his arms. She snuggled into his shoulder with a sigh, making his chest tighten.

He liked the feel of her in his arms a little too much.

The aftercare corner was set back behind the stairs, with plenty of squishy love seats, one big couch, and a smattering of oversized armchairs. There were stacks of blankets set between the furniture and two fridges—one on either side of the room—stocked with a variety of non-alcoholic beverages and snacks. Next to the fridges were shelves with more snacks that didn't need to be refrigerated.

The room was fairly empty at the moment, with only a few couples scattered around. David headed to one of the empty love seats. He settled Cassidy onto his lap, leaning over the arm of the loveseat to grab a blanket and pull it up and over them.

Veronica set his bag and her corset down on the couch beside him.

"Thank you, Veronica. Can you grab us a water and a chocolate bar?"

"You're welcome, Sir." She winked at him. Not a flirtatious wink. Definitely a 'I saw you had a good time' wink. A knowing wink. "And of course."

David groaned inwardly. The club gossip was definitely going to be making the rounds. He didn't usually do aftercare with the submissive on his lap. Snuggling wasn't so much his thing. Covering her up with a blanket, getting her a drink and a snack himself, making sure she was taken care of... that was definitely him.

Cuddling?

Not on the agenda.

But Cassidy felt so nice snuggled up against him, and she hadn't shifted when he'd sat down.

So, he kept his mouth shut as Veronica fulfilled his requests, then scampered out of there, a gleam in her eyes. He was going to have a lot of explaining to do to the rest of his team tomorrow. Maybe to Lincoln, too.

It wasn't like Cassidy was the normal run of submissive, though. She had been through some shit. He had to make sure she was taken care of. And it wasn't like he *never* cuddled. He did if it was what the submissive needed. Granted, Cassidy hadn't specifically *said* she'd needed it, but a good Dom also paid attention to body cues and didn't only go by verbal agreements.

He'd checked in with her throughout the scene, and she'd said green the whole time. If, at any point, he thought she'd been pushed far enough or that she was in a headspace where she didn't really know what she was saying, he would have called everything to a halt. It wouldn't matter that she was still saying green.

Same thing could go for aftercare. She was all woozy and snuggly and showing him what she wanted rather than having said it out loud. As a good Dom, it was his duty to provide her with what she seemed to need. Especially since he'd dropped the ball on negotiating what aftercare would look like before they scened.

So, he had to go by instinct and what she was showing him she needed.

And if he enjoyed the cuddling more than he ought... well, that might be due to his lingering erection. Because he'd been aroused, but he hadn't gotten off. Even though he'd gotten her off. Because she was the client, and they weren't going to get involved.

Which showed strength of character.

Sure, David. Everyone is definitely going to buy that.

They would. He would make sure of it. The next time he saw her, he would treat her just like any other client. And if they scened together, he would make sure that it never went any further than tonight had. Maybe he would even find her someone else to scene with, now that he was more familiar with her needs.

Right now, he would cuddle her as was his duty.

Then, he'd take a few days to get his head on straight. Maybe more. Not avoiding her, exactly, just giving them both a bit of separation to make sure there wasn't any confusion about *what happens in the club, stays in the club.*

Now that he had a plan, David relaxed and leaned back against the couch. He always felt better when he had a plan.

Tomorrow, he'd help his grandmother with her interviews, then take her to church on Sunday and spend some time getting things done around his house. By Monday morning, he'd have his head on straight again.

In the meantime, he'd enjoy the feeling of having a soft, sweet submissive happily burrowed into his chest.

17

———

CASSIDY

Cassidy missed friends.

To be perfectly honest, it wasn't like she'd been *best* friends with any of the Stronghold girls. They'd all been welcoming, happy to include her, and watching out for her... but it had been more like they'd been protecting her, and she'd been worried as hell she was going to get one of them hurt.

So, it made her feel a little bad to know that what she was really missing was what they could do for her.

Namely, she wanted someone to talk to about last night.

With David.

Who had given her a mind-blowing orgasm, cuddled the fuck out of her, then put her in Jensen's car without a second glance. To say she was confused was putting it mildly. Yes, they'd said it would be platonic before the scene even started, but...

But then, it hadn't felt very platonic.

Then he'd held her like he cared. Though, from the way his cock had been pressed against her the whole time, maybe it had just been arousal?

Her instincts were telling her that he'd been as into her as she was into him.

She didn't trust her instincts anymore, though. Not since Don.

A third party to talk things out with would be really helpful right now. Unfortunately, she didn't have a therapy appointment until Monday.

Sighing, she forced herself to get out of bed and go downstairs, wondering if Jensen or Mick would be there. Probably not Mick; it was after the time when he said he'd be going to the farmer's market this morning... Jensen had said he was going to go help him set up, and he'd be back after. Someone was supposed to be downstairs to guard her until he did. She just didn't know who.

Maybe it would be Claudia.

"Hello?" she called out as she went down the stairs, trying not to feel too much like she was in a horror movie. There was no reason to think that she was going to walk downstairs and find her guard in a puddle of blood, then be grabbed from behind by Don. No reason at all.

Thanks, brain.

"Good morning!" Jensen called out from the front room. Cassidy walked over to see him lying across the couch, yawning and rubbing his eyes. "You're up."

"I'm up. Are you up?" She couldn't help but tease him; he'd obviously come back from helping Mick set up, then fallen right back asleep.

"I'm up. Sort of." He groaned, not quite making it to sitting and falling right back down. "If you need me, I'll be up."

"You're fine." Since he wasn't on the couch in a puddle of blood with a slit throat, Cassidy had every confidence that if Don did come barging into the house—somehow bypassing all the security systems —Jensen would be up immediately. "I wasn't sure you'd be here."

"Ah, well, I helped load up the car, then when David got here, he said it made more sense for him to go help Mick than for me to leave and come back since he had to be out and about, anyway."

"Oh... that makes sense." Cassidy tried to decide how she was feeling at hearing that David was supposed to be her guard this morning but had opted out of it. If he was already going to be out and doing things, then it probably did make sense. So, there was no reason to feel disappointed that he hadn't stayed. She'd been asleep, anyway; she wouldn't have even known. She gave her head a little shake. "I'm going to go eat some breakfast. Are you hungry?"

"No, thanks, I grabbed a brownie this morning when I was helping load the truck." Jensen yawned again, throwing his arm over his face to shade his eyes from the light that was coming in from the big window at the front of the house. The couch he was on faced away from it, but there was still a fair amount of light coming into the room.

Amused, Cassidy wandered back to the kitchen.

She had to admit, Jensen's relaxed stance made her feel more confident, too. Sure, he felt safe here because it was his house, but his house also came with reinforced windows, a top-of-the-line security system, and he himself was deadly. Cassidy was still learning how to defend herself, but she was determined to get better.

The kitchen was empty and clean. Last night it had been full of containers of baked goods, but she hadn't eaten any. Hopefully, Mick wouldn't sell out, and she'd get a chance to eat some later. Or she could make her own.

Maybe if she had a good job interview today.

She glanced at the clock on the oven. Oh, wow. She'd slept later than she'd meant to. There were only a couple of hours before she needed to be there. Which meant she needed to eat, get dressed, and get herself together, especially because this was a job she actually wanted. She needed to make a good impression.

If she didn't get it, she didn't get it, and she'd keep trying for one of the other jobs, but she also needed to know that she'd put her best foot forward.

Okay.

Breakfast.

Going to the fridge, she noticed a plastic container on the counter next to it that hadn't been there the day before. The top was clear, and she peeked in.

Brownies.

Her stomach rumbled.

Oh, Mick was so sweet! He must have left the brownies there for her. He'd been up when she and Jensen had gotten home last night, and she'd gone right to bed. It was so incredibly thoughtful and so incredibly him. Hip against the counter, she picked up the container and popped it open.

Chocolate.

Screw it. It was Saturday morning, she was feeling good, she'd had a great if confusing night the night before, and she wanted a brownie for breakfast. She was an adult. She could do that.

Thinking about how disapproving Don would have been only made it even better. She could picture his scowl in her head.

Brownies weren't breakfast. They were empty calories. Treats to be earned, if she ever earned one—which she never did, according to him.

Picking up the brownie, she defiantly popped it into her mouth.

Yum.

Chocolate-y goodness.

There was another flavor there, too, something she couldn't quite define. It didn't taste bad, just a little odd. Maybe these were gluten free or something? Or maybe it had just been so long since she'd had a brownie. She couldn't remember the last time, in fact. Even though she'd started eating some junk food again after leaving Don, she had mostly stuck to cakes and pies.

She should start eating more cookies and things.

Finishing off the piece, she decided to take a second one.

Two brownies for breakfast. Utter decadence. And another symbol of her brand-new life.

David

Having successfully avoided accidentally running into Cassidy this morning by helping Mick load up and unload at the farmer's market instead, David headed over to pick up his grandmother. Jennifer had helped fill up a whole slate of interviews for today, and he'd asked Jaxon to do the background checks. He'd meant to do them himself, but he'd been so busy this week that he'd had to pass it off.

He'd bought a pack of cookies from Mick, knowing that his grandmother would be happy to have some sweet treats for the afternoon. Though he'd made triple sure they weren't pot cookies before taking them. Mick had offered him some pot brownies this morning.

Mick insisted that his brownies were for personal use only and that he wasn't going to try to get himself in trouble by selling them at the farmer's market. Still. David had eyed the cookies with suspicion at first, no matter how Mick reassured him.

He was pretty sure they were okay because Mick knew David would be pissed as hell if they weren't. Especially since they were for his grandmother.

Knocking on his grandmother's door, he wasn't surprised when she answered it, beaming, even though it was very different from how she usually looked when they had to interview new companions for her. The fact that she was going to get to choose her own companion-for-hire obviously made her feel very happy.

He almost felt guilty about not letting her choose in the past.

Almost.

Until he remembered some of the people she'd been drawn to.

"David!" Beaming, she went up on her toes, and he bent down obligingly for a kiss on the cheek. He did his best not to sigh at her outfit. A t-shirt and track pants weren't exactly inappropriate, but she wasn't exactly dressed to impress either. Her shirt was purple, had a stack of books on it, and said STFUATTDLAGG. David was not going to ask. He had a feeling he did not want to know the answer.

"Hi, Grandma."

"I'm so looking forward to this," she said, chuckling and closing the door behind him. She was practically rubbing her hands together with glee at the thought of choosing her own person. Jaxon had better have done a really good job with those background checks because David was going to be stuck with whoever she chose. "The temps the agency sent over were fine but boring."

"Boring isn't necessarily bad."

"Not for you, but I refuse to be bored." She shook her head, tutting. "Once you get to a certain age, you want to make sure you're enjoying your life because you've only got so much of it left. It's not like when you're young and think you're going to live forever."

David couldn't help but remember some of the missions he'd gone on where he'd been quite sure he wasn't going to live another day, much less forever. Definitely not things to say to his grandmother, though. She'd had enough stress while he'd been overseas and completely out of touch, knowing she wouldn't know what was happening to him until he either came home or she got the dreaded call.

Besides, things were a lot safer now. He *didn't* think in terms of his life possibly ending precipitously anymore. In his head, he had a nice, long life laid out ahead of him still... one that included his grandmother.

He frowned at her as she sat down on the bench in the front hall to pull on her shoes. Her purse rested beside her on the wooden seat that his grandfather had carved.

"Is there something you're not telling me?" he asked. Demanded to know, really. "Did you have a doctor's appointment this week?"

"I'm fine. Stop fussing." She waved one of her hands at him, putting her foot down and wiggling her leg back and forth to make sure her shoe was firmly on. "I'm just aware of my age and what I want for the rest of my life. My patience for everything has gone down. I'm not going to spend all my time around someone whose company I don't enjoy, whether they're a boyfriend, a companion, or a friend."

"So, I guess you enjoy my company?"

"You're my grandson. You're different."

David narrowed his eyes at her.

"So, you don't enjoy my company."

"I would if you'd get that stick out of your butt." She smiled gleefully as he sighed, getting back to her feet. "Thankfully, you and your butt stick don't get to choose my companion this time."

David growled under his breath. Him and his butt stick... for fuck's sake.

At the same time, he couldn't help but think about the vapors his mom would have if she heard her stepmother talking like this, and that helped bring his sense of humor back online. He couldn't blame his grandma for wanting someone she was more compatible with.

"Okay, Grandma, let's get you and my butt stick to the coffee shop." Which was where they'd be holding interviews.

She cackled when he said 'butt stick', even though she'd said it first.

Shaking his head, David couldn't help his own small smile as he followed her out the door. He really hoped they could find someone she was happy with and who didn't make his head want to explode.

18

CASSIDY

Something was wrong.

Something was very wrong.

She needed to leave for her job interview, but something was very wrong.

And not wrong in the way that said 'danger.'

She couldn't stop giggling.

She felt woozy. Not dizzy. Woozy. Like her vision was zooming in, then zooming back out, wavering around the edges. It made it kind of hard to walk.

"Cassidy, are you ready to go?" Jensen called from the front hall.

She stared at herself in the bathroom mirror, gripping the sides of the sink.

"Coming!"

Did her voice sound weird? She couldn't tell.

Crap, crap, crap.

She had to go.

She needed this job.

She didn't know what was wrong, but she knew she had to go.

Let go of the sink.

Were her eyes red?

Let go of the sink.

"Everything okay?"

"Coming!" She let go of the sink.

Found the doorknob. Turned it.

Focus, focus, focus.

One foot in front of the other.

Everything's fine. Just keep moving. Don't stop, won't stop.

Oh God.

She managed not to stumble as she made her way out into the hall where Jensen was waiting for her. He glanced up from his phone and put it in his pocket.

"Ready?"

"Yeah." One foot in front of the other. Jensen obviously didn't realize anything was wrong. Maybe she was sick? Maybe there was a tumor in her head, and it was making everything wonky.

For some reason, that made her want to giggle, but she suppressed it.

One foot in front of the other, out to the car.

Right foot. Left foot. Right foot. Left foot.

Open car door.

Sit down.

Okay, it was more like a controlled fall, but she made it! Hooray!

"Are you alright?" Jensen asked, sitting down in the driver's seat.

"Great!" She beamed at him. "Everything is great. Isn't there a song about that? Everything is great?"

"I think it's called Everything is Awesome." He eyed her. "You seem a lot more excited than you did earlier."

"Oh... well... you know. Job. Money." She waved her hand in front of her.

"Right. Um... seatbelt?"

"Right!" Crap, she'd forgotten her seatbelt. Concentrating, she managed to wrangle it over her body and click it into place. Click, click. She giggled again.

Cassidy stared out the window, pressing her hands into her lap to keep them from moving around the way they wanted to. The car started and began to glide down the street.

"It's Cuppa Joe's coffee shop, right?" Jensen asked.

"Yeah." The name had stood out, so she remembered it, even though her brain wasn't working properly right now. Maybe coffee would help whatever was going on with her. It couldn't make things worse, right?

"And this is for the companion position?"

"Yeah... I'll need to drive if I get it, but that's okay because she's apparently got her own car. She just can't drive it around. As long as I don't get pulled over, I won't come up in the system." She would make sure she was always obeying all the traffic laws to keep that from happening.

"Even if you do, just let one of us know, and we'll have Lincoln pull some strings."

Cassidy gave him a thumbs-up.

Oh my God, what's wrong with me?

She put her hands back in her lap. Would sitting on them be suspicious?

Sitting on them would probably be suspicious.

"Are you sure you're okay?"

Crap. He was onto her.

"Fine!"

A long silence filled the car as Cassidy stared straight ahead out the front window. She should do something. Anything. Something to prove that she was as fine as she was claiming to be.

Act normal.

How did she normally behave? How did she normally act?

What did she normally do with her hands?

"Cassidy," Jensen said slowly. "Did you happen to eat one of the brownies next to the fridge?"

The question was so out of left field, it took her a moment to process it.

"I'm sorry, were they for something specific? I thought they were leftover from last night and that they were up for grabs because last night Mick said that we could—"

"Cassidy, those are pot brownies." The car came to a halt at the red light, and Jensen leaned forward, banging his head against the top of the steering wheel—deliberately. "Oh, fuck. I totally forgot to warn you."

"Pot brownies? Oh my God, I'm *high?*" She'd never been high before. She'd never done any kind of drugs before. Mick had offered a vape before, but she hadn't, though the brownies... "Oh God... is pot legal here? Am I going to be in trouble?"

"Well, you can't take a pee test for a couple of weeks, I think." Jensen shook his head. "Medicinal pot is legal, but recreational isn't, so just... you need to keep it to yourself. Crap. Maybe we should reschedule."

"No! What if someone else gets the job? This is the one I actually want. I'll... I'll focus. It'll be fine."

The light turned green again. Jensen sighed but put his foot on the gas pedal.

"Shit... I'm sorry. If this doesn't work out, I'll help you find another job that you want. So will Mick. In fact, I'll put him in charge of it." Now Jensen was babbling, which at least helped her keep her mouth shut.

He pulled off to the side of the street, and for a moment, she thought he was changing his mind and was about to turn them around before he nodded toward a cute storefront with a green awning and a huge cup of coffee painted on the window with steam rising from the mug.

"That's it. Are you sure? We can call and see if you can reschedule."

"No, we're here. Let me just do it. It'll be fine."

This so wasn't going to be fine. She should listen to Jensen and turn around right now, but for some reason, the words coming out of her mouth didn't quite match up with her thoughts. Or maybe it would be fine?

"Okay, come on. I don't think anyone who doesn't know you will notice. It took me a bit to realize something was wrong." Jensen huffed and opened his car door. "I'll get you something to drink and eat. That might help."

That actually made her feel a lot better. If he hadn't immediately realized that something was wrong, then someone she didn't know shouldn't. She could totally do this.

Focusing on the door handle, Cassidy grasped it and pulled, then pushed the door open. *I've got this. I've totally got this.*

Jensen came around to help, closing the door behind her and offering his arm for her to lean on. Which helped. Moving was definitely harder than not moving. She'd be fine once she was sitting down.

"Okay, who are we looking for?" he asked, guiding her toward the door to the coffee shop.

"Mrs. Brenda Jamieson. Jennifer said she'd be sitting in the corner next to the cupcakes, and she'd be wearing a purple shirt."

"Got it." He pulled the door open, angling himself so she could walk in while still on his arm. Her gaze skittered around the inside of the shop, which was very cute. Lots of small tables, little nooks with couches and armchairs, and even some bean bags around a low table near a bookshelf.

The far side of the shop was where the workers were, behind a display case of various baked goods—the cupcakes were on the far right. She found the purple shirt, which was on a woman sitting next to a big redheaded man, another man sitting across from them.

"Oh, fuck," Jensen whispered, at the exact same time her heart dropped into her shoes.

That wasn't just any redheaded man sitting next to the older woman in the purple shirt.

That was David.

Oh, fuck.

DAVID

The interviews were not going well from his grandmother's perspective—she hadn't liked any of the interviewees so far—and they weren't going well from David's perspective because she wasn't going to choose any of them. All of them passed his parameters... well, except the guy currently sitting in front of them, who apparently did not take the hint that it was time to go.

He could tell his grandmother was not into him, even though Ted was doing his best to be charming. Unfortunately, he didn't have nearly the charisma he thought he did.

"Thanks for coming in to meet with us," David said for the fourth time, more forcefully this time. "We'll give you a call." Also said for the fourth time.

Ted beamed at him from across the table, lifting his hand to run it through his long blond locks and winking at David's grandma.

"Great! I think we could get along really well." He winked again. He did a lot of winking. That or he had a condition that made his left eye spasm. A lot. "I know I would love to spend more time with you, Brenda. Have you ever—"

Crap, this was how he'd kept things going every time, just changing the topic of conversation to something else instead of getting up.

"Ted, you're done. My next interview is here." Grandma's voice was flat. She'd been excited over Ted's blond good looks when he'd first arrived; that she was so ready to kick him out of his seat meant his personality had really failed him miserably. "She needs your seat."

"She is?" David looked down at the pile of files he had in front of him. Dammit, Ted had overrun his time to the point where David hadn't been able to give it even a cursory glance ahead of time. His grandma had looked at them in the car.

"Yup, right there. Hello, dear!" His grandmother waved, calling to someone across the shop. Ted turned around to look, too. Peering past him, David froze.

Cassidy and Jensen were the only two people standing just inside the door, and Cassidy was the only 'she'.

Dropping his head down, he yanked out the next file and opened it. Cassidy's headshot stared back at him from the very top. The same one used on the file Lincoln had shown him before they'd ever met.

Inwardly, he groaned.

So much for taking some time to get his head on straight before he saw her again.

"Bye, Ted," Grandma said cheerfully. "You need to move out of Miss Simone's seat."

"Oh, uh, alright then." Ted cleared his throat. "I look forward to hearing from you."

No, he didn't. And as punishment for putting Cassidy in the line-up without warning David, he was going to make Jennifer call the man to let him down. He had a feeling she'd snuck Cassidy in without telling him because she wasn't sure how he'd feel about it. She was right. He didn't know how he felt about it.

Especially after last night.

He was supposed to be staying *away*, not lining up a job with his grandmother for her.

Taking a deep breath, he lifted his head as Ted *finally* vacated his seat.

"Here, miss. Good luck." The smirk on his face and the smugness in his voice indicated the exact opposite, as if he was trying to hint that he already had the job in the bag and she was wasting her time.

Which she might be, but not because of him.

"You've got this," Jensen muttered in her ear as he sat her down. Cassidy was pale as a ghost. "I'll go get you a coffee and a muffin."

Mutely, she nodded.

"Hello, dear. Don't worry, I don't bite," Grandma said, leaning forward and smiling at her reassuringly. Cassidy stared at her, her eyes seemingly twice the size as they normally were. Was it just him, or were the whites a little pink? Shit, had she not been able to sleep last night because of what happened between them?

"Hi," Cassidy whispered and then cleared her throat and tried again. This time, her voice squeaked. "Hi."

"Hello, I'm Brenda." Grandma beamed.

"Grandma, this is Cassidy," David said when Cassidy kept staring at them, her gaze darting back and forth between them. She looked like she wanted to run. Had she not realized that the interview was with him?

Maybe Jennifer had left them both in the dark. Dammit. She was lucky she wasn't a member at the Outlands because he would have paddled her ass for this trick—or found someone to do it for him. She was too much like a little sister to him for him to imagine paddling her himself, but he would happily hand her off to someone else after this. Unfortunately, since she didn't come to the club because of her parents, he was stuck with giving her duties like calling Ted to let him know he hadn't gotten the job as punishment.

"Oh, you know each other?" Grandma asked, looking back and forth between them, obviously delighted. David groaned inwardly. She was both completely incorrect and way too correct in her thinking.

"Cassidy is a client of Black Fox," he said sternly, giving his grandmother a look. She didn't need to know anything about what had happened between him and Cassidy last night, even though the look she gave him made him feel like she *just knew*, anyway. "She does need a job, though I didn't know she'd be applying for this one."

"I wanted to be a nurse," she blurted out, then pressed her lips together so hard, the skin around them went white.

David stared at her. She was not acting like herself at all. Even with her surprise at seeing him there, even with last night, this is not the kind of behavior he would have expected from her. At her most upset, she'd still been calm and composed. Right now, she was jittery. Nervous. Still looked like she was about to run.

It couldn't just be about last night.

Could it?

"So, tell me about yourself, dear. Do you like to read?" Grandma was on a mission to draw Cassidy out. He could already tell that she liked Cassidy more than anyone else they'd talked to today. Maybe he'd made a mistake in letting her know that he and Cassidy knew each other, but hiding it wouldn't have been right.

"I do." Cassidy blinked rapidly. "Um. What do you like to read?" Her gaze dropped down to Grandma's shirt, and her eyes somehow managed to get even wider. "Holy crap... do you know what your shirt says?"

"Yes," Grandma said, sounding pleased, at the exact same time David spoke.

"What does it mean? Wait, no, I don't want to know."

Unfortunately, as he said the second part, Cassidy was already answering.

"Shut the fuck up and take that dick like a good girl."

She slapped her hands over her mouth, looking like she wanted to sink into the floor, but it was already too late. David choked on absolutely nothing, wishing he could carve the knowledge that his grandmother knew what it meant out of his head. He also knew that something was really wrong.

Jittery, reddened eyes, looking like she was trying really hard to focus...

"Are you high?" He could hear the disbelief in his voice as he asked the question. Why on earth would she have gotten high this morning, but all the signs were pointing in one direction?

Cassidy froze, staring at him, hands still over her mouth like she couldn't figure out whether to lie or tell the truth.

Grandma slapped her palm against the table.

"You're hired!"

"*Grandma, no.*"

19

David

"It was an accident," Jensen whispered, shooting a surreptitious glance over to the table where Cassidy was sitting with David's grandmother, hungrily tearing apart the muffin he'd gotten her. Grandma was chattering about something, looking very pleased. A vein pulsed in David's temple, and his jaw felt like it was locked into place. "It's not her fault; she didn't realize Mick had made pot brownies, and I didn't warn her because I thought she was eating breakfast. Who eats brownies for breakfast?"

They wouldn't be David's first choice, either, but he had a sister, so he knew there were certain circumstances under which he could imagine her eating a brownie for breakfast. That time of the month. After a really long trip. During times of great stress.

After a breakup.

Crap, was this his fault?

Not that he and Cassidy had broken up, but...

Stop trying to figure out why she ate them. It doesn't matter.

What mattered was that his grandmother obviously liked her and wanted to hire her, even though she'd shown up high to the interview. *Be honest*—because *she'd shown up high to the interview.*

Groaning, he closed his eyes, pinching the bridge of his nose.

"She really wants this job, Ginger. Your grandma seems to like her. She'd probably be good at it." Jensen was speaking earnestly, quickly. "It'll get her out of the house regularly and earn her some money, which you can handle paying her through the firm, so we can keep her hidden."

"What if her ex comes looking for her and finds her with my grandma?" David asked, even though he knew the chances of that were extremely low.

"Are you telling me you don't have safety measures set up for your grandma?" Jensen asked archly.

Of course, he did. The security system on her house was just as good as the one on his apartment, and he had access to it. He'd be able to check in on them throughout the day. Plus, his grandma had a panic button. And a panic room. She'd called it overkill, but it had made him feel a lot better.

Those were safety measures that Cassidy wouldn't necessarily have access to if she was hired somewhere else.

"I'll have to tell my grandma about the danger," he said gruffly, already knowing she wouldn't consider it a deterrent. She'd probably just want to hire Cassidy even more.

"You know there's not that much danger." Jensen shook his head. "I feel like we've already gone way overboard. There's no reason to think her ex is coming after her at this point, if he even knew where she was, which he doesn't."

"I know." David sighed. "It's the only reason I'm even willing to consider it."

That and he'd promised his grandmother that she could make the choice this time. He really should have held out for a veto before giving her a blanket agreement.

Looking over at the table where Cassidy was nodding along with whatever his grandmother was saying, he wasn't sure it would have mattered if he'd had veto power. His grandmother was obviously taken with Cassidy, and... how was he going to tell Cassidy no?

If he did, she might think it was because last night had affected him in some way. Which it had, but he didn't want her or anyone on the team to know that. So, he had to act like it hadn't affected him. Which meant not overriding his grandmother's choice.

Fuck.

Her showing up high to the interview might have been a good reason not to hire her if his grandmother hadn't decided that was a good thing. Or the danger that her ex represented, but there was no reason to think he knew where she was right now. And at least with her, he knew what the downside was, which was something he couldn't calculate with someone else.

Any of the other applicants could also have someone dangerous in their lives, and he just wouldn't know about it. With Cassidy, he knew.

Was he making excuses?

Yes. Yes, he was.

"At least with her, you know what the downside is," Jensen said, echoing David's thoughts. "And you know she's not going to steal from your grandma or disappear on her. It sounds like your grandma's book club isn't going to scare her off, either."

No, Cassidy wasn't going to be scared off by a bunch of old ladies reading about unusual kinks. If Stronghold and Marquis were anything like the Outlands, she'd seen enough old ladies engaging in all kinds of kink at the club. He would have to warn her not to mention the Outlands to Grandma or her book club.

It wasn't that they wouldn't be welcome if they wanted to actually explore kink, but they would be far more interested in watching and commenting than participating. Which he was grateful for because, as open-minded as he tried to be, he didn't want to belong to the same kinky sex club as his grandmother.

"No, I don't think much will scare her off," he murmured, other than himself.

"Are you worried it's going to make things weird after last night?" Jensen asked. "Because we'd all understand if it did."

His grandmother wouldn't understand.

Cassidy might understand all too well. So would his team.

The whole point of keeping things at the club was that what happened at the club wasn't supposed to affect his decisions outside of the club. If he told his grandmother that she couldn't hire Cassidy and the real reason was that he was wildly attracted to her and wanted to scene with her again, that would be letting it affect his decisions.

Besides, it wasn't like it was his choice, anyway.

<u>CASSIDY</u>

"Have you read any Daddy Dom books? Or age play?" Brenda asked eagerly, her blue eyes sparkling with delight.

Cassidy was trying very hard not to get attached already, because she could tell that David wasn't happy about her showing up to interview for the job. Plus, the fact that she was high. Although she felt like she was coming down from the high at least. The food and drink were helping.

Or maybe that was just wishful thinking, but hey, she'd take it, especially if it helped her act more normal. She couldn't believe what a fool she'd already made out of herself today.

She shouldn't have eaten the brownie. *Brownies.* This is what she got for being greedy.

"Cassidy?"

Shoot. She might not be as not-high as she was hoping.

"Yes, sorry, yes." *Focus.* "Rawhide Ranch. Laylah Roberts. Stella Moore. Pepper North. Kate Oliver. Allysa Hart." Crap, she was just listing off some of her favorite authors instead of engaging in conversation. "What about you?"

"Oh, yes, all of them," Brenda said cheerfully. "And Maren Smith, Rayanna Jamieson, and Honey Meyer. Do you know any more obscure authors? I'm part of the Dirty Daddies Party Room, so I'm always finding more there, but with as much as I read, I'm always on the lookout for more. It's my favorite kink to read about. Have you read any hucow?"

"Hucow?"

"Yeah, human cow. Milking."

"Um, you mean like *Morning Glory Milking Farm*?" That was the only book that came to mind.

Brenda brightened immediately, reaching for her phone and swiping on the screen to write down the title. She'd done that a few times already with some of Cassidy's suggestions. Cassidy wouldn't mind writing down some of Brenda's, too.

"I haven't heard of that one before. That sounds like fun. Minotaurs and milking, huh?"

"Yeah, um, it's the heroine's job."

"Oh, I like that. Hucow is breast milk milking, though, like a human cow. You said you read Stella Moore, right? She wrote one, Daddy's Naughty Little Hucow. Vivian Murdoch has a whole series about aliens who want hucow brides." Brenda cackled gleefully at the expression on Cassidy's face. "Yeah, I wasn't sure about it either, but my book club read His Favorite Hucow, and I went down a whole rabbit hole."

"Your book club read that?" For some reason, she hadn't put Brenda's reading habits together with her book club. She'd assumed Brenda was reading the really shocking smut on her own, not that she was finding it through her book club.

"Oh, yeah, that's why my last companion quit. She couldn't handle my book club." A statement that was said with utmost pride and a lot of amusement. "I don't think you're going to have that problem."

"Oh." Cassidy blinked. "No, I'm not bothered by kinky romance."

It had been those books that let her know she wasn't alone in the world in her desires, that there wasn't something wrong with her for what she wanted, for what turned her on. It had also been those books that had made her start questioning things about Don and the way he treated her. Those books were why she'd dared to say 'red' at Stronghold, hoping someone would help her. Sure, they were fictional, but they did a lot of good, too.

"Good. This month, we're reading something a lot tamer—

Masters of Restraint by Ines Johnson—but it's really good. Three men to one lucky lady. No milk or anything, but they can fill all three holes at the same time."

Cassidy laughed. Brenda's plain way of speaking was hilarious and something she envied.

"I think I've only read her vampire books. I'll have to add that one to the list."

"Ooh, maybe I'll suggest vampires for next month." Brenda tapped her finger against her lips, then brightened as she looked over Cassidy's shoulder.

Immediately, Cassidy tensed. She knew that David must be coming up behind her. It was in the way Brenda smiled, in how her eyes softened.

"How are you two doing?" David asked, turning sideways to slide between the two tables so he could sit next to his grandmother in the booth. His green eyes were serious but not condemning. Jensen had pulled him away, saying he would explain everything.

Cassidy could only hope David understood.

She really, really hadn't meant to get high before this interview.

Though, she wasn't sure he'd want her around his grandmother, anyway. Everyone who was interviewing her was supposed to have been informed of her particular situation, but she had planned to make sure of it, anyway. She was feeling safe, but that didn't mean she would put someone in a situation they weren't prepared for.

"Wonderful. I love her. She's going to be part of the book club with me," Brenda said gleefully, as if it was a done deal.

Biting her lower lip in worry, Cassidy kept looking at David. He was looking at his grandmother.

Was the fact they'd scened together last night and things had gone a little farther than they'd meant to going to be part of his decision? Yes, she had a crush on him. That didn't mean anything.

She wouldn't let it mean anything.

She liked him. She was attracted to him. But she'd do a really good job of taking care of his grandmother even if he was a total jerk to her. She liked Brenda. No matter what happened between her and

David, she would do a good job taking care of Brenda. If she got the job, that was.

Which she wasn't sure of, even though she wanted it even more now that she'd met Brenda.

"Oh, yeah?" David asked tiredly, leaning back against the booth. He looked tired but also resigned. He smiled at Cassidy. A really nice, sweet smile that made her feel a little melty.

Did that mean that she had the job?

Hope started to rise up in her chest.

"Yup." Brenda winked at Cassidy. "You said I could choose my next companion, remember?"

"I remember." David's smile became a little crooked. Seeing this softer side of him with his grandmother was not helping her crush at all. It was making it way, way worse. His gaze met Cassidy's. "I guess you're hired."

"Thank you! Thank you so much. You won't regret it."

She hoped.

20

———————

CASSIDY

Despite everything, Cassidy was incredibly excited to have a job. Brenda seemed wonderful. She was aware of the danger of Cassidy's ex but reassured her that she would be perfectly safe at home. David had her schedule, and any time they went out, someone from the team would be there with them, but at her home, it was just as secure as Jensen's.

Maybe more.

Brenda had promised to show Cassidy the panic room first thing when she came over on Monday. She made it seem like an adventure. Her casualness about everything made Cassidy feel even better.

Back at Jensen's, she flopped onto the couch, breathing out a sigh of relief.

"Well. That could have been better, but it could have been worse." He grinned down at her sheepishly. "How are you feeling?"

"Relieved. Excited." She giggled.

"Not pissed at Mick?"

"It wasn't his fault. I shouldn't have eaten a random brownie without asking." She groaned. "Who eats brownies for breakfast?"

"He should have labeled them or something. If he leaves any

more food around that has pot in it, I'll make sure he puts something on it, so you know before eating." Jensen patted the top of her head right as her phone rang.

Rolling over, Cassidy reached to the coffee table and picked it up. Kincaid's name was on the screen, and she lit up.

"It's Kincaid!"

"Okay, you get that, and I'll go find Mick to yell at him."

Cassidy grinned at him. Maybe she wouldn't find it as funny later, but right now, she was really happy. Heck, maybe she should thank Mick. Brenda had been delighted that she was high. It might have even been what tipped the scales to her being hired. Cassidy shook her head as she lifted the phone to her ear.

Brenda was probably going to run her ragged, but she was looking forward to it.

"Hey, Kincaid! How are you? I was going to call you tonight!"

"You were?"

The surprise was evident in his voice, and she was gleeful at having good news to give him. Also, she was maybe still a little high.

"Yeah, I wanted you to know that I finally got a job! I applied for a job being someone's personal assistant, and I got it... and you'll never guess who it is... David's grandmother. He didn't want her to hire me, but she did, and now I have a job!"

She did a little happy dance in place since there was no one there to see her do it. It had been so long since she'd had something really good to celebrate, it was hard to stay still.

"Is David giving you a hard time about it?"

Cassidy giggled. She was pretty sure David had wanted to, but...

"No, she won't let him. She's amazing. And, to be fair, he had good reason for not wanting to hire me. I kind of accidentally showed up to the interview high." She giggled again at Kincaid's reaction. She could actually hear him sputtering.

He and David were more alike than either of them probably thought.

"You *what*? How do you *accidentally* get high?"

Yup, he sounded just like David. She didn't want to get poor Mick into more trouble than he already was, though. Time to change the subject. Kincaid must have called for a reason, right? She'd tell him the full story later.

"Oh, it's kind of a long story... What did you need?"

There was a pause on the other end of the phone, and Cassidy stilled, her heart dropping in her chest. The urge to dance had disappeared.

She'd been riding such a high, in more than one sense of the word, her brain hadn't caught up with what was happening. The likelihood of Kincaid calling just to chat... His pause made her even more nervous.

"Cassidy," he said gently, the way someone did when they were about to say something terrible, "I have some... well, we're not sure it's bad news yet, but it's not good news."

"Oh... oh. Damn." At least it wasn't bad news, but she couldn't quite muster up joy for 'not bad' news. "What did he do now?"

"We're not sure. He seems to have disappeared. He hasn't shown up for his job, although he didn't quit. The lease on his apartment ended, and he's no longer there." Kincaid sighed. "We're not sure where he is. We're going to do our best to find him quickly and make sure he's nowhere near you, okay?"

Cassidy took a deep breath and let it out slowly before she answered. "Okay. Do you think he's coming here?"

"There's no way of knowing. Maybe he pissed someone off and is on the run. Maybe he got a new job somewhere else and needed to move and didn't care that he was leaving someone in the lurch."

"Or maybe he figured out where I am and is coming after me here," she said quietly. She slowly sank down onto the couch and lowered herself onto her side, her elbow up in the air, holding her phone against her ear. Laying down felt like the right way to respond to the news that her ex was in the wind.

"Maybe."

"Do you think I should quit my job? I don't want to put Brenda in danger." The idea that that sweet old lady could end up hurt because of her...

"No." Kincaid said it firmly enough that it made her feel a little better. "There are a lot of other things it could be. But I do want you to keep an eye out, just in case. I'm also going to let Lincoln and David know that Don has fallen off our radar so they can keep an eye on you."

"I'll tell Jensen tonight, too." She sighed again. "This sucks."

"It really does. I'll keep you updated as I get new information."

"Thanks, Kincaid, I appreciate it." She did, but she just wanted to get off the phone now. Sit and think. Process.

Decide if she was going to quit the job she'd just gotten today. Despite Kincaid's reassurances, she wasn't ruling it out.

"I'll call you when I know anything new."

"Okay, thanks. I'll talk to you later."

"We'll find him. Bye, hun."

"Bye."

She swiped to end the call, then dropped the phone on the floor, where it landed with a dull thud on the carpet. Turning her head into the cushion she'd laid down on, Cassidy let out a muffled scream as tears sparked in her eyes.

Why me? What did I do to deserve this?

---

*D*AVID

Fuck.

What had he done in his life to deserve this?

Groaning, David put the phone down and heaved a sigh. Dammit. It was like the entire universe was conspiring against him.

It could be nothing. Maybe the asshole finally got the hint and left.

Or maybe he left to go looking for Cassidy.

Of course, then the question was, where would he have gone looking?

Kincaid had promised that he and the others were proactively looking for the man. They'd put the submissives on seeing if they could figure out where he might be. Considering most women he'd met were as good—or better—than law enforcement when it came to hunting someone down online, David hadn't scoffed at the idea. Though he would also be putting his own person on it... unfortunately, Jaxon was already buried in work, so having extra eyes was a good thing.

He couldn't help but wonder how Cassidy was feeling. What she was thinking.

If she was afraid.

Glancing at the clock, he could see it wasn't too late. He'd pretty much finished the workout he'd planned on doing. He could swing by Jensen's on the way home. Just to make sure Cassidy was okay.

Decision made, he hit the shower, changed, and got in his car to head to Jensen's. On the way, he fielded a call from Lincoln—who had also heard from Kincaid. He let Lincoln know that he was on his way over to check on Cassidy. He also admitted that his grandmother had hired her. Lincoln recommended they stay out of public spaces, which was a rule David had already thought of, so it was easy to agree with.

He didn't want to take the job away from Cassidy if he could help it, and she would be just as safe with his grandmother as she was at Jensen's. Possibly safer, considering there would be no pot brownies lying around.

At least, there better not be.

Part of her job was going to be making sure his grandmother didn't decide that pot brownies were a good thing to try. Something that he wouldn't put past her now that she'd heard about them from Cassidy.

Still, before he talked to Cassidy, he should talk to his grandmother, so he called her as soon as he got off the phone with Lincoln. She responded to the news in about the manner he expected.

"Are you making this up so that she can't work for me?"

If they were blood-related, this was where he'd say he came by his paranoia. David sighed.

"No, Grandma, she can still work for you. I just want you to be aware of the possible additional danger and the new rules. Cassidy can show you how to order groceries or anything else from the store that you need online, and you two are not to go out to community spaces."

"But we can still go over to other people's houses?"

"Yes."

All of her friends lived in areas where there were a lot of nosy neighbors. They didn't have one Mrs. Tulieman watching the street; they had a dozen or more.

"And to the community center for Bingo?"

"Yes." The community center was in the retirement community and was not somewhere anyone could walk around unnoticed. The seniors took note of everyone and everything. If Douchebag showed up there, unattached to any of the residents, they would know. Plus, it was hardly the kind of place he should think to look for her.

"I can still go to book club?"

"Yes." David did his best to hold in his sigh. He pulled up in front of Jensen's house, putting the car in park and leaning back in his seat while he waited for his grandmother to run through her questions.

"And mahjong?"

"As long as it's at someone's house or the community center."

"And crochet club?"

"Since when did you join a crochet club?" David frowned. That was a new one to him. He'd never pictured his grandmother as the type of grandma who would crochet or knit. He was having trouble imagining it.

"I just joined. Last week we made crochet butt plugs." The glee in her voice was obvious.

With a groan, David leaned forward to bang his head against the top of his steering wheel. Yeah, okay, he could imagine that. Unfortunately.

"Next week, we're making crochet cocks."

"I'm going to pretend you said socks."

"No, I said—"

"Anyway," he interrupted her loudly. "Any activity you want to take part in that is not out in public is fine. If you want to do something like shopping in a store, going to the library, or those craft fairs you like, we'll need to know ahead of time so we can schedule a guard, which is the same as before."

"That's about the same as what you already told me, isn't it?" His grandmother sounded amused.

"Close enough, but I wanted you to be aware of the possibility that her ex really is looking for her and that we don't know where he is or how to track him. And to be extra careful any time the two of you leave the house."

"That's fine, dear." The dismissive way she said it had him a little worried that she wasn't taking the situation as seriously as he might like, but at least she was forewarned. Cassidy would take it seriously. "I still want her as my companion. I'll see you for church tomorrow?"

"See you tomorrow morning," he confirmed before they said their goodbyes and hung up. He didn't waste any time getting out of the car and heading up to the front door where he knocked before punching in the code on the door to let himself in.

He was greeted on the other side by a scowling Jensen in a fighting stance.

"You couldn't take two seconds for me to verify it was you?" Jensen complained.

"Sorry. It's just a quick stop. I need to get home." David looked as apologetic as he could make himself, considering he didn't feel apologetic at all.

"It's David?" Cassidy's voice preceded her down the staircase. She peeked around the corner before descending. The high from the pot brownies had definitely worn off. He hadn't realized how much it had changed her demeanor, how much it had relaxed her before he saw the difference between then and now.

That or the news that her ex had gone underground had made her even more tense than before, which was entirely possible.

"Hey. I talked to Kincaid, and I just wanted to swing by and check on things." He didn't mention that 'things' was really her. Instead, he tore his gaze away from hers, looking around as if taking in the house as a whole.

The urge to reach out and touch her, to pull her into his arms and reassure her that everything was going to be okay, was stronger than he'd anticipated. If Jensen wasn't there, he didn't know if he would be able to resist. Thankfully, the presence of one of his team members helped him stay professional.

"Everything's fine," Jensen reassured him, eyeing David somewhat suspiciously. He knew that this wasn't David's normal mode of operation. "Situation normal."

"I'm fine," Cassidy said, though she was looking at him anxiously. "Unless... am I fired?"

"You are not fired. My grandmother has been updated, and she's very happy to keep you on... in fact, she accused me of trying to keep you from her." He let his wry amusement show, which made Cassidy smile, and that made his effort worth it. "We're going to try to limit how much you go out in public, so we'd prefer online ordering to going to stores... that kind of thing. But you can still accompany her to her friends' houses and the center in the retirement community without having to take extra precautions. There's no way anyone could follow you there without the residents being completely in their business."

Her shoulders dropped as her tension released. Guiltily, David realized that a lot of her anxiety had been over her job. Still, she wasn't entirely relaxed.

"Does Brenda understand the danger?" Reaching up, she rubbed her forehead. "Maybe I should just stay here. That would be safer, right? I don't want to put anyone else in danger, especially not your grandmother."

"Hey." David moved forward, reaching up to take her hand and pull it down away from her forehead, squeezing her fingers with his. His voice gentled as he looked down at her, her gaze still not quite meeting his. "I wouldn't let you do it if I thought it was unsafe. Don was a douche, and he was harassing your friends, but he hadn't escalated beyond that. There's no reason to think that he'd harm my grandmother... if his disappearance even has anything to do with you. Do you want to live your whole life based on what he might do?"

"No." Now, she did meet his gaze. Hers was somber. "But I don't know that I'd be able to forgive myself if anything happened to Brenda."

"Trust me, my grandmother would tell you that she's an adult who can make her own decisions. It wouldn't be your fault if Don did something. It would be Don's. And even though we've taken a lot of measures to get you out of D.C. and keep you safe, it's because we're trying to be proactive rather than waiting 'til he escalated further and harmed you." Her fingers gripped his more tightly as he spoke, and he moved in a little closer, his other hand coming up to hold hers between his.

"That doesn't mean he's guaranteed to harm you or anyone else. There's every chance he just decided to move elsewhere. And we will find him, but there's no reason to think he's headed here or, even if he somehow magically knew where you were, that he's reached the point of violence toward anyone."

Cassidy let out a long breath.

"I know. Logically, I know, but..." Her voice trailed off, her free hand lifting to press against her stomach. "Sometimes, my brain only pushes the nightmare scenarios at me."

Sliding one hand up her arm, trying not to think too much about how silky soft her skin was, David rubbed up and down to soothe her.

"Let me think about those scenarios. You just concentrate on you. We've got you." His voice had gentled. Softened to something almost intimate. Her gaze was trained on his, her nearness making his entire body tingle as he shifted closer to her again. They were almost touching.

And she wasn't moving away.

Her chin was up, head tilted back, almost like she was inviting him in for a kiss.

Their faces were mere inches away.

Jensen cleared his throat.

Cassidy jumped as if she'd forgotten he was there. David *had* forgotten, for just a moment, but he managed to keep from jumping, though he did take a step back. Dropping her hand, he took another step, raking his hand through his hair. He was far too aware of the amused expression on Jensen's face, the man's arms crossed over his chest as he raised one eyebrow.

David felt his face flame. Most times, he didn't mind being a redhead, but sometimes, like now, he wished he didn't blush so damn easily. He was mostly unflappable, but when something did get to him, everyone knew it.

"Anyway, uh, like I said, I was just dropping by to make sure you are... that everything is okay." Fuck, he needed to get out of here before he made a bigger fool of himself. "My grandmother is looking forward to seeing you on Monday."

"I'm looking forward to seeing her, too." Cassidy had recovered, though her cheeks were pink, too, and she was avoiding his gaze again.

Time to get out of Dodge.

"Great. Jensen, I'll see you on Monday."

"Sir, yes sir," Jensen replied a little too cheerfully, stopping just short of actually saluting.

Fuck.

David was going to be avoiding the team's group chat today.

21

———————

"See? It looks just like a butt plug, right?" Brenda asked gleefully, holding the crocheted pink plug out for Cassidy to see. The craziest thing was that it really did, other than the bead eyes and the little mouth that decorated it. That kind of killed the illusion.

"It really does," Cassidy agreed, although she wasn't sure she was supposed to be admitting to Brenda that she even knew what a butt plug looked like. She was pretty sure David wouldn't accuse her of corrupting his grandmother since he already knew what she was like, but she wasn't sure where the lines for herself were.

"Next week, we're making cocks," Brenda said, focusing on the plush plug, turning it back and forth in her hand and grinning. She was obviously very proud of it and thoroughly enjoyed trying to make people uncomfortable with her creation. Cassidy found her hilarious. "They'll have cute little balls and everything. Want to make one, too?"

"Sure, why not." She'd always wanted to learn how to do things like crochet, though she hadn't pictured sex toys and male genitalia as the outcomes. Still, making anything would have to teach her the basics, right? And she could send crochet dick pics to Kincaid, which would probably make him feel better about how she was doing.

He'd already texted her this morning to check on her, and she'd reassured him she was fine. It wasn't a total lie.

She was as fine as she could be under the current circumstances.

The current circumstances being that she was torn between being terrified that Don would show up at any moment while simultaneously hoping he'd disappeared for some other reason that took him far, far away from her, while being extremely happy she had a new job, worried for Brenda if Don did show up, and brutally confused about David. Who'd seemed like he was going to kiss her when he'd shown up to check on Saturday evening but then had gone MIA again.

At least she knew where he was working. Just nowhere near her.

"We're going to have fun," Brenda said approvingly. "Now, let's order some stuff online and see if we can find something that will make David's head explode."

Brenda was not wrong about having fun. It was Cassidy's favorite job she'd ever had.

The mornings started with making breakfast for her and Brenda, then Brenda liked to watch some kind of television show. Even though they were using subscription services, the most she would watch was an hour—she did say she'd made an exception for *Sherlock* —because she didn't want to watch more than two episodes in a row. The idea of sitting and binging a whole season, rather than waiting in anticipation until the next episode, was not her 'cup of tea.'

She was currently halfway through the first season of Dexter, which Cassidy reassured her she'd already seen. It had been a while, but she and Don had watched through Season Four. Watching the show was one of her good memories of him, the kind of thing that had kept her hanging around, even after the red flags had started popping up.

It was always a little strange remembering the parts that were good. Somehow, it made her feel both better and worse. Better because at least she knew it wasn't like she'd been taking constant abuse and unable to see it... worse because she knew that was how he'd trapped her.

Abusers weren't abusive all the time. Especially not at the beginning.

If they were, it would be easy to leave them.

Sitting and watching with Brenda was cathartic, though, replacing the memories she had of watching with Don. Pushing them a little further back.

The show also let her fantasize. There was a brief moment where her brain went down the path of what would happen if Don caught her and Brenda here. Imagining how he'd disable Cassidy so he could take out Brenda, dragging Cassidy away while Brenda lay bleeding on the floor. She'd never know whether the other woman died or was saved. Who would find her.

If David would be the one to enter the house first.

Heart in her throat, Cassidy blinked away the tears and focused on the show.

Which, of course, made her think about Don's disappearance. It was probably too much to hope that someone had Dextered him. And wasn't she a shitty person for thinking about it?

Shouldn't she just want him to leave her alone?

Sure, leave me alone so he can go and terrorize someone else.

She'd rather the guilt from being relieved that he was dead than finding out he'd gone on to hurt someone else.

It sucked that the justice system wouldn't do anything to him until he had.

No wonder people loved shows like *Dexter*.

They could cheer on the bad guys meeting a bloody end without any guilt because it was all fictional. She would be wracked with guilt if Don turned up dead, but she would also be secretly grateful. Wildly relieved.

So, watching Dexter gave her mixed feelings, but it also felt good in a way to be doing something that had so many memories attached to it. Like she was watching in defiance of Don.

After TV time, Brenda liked to read or sit and do some Sudoku or a crossword puzzle to keep her mind sharp.

Then, it was time to make lunch, after which Brenda took a short nap. The afternoons were dedicated to Brenda's various activities. Monday was book club, Tuesday was Mahjong, Wednesday was crotchet club, Thursday was yoga class, and Friday, there were alternating activities at the community center. The last thing they did every day was go take a self-defense lesson with Claudia. When Cassidy had mentioned the lessons, Brenda had insisted she wanted to join, so now that was how they ended their days before Cassidy took Brenda home and made dinner before leaving.

Since they weren't going anywhere other than the retirement center and Black Fox, Cassidy had been cleared to drive and given a car... the first week, someone was always with them, whether it was Jensen, Claudia, or Drew. David did not come. She knew through the others that he was gearing up for an important fundraiser. All of them were, of course, but the responsibility was on him.

Week one passed without incident. Don didn't show up anywhere. They still didn't know where he was, but if he was anywhere in Pittsburgh, he wasn't showing himself. Cassidy spent her days with David's grandmother, her evenings with Jensen or whoever was guarding the house that night, and Thursday night at game night for a rousing round of Seven Wonders.

They really should call it Game and Gossip Night.

"So, how is it going working with David's grandmother?" Yasmine asked slyly, casting her gaze at Cassidy in between examining her cards. "Is it awkward after your scene last week?"

"It's not like she scened with his grandma," Ashley, Lincoln's wife, pointed out. She'd joined them this week and added a surprising dollop of sass to an already pretty sassy group, much to Cassidy's amusement. She was also the youngest of the gathered women, and all of them were genuinely amused by her. "Why would it be awkward?"

"Uh, because she scened with the woman's grandson right before getting hired."

"Yeah, but his grandma doesn't know that. Wait, does his grandma know that?" Ashley's head swiveled around so she could look at Cassidy with wide eyes of surprise.

"No, she definitely does not know that." Though she'd dropped several hints about how David was a very 'good boy' and would make someone a wonderful life partner if he would just slow down enough to make time for someone else. There was no way Cassidy was going to admit to Brenda that she and David had any kind of relationship outside of him being in charge of the team that was protecting her.

Because they didn't.

Not really.

And she definitely didn't want his grandmother putting pressure on him to start one.

They'd agreed to keep things to the club, and she'd meant it.

"So, it's not awkward?" Yasmine asked curiously.

"No, not really. I haven't even seen David since she hired me." Which was disappointing, but she understood. He was busy with work. And they weren't in a relationship anyway, so she didn't have any expectations about seeing him. It was just that she'd kind of hoped to.

It was probably better this way, though.

"Things have been pretty crazy this week," Claudia said as they passed the last set of cards for that round. "I don't think any of us are going to make it to the club this weekend. There's too much going on. Okay, everyone ready to reveal?"

"Ready." Cassidy chimed in with the others, relieved at the turn of conversation, though she had mixed feelings hearing about the club. Especially when Yasmine and Naomi asked if she wanted to join them there the next evening.

Since she knew Naomi wouldn't be scening without Drew there, so Cassidy would have someone to hang out with regardless, she said yes.

DAVID

Knowing Cassidy was at the club when he was at work was grating on David, but there was nothing he could do about it. He'd asked Gavin to text him regular updates on how she was doing. Drew had picked her up so he could take Naomi there at the same time, providing guard duty to both of them on the way.

Once he'd dropped them off in the club, they were safe as could be. All the Dungeon Monitors knew to keep an eye on them. Gavin knew to keep an eye on them.

He'd also hired Mistress Cyana, a private investigator with a punishing left hook, to keep an eye on them for the evening. A task she'd happily taken up. She was really a two-person team since she would likely have Master Aiden with her, the Dom turned submissive for his mistress. He was also protective as hell and just as sharp.

David had literally done everything he could to ensure Cassidy stayed safe that evening; he just needed to trust in his people.

"David, do you have a minute?" Lincoln's voice came from behind him, and David turned from where he'd been looking at the recent text he'd gotten from Gavin, reassuring him that Cassidy was still sitting at one of the tables with Naomi, Yasmine, and a few of the other club subs. A few Doms had approached her, but she'd turned them down.

Which meant he could focus a little easier, sliding his phone into his back pocket as he faced Lincoln, the petite woman standing next to him, and the contingent of security she already had around her. He recognized Senator Aditi Marlin immediately, though she was dressed more casually than when she was on television, in a white button-down shirt and blue jeans.

"Hi, sorry, I was just checking on something," David said with a smile. It was true, he just hadn't been checking on anything to do with the fundraiser.

"Of course." Lincoln nodded. "I'd like to formally introduce you to Senator Marlin. Senator Marlin, this is David, the head of my team who will be running our part of security for the fundraiser."

"Nice to meet you, David," Senator Marlin said, reaching out to shake his hand. He took her hand and was pleased by the firmness and grip of her handshake. Not that it always meant anything, but he had to admit he found a good handshake to leave a good impression.

"Nice to meet you too, Senator. Thank you for placing your trust in us."

"I've heard nothing but good things." She smiled widely at him as he let go of her hand, her statement completely sincere.

The warmth in her focused gaze made him feel like she was truly paying attention to him, and he felt a snaking tendril of guilt that he'd been texting about Cassidy when she'd walked up to him.

"I appreciate the extra help, though I hope it won't be necessary."

"That's definitely the goal," Lincoln quipped. "We'd like you not to even notice that we're there."

Senator Marlin laughed. "That sounds perfect."

She moved on, and Lincoln gave David an approving nod, which relieved him of some of his guilt over texting Master Gavin about Cassidy rather than paying attention to his job. He needed to get his head on straight. Thankfully, so far this evening, there were no surprises, and it seemed like the fundraiser should run smoothly next week.

David let out a long, slow breath, slowly emptying his lungs of air as he refocused himself.

There was no reason to keep checking in on Cassidy. Everything was fine. Everything had been fine all week.

If she scened with someone else tonight, that was none of his business.

"Hey, Ginger, was that the senator?" Drew came up from behind David, watching the pack of people moving away with interest.

"It was. You just missed meeting her."

"Damn. I would have liked to grab a picture. Maybe later. Naomi is a big fan, and she's already jealous that I'm working security."

David chuckled. He could absolutely picture that. Senator Marlin was well known for the work she did advocating for women. With the work Naomi did, she always had her finger on the pulse of the politicians who might affect the women's shelter.

"I'm sure we can arrange to get you a picture sometime."

"Think there's any way you could get Naomi into a meet and greet with the senator?" Drew asked, still watching after the group. There was something in his voice that made David raise his eyebrows.

"I can look into it. Is there something going on?"

One shoulder went up in a shrug that indicated a casualness David didn't quite believe.

"Just the same old, same old. Naomi got her period again today." Drew sighed, and David reached out to clap him on the shoulder. Drew slanted a glance at him. "Thanks for letting Cassidy go to the Outlands tonight. I think Naomi needs the distraction."

"Of course." David's heart hurt for Drew and Naomi. The IVF was not cheap, nor was it easy on either of them every time it didn't take. They didn't seem ready to give up yet, but he knew it was a struggle for them, and it seemed to hit harder every time. He squeezed Drew's shoulder. "If there's anything else we can do, let us know."

"Thanks. I think we're okay for now." Drew smiled wryly. "Maybe next time, you can throw us a celebration."

"I hope so." He really did. Drew and Naomi would make great parents.

"What are you two just standing around for?" Claudia barked as she walked by, frowning at them. "I thought we were supposed to be working."

Both David and Drew chuckled, snapping to attention.

"Yes, ma'am, Scary ma'am." Drew saluted. Since he immediately covered anything other than his amusement, David could only deduce that he wasn't ready to talk about things with the entire team. Which was fine.

David certainly wasn't going to talk out of turn. When Drew was ready, he'd tell the rest of the team.

22

Cassidy

It was a dark and stormy Saturday morning when David appeared at Jensen's door, and Cassidy was not prepared. She hadn't known he was coming, or she would have actually gotten dressed. He'd shown up without warning, ringing the doorbell. If she'd jumped up to run upstairs and make herself look more presentable before he came inside, Mick and Jensen would have known something was up.

So, she had to sit there with her bedhead, no makeup except the bit that was smudged under her eyes after not coming off when she washed her face the night before, wearing a ragged t-shirt that went down to her thighs and some flimsy pajama pants, pretending to be unaffected by his presence. The truth was, she was hyperaware of it.

Last night at the club had been fun, but it had also hammered home that she wasn't really interested in scening with anyone but him. Which was probably a good reason to try to scene with someone else, but her heart hadn't been in it.

Plus, Naomi had been pretty down. She'd eventually told them that the latest round of IVF hadn't taken, which had made her depressed. There was no way Cassidy was going to leave her side after that just to scene with someone she didn't actually want to scene with.

Pretending to be focused on the pancakes she was eating, she glanced up and smiled a greeting as Jensen walked back into the room with David trailing behind him.

"Good morning," David said, his gaze moving over her and Mick, including them both in his greeting.

"Morning," Mick mumbled. He was in a bad mood because the weather was bad enough that the farmer's market had decided to close. Normally, rain didn't keep them down, but the wind was howling and blowing hard enough to make things dangerous. Which meant that all his baking was for naught.

"Good morning." She made herself meet his gaze, keeping her smile on her lips even though what she really wanted to do was crawl under the table and hide herself until he left. Why couldn't he have seen her last night at the club when she was all dolled up? Why did he have to come over *now*?

"Want some pancakes?" Jensen asked, taking his seat at the table again without waiting for David's answer. "There's also muffins and coffee cake if you're interested." He gestured at the plate of pancakes that was sitting on the table, along with the butter and syrup.

Mick grunted, scowling into his coffee at the reminder that they had a bunch of baked goods sitting around that were going to need to be eaten by someone.

The dining room table was huge, seating ten people normally. One at each end and four on each side. She, Jensen, and Mick had taken over an end, with Jensen at the head of the table and Mick across from her. At that moment, she was facing all the men. Mick was seated closest to the doorway David and Jensen had come through. It would make the most sense for David to sit down next to Mick.

"Thanks, that sounds great," David said, walking around the table and pulling out the chair next to Cassidy.

It felt like all the little hairs on the left side of her arm suddenly stood to attention, his presence attracting them like moths to a flame.

Down girl. It doesn't mean anything.

Right? Except it really would have made more sense for him to sit next to Mick. But here he was, sitting next to her, his right arm brushing against her left as he leaned forward to snag a pancake in his hand and roll it up without any butter or syrup or anything.

"Let me get you a plate." She jumped up from her seat before any of them could tell her not to, needing a minute to compose herself. Her hyperawareness of him beside her was kind of disturbing. She needed to get a grip.

He wasn't here for her. At least, not like that.

In the kitchen, hidden away from the rest of them, she took a couple of deep breaths. There was no reason to get worked up. She looked like shit, anyway. It was part of the freedom of being single. She would never have dared let Don see her like this unless she wanted to spend the day listening to snide comments about how she was letting herself go.

From the moment she woke up until she went to bed, she was supposed to look perfect.

None of the guys here had said anything... but none of them were in a relationship with her, either. Including David. Which is why she shouldn't care what he thought about how she looked.

Last deep breath.

She picked up a plate and walked back into the dining room, where the guys were chatting about the fundraiser prep. David was sitting right where she'd left him, taking up more room than he had any right to on her side of the table. Why did the chair beside him suddenly look so small? One elbow propped on the table, he held the rolled-up pancake in his hand, several bites already taken out of it.

Pretending she wasn't a bundle full of nerves, Cassidy rounded the table, walking behind Jensen to return to her seat. Every step closer to David made her body buzz.

"Here you go," she said, sliding the plate in front of him as she sat down in her chair. It felt like everyone could see how affected she was by his nearness, but none of them were looking at her oddly. Mick wasn't looking at her at all and Jensen barely paused in recounting his assessment of the security measures.

"Thanks." David's smile made her stomach flip over.

God, she was pathetic.

Doing her best not to squirm in her seat, Cassidy made herself focus on finishing her breakfast, hoping that none of the Doms around her noticed how antsy she was.

DAVID

Coming over this morning might have been a mistake, but he'd wanted to see Cassidy. Gavin had told him that she had stayed in the main area with Naomi and Yasmine the entire night, which had made him feel a little better, but he'd still wanted to see her.

It made sense to personally check in on her at least once a week. Especially since this week, he had a really good excuse.

"How are things going with my grandmother?" he asked her. "Any problems?"

"With Brenda? No." Cassidy laughed, turning her head slightly toward him to answer. "It's the best job I've ever had, to be perfectly honest. She's a lot of fun."

"I'm guessing her book club didn't put you off at all."

"Not even a little. I got a bunch of new book recommendations to add to my to-be-read list when I went there." She shook her head. "I will admit, even after meeting your grandmother, I did not expect book club to be quite so filthy."

"What do you mean?" Jensen asked. "What are they reading?"

"Very naughty romance, and they are graphic in their criticisms. This week, there was an argument about whether they'd liked having their breasts played with while they were lactating."

"Oh, for fuck's sake," David muttered while both Jensen and Mick choked on their food. Whatever they'd been expecting her to say, it clearly wasn't that. David wasn't all that surprised, but then, he knew his grandmother. He just didn't have a habit of repeating what she said to his teammates.

"What?" Mick sounded utterly horrified, which, of course, only encouraged Cassidy. She definitely had a bit of brat in her.

"You know, after they had babies. They were reading a hucow book."

"Hucow?" Jensen's face would have been hilarious if David wasn't already so traumatized by knowing it was his grandmother reading these books.

"You know, human cow."

"No." Mick shook his head. "No, I did not know, and I'm not sure I wanted to know." He pushed his plate slightly away from him, making Cassidy giggle again.

"Oh, yes. They are all very frank about their sex lives and which of their husbands wanted to taste their milk."

"Stop right there." David twisted in his seat to give her a stern look, trying not to let the ends of his lips curve up when she grinned at him, eyes sparkling with mischief. Damn it. She was even more attractive when she forgot to be shy or hold herself back. "I do not want to know what my grandmother said."

"Normally, I would be all for torturing Ginger, but I'm not sure I can handle this conversation, either," Jensen said.

"Thank you, Baby," David responded dryly, keeping his focus on Cassidy, who looked like she was considering disobeying his order. "I mean it, Cassidy. Not another word, or you won't sit for a week."

Shit.

He hadn't meant to say that.

Even worse was the way Cassidy lit up.

She was considering it.

Which made him feel a little better.

He didn't want her afraid of him or feeling like she couldn't sass him—and he didn't know exactly how her ex had abused her. Whether or not he'd threatened her in that way.

Either he had not, or she trusted David more than he realized because the unholy light of mischief in her eyes said he'd just thrown down a challenge she was interested in accepting. His body tightened in interest, his cock stirring with anticipation.

He needed to shut this down before it went any further. And not just because he really didn't want to hear about what shenanigans his grandparents had gotten up to.

"I will make you sit and do lines about oversharing."

Immediately, the mischief went out of her eyes, and she pouted at him for cutting off her fun. At least now, he knew what was an actual punishment for her because a spanking clearly wasn't.

"Do lines?" Mick asked, obviously confused.

"Like writing out 'I will not share what I learn about Ginger's grandmother's sex life' a hundred times," Jensen explained, making David scowl at him. He grinned cheekily. Laps for him next workout session. Jensen liked lifting weights, but he hated running.

"*Oh*. That makes more sense."

The tone of enlightenment had David wondering what kind of lines Mick had been thinking of. No, wait, scratch that. He was pretty sure he could guess. Inwardly, he sighed. As if he'd have Cassidy doing lines of cocaine or something. For fuck's sake.

If he didn't know any better, he'd think Mick didn't have a thought in his head.

"Anyway. Anything weird happen this week? Anything that might make you think that Don is around?"

Cassidy shook her head, her expression sobering, which was unfortunate but necessary. He'd wanted to check in with her on multiple levels, and this was one of them.

"No. I'm hoping he's gone somewhere else." She put her fork down, even though it still had a bite of pancake on it. "Though, then I feel guilty because if he's gone somewhere else, that means he might have found someone else to hurt."

Which echoed David's initial thoughts when he'd first gotten her file so much that now, he felt extra guilty. It wasn't that she wanted someone else to suffer; it was just that she didn't want to suffer, either. Which no one could possibly blame her for.

The only person to blame for all of it was Don.

"Or maybe he pissed off the wrong person, and now he's sleeping with the fishes," Mick mused. "That would solve all of our problems. Though I hope they find his body soon, if that's the case, so you know you don't have to worry anymore."

Cassidy tilted her head at the other man, her expression lightening to one of amusement.

"That is very sweet in a very macabre sort of way."

"I'm just saying. Doubt he would be missed by anyone." Mick shrugged.

"He'd be missed by his mom." Cassidy sighed, rolling her shoulders as if to roll some tension off her.

David squashed the impulse to reach out and rub them for her to help. Touching her outside the club wasn't going to do either of them any good.

"She was not the type to see any fault in her baby boy. It was always my fault."

"Sounds like she created the problem, so you'll have to excuse me if I don't care that she'd miss him."

"He's not wrong," Jensen chimed in.

Cassidy pressed her lips together, as though she was trying to figure out if she should argue with them—or maybe how to argue with them—because they had a damn good point. Not that kids could never defy their parents even when they were born with a silver spoon in their mouth—David liked to think that he was proof of that —but some parents did not do their kids any favors.

He'd lost a number of friends over it over the years when they felt like just because they could get away with doing something, that meant they should do it. No matter if it hurt someone else. Which was probably part of why he'd ended up enlisting—he hadn't wanted to go through life buying his way out of any trouble he was in; he'd wanted to help people.

Still did.

Like he was going to help Cassidy right now by changing the subject, so she didn't have to dwell on her shitty ex.

"What are you going to do with all the baked goods you've got?"

David asked, directing the question at Mick. Immediately, the other man scowled again, obviously put out by the reminder of this morning's lost income.

"Not sure yet." He sighed.

"I can buy some of them and take them to my grandmother's church tomorrow," David offered. "She's in charge of the after-service refreshments."

Immediately, Mick perked up. "That would be great!"

For the rest of breakfast, David managed to keep the topic of conversation away from Cassidy's ex. He also kept an eye on her. She was a lot more relaxed with Jensen and Mick than she'd been a week ago, which was good. More relaxed with him, too, in some ways.

Not so much in others.

If he had to hazard a guess, he would say that she was just as aware of him as he was of her on a physical level. Being this close to her without touching her made him feel itchy, yet it was better than not seeing her at all. It wasn't long before he ran out of reasons to stay, though. Plus, he needed to meet Mason and Claudia at the gym for their Saturday workout.

Cassidy walked him to the front door. Looking down at her, David wrestled with his conflicting feelings. He was playing with fire, and he knew it... but so far, he wasn't getting burned. He was keeping her at a distance, despite the scene they'd had at the club.

Maybe he wasn't doing as poorly as he thought at resisting temptation.

Surely, it would only get easier. Practice makes perfect.

"Let me know if anything happens this week," he told her, opening the front door.

"Aren't you kind of busy with the fundraiser this upcoming weekend?"

He came to an immediate halt, giving Cassidy his full attention, facing her, though his hand was still on the doorknob. As soon as he focused on her, her gaze averted, hands coming together in front of her, the very image of a submissive who knew she was doing something she shouldn't.

"Cassidy. Look at me."

Reluctantly dragging her gaze back to his, her expression was slightly mutinous. He raised his eyebrow at her.

"If anything unusual happens this week, if anything that worries you happens this week, you are going to call me." It was a command, not a suggestion. "Got it?"

"Yes, Sir." She huffed right after she said the words.

"Good girl."

The light that sparked in her eyes was a completely different kind than the mischief he'd seen earlier, and his body reacted accordingly. Fuck, he needed to get out of here.

"Have a good rest of the weekend," he said, moving as quickly but as nonchalantly as he could.

"You, too," she called from behind him before the door could close.

It would be a hell of a lot better of a weekend if he could do what he wanted to her... but...

Do not get physically or emotionally involved with the client.

He'd already bent the first half of the rule; the least he could do was follow the second half.

23

———————

DAVID

"Well, that was a bust," David said disgustedly, tossing the file on their most recent interviewee on Lincoln's desk. They needed to hire more people, but it was just as important—if not more—to hire the *right* people. Jason D. Vince had not been the right person.

"It was," Lincoln agreed, sighing as he leaned back in his chair. "Definitely not what I'd hoped for."

Underqualified, overconfident, and far too easily swayed to say whatever he thought the boss would agree with, Vince was not the kind of candidate they were hoping for. David was surprised he'd gotten as far as an interview, to be honest.

"Who recommended him again?"

"No one." Lincoln grimaced. "Unfortunately, Marshall has been poaching the best candidates before we can even get to them."

Fucking Marshall. David scowled. "Well, if they're going to work for Marshall, they're probably not the best candidates, anyway."

His boss shot him a look.

"You know as well as I do that Marshall is good at putting on a front. They probably won't realize what an unethical bastard he is until it's too late. Like me." Lincoln made a face. Considering

Marshall had both stolen from the company *and* slept with Lincoln's now ex-wife, that was putting it lightly.

David felt a smidgeon of guilt because he knew that Lincoln and Marshall had been good friends for years before Marshall finally crossed too many lines. But David had never liked him.

He was too smart to say 'I told you so' about the man, even though he'd wanted to.

"So what are we going to do?" he asked. Better to discuss a solution than all the ways in which Marshall Devlin sucked. That could go on for hours without them getting anywhere.

"I'm not sure." Lincoln picked up one of his pens, holding it between two of his fingers and tapping each end of the pen against the desk as he moved his fingers up and down. He stared into space while he thought. "I don't want to stoop to Marshall's level."

"It wouldn't be stooping to his level to start letting it leak more broadly about why he's no longer with Black Fox," David countered. Something that he'd said before.

Lincoln had quietly let their contemporaries know that Marshall had been embezzling, but it hadn't made the papers, and nothing had been said to any of their clients. All of whom would have been likely to spread the word to their friends, depriving Marshall of contacts... which would have been for the best.

To be fair, David didn't think Lincoln had expected Marshall to start his own competing security firm in Pittsburgh. He'd expected Marshall to have enough shame to flee the city and start over elsewhere. But, as far as David could tell, Marshall never felt any shame. He was convinced he was the one who'd been wronged. Which just went to show how fucked up his moral compass was.

"I'll think about it." Lincoln was frowning, though, which meant he wasn't going to do it. Not yet. Saying that he'd think about it was already a more open-minded answer than the last time David had suggested it, so maybe one day.

David understood. Lincoln wanted to take the high road. Unfortunately, too many people were all too willing to believe the shit Marshall was shoveling. Lincoln also didn't want Black Fox's reputation to be affected by people knowing that one of the partners had been embezzling from them... and they hadn't noticed right away. Lincoln didn't think admitting that would engender trust from the clients. But Marshall was already doing his best to shit on Black Fox's reputation; telling the truth was hardly going to hurt them more at this point.

It meant that Marshall had gotten off with basically no consequences other than being removed from Black Fox, and no one outside of the firm knew why he'd been ousted. He was a smooth enough talker that he'd managed to allay people's suspicions.

Which was frustrating as hell.

It really grated that they, the people who were trying to do the right thing and not be shitty, were the ones losing out to someone who was willing to lie, cheat, and steal to get whatever he wanted. Yet people didn't seem to look deeper than the surface or question why he was offering so much money for them to get on his side.

David didn't really blame anyone who took Marshall's very generous job offer. Marshall had already made it clear he'd be happy to poach Black Fox employees with a shit ton of money. Thankfully, they knew better than to drink from the poisoned chalice.

Others, who hadn't had personal experience with him, didn't.

But it still grated.

"How are things going with Cassidy?" Lincoln asked. "You said you pulled some of the daytime protection from her?"

"We don't have enough people to cover her full-time," David replied, trying to ignore the trickle of unease that went through him at the admission. Strangely, it did make David feel better that Cassidy was with his grandmother, knowing they were taking care of each other. He didn't estimate the danger to his grandmother to be very high, but even if Don did show up, they were well protected. Lincoln knew David would drop everything to go running if his grandmother's alarm went off.

The whole team would.

"There hasn't seemed to be a reason to keep someone on her every day, all day," David continued. "She and my grandmother only go to the retirement center, my grandmother's house, and here for self-defense lessons. Which Claudia said they've both been very dedicated and progressing nicely. So far, her ex hasn't shown his face anywhere. He's practically disappeared off the face of the planet as far as we can tell."

"Kind of like what we did to her," Lincoln mused, rubbing his hand across his chin.

"Yes. And so far, no sign of him."

"Hopefully, he's gone for good, though I would like to know where he is." Lincoln shook his head. "Stalking cases are never easy."

That was an understatement. If Don never resurfaced, Cassidy would have to spend her entire life wondering if he would suddenly appear out of nowhere. Not exactly a fun way to live. David wouldn't be able to relax, either. Just in case.

<u>Cassidy</u>

Driving home from Brenda's, Cassidy couldn't help but smile when a call came through from Yasmine. She missed her friends from Stronghold, but she was really enjoying the new friends she was making.

Tapping the button on the dash to answer the call, she cheerfully answered, "Hello!"

"Hey Cassidy, how are you?" Yasmine's warm voice filled the car.

"Pretty good. On my way home from work."

Behind her, a grey car moved into her lane, closer than she would have liked. Her shoulders tensed, and she shook them out. Some people were jerks, riding others' bumpers. It didn't mean anything.

"Do you have a minute to talk?"

"Sure."

She wasn't doing anything except driving. Well, and now trying to get a look at the jerk who was riding her bumper.

It was a man, she was pretty sure of that, but he was wearing a red baseball cap and a pair of big sunglasses, which obscured the upper half of his face. The lower half was covered by a light-colored mustache and beard.

Don could have grown a mustache and beard.

Oh. My. God. Paranoid much?

"So, my parents have come to me with a proposal, and I'm thinking about doing it, but part of me thinks I must be crazy for even considering it. I'm looking for a completely unbiased third-party opinion, and I feel like you might be the closest I have to that who also won't judge me."

"Okay." Well, Yasmine officially had her attention, which was good because she didn't need to be making up scenarios in her head about the random jerk in the car behind her. Because that's exactly what he was—a random jerk. Not Don in disguise.

Unless he is.

Stop it. Focus on Yasmine.

Yasmine sighed, long and deep, like she was reluctant to get started talking. While she did that, Cassidy switched lanes to see if the grey car would follow. A moment later... it did. Still riding her ass.

Cassidy tensed up even more. Should she get off the phone and call David? Should she ask Yasmine to call David?

"Okay, so you know I said I was the queen of bad dates, and that's why I don't date? Or get involved? Well, my parents think they have a solution to that. They want to arrange my marriage." She said the last sentence so fast, the words blended together, and Cassidy jerked her attention back to the conversation.

"They want to what?"

"Oh... crap. It's crazy, isn't it? I knew it was crazy, and it sounds even crazier when I say it out loud."

"I mean, not necessarily. I just... what do you mean? Like, to a stranger?" With her attention divided between Yasmine's announcement and the man in the grey car behind her, she was feeling frazzled, but she didn't want to let her new friend down. And she was also interested. Plus, she wasn't convinced the guy behind her was actually a threat. He was just riding her bumper like a jerk.

That didn't mean he was Don.

"Well, I'd meet him beforehand. Apparently, my parents know a guy, who is local, who has asked his parents to arrange his marriage. My great-aunt and great-uncle's marriage was arranged, and they're very happy forty-some years later, but I don't know anyone of my generation who has done it. But that would break my bad date curse, right? No dating, no getting involved, just... straight to the planning the wedding. No opportunity to fuck it up."

"Other than meeting him beforehand."

"Yeah, but that won't be an official date. Just a meet and greet." There was a yearning in Yasmine's voice that made Cassidy's heart ache a little. It sounded to her like Yasmine wanted to do this; she just needed someone else to tell her that it was okay.

Glancing in the rearview mirror, Cassidy breathed out a quiet sigh of relief as the grey car turned off. He must have gotten over into this lane with her because he was making the turn soon. He was just a tailgating jerk who didn't use turn signals. Figured.

"I think it doesn't hurt to at least meet him. See if you think this might be a good alternative. Would your parents set you up with someone they didn't think would be a good match?"

"No. Not that I would have trusted them with my romantic life in the past, but I've proven that I don't have a good picker. Maybe that's the trick—I need someone else to pick for me." Yasmine laughed, though there was a touch of bitterness to the sound. "So, you don't think it's nuts to let my parents pick out my possible groom?"

"No more nuts than other ways people meet and get married." Cassidy shrugged, even though Yasmine couldn't see her. "Right now, most people trust a computer or app algorithm. That doesn't seem any less weird than trusting your parents, as long as they're good parents."

She wondered who her parents would have picked for her if they'd been alive. Someone better than Don, probably. They would have been horrified to know how he'd treated her.

"You've got a point. Okay." Yasmine took a deep breath. "Okay, I can do this. Just the meet and greet, at least. I don't have to make a decision until after that. Maybe I'll meet him, and it'll be an immediate no. Or maybe he'll end up being the man of my dreams."

"That's the spirit," Cassidy teased. "Who knows, maybe you'll start a trend."

That made Yasmine laugh.

"Doubtful, but who knows? At least I feel a little better now. Thanks, Cassidy."

"Any time." She was pleased she'd been able to help, though she didn't feel like she'd done much.

"Anything going on with you this week? Like with David?" Yasmine's tone had turned slyly teasing. She'd been the first one to comment on the fact that Cassidy hadn't scened with anyone last Friday when David wasn't there.

"No, he's been busy. I've seen more of you than I have of him. Which is fine because we're not... you know."

"Wildly attracted to each other and fighting it tooth and nail?" Yasmine laughed when Cassidy made a noise of rejection, though she couldn't find the words to counteract what felt like the cold, hard truth. "We're all thoroughly enjoying watching you two figure it out."

"We can't possibly be that interesting," Cassidy complained. Apparently, the Outlands were just like Stronghold and Marquis when it came to the gossip. At least Yasmine hadn't mentioned anyone placing bets like they often did back in D.C.

"Maybe we're just bored."

"You must be." Cassidy couldn't deny that she wanted to get to know David better and not just inside the club, but she also wasn't going to throw herself at him if he wasn't interested. That would just make things even more awkward, especially since she was working for his grandmother. Pulling in front of Jensen's house, Cassidy parked the car, happy to find a space open so close. "I just got home, so I will have to talk to you later."

"You can run, but you can't hide," Yasmine teased. "We'll talk later!"

Shaking her head, Cassidy got out of the car, casting a quick look up and down the street. There was no sign of the grey car that had tailgated her. Not that she should expect there to be one. But it had occurred to her that if Don knew where she was, he could have been following her, then turned off to make her think it wasn't him, only to come back around again once she was at Jensen's.

Talk about paranoid. Thanks, brain.

Across the street, Mrs. Tulieman was out on her front porch. Seeing Cassidy looking in her direction, the older woman waved. Feeling a bit more reassured that the neighbor had her eye on things, Cassidy waved back and went into the house.

David had wanted to know if anything weird happened... Should she call him? Or tell Jensen?

No. Being tailgated wasn't weird. It happened to people all the time. She was just more paranoid about it than usual. At best, she'd come off as an alarmist, especially since the guy hadn't followed her for more than five minutes. It was obviously a coincidence, not something to be reported to her security team. Plus, she didn't want David to think she was making up reasons to call him.

How embarrassing.

Shaking her head again, she made her way up the walk.

There was no reason to say anything to anyone.

No reason at all.

24

———————

DAVID

The fundraiser was over. It had gone off without a hitch. Thank God.

They'd all gone over to Jensen's afterward to celebrate. Well, not 'all.' Lincoln had gone home to Ashley. But David, Drew, Claudia, Mason, and, of course, Jensen since it was his house. After all the man-hours, it was nice to know that one of their biggest jobs was out of the way. Though the senator had mentioned that she might want to hire them for future events as well.

They'd be more than happy to work with her again when the time came, but for now, it was another big job finished that they could celebrate.

"Is Naomi okay with you being out with us?" Mason asked Drew as they headed up the walk.

"Yeah, I asked her if she wanted to come over, too, but she wasn't feeling up to it." Drew shrugged, but the concern in his expression was clear. "Last week, she wanted distraction. This week, she's wallowing. I'm just trying to let her do whatever she feels she needs."

Clapping Drew on the shoulder, Mason nodded.

"Sorry, Sporty. If you need me..."

"I'm good right now, thanks. It'll help that this job is over now, and our schedule is freed up some." Drew glanced over at David on his other side as they walked up the steps to the porch, following Jensen and Claudia. "I know you and Lincoln were interviewing people this week. Anyone good show up?"

David shook his head grimly.

"I'll tell you about it inside." That way, he could let them all know they were pretty sure that Marshall was responsible for the lackluster candidates they were receiving. Though, thankfully, the former partner didn't seem to have managed to damage Black Fox's reputation with clients—they were still fielding just as many calls as usual.

Unfortunately, having to turn some of them down due to no longer having three teams might affect them in the long run, but Lincoln was prioritizing current clients. It wasn't like growing the company was an option at the moment, anyway; they needed to get back to the level where they'd already been. That or accept that they were just going to be smaller now.

David still wasn't sure which direction Lincoln was going to take the company.

Once they were all in and had a drink, they'd gathered around the island in the kitchen. The caterers had given Claudia a tray of food that she'd brought with her for them to snack on, and Jensen found the baskets with Mick's leftovers from the farmer's market that morning. There was no sign of Mick or Cassidy, who were probably both already in bed.

Which he was not disappointed about, at all, and he had definitely not been hoping that he would see Cassidy while they were here.

Giving everyone the update on the candidates who had been applying and where he and Lincoln thought the good candidates were going had everyone cursing loudly.

"Fucking Marshall," Claudia fumed. "I should have kicked his balls into next week when I had the chance."

"He's always been jealous of Lincoln, you know," Mason said, taking a sip of his beer. Leaning back against the counter with his arms crossed over his chest, he had his 'thinking look' on, which meant he was working something out. "Jealous of Lincoln and Harris' relationship."

"But they're brothers..." Drew frowned.

"Jealous of the fact that his name wasn't on the company."

"Because he didn't start it, he came on after Lincoln and Harris created it." Drew interrupted again. Mason ignored him and kept going.

"Jealous of his family, his friends, basically everything Marshall saw as a success."

"Is that why he slept with Lincoln's wife?" Jensen asked, making a face. None of them had been a fan of the former Mrs. Black, even before her infidelity. How Lincoln had ended up with such a self-involved, self-aggrandizing woman was a mystery to David.

Then again, Lincoln's ex was the female version of Marshall, and Lincoln had been best friends with Marshall for decades. Despite being former military, Lincoln had a very soft spot in his heart for hard-up cases. Maybe there was just something about him that drew shitty people who thought they could use him.

"Probably," Mason answered Jensen. "I think it certainly gave him a rush to steal from Lincoln, both money and his wife. He would see it as making himself better than Lincoln. The fact that Lincoln's wife was planning to leave him for Marshall..."

"Yeah, but they didn't make it a year after she and Lincoln split up," Claudia pointed out.

"Likely because Lincoln already had a replacement lined up. A much younger one. I doubt Marshall had much interest in Janet after he realized that Lincoln didn't. Especially since he would see a young woman like Ashley as the bigger prize." Mason made a face.

"Ew, of course, he would," Drew said, scowling. "That's not why Lincoln fell for her."

"We know that, but society views age-gap romances like that in a certain way." Claudia rolled her eyes. She pitched her voice into a falsetto. "Much older man, younger woman, oh wow, he must be such a stud."

"So, you think that starting his own company and offering outrageous amounts to the people we'd be interested in hiring is another manifestation of his jealousy?" David asked, wanting to make sure he understood what Mason was saying.

"Ooh, look at you, using the big words," Drew teased, making them all laugh.

"Yes, that's exactly what I'm saying," Mason replied, ignoring Drew other than for a brief chuckle. "I think he's still trying to steal what Lincoln has. But with even more motivation than before since he got kicked out of Lincoln's inner circle and now that his animosity has free rein. He doesn't have to hide it anymore."

"Well, that's just great." Claudia sighed. "Because we needed something else to make our lives harder right now."

"Honestly, if we could just get a tech person for our team, I think that would help a lot. Lincoln isn't taking cases at the rate we would have for three teams. We may end up being a two-team firm, which would be fine," David said. "At least for a while, until Marshall shits the bed again, and his goes belly up."

"We can only hope," Jensen muttered, taking another swig of his drink. Then he straightened up, his gaze going behind David. Immediately, David's senses tingled, and he turned to see who Jensen was looking at, even though part of him already knew. "Sorry, did we wake you up?"

"Not really, I woke up to use the bathroom and was having trouble falling back asleep when I heard voices." Cassidy stood in the doorway to the kitchen, looking adorably disheveled. Her dark hair was pulled back into a messy bun. One long tendril had escaped confinement and was draped over her shoulder, while there was a crease on one side of her face from her pillow. She was wearing a tank top and shorts, both of flimsy-looking material but thick enough that he couldn't see her nipples through the top. "Figured I'd come see who was here since I couldn't sleep."

"Come join us," Claudia said, stepping back to make space for Cassidy between her and David. The Domme winked at him.

Interfering friends. He didn't know why he was surprised. It didn't bother him as much as it probably should have.

He'd seen Cassidy several times over the week, always in passing at his grandmother's, and they'd chatted. Done their best to ignore his grandmother's meaningful looks. Kept their distance.

Which meant he didn't feel like he needed to worry so much right now, no matter how attuned he was to her presence as she came to stand between him and Claudia.

"Beer?" Jensen asked her.

"Just water, thanks." She smiled at Jensen as he moved to get her a glass. "So, how was the fundraiser?"

Cassidy

Sometimes, not being able to fall asleep wasn't the worst thing in the world. Especially when it meant coming downstairs to find a kitchen full of hotties... and one hottie in particular. Part of her had thought about sneaking back upstairs, but then Jensen had seen her, and she'd figured she might as well stay.

It was fun listening to them talk about their job and hanging out together. She'd seen David at his grandmother's during the week, but this was a different side of him. The team leader. He listened as much as he talked, and he was a lot more blunt with them than he was with his grandmother, but it was just as obvious how deeply he cared about them.

Eventually, Drew left, then Claudia. Mason, Jensen, David, and she moved to the living room, which was good because she was starting to get tired.

Somehow, she ended up on one couch with David while Mason and Jensen took the other. They were arguing about something from a reality TV show. Not something she'd watched, though she was amused by how passionately opinionated they both were. David was listening and watching them with an expression of incredulity on his face.

Cassidy couldn't help but giggle, pulling one of the cushions onto her lap and curling up around it. He slanted a glance her way, catching her eye as if to say, 'Can you believe them?', making her giggle even harder. She reached up to cover her mouth with her hand to try to keep Jensen and Mason from hearing her.

Fortunately, they were way too engrossed in their debate to realize she was laughing at them.

The corner of David's mouth tipped up, and he leaned back against the couch, throwing his arm along the back of it. They were far apart enough that his arm wasn't behind her, though it would be if she scooted over one place. She ignored the desire to do so.

"How's your week been?" he asked. "Nothing weird that I should know about?"

He asked the same question every time he saw her. Cassidy shook her head, bemused. Nothing weird had happened since the day she'd been tailgated.

Which wasn't weird. Get over it.

She hadn't told him about it, and she sure as heck wasn't going to bring it up now, especially since it hadn't happened again.

"Weirdest thing that's happened is Mick had a date last night," she said, grinning.

David blinked.

"Mick, as in Jensen's cousin Mick? *That* Mick?" Obviously, he knew it was that Mick, but his reaction was akin to hers and Jensen's.

"Yeah, apparently, he met her at the grocery store, and they hit it off." Cassidy hoped she got to meet the woman one day because Mick was not someone she would have thought would ask out a woman he just met. Or that she would say yes. Mick was delightful, but he was kind of a himbo. Cassidy did not see him as the type to have a lot of game. Now, she had to wonder if she'd misjudged him or if he'd just found the right kind of woman for whatever line he'd used.

"What's her name? Maybe I can look her up." David started to reach for his phone. Laughing, Cassidy held out her hand, waving to stop him.

"I'm not entirely sure. He was talking pretty fast while he was telling us about it. It starts with an 'N', which is the only thing I'm sure of."

"Darn. Not quite enough to go on." David sighed. "Once you get me a name, I'll do a check and make sure she's good enough for him."

Okay, well, that was adorable.

"Do you do background checks on all your friends' dates?" Though, she wasn't sure that David would actually quantify Mick as a friend, which made the gesture even sweeter.

"Yes."

The blunt, unapologetic answer made her snort with laughter. Actually snort. Good Lord. She was overly tired and should go back to bed, but she didn't want to. She wanted to stay up and keep talking with David. She was enjoying it.

Jensen and Mason were there, even if they were having their own conversation, so surely there was no harm in it.

They talked about how he'd ended up joining the military, then Black Fox. Cassidy had already heard some of it from Brenda. She knew the family was mostly estranged, with David's sister being the only connection he had with his parents. She ached for him.

Her parents were gone, but at least they'd had a good relationship when they were alive. Never once had she thought they wouldn't support her or that they'd only love her if she acted the way they wanted her to. There was nothing she could do to disappoint them so badly, they would turn away from her.

The longer they talked, the more tired she became. She turned to face him on the couch so she could lay her head against the back cushion and rest a little, which didn't help with how tired she was. It did mean she could stare at him. With her legs tucked up while she was curled up, they were still pretty far apart, but eventually, she felt the need to stretch.

Leaning back slightly, she did her best not to touch him with her feet.

To her surprise, instead of shifting away or looking bothered by the nearness of her feet, he grabbed one leg by the ankle. Before she could protest or ask what he was doing, he had it propped up on his thigh and was pushing his thumbs into the center.

"Oh God... you can stop that never, thank you."

"I figure you've probably been on your feet a lot, keeping up with my grandma." He chuckled.

"Not that much," she admitted, feeling a little guilty, as if she was getting a foot massage under false pretenses. "But I can't remember the last time anyone gave me any kind of massage. That feels amazing."

"Well, then it's past time you got one." He tilted his head at her, still rubbing his fingers over her feet in a way that made her want to whimper. She didn't have a foot fetish, but she was starting to think she might have one for foot massages. Or maybe it was just David having his hands on her in any capacity. "Do you like massages?"

"Who doesn't like massages?"

"Claudia, for one," David smirked. "She doesn't like being touched when she's face down on a table with someone behind her."

"And she doesn't like being relaxed," Mason interjected into the conversation. Apparently, David giving Cassidy a foot massage had drawn his and Jensen's attention. "It makes her feel too vulnerable."

"That's why she's Scary," Jensen muttered.

"I'm not a huge fan of them for similar reasons, but I'm not as wound up about it as Claudia is," David admitted, making Cassidy shake her head in amazement. "So, if you like them, why has it been so long?"

"Don, of course." She sighed, rounding her shoulders as if that would deflect the weight of any possible judgment. None of them reacted, though. "He thought it was a waste of money." Though he'd been insistent that she massage him whenever he wanted it. Because he was the Dom, and she was there to serve him.

Obviously, that was not the kind of Dom that David was.

She didn't mention that part.

"What a dick." Jensen scowled.

"We already knew that," Mason pointed out, amused. David

stayed silent, but he pulled her other foot up onto his lap, like he wanted to make the point that he would be tending to that one next.

Cassidy smiled sleepily at him.

The conversation wound around her, but she couldn't keep up with it anymore. She was too tired. The rubbing of her feet felt too good. She didn't know when she fell asleep; she just slowly drifted off to the soothing sound of low male voices, knowing they were there to protect her.

At some point, she woke up enough to know that she was being carried up the stairs, and she didn't have to open her eyes to know that David was the one with his arms around her.

She just wished that he could have crawled into bed with her instead of placing her down and walking away.

In her dreams, he stayed.

25

———————

CASSIDY

Someone was tailgating her again. Another man with a baseball cap and glasses on. But it was a different car. Different baseball cap. This one was black. So, it made no sense to think it was the same man.

Yet she couldn't shake the idea.

Because her anxiety sucked, and she was a paranoid mess.

Every street that he followed her, she wound tighter and tighter, especially as she got closer to Jensen's house.

Should I call David?

It was probably just a coincidence.

Maybe she should call Jensen. Or Mick. Hopefully, one of them would be home.

I should probably call someone, right? Or should I? And tell them what —I'm being tailgated, as if that's not something that happens to everyone who gets on the road, every single day.

Her heart felt like it was slowly working its way up from her chest and into her throat, making it hard for her to swallow. If she hadn't been gripping the steering wheel so tightly, her hands would have been shaking. It felt like sweat was starting to pop out around her hairline as her pulse raced. She could feel a single drop trickle down the side of her temple.

Who do I call?

What if I'm wrong?

Mick. She should call Mick. Out of everyone she could call, he was the most likely to be home and not doing something important.

She was just reaching for her phone when the car suddenly moved into the left lane and out from behind her. It sped past as all her muscles turned watery with relief, racing ahead to make the left turn at the yellow light before it could turn red.

Coming to a halt, Cassidy felt tears spark in her eyes as she sucked in deep breaths to calm her nervous system. Since she was at a red light, she put her head against the steering wheel.

Maybe she should see if someone could start driving her again.

But no. They were busy. That was the whole point of driving herself. And it wasn't like she had to go far. She just needed to get herself together and stop being such a drama queen about someone riding her bumper, especially since it had been two different cars.

Of course, two white guys wearing baseball caps and sunglasses would look similar. But she'd been making up a whole scenario in her head because she couldn't just be normal.

That or both times it's been Don, and he's trying to lull me into a sense of complacency about being tailgated, so I don't get suspicious when he follows me all the way somewhere.

Or it's Don, and he's trying to scare me. To panic me. Just for fun or because he's hoping I'll make a mistake.

Yes, thank you, brain, for both of those scenarios.

As if Don was some kind of mastermind who had figured out where she was and was so obsessed with her, he had followed her just to mess with her.

The far more logical explanation was that it had been two totally different cars driven by impatient jerks who didn't care about tailgating people. It happened every day, all the time, to lots of drivers. There was no reason to get worked up about it.

She didn't need to bother David or Jensen with her drama, but she was definitely going to be bringing it up during her next session with her therapist. Mistress Julie had already helped a lot with Cassidy's anxiety. She could reassure Cassidy that she was overreacting, then help her with regulating herself when her brain wouldn't leave things alone.

<u>D</u>AVID

Walking into Black Fox's office, David nodded hello to Jennifer. She was on the phone with someone, her register higher than normal in the chirpy tone she used for customer service.

Jensen was just coming out from the hall on their side of the office, and he grinned when he saw David.

"Hey, Ginger."

"Baby. How's Cassidy doing?" He hadn't seen her or talked to her since the night he'd given her a foot massage, then put her in her bed and manfully walked away. Just to prove that he could. Which he had. So, he was doing a good job of not doing anything he wasn't supposed to do.

"Good." Jensen hesitated, and David's senses went on high alert.

"What?"

"It's probably nothing, but Mick said she was acting a little weird when she got home the other day."

"Which day?" He knew his tone had changed to a little aggressive, but he'd caught Jensen's smirk on Monday when he'd asked about her, after giving her a foot massage on Saturday, and he'd forced himself to back off asking every day. Now, he was wondering if that had been a mistake.

"Wednesday night."

"I was going to say it couldn't have been yesterday," Jennifer said. She'd gotten off the phone. "She was totally normal at game night."

"Which is why I didn't report anything." Jensen shrugged, leaning against the large wooden frame wrapped around Jennifer's desk and propping his elbow on it to make himself look more casual. "She was fine. I didn't notice anything. Mick said it was just when she first got home, she was kind of snappish and seemed a little shaken. When I checked in with her after he told me that, she just said she was fine."

'Fine' was such a loaded word that could mean so many things. Or it could mean that she was fine.

"She really did seem fine yesterday," Jennifer said, looking back and forth between David and Jensen with a slightly worried expression on her face. Like she thought Jensen might be in trouble or something. "She was laughing and enjoying herself. She didn't say anything had happened."

Which meant it was probably nothing. Maybe Mick was just misreading things. Maybe she'd been experiencing a bout of homesickness and hadn't wanted to talk about it. David rolled his shoulders. There was no reason to get all worked up over what could have been literally anything, not something necessarily nefarious.

Rolling his shoulders only loosened some of his tension, and he gave his neck a quick jerk, making it crack. Jennifer made a face.

"I hate it when you do that," she muttered.

"Sorry." He wasn't really, though. He did feel a little better now. He looked at Jensen. "Do you know if she's going to the club tonight?"

"She is." Jennifer answered him rather than Jensen, who had opened his mouth but closed it again when Jennifer got there before him. "We were talking about it yesterday at game night."

"Does that mean you're finally coming, too?" Jensen asked, so nonchalantly that he might have well screamed that he was invested in the answer. David had been watching the two of them tiptoe around each other for ages. "Master Gavin *is* supposed to be out of town this weekend."

"Why do you want to know?" Jennifer asked, tilting her head and focusing on him.

Jensen shrugged with one shoulder.

"You know. So I can keep an eye on you."

If David could have face-palmed without being obvious, he would have. While he understood Jensen's reasons for not asking Jennifer out—her age, her position at the company, the fact that they had to see each other on a daily basis—it was clear they were attracted to each other. Which meant that was not the answer she was looking for.

Her eyes narrowed at Jensen, and she sniffed derisively, tossing her long black hair over one shoulder.

"Keep an eye on me. You mean like, watch me if I decide to scene with someone?"

"Like making sure you don't choose the wrong person to scene with. Keep you from getting in over your head on your first visit. You know, like a big brother."

Oh, shit. David froze in place. He should start backing away, but he was afraid that would draw attention to him.

"You want to be my big brother in a BDSM sex club?" Derision dripped from her voice.

David eased back, just shifting his weight, waiting to see if either of them noticed his movement, but they were too locked in on each other. Jensen's skin was brown enough that he couldn't really flush, not like David, but David was pretty sure he would be blushing if he could.

"I mean, not like in an incestuous way."

"It doesn't matter, anyway." She waved her hand at him, turning her attention back to the computer to her right and away from both Jensen and David. David took a cautious step back. "I'm not going tomorrow night because I have a date."

"You have a date?" Jensen straightened up immediately, glaring at the back of her head. David took another step back. And then another.

"Yes, Jensen, I have a date. *Some* men are willing to admit that their feelings for me are more than brotherly."

Oh, shit.

David backed up as fast as he could to get himself out of the danger zone. Every good soldier knew when it was time to beat a strategic retreat.

Cassidy

"Thanks for the ride today," Cassidy said to Naomi as she got into the car. Buckling in her seatbelt, she waved goodbye to Brenda, who was watching from her front door. Brenda waved back, smiling cheerfully, then turned to go inside, shutting the door behind her.

"No problem," Naomi replied cheerfully. She was still in her work clothes, though she'd taken off the jacket to her grey suit and was wearing just the peach shell that had been underneath. Her hair was pulled back in a neat bun. "It's not out of my way at all. Plus, it's not like you can control when you get a flat tire."

"At least we made it back to Brenda's." Cassidy sighed. She'd taken the older woman out for a quick stop to get an ice cream. It wasn't at the retirement community, but she figured that since it was also out of their routine and no one would be able to predict it, it would be safe enough. At some point, she must have run over a nail or something because, by the time they got back to Brenda's, the tire was already low on air. While she waited for the tow truck to come get it, it completely ran out of air.

She'd called in to Black Fox when it first happened. Jennifer had been concerned, but Cassidy reassured her that there was no reason to think it was anything other than happenstance. Neither she nor Brenda had seen anything suspicious while they were out. Cassidy couldn't imagine how Don could have known where she'd be to do something like that when it had been an impulse trip.

Drew had come out to take a look, then reassured Cassidy that everything seemed fine and that Naomi would come pick her up at the end of the workday. He had another job to get to. Cassidy had been grateful he'd taken the time out of his day to come look at it personally before arranging for the tow.

"Thank Drew for me, when you see him, for looking after me today."

"You can thank him yourself." Naomi turned onto the next street. "We'll be at the club tonight."

"Oh, good." Cassidy slid her sneakers off, resting her feet on top of them. She'd had them forever, and they'd always been very comfortable, but they were starting to wear out... and sometimes, after a day of wearing any shoes, she just needed to feel free of them. "Um... do you know if David will be there?"

Noami smirked, shooting her a sidelong glance.

"I happen to know that he will, yes. I also happen to know that he asked Jennifer if you would be there."

"Oh. Um. Great." Cassidy gave her a thumbs-up, trying to ignore the red-hot blush now heating her cheeks and making Naomi laugh. It was good to see her laugh. She'd still been a little down last night at game night, but it seemed that today, she was feeling better. Cassidy couldn't imagine how hard the ups and downs of IVF were, but she hoped that it would be permanently up for Naomi and Drew soon.

She'd rather be embarrassed and see Naomi laugh again.

"So, are you finally going to admit that there's something going on between you two?" Naomi asked, grinning widely, though her focus was on the road.

"I don't know what's going on between us or if anything even is." Cassidy sighed. "I'm not going to deny that I'm attracted to him and that I would like to get to know him better." Though their conversation on Saturday night after the fundraiser had done nothing to make her like him less, that was for sure. And he'd given her a foot massage. And carried her to bed.

If she spent too long thinking about what it all might mean, she'd drive herself crazy.

"The fact that he's asking if you'll be at the club is a good sign. He's always so controlled—he normally doesn't do anything without thinking it through thoroughly—but with you, he doesn't seem to be able to help himself. He could have just waited 'til he got to the club to see if you came, too, but he wanted to know beforehand."

Hm. Did that mean that he'd thought through giving her a foot rub and decided it was the course of action he wanted to take? Or was it like Naomi said, and he hadn't been able to help himself?

Which was better?

She was about to tell Naomi about Saturday night when the other woman cursed under her breath, glancing up into the rearview mirror.

"What?" Cassidy asked, all of her nerves going on high alert. She twisted in her seat, trying to see behind them.

"Just some jerk riding my bumper. He's already moving, though." Naomi shook her head.

The grey car was in the other lane, zooming past them as Naomi spoke, going so fast that Cassidy couldn't get a good look at the driver. He might have been wearing a hat and sunglasses… it was too fast, though, and Naomi partially obstructed her view… she couldn't really tell.

"I hate jerks who do that. There was plenty of room in the other lane for him to move over. He didn't have to try to go straight up my tailpipe."

"Right." Cassidy sat back in her seat, her heart rapidly pounding in her chest.

It probably wasn't the same person who had tailgated her before, even though it was a grey car again. She was just being paranoid. The cars had been different. And this wasn't even her car. It was Naomi's. How could anyone know she was inside it? She was just overthinking everything because she was scared. Naomi obviously didn't think two thoughts about it. She was already back to chatting about the office gossip.

Apparently, Jensen hadn't been too happy that Jennifer was going out on a date tonight.

Last night, Jennifer had told them she'd been asked out, but she hadn't accepted yet. She'd been thinking about it. Obviously, Jensen had done something or said something to change that.

Cassidy pushed a smile onto her lips and tried to focus on Naomi.

She needed to stop freaking out over nothing.

26

David

Since he hoped he would be scening with Cassidy today, David had brought his kit to the Outlands rather than relying on the smaller one he kept at the club. A black duffle bag with his favorite toys and implements neatly packed inside... though he wasn't sure what he would actually use.

They didn't know each other that well; he'd only scened with her once before, and he'd been exploring her reactions and responses. He hadn't been trying to push any boundaries; he'd just been trying to learn about her. For a second scene, he could push her more, but he would probably still want to keep things pretty basic.

It would also depend on how much she was willing to do with him.

If she said yes to scening this evening at all.

He didn't think she would say no, though.

They were attracted to each other.

They also both understood that things needed to be kept in the club.

That they'd done such a good job of keeping their attraction to the club, despite moments where things could have become more intimate—like on Saturday—meant they could probably push things a little more in the club. As long as they communicated clearly where they stood.

Was some of this coming from his dick wanting to get inside her? Probably.

Definitely.

But he could handle his dick.

He'd already proven that when he'd given her a foot rub and kept it completely platonic, even after carrying her to bed. He hadn't called her the next day or tried to keep things going. After the way Jensen reacted on Monday, he hadn't even asked after her every day. He hadn't had time to stop by his grandmother's to see her, and he'd been fine.

So, if they wanted to take things to the next level in the club, there was no good reason not to.

Do not get physically or emotionally involved with the client.

But they'd already done more physically than he should have, and it hadn't changed anything afterward. There was no reason to think that it would after a second time. Plus, she wasn't *really* a client. Not in the strictest sense of the word. She was different.

Hence why she was living at Jensen's house instead of somewhere else.

Rules had already been bent for her; a few more wouldn't hurt anyone.

Hell, if anything, she'd be more protected if he was sleeping in her bed.

Nope, stop that. Keeping it to the club.

Right.

But he was just saying.

"Hello, Master David." Eben smiled as she greeted him before looking at her computer to check him in. She had her hair down, brushing her shoulders as she usually did. Today, her shoulders were bare, and she was wearing a steampunk-style leather corset several shades darker than her skin, with shiny gold buckles glinting when she moved. They matched the gold earrings dangling down alongside her naked throat. "How are you doing this evening?"

"Pretty good, thanks, Eben. And yourself?"

Her smile widened in appreciation that he'd asked.

"Good, thank you, Master David. Enjoy your evening."

"Thank you. Ah... Eben? Has Master Jensen and his guest checked in yet?"

Mischief sparked in her dark eyes. Dammit. Yeah, he sounded about as credibly nonchalant as Jensen had when he'd been speaking to Jennifer earlier today. He was sure that club gossip about him and Cassidy was already doing the rounds.

A new submissive to the club was always watched by everyone with curiosity. Add in that David had scened with her when he never scened with new members, then she hadn't scened with anyone else when he wasn't there... asking after her was a big old 'something is going on' flag.

Oh, well. Whatever.

The gossip would have already started flying again when he scened with her this evening. It couldn't get any worse, right?

"Yes, Master Jensen and his *guest* have checked in. That would be Cassidy, right?"

"Yes, but don't mention her name to anyone else who asks about her. And if they ask for her by name, she's not here," he said immediately.

Eben sobered.

"I know," she replied. "I only said it because it's you. Normally, I wouldn't answer any questions about members or guests being inside or not, but Master Gavin said you should be kept apprised of where she is at all times."

"Okay, good. Thank you." That made him feel better. Eben was a good girl, but sometimes people could be too trusting with the information they handed out, not realizing the person they were talking to had bad intentions. He had never asked about anyone being present in the club before, which was why he hadn't known the protocol.

Yeah, he could understand the gossip and interest in him and Cassidy.

Giving Eben a nod, he turned away and headed into the club, nodding at the Dungeon Monitor guarding the door. David Moore, who David liked to think of as "other David." He was pretty sure that the DM was part of the reason the club submissives had given him the nickname Master Ginger, to differentiate between the two Master Davids. None of them dared call him that to his face, but he knew they did it when they were talking about him—then they'd ended up giving the rest of his team Spice Girl names, too.

Other David nodded back a greeting as David passed him.

Walking into the club always felt like the rest of the world was falling away. He could walk a little easier, breathe a little easier, and just focus on what was happening right in front of him. It was an oasis away from all the problems in the world and a place where he didn't have any responsibilities other than to the submissive he paired with for the evening.

He spotted Cassidy right away, sitting at a table with Yasmine, Naomi, and Ashley. Jensen, Drew, and Lincoln were just beyond them, talking to Master Aiden, who was behind the bar. The three men were keeping an eye on the ladies while obviously deep in their own conversation. While he watched, Cassidy threw back her head and laughed at something Naomi said. Her long, dark hair had been pulled back in a high ponytail again, the ends of it brushing across her upper back as she moved.

She looked gorgeous in a lacy black chemise that hugged her curves and the same shoes she'd been wearing the last time. There was a lot of bare skin showing, and he couldn't help but wonder if those were the only things she had on. Maybe a thong underneath.

Blood was already racing to his dick, and he'd barely stepped into the club.

As if she'd heard him walk in, even though it was impossible, Cassidy sat up a little straighter and turned her head. Their gazes clashed from across the club.

Yeah, they were keeping everything to the club, but if he could step up what they were doing inside it, he sure as hell was going to do that.

<u>CASSIDY</u>

The feeling of eyes on her made her skin itch, but because of where they were, it wasn't in the way that made her want to run and hide. Sitting up, Cassidy looked around, anxious excitement welling up inside her. Right at the entrance to the club, she saw him.

Master David was wearing a pair of leather pants with a black button-down, unbuttoned at the collar and the sleeves rolled up to his elbows. All that dark fabric contrasted heavily with his skin and hair, making both appear even brighter, despite the low lighting in the bar area of the Outlands. His gaze met hers, and she knew he was the one who had been looking at her.

The movement of sitting up made her nipples brush against the lacy fabric of her chemise, the sensation teasing the little buds to hardness. Cassidy was already feeling pretty wound up, just being in the club, knowing he was coming tonight.

Had she dressed for seduction?

Absolutely.

But only if he was interested.

From what Naomi had said, he was.

He looked pretty interested right now.

"Girl, he looks like he wants to eat you up," Yasmine murmured, fanning herself.

"Holy shit," Ashley said. "I've never seen him look at anyone like that. Have they been doing this the whole time?"

"Yes," Yasmine and Naomi chorused.

"Shh," Cassidy hissed as Master David came closer, her heart starting to beat a little faster in her chest at his approach. He was completely intent on her, moving through the crowd with an intensely focused stare, a large black duffel bag hanging from his hand. Wondering what he had inside there made her nerves flutter.

The table fell silent when he reached them, and she could feel her friends' eyes on her, eagerly awaiting what was going to happen next.

"Ladies," Master David said, nodding his head as he glanced around the table before refocusing on Cassidy.

She managed to smile at him, though it felt as if her heart was beating triple time in her chest now. His nearness just made her senses go even more haywire.

"Could I steal Cassidy from you for a moment?"

Hopefully, more than a moment.

"Oh, feel free to talk to her right now," Ashley said sweetly. "Just pretend we're not here. We don't mind."

"I'm sure you wouldn't," Master David said dryly, leaning to set his bag down under the table right next to Lincoln and Drew's. Straightening, he held out his hand to Cassidy, silently offering to help her down from the high-top chair. Shooting a glance of apology to her disappointed friends, she took it.

They'd just have to hear about the conversation later.

Not that Master David took her far. Only a few steps away from the table, putting them in their own little space between the small clumps of people, so they could have a semi-private conversation. She did notice that he deliberately put his back to the table where Naomi, Yasmine, and Ashley were probably straining their ears, trying to overhear.

The silky chemise slid around her body as she moved, the lace rubbing her nipples to even further hardness, and she could feel the wetness from her pussy soaking the miniscule fabric of her thong. The string between her cheeks wasn't the most comfortable at the moment, but there was no way she was going to reach back to fix it right now. She'd rather die.

Master David tilted his head as he looked down at her, examining her, studying her expression. It felt a little like being under a microscope, and she could feel a blush starting to heat her cheeks.

"Cassidy. How are you feeling?"

She stared up at him.

"I'm good." Should she say something about the tailgating? No. Even if he didn't laugh at her for making such a stretch, she didn't want him thinking she was trying to make up drama so that he would pay attention to her. She already had his attention. If it happened again, in her own car, she would say something. Today had to have been a coincidence, and the guy had barely been behind Naomi for more than thirty seconds. "How are you?"

A little smile curved his lips.

"I'm good. I was wondering if you would like to scene with me again this evening."

"Yes, Sir." She nodded, putting her hands together in front of her to keep from fidgeting. "I would like that."

Heat flared in his eyes.

"We should discuss what you're comfortable with doing in the scene. Last time, we had negotiated keeping it platonic, but we pushed the bounds of that. Tonight, I want to lay down some clear expectations for how far we can go."

"So, you're saying we could scene platonically *or* non-platonically?" That was unexpected. She'd thought she'd have to do more work than simply show up in a silk nightie to convince him to have sex.

"Whichever you're more comfortable with."

Crap. Why wouldn't he just say what he wanted?

"Well, I don't want to make you do anything you don't want to do."

He blinked at her, an almost patronizing expression flitting across his face as he looked her up and down. The sides of his lips quirked up in pure amusement.

"You can't make me do anything I don't want to do."

Physically, that was probably true, but he hadn't really stated a clear preference for what he wanted from her tonight. Cassidy scowled up at him. How hard was it for him to just say he wanted to bang?

"Well, I don't want to say non-platonically if you want to keep things platonic." She could hear the little bite in her voice. He was starting to frustrate her.

Just say that you want to fuck me so I can say yes!

"Do you *want* to keep things platonic?" There was some frustration starting to grow in his voice and eyes, the same frustration she was feeling. It would probably be undignified to stomp her foot.

"Yeah, if you're not interested in non-platonically scening with me."

He moved so quickly that she squeaked in surprise as she found herself being hauled up against his hard body.

His *very* hard body.

That was *very* hard *everywhere.*

Her breath caught in her throat as her senses went haywire, her hands pressed against his chest, the rest of her squished against him.

"Does this feel like I'm not interested?" He growled the words, his cock digging into her stomach, fingers into her hips. The silk of her chemise felt gossamer thin between them. He was big and hot and hard, and there was no denying he wanted her.

Her brain had fuzzed out and stopped working, and she knew the words that came out were nonsensical considering the situation, but they came out, anyway.

"So, you want to scene non-platonically?"

"For fuck's sake, stop saying that word."

Lowering his lips to hers, he captured them in a kiss that seared her from the inside out.

Cassidy whimpered.

It had been so long since she'd been kissed.

Much less a really *good* kiss like this one.

Firm. Confident. Eager. Filled with heat and desire. The attraction between them snapped and popped around them, the very air feeling like it was full of sparking electricity. A kiss that could melt insides and panties simultaneously.

The best first kiss of her life.

If she could freeze a moment of time in her life, this was the one she would choose.

But every moment ends, and Master David broke away from the kiss, leaving her breathless and needy, leaning against him because her knees had gone too weak to hold her up properly. She stared up at him.

"Cassidy, just to be completely clear, I want to scene with you tonight. Non-platonically."

Finally.

"Yes, Sir," she whispered.

27

———————

DAVID

Time to just admit what he freaking wanted. Talking around it hadn't helped. It just made him frustrated as hell. Yes, it would be easier to give Cassidy what she wanted rather than admit what he wanted, but since she wasn't willing to admit it, either...

He was very aware of how ridiculous they'd sounded going around and around like that and was very glad their friends had not been able to hear them.

They had, however, seen the kiss, just like the rest of the people on this floor of the club. Several catcalls and cheers were already coming from behind him. He sighed as he draped his arm around Cassidy's shoulders, keeping her close even though she was no longer pressed up against him.

Drew, Jensen, and Lincoln had rejoined the table, no longer at the bar. Drew and Jensen were grinning. Lincoln raised his eyebrows at David, but the slight smile on his face was more amused than anything else. He didn't disapprove. One of the little knots in David's stomach undid itself.

If Lincoln approved, then that was fine, right?

He wasn't doing the wrong thing by scening with Cassidy at the club.

Non-platonically.

This is what happens when you don't just admit to a woman that you want to fuck her. You use words like non-platonically.

Though he wouldn't feel the need to dance around it so much anymore. Cassidy had said yes. He'd already proven to himself that they could keep things to the club. His boss knew what was going on. No one else seemed to think David was doing anything wrong; they were all cheering him and Cassidy on.

He could still feel some of his internal reservations making him want to hesitate, but right now, he was just going to go with the flow. Which was not his norm, but this wasn't exactly a normal situation. If it was a normal situation with a regular client, he would never have put his hands on her.

"Thank you all for your support," he said sarcastically, shaking his head as he went to retrieve his bag. "We'll see you later."

"Go on, you two crazy kids," Ashley said, making everyone laugh since she was the youngest person at the table. She shooed them with her hands. "Have fun. I know I'm going to. Lincoln owes me a *really* good time tonight now." She grinned up at her husband, who sighed and shook his head.

David paused.

"Wait, were you two betting on us?"

"Just a small one." Ashley tossed her honey-streaked brown hair, clearly smug in her win. "I told Lincoln you two had a thing for each other."

"And I told Ashley that you would never unbend about the rules enough to actually make a move on it." Lincoln smiled. "I'm not sorry to see I was wrong."

The rules were the rules for a reason, which was something he'd said to his team often enough. And to Lincoln more than a few times. This time, David pressed his lips together to keep from saying it. Because he was bending the rules a bit.

Picking up his bag, he shook his head at his friends, his arm still around Cassidy as he began to lead her toward the stairs. She looked up at him curiously, letting him guide her through the tables.

"What rules are we breaking?"

"Getting involved with clients. Though you're not technically a client. You're different." Yup. That was his reasoning for why it was okay in this one situation. Things were different, so she could be treated differently. "That's why I want to keep things inside the club, though, for now. It makes things easier."

"That makes sense." She nodded, though she appeared thoughtful. The hair from her ponytail brushed against the back of his arm as they walked, making all the hair there stand at attention. "You thought you were going to get in trouble for scening with me."

"It was a possibility, but Lincoln doesn't seem to have a problem with it. Like I said, you're not our usual kind of client." They reached the top of the stairs, and he shifted his arm so she could hang onto it while she walked down the stairs in those high heels rather than be tucked under it. She smiled gratefully at him. "We should talk about limits, though. Are there any areas of your body that you want off limits? Anything that's not on your sheet that you want on your hard limits tonight?"

Then she said the words that he most wanted to hear.

"Nope. I'm all yours, Sir."

His groin tightened. Some of his erection had subsided when the kiss had ended, and he'd had to face the group, but now it was back with a vengeance.

Fuck, he wanted her bad.

And now I can have her.

He just needed to figure out what he was going to do with her first.

Cassidy

Holy fuck, holy fuck, holy fuck...

Every inch of her body felt like it was hypersensitive as they walked down the stairs. Her breasts bounced under the lace, rubbing her stiff nipples against the material that felt scratchy as it stimulated sensitive tissues. She could feel the heat of his body against her arm, his pant leg occasionally brushing her bare one.

She didn't know if he realized what a big deal it was for her to offer up anything and everything to him. At Stronghold, she hadn't done that with any of the Doms.

But she wanted him.

And he'd said they had to keep things to the club *for now*.

Which meant maybe, in the future, they wouldn't have to. Like, after she was no longer a client. Now that she was sure that was why he'd been holding back, and she'd seen that Lincoln was fine with them being together in the club, she didn't want to hold back anymore. She wanted it all.

All the pleasure. All the torment. All of him.

"Let's check if any of the private rooms are open," he said, leading her over to the wall where the doors were. She hadn't gotten a good look at them last time because she'd been a little distracted. Next to each door was a small placard with different labels on them.

In use.

Reserved.

Reserved.

In use.

Reserved.

Open.

Master David halted in front of the last one, a grin spreading on his face.

"Perfect," he murmured, releasing her long enough to open the door. He stepped back, holding it open so she could precede him inside. Not that she needed any encouragement. She was as curious about the room as she was eager to scene with him.

She'd never scened in any of the private rooms at Stronghold or Marquis, though she'd watched others inside them. Don had wanted to be out in the main Dungeon where everyone could see them. That was what had given her the opportunity to escape. If he'd taken her to a private room, she wasn't sure she would have had the courage to say 'red.' Not when she could imagine what he could do to her in the time it took for someone else to get to the room.

There was a part of her that was a little concerned about being in a private room with Master David, but she knew that was Don's shadow on her current life, and she wasn't going to let that make her choices for her. She wanted to have sex with Master David tonight. She appreciated that they weren't going to have an audience for their first time together.

The room wasn't large—she didn't expect it to be—but it had everything they could need in it. In the farthest corner was a full-size bed, small enough that it didn't take up the entire room but large enough that two people could easily fit on it. Especially for sex. In the center of the ceiling a D-ring was bolted to the ceiling, chains currently dangling down from it with cuffs attached to the ends.

There was a St. Andrew's cross to her right, in the corner opposite the bed. The door was in another corner of the room, so that she walked in toward the cross. Along the left wall adjacent to the club was a large wardrobe, several open shelves, and a peg board. Considering what was displayed on the shelves and peg board, she could only imagine what types of toys and implements were in the wardrobe.

Turning to look behind her, she could see Master David doing something to the sign on the wall next to the door, his foot keeping the door open. Finishing up, he started to come inside the room and smiled when he saw her looking at him.

"Changing it to 'in-use'," he explained.

Right. That made sense. Cassidy nodded, nervously waiting for him to join her. Closing the door behind him, he put his bag down next to the wardrobe, studying her again. She clasped her hands behind her back, trying not to wilt under his scrutiny.

The closed door shut out the sounds of the club, of the other people, turning them into muffled white noise rather than anything legible.

They were alone.

"I don't know how it was at your last club, but the sound in here is hooked up to the security system," Master David explained, walking forward and putting his bag down. His expression was serious as he looked down at her, her head tipping back to meet his gaze. "If you say 'red,' the Dungeon Monitors will hear it and automatically pull up the video for this room—which means they're watching right now since I said it. They monitor everything and will come running if necessary."

"Oh. Okay. Thank you." Stronghold had a very similar system. Cassidy decided not to point out how much damage could be done to a person in sixty seconds while they waited for the DMs to appear. The safety measure was better than nothing. At least someone would be on the way.

Watching her, Master David's lips quirked as if he knew what she was thinking.

"I'm not going to use any restraints again this evening," he said reassuringly. Cassidy felt a brief spurt of disappointment. "You're just going to have to be a good girl and hold yourself in place for me."

Oh. *Oh.*

Well, when he put it that way.

Heat flowed from her lower body up to her cheeks, leaving them hot pink and right back down again as she did her best not to squirm in place.

"Yes, Sir," she whispered and watched a similar heat flare in his eyes. Her body felt like it was pulsing in anticipation of what was to come.

"Okay, little spark. Now, I want you to take off that little silk thing so I can see what you have on underneath."

Not much.

Her mouth felt suddenly dry, but this was what she'd wanted. What she'd hoped for. And why she'd worn something that was so easy to take off.

Hooking her thumbs under the thin strings of her chemise, she tugged them off her shoulders and let the silk slide over her body. Watching him watch her, she could see the desire in his expression grow as the tiny bit of clothing between them fluttered to the ground, leaving her in nothing but her favorite heels and a miniscule thong. The tiny scrap of triangle fabric and strings wasn't really functional; it was mostly for show.

For tantalizing.

Going by the look in Master David's eyes, it worked.

She stepped out of the little circular pool of silk that was at her feet, one step closer to him.

"Good girl." His voice was lower than before, rougher, and her body thrilled to the sound of it. She was pretty sure she saw his hand twitch, as though he wanted to reach out to touch her. "Now, I want you to lace your fingers together behind your head and stand with your legs shoulder-width apart."

A classic submissive pose, one she'd stood in many times. Cassidy raised her arms, lacing her fingers behind her head with her elbows spread wide. She shifted her feet apart, feeling the coolness of the air in the room flowing across her inner thighs and the damp silk over her pussy.

The position made her breasts thrust out in front of her, as if she was offering them up to him... which, in truth, she was.

Touch me, hurt me, play with me.

Her breath stuttered in her throat.

Despite the scenes she's done at Stronghold, post her Douchebag Don era, she hadn't felt this level of excitement, this level of anticipation, until Master David. He was the difference, or at least, her attraction to him was. He made all the difference.

"Very pretty," Master David said, stalking up to her. Rather than coming to a halt in front of her, he moved around her. The first time, he was looking her over, inspecting her, making her blush at the closeness of his attention. Her nipples puckered, hardening further as her anticipation grew.

The second time he moved around her, his hands reached out to explore. Touching her. Caressing her. Heat flared everywhere his fingers landed, making her want to squirm even more. She couldn't press her thighs together to put some pressure on the aching parts between them without disobeying, though.

He paused behind her, running his hands over the globes of her ass, squeezing them together, then releasing. A short, sharp smack against her right cheek made her squeal, but she held her position.

"Good girl."

A second smack against her left cheek evened her out.

Cassidy let out a little moan.

She wanted more, and he knew it.

But apparently, he was a teasing jerk.

Rather than giving her more spanking, he stepped up behind her, the leather of his pants rubbing against her ass, and placed his hands on her hips. She could feel his hot breath against the back of her neck before his lips suddenly brushed over the sensitive skin, and she gasped. Her hands were clasped against her head, just above where her hairline ended, leaving her neck totally exposed.

Leaning back against him, she felt the ridge of his cock pressing between her cheeks, his hands sliding to her front to splay over her lower stomach. His lips moved down the side of her neck, distracting her from any consternation she might have normally felt over him touching her stomach. Don's voice, criticizing the small pooch she'd never been able to get rid of no matter how he'd starved her, tried to rise up and was banished by a rush of sensation as Master David rocked his hips against her from behind.

Whimpering, she leaned back against him. He caressed her stomach, that part of her that had been so maligned by her ex, before moving his hands up to her breasts. His lips moved over the side of her throat, encouraging her to lean back against him as he cupped her breasts with his hands and squeezed.

The needy ache shot straight through to her core, making her gasp. His fingers closed around her nipples, pinching the sensitive buds tightly, and Cassidy shuddered.

He'd barely gotten started, and she was already ready to drop to her knees and start begging.

28

———————

Beautiful. Sensual. Wildly responsive.

Everything he'd remembered from their first scene together and more because this time, he didn't feel like he had to hold back. He could touch Cassidy as much as he wanted. Put his hands wherever he wanted. His cock wherever he wanted.

His cock was dying to be inside her.

He rocked his hips against her again, feeling her push back against him, his hands full of her breasts as he ran his tongue along the side of her throat. Pinching her nipples tightly between his fingers, he gave them a little twist and felt her whimper as much as he heard it.

Fuck.

He wasn't going to last if they kept this up.

There was only one solution.

He needed to take the edge off so he could take his time.

Releasing her nipples, he massaged her breasts one last time, giving the side of her neck a final kiss. He rolled his body to help her straighten up again, which she did with a sigh, following his non-verbal lead. Sliding his hands back down her sides, he gave her ass another two swats—one for each cheek—before continuing his walk around her.

When he came to the front of her, and she tipped her head back to look up at him, he could see the glaze of desire over her hazel eyes. Her lips were slightly parted as she panted for breath, cheeks flushed with heat and need, her nipples hard and standing at attention. The flush on her cheeks went down her neck all the way to her upper chest, her skin light pink as if it had just been flogged.

David couldn't help himself. He leaned forward to kiss her, brushing his lips over hers, though he deliberately didn't deepen the kiss. He'd had enough trouble controlling himself when he was behind her. He didn't think he'd be able to handle himself the way he wanted if he kissed her fully now.

With his lips still hovering over hers, he slid one hand around the back of her neck, and his fingers brushed against hers where her hands were still in place. Cupping the back of her neck, he met her gaze with his own, holding them in place.

"On your knees, sweetheart. And drop your hands down behind your back."

They were standing close enough that he could see her pupils dilate at the order. Her little pink tongue darted out to lick her lips, then her arms dropped down, hands going behind her. He kept his hold on her neck, helping her keep her balance as she lowered herself to her knees, head tilting back to continue looking up at him as she went.

Fuck, she was so damn pretty.

Still holding on to her with the one hand, David used the other to open his belt and then his pants, freeing his cock. He didn't miss the interest that flared when he undid his belt, but that was going to have to wait for a different day.

"Open up, little spark. I want you to show me how good you can suck my cock." He paused, examining her, waiting to see if she would request a condom or that he not cum in her mouth. Cassidy did neither. Instead, she opened her mouth, leaning forward almost before he was ready.

She managed to get a long lick up the underside of his dick, making it jerk in reaction.

Since she was so eager, there was no reason for him to hold back.

He slid his hand up to wrap around her ponytail, giving him some semblance of control, watching avidly as he allowed her to do whatever she wanted.

Again, her tongue darted out, licking up the length and around the crown of his cock, making him groan. With his free hand, he reached down to fondle her breast, his hips thrusting forward between her open lips at the same time. She hummed in appreciation around his dick, sending the vibrations straight up his spine in a tingling rush of pleasure.

Fuck.

No need to tell her what to do.

She slid her lips down the length of his cock, tongue and throat working, sucking him hard. It felt like his knees were about to buckle, and he kind of wished he'd sat down on the bed before letting her do this... but there was also something about being mostly dressed and standing over a pretty, mostly naked submissive kneeling in front of him.

Plus, now that they were here, he didn't want to move.

So, he braced himself against the pleasure and shuddered as her mouth bobbed up and down on his cock. His hand on her ponytail wasn't doing much more than holding on for dear life at this point.

"Fuck, that's good, sweetheart," he said hoarsely as she took him deeper, sliding her lips down to near the root. Her tongue flicked along the underside of his cock, massaging its length, and her head tilted back to look up at him, meeting his gaze.

Such a pretty fucking picture. David pinched her nipple in reward, making her squeal around his cock, the sound muffled by the thick meat between her lips.

"Now, hold still so I can fuck your pretty little mouth. If you need me to stop or slow down, just smack my thigh."

She made a little whimpering noise that traveled along his dick.

Strengthening his grip on her ponytail to hold her in place, he let his hips slide back before plunging forward, his cock sliding over her tongue all the way until her nose was pressed into the red curls just above his cock. He could feel her momentary struggle, the way her throat worked around his cock, fighting against her gag reflex, then he pulled back again to give her a moment to breathe.

He thrust in again, fucking her mouth the way he wanted to fuck her sweet little pussy. Tears gathered in her eyes as he cut off her airway again and again, his cock easily sliding over her mouth and down her throat as she relaxed into the face-fucking. She hummed as he used her mouth, her gaze unfocusing as she went into a subspace-like haze. She was completely intent on pleasuring him, and it was the hottest fucking thing he'd ever seen.

"Fuck... I'm going to cum, Cassidy..." He was about to say that if she didn't want to swallow, she needed to pull back now, but the moment he said the words, her eyes flared, and she started moving with him instead of passively letting him use her mouth. It was like she was trying to swallow him whole.

Fuck.

He couldn't even get the word out as his breath strangled in his throat, his hips thrusting forward to bury himself in her. Muscles worked around the head of his cock, massaging it as pure heat pulsed through him. He could feel each jet of cum coaxed out by her tongue, shooting straight out from his balls and down her throat.

CASSIDY

Swallowing convulsively, Cassidy felt Master David's cock slowly start to soften against her tongue. Not that that stopped her.

She'd always had a bit of an oral fixation.

Don hadn't liked oral, though—giving or receiving—and she'd never understood why, though she'd eventually been grateful that there was something he hadn't been able to ruin for her.

Master David's hand gentled around her ponytail, no longer gripping her hair quite so tightly, and he sighed out a long breath as he relaxed. Cassidy felt that breath down to her toes. Knew that she had been the one to make him feel that way, to make him feel good. Pride and pleasure filled her in equal measure.

She suckled until he pulled away, only then reluctantly letting his half-hard cock fall from her lips, leaving her panting and aware of the growing ache between her thighs. What could she say? Pleasuring her Dom got her off. At least, it had used to. And now, with Master David, that pleasure was returning in a way that was sexual as well as emotional.

She'd missed this.

"Good girl."

Cassidy's insides clenched. She was pretty sure she was never going to get tired of hearing him calling her that in a raspy voice, as if she'd completely undone him. His hand caressed the top of her head, and she closed her eyes for a moment, luxuriating in his praise. The taste of his cock and cum lingered on her tongue, salty and sweet.

"Now, stay right here. I want to get some toys, so I can take my time playing with you." His hand slid around the side of her face, down to cup her jaw, tilting her head back. Cassidy opened her eyes so she could look up at him, meeting his gaze.

The fire in his eyes was banked but not gone. He was calm and controlled again, but the desire was still there.

Oh.

He'd gotten off in order to get control of himself again. She'd been that close to making him lose it.

Yes, she was a smug little submissive sometimes. She couldn't help the curve of her lips as she smiled up at him. Not that he seemed upset. He pressed his thumb against her lower lip before releasing her with only a slightly admonishing look as if to tell her not to get too cocky.

Hands still locked behind her back, she kept smiling as he released her and turned to go get his bag. Though she couldn't see exactly what his hands were doing, she knew he was closing the front of his pants, tucking his cock away. Bending to pick up the bag, when he turned around, she could see that he hadn't re-buckled his belt, and it hung loosely, like a tantalizing threat.

Cassidy ducked her head.

Did she want him to use the belt? She wasn't sure. He could make it good, she felt confident about that, but she didn't know if that's what she wanted tonight.

What she really wanted, deep down, was to be his good girl. She was on a roll with that so far, and she didn't want to ruin it.

The bag was set down beside her, the items inside rustling as they settled, making her wonder what was in there. What implements did he like to use? What toys? And which was he going to use on her now? Anticipation swelled, making it hard not to squirm in place.

Although the need to squirm might also be because her knees were starting to hurt from kneeling on the vinyl flooring, it was mostly from the growing ache between her legs. On her knees, she was able to put a bit more pressure on the part of her that needed it, but not enough to get anywhere near completion.

Master David's eyes narrowed as he looked down at her.

"Spread your knees apart, Cassidy."

Damn all too-perceptive Doms.

Huffing, she spread her knees apart, trying not to whimper as she felt the coolness of the air brushing over her *very wet* thong. The fabric felt like it was clinging to her pussy, and she wanted to rip it away—or press her fingers against her clit and get the relief she needed—but of course, she couldn't. Not without disobeying Master David.

This was why it could be easier to be restrained; honor bondage could be a pain in the ass.

She would trust David to restrain her.

"Let's start with these." He lifted a pair of spring-loaded nipple clamps up from the bag. They glinted silver, tipped with rubber, and a chain hanging between them. Cassidy's nipples felt like they tightened even more at the sight.

They were just like the ones he'd put on her last time, but this time, he didn't bother with a looser setting. Crouching down in front of her, he held them where she could see they were on the tightest setting from the beginning. Cupping her breast in one hand, he rubbed his thumb over her nipple, making her whimper as her pussy clenched in response.

He shifted his hand, and the tight pinch of the clamp made her gasp. The rubber tip was a lot cooler than his fingers, not that it mattered because it warmed against her skin quickly. The heat of her need made the little bud pulse in the tight grip. A moment later, he was cupping the other breast, teasing that nipple to hardness and repeating the process.

The need to press her thighs together and relieve some of the ache between them was nearly overwhelming. She shuddered, closing her eyes and breathing through the stinging pain that was somehow transmuted to pleasure as it moved from her chest through the rest of her body. The throbbing echoed from her nipples straight down to her clenching pussy.

"Very pretty, little spark." Master David tugged on the chain gently, making her breasts bounce, the clamps pulling at her nipples, then releasing. Cassidy moaned, gripping her fingers tighter behind her back to keep from grabbing his hand and holding on. "Now, I want you on all fours. I have one more piece of jewelry for you."

Something in the way he said it, she just knew. Whatever it was, it was going in her butt.

Letting out a shuddering sigh, she leaned forward onto her hands, giving her legs some relief from the kneeling position. Master David rocked back on his heels, reaching into his kit and pulling out a small, silky blue bag. When he revealed the metal plug waiting inside, the light in the room glinted off the pink heart-shaped crystal base of the plug.

Yup, it was going in her butt.

Cassidy dropped her head, hiding her smile. It had been a long time since she'd had a Dom scene with her like this, long before Don, who hadn't believed in plugs at all—but also hadn't been much more interested in her ass than he had in her mouth—but her instincts were still intact.

Sometimes, Doms could be so predictable.

29

———————

CASSIDY

It only took him a moment to shift the string between her buttocks, then the cold, wet tip of the metal plug pushed against her bottom hole, stretching it and making her gasp as the chilly toy began to push inside her. She rocked back against it, taking it deeper, feeling her tight ring stretch around the tapered length. The chain hanging from the clamps on her nipples swung gently beneath her, tugging on the little buds and adding to the sensations.

Master David's hand came down to rest on the small of her back, making her freeze in place, which was likely the intention.

"Deep breath, sweetheart."

She automatically did as he ordered, then gasped as the plug pushed all the way in, the heavy toy settling inside her. It felt good and strange at the same time. Her bottom clenched around it in little spasms as Master David twisted it back and forth inside her. All the little nerve endings around her entrance felt like they'd ignited.

"Very pretty." He commented, pulling gently, then pushing it back in, making her moan a little; she wanted him to be doing that to her pussy. "How does it feel, Cassidy?"

"Good, Sir." She breathed out the words, feeling like there wasn't enough air in her lungs to speak normally. Another thrust of the plug rocked her forward, swinging the nipple chain again, and her pussy clenched emptily.

"Good. Let's get you up on your feet, then I want you on the cross."

He shifted on his feet, moving to her side and holding out his hand for her to take so he could help her up. Moving with the plug inside her and the clamp chain hanging down just added to the need already sizzling inside her. Even the smallest movement caused additional stimulation.

Taking Master David's hand, she got to her feet, feeling a little unsteady as her knees protested the change, and she got her heels under her again. She could feel the string of her thong resting against the side of the plug, slightly off-center now that there was something in its way.

Master David moved with her, guiding her to the St. Andrew's cross on the side of the room, positioning her where he wanted her. Facing the cross, back to him, hands up on the higher portions of the wooden X. She could lean against it if she needed to, though her breasts were right at the center of the frame, and doing so would squish her clamped nipples against the hard polished wood.

"Keep your hands right here, little spark." His hands put hers where he wanted them before sliding down her arms, skimming over her sides and down to her ass. Cassidy's hips thrust back at him, but he just chuckled, giving her bottom a little, unsatisfying pat before moving away.

She wanted to scream in frustration.

Apparently, getting him off quickly meant he could take his time edging her.

The big jerk.

———

<u>DAVID</u>

One orgasm had taken the edge off, but his cock was already

heading right back to full mast as he got Cassidy exactly how he wanted her. She swayed as she walked, partly from her time kneeling, partly from the heels she was wearing. He knew she was probably expecting to be flogged or spanked... he was looking forward to surprising her. Part of the reason he wanted her facing away from him to start with was so that she couldn't see what he was planning right away.

Going back to his kit, he pulled out the small finger vibrator, slipping it over the first two fingers of his left hand. It was just a little bullet vibe as a silicone ring, with two ring spaces to keep it steady. He put it on so the vibrator was on the palm side of his hand. Then he picked up his other toy of choice for the evening—the Wartenburg pinwheel, which had four of the spiky rolling wheels on its end.

The four wheels would spread out the pricking, tingling sensation rather than isolating it with one wheel. He had one of those, too, but right now, he wanted to play with the four wheels. Although flogging her first would make her skin even more sensitive, since this was their first time playing with it, he wanted to start from scratch and see how she reacted.

Nothing on her forms indicated she had any special interest in or aversion to the wheel. Most of the abuse her ex had heaped on her had been with impact implements. The wheel felt like a good choice for sensual play, which was exactly what he wanted for tonight.

He didn't want anything that might remind her of her ex.

Getting back to his feet, he looked over at Cassidy, who was shifting her weight back and forth in impatience. If she had looked over her shoulder, trying to peek, he hadn't caught it.

Lucky for her.

"Okay, sweetheart," he said, coming closer. "You're going to have to let me know if anything becomes too much."

"Yes, Sir." Her shoulders tensed, then she rolled them, loosening them. He could see the deep breath she took in, deliberately working to calm her nerves. Need surged through him, but he pushed it down. At least he was able to push it down instead of it riding him the way it had at first.

Kneeling behind her, he placed the pinwheel against her calf, just above where it met her ankle. She flinched at the sensation, though whether it was from the coolness of the steel or the prickling of the spikes, he couldn't tell.

"Oh!" Her little gasp made his cock jerk. Moving his hand, he ran the pinwheel up the back of her leg, grinning as she let out a little squeal, trying to move away from the sensation only to be stopped by the cross. There was only so far she could go, even with pressing her body against the wooden frame.

Running it up the back of her left thigh, he moved it across the sensitive skin between her thigh and bottom. Her cheeks clenched, the pink heart flashing between them, and she went up on her tiptoes, gasping again as she tried to escape the prickling. David ran it down the other side of her thigh to her knee and then lifted it away.

"What is that?" She asked the question in a breathless voice, her ponytail swishing as she tried to peer over her shoulder without moving her hands from the spots he'd put them in.

She'd never experienced the wheel before?

David grinned.

Oh. This was going to be fun.

"What do you think it is?" he asked rather than answering her right away. He placed it against her other leg, at the same starting point that he'd used for the first, and began to run it upwards. Again, she gasped, writhing, unable to answer him while she desperately tried to hold herself in place the way he'd told her to. "What does it feel like?"

He ran it under her buttocks and then back down the other side of her thigh.

"It feels like... I don't know... it tickles, but it hurts, too..."

"Do you like it?" This time, he ran it up the inside of her spread thigh and then across the wet silk of her thong, making her shriek despite the thin protection the fabric provided. Then he ran it back down her other inner thigh.

"I don't know."

No one could say she wasn't honest. David flicked the

vibrator on with this thumb and slid his left hand between her thighs, tracing it over her plump pussy lips, then pressing it firmly against her clit—but only for a moment before he turned it off again. Her moan of erotic disappointment made his cock throb.

<u>*Cassidy*</u>

Oh my God, what is he doing to me? She'd been prepared for a flogging or a spanking, maybe even a cropping. She knew he'd probably torment her some more, withholding from giving her an orgasm right away.

She hadn't expected this.

It wasn't electricity. There was no buzz, no hum until he'd turned the vibrator on, but that was the closest thing she could think of to the sensation running over her. She didn't know what it was, much less if she loved or hated it.

The sensation had all her nerve endings prickling. It had tickled, but it had also hurt in a way that made her skin feel both extra sensitive and extra sensational. She felt so *aware* of her skin. Something else that reminded her of a violet wand. But it wasn't one; she was sure of that.

The vibrator was no mystery, just sexual torture. Her clit was humming and throbbing between her legs, her ass clenching around the plug. The tips of her nipples felt sore from where they'd rubbed against the hard wood of the frame, her breasts pulsing in time with her clit from the ache of the clamps.

"Let's try this," Master David murmured, then the prickling ran over her buttocks vertically. Up and down, up and down. Thank God, he hadn't spanked or flogged her before doing this. She wasn't sure she would have been able to remain still.

As it was, every time he hit a particularly sensitive spot—mostly near the crease or where her thighs met her curves—she went up on her toes, trying not to move her feet or hands. It pricked and prickled, leaving a line of tingling near-pain everywhere it went. Her skin hummed.

Then he would stop, pulling it away, and that was the worst part... because that meant his hand went back between her legs. The vibrator was brutally strong, too strong for her to get off immediately when he would press it against her clit, yet he always seemed to know exactly when to pull it away. It was complete torment.

Cassidy danced in place, up and down on her toes, writhing against the sensations.

"David! Sir! *Please!*" she begged as he pressed the vibrator against her clit again.

Chuckling, he rubbed it against the little bud, the vibrations making her toes curl, before pulling it away again.

"Okay, little spark," he said while she quivered in anxious need. What was the girl version of blue balls? Because whatever it was, that's what she had right now. The need to orgasm *hurt.* Edging *sucked.* "Let's get you turned around."

Cassidy could weep because that didn't sound like she was going to get her orgasm. At best, she was finally going to find out what he was using on her that was making her feel like she was going to jump out of her skin.

Unsteady in her heels while she was so overcome with the sensations, she managed to turn herself around with only a little assistance from Master David.

On one hand, he had the vibrator attached to his fingers with what looked like a double ring. In the other, he held a metal instrument with a long handle and prickly wheels at one end of it, like a pizza slicer but with spikes. She'd seen them before, though never with four wheels; she'd only seen it with one... her brain struggled to actually work before the word finally popped into her head.

Wartenberg wheel.

So, that's what that felt like.

She wasn't sure if she loved or hated it.

Lifting her gaze to meet Master David's, a little shiver went through her at the hot, sadistic gleam in his eyes. Her tongue flicked out to lick her nips nervously, and his gaze dropped down to them for a moment before meeting hers again.

"Hands up on the cross, Cassidy. Feet apart." His voice was low, harsh, and needy. The same need that was pulsing through her.

Cassidy stepped back, leaning against the wooden frame and lifting her hands in position. Her nipples ached as they were thrust toward him, and the humming between her legs had barely dissipated. David's eyes glowed as she obeyed him.

"Good girl."

Stepping forward, he bent his head to brush his lips over hers again. The tips of her nipples were abraded by his wiry chest hair and then crushed as he leaned into her, taking her mouth in a passionate kiss. Cassidy kissed him back eagerly, needily, her tongue dancing with his, ignoring the twin spikes of pain from her clamped nipples. Her lips clung to his as he slowly ended the kiss and pulled away.

Stepped back.

Her nipples were throbbing. Her pussy was throbbing. *Everything* was throbbing.

She wasn't sure if she wanted to murder him or fuck him.

Then, staring directly into her eyes, he ran the little row of wheels up the center of her right thigh.

Murder, then.

She sucked in a breath, shuddering as the spiky wheels pricked her stomach, her sides, and up to her breasts. Throwing her head back, she panted as she worked her way through the sensation, doing her best not to squirm out of place. Also not to reach up and grab the awful wheel from him.

If this was his way of making her wish that he would just tie her up already, it was working.

The pressure on her right nipple released, and she cried out because she hadn't been expecting it. The left throbbed, protesting as the chain swung from it, the other clamp like a little weight tugging it. Master David's wet mouth closed around the freed nipple, sucking hard on the tender little bud.

"Oh! Please, *Sir!*"

He ignored her, suckling harder and then lifting his mouth just to run the pinwheel over the overly sensitive bud. Cassidy screamed, lifting her hands for just a moment before pushing them back down again, panting in pain.

Then the asshole released the clamp on her other nipple and did the exact same thing, leaving her a quivering, panting mess of sensations. She wasn't going to be able to last much longer.

30

By the time Master David was done torturing her breasts with the damn wheels, Cassidy was ready to scream. Her nipples felt raw, sore, and so sensitive that the slightest brush made her jump, much less the spiky wheels.

"Okay, beautiful," he murmured finally. "Stand right there."

As if she was going to go anywhere else?

Not that she would dare ask such a question out loud.

I would like my orgasm now, please.

He put the vibrator and wheel back into his bag, then came back to where she was standing. Cassidy squeaked as he swept her up into his arms like they were on the cover of a romance novel. Her arms automatically went around his neck. Even though her whole body was humming with need, a little part of her wanted to swoon at being picked up and carried in such a way. The room wasn't very big, so he didn't have to go far to reach the bed.

Laying her down on it like she was something precious, he wasted no time in removing her thong, though he left her heels on, eyeing them with approval. Then he straightened, shucking off his shirt as he did so. Cassidy just watched, trying to ignore the demands of her body as she enjoyed seeing him strip down. He was all long lines and hard muscles, his cock already thick and long again.

Yay! Orgasm time!

Getting onto the bed, Master David loomed over her, his lips coming down to meet hers. She reached up for him, tilting her head up to meet his kiss, luxuriating in the feel of him against her needy body. Once again, Cassidy found herself squealing as he did the unexpected, and they rolled together, ending with her atop him, straddling his cock.

Lifting her head up from the kiss, she stared down at him in surprise.

Don had *never* let her be on top. And she knew that wasn't in any of the files or surveys she'd filled out—not for Black Fox, not for the Outlands.

Master David's hands, which had been on her hips when he'd flipped them around, slid up her sides to cup her aching breasts. He massaged them in his warm hands, an entirely different sensation than the prickling wheel, like a warm balm after the tingling pricks.

"Ride me, sweetheart." His smile was warm, his voice husky. His hips lifted, rubbing the tip of his dick against the slick folds of her pussy. "Use me for your pleasure."

Normally, if she wasn't so on edge, so damn needy, such an order would have flustered her. She wouldn't have quite known what to do.

Right now, though? With the need riding her in a manner she'd never experienced in her life? With a Dom inviting her to take what she wanted, needed, from him?

It was the hottest offer she'd ever been given.

Lowering her mouth to his for another needy kiss put her body in a position where the end of his cock was right up against the entrance to her body. She reached down between them to help position it in exactly the right spot before she let her weight fall, sliding her body down onto his cock.

Oh, fuck... yes...

He was thick and hard and felt oh so good as she sat down on him. Her pussy felt tight, as if he was huge inside her, and it took her a moment to remember the plug that was in her ass. She'd almost forgotten it amid all the other sensations assaulting her senses. Now, she was hyperaware of it again, taking up space alongside the cock that was sliding inside her.

"Oh God…" she gasped, shuddering as she bottomed out, her pulsing clit rubbing against Master David's hard body.

Master David chuckled. "Don't stop there, little spark."

He pinched her sore nipples, making her gasp and clench around him and the plug.

The need he'd built up inside her with the vibrator, tormenting her by never letting her go over the edge, was surging up inside her. She couldn't stop if she wanted to.

Use me, he'd said, and she did.

Up and down, grinding herself against him, it felt like barely moments before the first wave of her orgasm hit her. Ecstasy burst over her, her body convulsing as fireworks exploded inside her. She cried out his name, shuddering atop him, feeling him thrusting up into her, massaging her breasts through the waves of erotic rapture.

The sheer relief of release was enough to make her feel boneless, much less the actual pleasure.

She slumped over him, panting, her pussy still squeezing around the relentlessly hard cock inside her.

He hadn't come yet.

Hands squeezed her breasts, massaging, coaxing.

"Keep going, sweetheart. Ride me." The low command had her moving again, despite how watery her muscles felt.

This time, she moved slower, more deliberately, rocking up and down on his cock. Savoring the sensation. This time, her orgasm was a slow build, though its foundation was solidly planted on her previous paroxysm of pleasure. Master David helped, sliding his hands from her breasts to her arms, down to her hands.

Cassidy moved up and down on his cock, her thigh muscles burning, her fingers entwined with his as he assisted her movements. His gaze moved up and down her body, helping her to keep up the pace, enjoying the way he watched her.

Pleasure built, syrupy slow and hot, coiling and coiling inside her.

When she cried out the second time, her head fell back, her body clenching and pulsing around his cock and the plug. The orgasm felt deeper, stronger, the waves pulling her under, tumbling her around, until she came back up gasping for air. Her clit buzzed and hummed under the sensual assault until she fell atop him.

Stretched out over his hard body, she could feel his hard cock still inside her as well.

He hadn't come.

Again.

"Up, Cassidy." His fingers stroked down the center of her damp back. "Ride me again."

Cassidy whimpered. Tried to push herself up with loose-limbed arms. Felt herself collapse back down on top of him. Her pussy spasmed. She didn't think she could come again. She didn't want to come again.

But she did want *him* to come again.

She didn't want to leave him unsatisfied.

She just couldn't get herself up again.

"I can't." She buried her head against his shoulder, feeling tears spring to her eyes because she couldn't do what he wanted her to. She'd disappointed him.

Instead of chiding her, he surprised her.

"Good, then it's my turn." He kissed her temple, and suddenly, they were twisting on the bed again, back the other way, his hard cock still lodged inside her. Cassidy clung to him, squealing as he flipped her over onto her back, leaving her staring up at him in surprise. Any shame about her inability to do as he'd ordered dissipated as he grinned down at her.

He'd meant to get her to the point of no return.

Relief flooded her, along with consternation, when he rocked his hips against her, making her pussy quiver. She was already so over-sensitive, so overwhelmed from the two orgasms in a row, she wasn't sure she could take anything more.

Not that she stopped him when he pressed her hands, still

entwined with his, into the bed on either side of her head and began to pound between her thighs. Keening, Cassidy arched her back, crying out at the sensual assault that was almost too much to bear.

DAVID

Hot need pulsing through him, David groaned as Cassidy quivered and cried out beneath him. He moved fast and hard, feeling her fighting the rise of another climax. Her pussy was sweet heaven, hot and wet and clamping down around him as she fought a third rise of ecstasy.

"Please..." Her head thrashed back and forth. "I can't!"

He knew exactly what she was talking about, but he was determined.

"Yes, you can, good girl," he crooned. Pushing her hands above her head, he adjusted the angle of his body, making her shudder and writhe as he hit her clit with every hard thrust home. "One more time."

A little wail rose in the air, and she shook her head again.

"I can't, I can't..." But her pussy was already starting to spasm around him.

David moved with hard, rough, deliberate strokes, the opposite of what she had been doing on top of him, stimulating her in an entirely different way.

"Oh God... David... please..."

"That's it, sweetheart. Come for me. Come all over my cock."

She screamed, heat flushing up and down her throat, filling her cheeks, and he shuddered as he felt her spasm around him. *Fuck.*

They raced across the finish line together, Cassidy sobbing from the extreme pleasure while David groaned, emptying himself into her. They rocked in unison, so deeply wound together, he could barely tell where he ended and she started.

His elbows hit the bed, bracing himself so his full weight didn't fall atop her as they slumped. He could feel, rather than hear, her whimper as his forehead bowed down to press against hers. The long, shuddering breaths she took in were testament to how affected she was.

The smallest movement on his part made her twitch and gasp. Not that he wanted to move much. He held himself fully inside her, slowly softening, though even the shrinking of his cock made her react. She was oversensitized in the most delightful manner.

David shifted to brush his lips against hers again. She sighed as she opened her lips to him—the happy, satisfied sigh of a satiated submissive.

Eventually, though, he had to disengage.

"Stay here," he murmured, pressing a kiss to her forehead when she started to open her eyes, moving like she was going to push herself up. "I'm going to clean up. You don't move a muscle."

Sinking back into the bed, Cassidy smiled as he pulled the covers up over her to make sure she didn't get cold alone in the bed. That meant he could take his time cleaning up, packing up his equipment, then returning to the bed with one of the wipes that was kept in the wardrobe to clean her up as well.

She'd fallen asleep.

David quietly cleaned her up and removed the plug, glancing at the clock on the wall. They had the room for another twenty minutes.

Waking her up would be wrong.

Right?

Aftercare was about what a submissive needed. She needed to sleep.

Did she need him to crawl back in beside her and wrap his arms around her?

Need might be a strong word, but she immediately snuggled into his arms, sighing and rubbing her cheek against the inside of his bicep as she settled into place. And damned if she didn't feel good there.

Lincoln already knew they were down here. Therefore, everything that happened tonight had his tacit approval. He had to know that Cassidy and David were going to sleep together tonight.

Did this still feel like something David wasn't supposed to be doing? Yes. But, surprisingly, he didn't feel any regret. Just a bit of resentment at the idea that someone would tell him he shouldn't have slept with Cassidy. He always followed the rules. That was who he was. He'd broken his parents' rules because their rules had been selfish, harmful. Their rules were all about benefiting themselves and not about the good of anyone else. David's rules were always about other people. Was it really so bad to break his rules just once? Especially with someone who didn't entirely fit the parameters of a client, anyway?

Yes, he was arguing with himself inside his head.

Cassidy shifted against him.

"Shh," he murmured, tightening his hold on her. "We have five more minutes."

"Mmm. And then what?" Her nose rubbed against his chest hair in a ticklish manner, one leg sliding between his as she tried to get closer to him. He couldn't tell how awake she was. Enough to be talking, but her words were slurred, as if she wasn't fully awake.

"Then I have to take you home."

"Mmm."

Take her home, but he knew this wasn't over. He couldn't take her out on an official date right now, but he already knew that keeping this to the club couldn't last forever.

For the first time in his life, he'd rather break his rules than follow them.

31

Cassidy

Waking up and stretching in her bed, Cassidy winced.

Everything hurt.

Inside and out.

Deliciously so.

Sore. Satiated. And a little lonely.

Being wrapped up in David's arms last night after the scene had been very, very nice. Unfortunately, she'd been too insensible afterward to do more than be packed away in Jensen's car and taken home. Jensen had been the one to help her get to bed, not David.

Hashtag: Disappointment.

But they'd agreed—keep it in the club.

She sighed.

Getting up, she winced some more. Certain parts of her were a lot more sore than others. It had been a while since she'd had sex, much less sex like *that.* Master David fucked like a God.

Putting on some comfortable clothes, she wandered downstairs. It was late enough that Mick was probably already going to be gone to the farmer's market, so she was surprised when she heard Jensen talking to someone in the kitchen. Frowning, she picked up her pace, not daring to acknowledge the little kernel of hope that had sprung up in her chest.

That hope was rewarded when she heard David respond to Jensen.

Why he was here so early, she didn't know, but she hoped it was for her in a good way. *That or Don finally surfaced somewhere.* Crap. She wished her brain didn't work the way it did, but it was better to be prepared for bad news and take it on the chin than to think David was here for her only to find out that it was for the bad way.

Taking a deep breath and inhaling the glorious scent of coffee in the morning, she hurried down the last few steps and into the kitchen rather than torturing herself, waiting to find out. David stood on the other side of the island, sipping from a large mug of coffee that had a large black mustache near the brim, comically making him look like an old-timey cartoon villain when held up to his mouth. Cassidy couldn't help but smile—then immediately tried to dim her smile because she didn't want him to think she was expecting anything from him.

Unless, of course, he wanted her to expect something from him.

But she didn't know what he wanted.

"Good morning," she said, trying to sound normal and not over eager or too shy. The fact he didn't look stressed out or worried helped her relax a little. If this did have to do with Don, it wasn't an emergency. That was good.

"Good morning," both of the men chorused, and she made sure to look at Jensen, too, so he didn't feel left out.

Jensen looked the way he always did in the mornings, his plaid pajama pants slung around his hips, showing off his chest. Despite the fact it was a very nice chest, it did absolutely nothing for her, whereas David, in his fitted black t-shirt and jeans, made her body quiver. Didn't matter that he was covered up and Jensen wasn't; the hormones wanted what the hormones wanted.

Maybe a little bit of her heart, too, although she refused to think about that.

We're keeping it to the club.

"How are you feeling this morning?" David asked, putting down the cup of coffee he was drinking and turning to get her a mug without asking. Why that made her heart flutter, she couldn't say, but the darn organ was doing a little butterfly dance in her chest.

"Good." She managed to get the word out with no stuttering and only minimal blushing as he poured her a cup of coffee, turning to push it across the island along with the sugar cup and creamer. "You?"

His smile would have been enough to make her go weak-kneed if she hadn't already been sliding onto one of the barstools. Good grief. It was like being in high school all over again. Her body throbbed in remembrance of the night before. Okay, maybe not *exactly* like being in high school.

But it was like having a high school crush.

"Good."

She ducked her head down again to fix her coffee without having to meet his gaze.

Jensen cleared his throat and straightened up from where he'd been leaning against the counter a few feet away from David.

"I'm just going to let you two chat... I'll be in the living room." He maneuvered his way around the island and past Cassidy, heading toward the front of the house. Cassidy pressed her lips together.

If he was trying to be subtle, he'd failed miserably.

David had been taking another sip of his coffee while Jensen moved. Now, he put it down on the counter with a little clink. It was just the two of them in the room, but the island was between them, which might be a good thing. For some reason, it made the tension in the room seem thicker, yet the fact they couldn't actually put their hands on each other without effort might be a good thing.

Something in David's eyes made her think he was having similar thoughts. Her breath hitched, and she lifted her own coffee cup to her lips to hide it. The first hit of bittersweet mocha hit her system, making her feel a little more awake and a little more human. It did absolutely nothing to ease the soreness of her body.

"So." David tapped his finger against the side of the mug. "I came over early today for a few reasons. The first of which was to see how you felt about last night."

Direct and to the point. Cassidy blushed, but she was determined to rise to the occasion.

"I really enjoyed the scene," she replied baldly. "It was everything I'd hoped it would be and more. Though I would not object to more impact play in the future, I liked trying new things, and that was a lot of fun."

He studied her intently as she answered, as if he was weighing his words. As often happened with him, she found herself wondering what he was thinking, if her answer matched what he'd hoped.

"When we first started scening, I told you it needed to stay in the club." He paused, and Cassidy felt a little tingle of anticipation, a little blip of hope on the horizon. "That's still the case for right now, but I felt like I should tell you that I..."

He hesitated, and Cassidy felt like she was literally hanging in air.

"You..." She prompted after a long moment, despite how uncomfortable he looked.

Taking a deep breath, David frowned at her, but it wasn't a disapproving frown exactly. More like he was trying to think of what he wanted to say, and he wanted to chide her for her impatience without actually saying it out loud.

"I would like to take you out on a date. At some point. In the future."

The staccato way he said it, like the words were being yanked out of him, didn't diminish the joy that she felt at hearing them.

"You do?"

The look he gave her was incredulous, as if he couldn't believe that she was questioning the fact.

"I do," he said firmly, shifting uncomfortably in place. He started to lift the coffee mug and then set it back down again. "I know it's not professional and—"

"Yes." Interrupting was rude, but she didn't really want to hear him list all the reasons why they shouldn't date. If he thought too hard about it, he might change his mind.

He stopped and stared when she cut him off.

"Yes?"

"Yes, I would like to go on a date with you." She smiled. "Sometime in the future."

"Okay, well. Good." He took a deep breath. There was something so adorable about a strong, confidant, dominant man who was just a little unsure of himself for a moment. Especially because she knew if she sassed him right now, he'd probably take charge of her immediately, bend her over the counter, and...

Well, maybe not with Jensen only a couple rooms away, it being his island and all. But a girl could dream.

<u>DAVID</u>

That wasn't the complete disaster he'd been afraid it would be. Was he really too hard on himself, the way Jensen had accused him of being just before Cassidy had come down?

Maybe.

Lincoln had said something similar when David talked to him last night after he'd gotten Cassidy to Jensen's car. He'd wanted to be upfront with his boss about his plans for the future with their client.

But he felt the pressure of being team lead in more ways than one. It was harder now that they were all civilians. The rules were looser. The expectations not as strict. There were more shades of grey and room for interpretation and all the things he hated trying to navigate. New relationships were at the top of the list.

He was incredibly out of practice when it came to romance.

Point in fact—the way he was going to change the topic of conversation right now.

"Great. Well. Okay. I look forward to that." He took a sip of his coffee, gearing up for the switch. "The other thing I wanted to talk to you about was your flat tire. Naomi mentioned it last night—is there a reason you didn't tell me about it?" He did his best not to sound accusatory.

"I... I wasn't sure it was something worth mentioning." She said the right words, but her gaze averted, flickering away from him as she lifted her mug to her lips, both hands wrapped around it. "And since Drew knew, I figured if it was, he would say something."

Suspicion rose up inside him.

"Well, Naomi said something to me." She hadn't been worried but had just wanted to mention it. Drew hadn't, though he had probably written up a report about it that would be on David's desk on Monday. He would tell Drew to let him know verbally, immediately next time anything happened with Cassidy. "Is there anything else you haven't thought was worth mentioning?"

"I've been tailgated a few times, but it was by different people." The words came out in a rush, and she made a face as she said them, like she was judging herself for thinking it was a problem.

"Tell me about it." David wasn't going to judge until he'd heard the details.

She went over the incidents—three of them, including one when Naomi had picked her up. That one was less suspicious, other than the fact that it had been after she'd gotten her flat tire.

"Did you get a look at any of their license plates?"

She shook her head.

"They were moving too fast after they came up behind me, and once they passed me, they turned off the road... and I'll be honest, I wasn't really thinking of it. I should have." Shrugging, she took another sip of her coffee, watching him warily, like she was waiting for him to either laugh at her or freak out. "I know it sounds paranoid to be frazzled over a few tailgaters. If it wasn't for Don disappearing, I would have just shaken my head at the drivers being jerks."

Rubbing his hand on his chin, David had to nod.

It sounded like they were probably different people.

"Next time, especially if someone else is in the car, mention it and try to get at least a partial license plate. Anything helps... though don't chase after the car." He gave her a strict look, and her expression was almost hilariously bewildered. Good, she hadn't been thinking about that. "It's probably nothing, but I prefer an abundance of caution to a lack."

Cassidy's shoulders relaxed—he hadn't realized how tense she was until they did—and she smiled at him as her expression softened.

"I didn't use to, but right now... my brain is constantly running a mile a minute with possible scenarios, all the time." She looked sheepish but also tired, and David couldn't help himself anymore. Moving around the island, he came to her side and put his arm around her.

She leaned into him, sagging even more as he held up some of her weight.

Fuck.

"One of my exes was stalked," he admitted. He hadn't meant to talk about Tasha, but he wanted Cassidy to know that she didn't need to be ashamed of being scared. He got it. "She ended up in the hospital after she got a restraining order. At the trial, he had several previous girlfriends come forward, too."

With a shuddering sigh, she put down her coffee cup on the island and fully turned into him, pressing her face against his chest and wrapping her arms around his middle. David hugged her back, holding her up and comforting her at the same time.

"I keep worrying about that," she whispered. "What if he goes after someone else? Kincaid said they were keeping an eye on him, but now that he's disappeared... what if he's not after me? What if he's just gone somewhere so he can start over where no one is watching him? What if he hurts the next woman even worse, and there's no one to help her?"

He could feel her trembling against him, and he tightened his grip on her. A little wave of guilt went through him as he remembered his first conversation with Lincoln about her. He'd wondered if she'd even considered what might happen to the women who came after her.

Now he knew.

It wasn't her fault, though. She wasn't responsible for Don's actions. She wasn't the one causing the problems. If he hurt another woman, it wasn't because of anything she did or didn't do. It was because he was a shithead, and society and the justice system were set up to allow him to get away with it. Just as he'd been thinking that it would be her fault for not going to the police, even though he'd known that far too often, the system didn't work.

Even if she'd come out on top and he'd gone away for assault, the likelihood of him spending any real time in jail was small. And then when he'd gotten out? What was to stop him from coming after her again? A piece of paper?

Yeah, the 'right' thing to do might be to press charges, but it wasn't a black-and-white scenario. Especially with how little use doing the 'right' thing actually was.

"All you can control is what you do," he murmured, smoothing his hand over her hair. "You're doing your best, and you need to keep yourself safe, too. You can't do anything about what he *might* do, though we're all doing our best there, too."

That was the honest truth.

The doorbell rang, and Cassidy startled, trying to pull away. David held her for another moment, then let her go, but he caught her hand. She already knew he liked her. They'd already bent the rules some.

"Are you expecting anyone this morning?" he asked. She shook her head, trying to peer around him. They could hear Jensen answering the door, talking to someone. It sounded like a woman. David turned to try to look out the doorway to the hall, keeping Cassidy behind him.

A moment later, the front door closed, and footsteps started coming down the hall.

David frowned as Jensen came into view, a bouquet of black roses in a black vase held out in front of him. Over the top of the funereal flowers, his face was set in a frown.

"Hey, guys. We have a problem." Jensen glanced at Cassidy. "There's no note, and the woman said the person who ordered them put in the order and paid for them by messenger. We'll have to see if we can track the messenger down, but..."

Shit.

It looked like Cassidy didn't have to worry about Don having moved on to someone else. She just had to worry about the fact that, somehow, he knew where she was.

32

———————

CASSIDY

"From 'I'd like to take you out on a date' to 'move in with me' didn't take very long," Cassidy joked because if she didn't joke, if she didn't find a way to laugh about this, she was going to completely fall apart.

David gave her a dark look. He didn't seem to have a sense of humor about the situation at all. From the moment Jensen had appeared with the roses, it was like a switch had been flipped.

No more Master David, no more Sweetly Awkward David—he'd morphed into Protector David, which was also hot. Though in a very different way. A very hands-off way.

He was focused. Tightly wound. Watching her every move.

Cassidy folded her hands on her lap as she sat on his couch, doing her best to contain her nervous energy. It was not quite as comfortable as Jensen's couch, which was so easy to sink into. It wasn't uncomfortable, either, just... more utilitarian. Just like the rest of his apartment. Which is where she was staying for the foreseeable future since Don apparently knew where she was.

She hadn't even been allowed to bring a bag of clothing with her since they didn't know how he'd tracked her. Nothing that had come up from Maryland with her. Everything had been left at Jensen's. So, she still had access to it; it just wasn't within immediate reach. Which meant there was no reason to feel like crying.

Other than Don stripping her of the rest of the very little she'd held onto. It was temporary.

No big deal.

Right now, she was wearing Mick's clothes since he was a little closer to her size than Jensen. The basketball shorts and t-shirt were baggy on her, but at least they weren't falling off her.

Claudia plopped down on the couch next to her.

"Ginger wants to take you on a date?" she asked, a slightly gleeful note in her voice.

"Now is not the time, Scary," David admonished, glaring at her. The whole group had snapped into work mode after the arrival of the roses. They all had an air of alertness she hadn't seen before, they were using each other's call signs, and even their tones of voice had changed. "Do not mess with me."

"I'm just trying to find out if you're going to be messing with her."

"We agreed that I would take her out on a date, eventually. Some-time in the future. So, if you bet something for this week, you lost." He said the words flatly, and Claudia made a face. "Now, leave her alone. I need her to go over the descriptions of the tailgating again."

Which was exactly what Cassidy had hoped to avoid. They'd already talked it through several times. After each time, David paced, shook his head, then wanted to go over it again. Hence making the joke about moving in together while he paced.

A knock on the door had both Claudia and David straightening on high alert.

"It's me!" The voice through the door was familiar, and it only took Cassidy a moment to place it before Drew opened the door, revealing she'd correctly identified Ashley. The pretty brunette smiled as she hurried in, seeking out and immediately finding Cassidy peeking at her from over the back of the couch. She had a duffel bag slung over one shoulder and a plastic shopping bag in her other hand. "Sorry, it took me longer than I thought to get everything because I figured you wouldn't want to wear my underwear, so I had to stop by the store for that."

Cassidy blinked.

"Your underwear?"

"I asked her if you could borrow some clothing. Just for a few days while we go over all your things," David explained. "You two are the most similar in size from our group."

"And I figured you wouldn't want to borrow underwear." Ashley wrinkled her nose, coming over to sit down on the other side of Cassidy on the couch. She gave Claudia a little smile.

Seeing her sit, David sighed, seemingly giving up on going a sixth round of "Is there anything else you remember?" with Cassidy now that she was flanked by Ashley and Claudia. He moved around the couch, heading for the table where Mason, Drew, and Jensen were sitting, reviewing security footage from Jensen's house from the past few weeks to see if there was something they'd missed.

Definitely not the way she'd imagined spending her Saturday morning.

Ashley leaned in conspiratorially.

"I know you guys are supposed to be keeping things to the club, but since you're staying here now, I got you some of the good stuff." She gave the little plastic bag a shake.

"Her ex just found her, and you think she needs sexy underwear?" David whirled around, proving that he had been listening.

"I'm just saying, it's a one-bedroom apartment, and the safest place for her to sleep is either right next to or under you," Ashley retorted. "Tell me I'm wrong."

Scowling, David turned away from her. Apparently, he was going to pretend he hadn't heard her. Instead, he leaned over Drew's shoulder, looking at something on the other man's screen. Drew gave him a glance, then shot another apologetic glance to Cassidy before refocusing. The moment he'd arrived, he'd apologized for not taking her flat tire more seriously, but honestly, she hadn't wanted him to.

It had been nice to have a night of not worrying about Don last night. If she'd been freaking out, thinking it was Don who had given her a flat tire, last night with David wouldn't have happened. At least this way, things had already shifted between them before she went on lockdown with him.

If she'd had to move in and *then* they'd slept together... would David have even slept with her under those circumstances?

Probably not. Even if he moved her in with him, he would probably have insisted on sleeping on the couch. It was the right thing to do. But Ashely was right—Cassidy would be safest with him at her side. That's definitely where she'd *feel* safest, and that had to count for something.

Though she hoped she wouldn't need sexy underwear to convince him of that. She wasn't sure she'd be feeling very sexy.

On the other hand, just in case Don catches up to me, I might as well enjoy myself while I can.

Before being kidnapped or killed or whatever he planned to do.

Maudlin thoughts, but that wasn't surprising. What was surprising was that they felt a little farther away. Like something that could happen but wasn't imminent. They were just thoughts. Her body wasn't reacting like it normally did, as if it was real or about to happen at any moment.

Because she felt safe here.

---

*D*AVID

"Maybe we should move her to Naomi's shelter?" Drew suggested, though it was more of a question than a statement. "That's not directly connected to any of us, and they're good at making people disappear."

"She's perfectly safe here," David growled, though deep down, he knew Drew's suggestion wasn't a bad one. It just wasn't the course of action he wanted to take at the moment. He wanted her here where he could see her. Where he could protect her. "Besides, until we know exactly how he found her, I don't want her unprotected. I also don't want to put anyone else at risk."

"They're used to it. He wouldn't be the first stalker ex they've handled," Drew pointed out, though he wasn't really arguing.

"I know, but she came to us, not to Peggy's House. If we need to, we'll use them, but our workload has lightened a little, and they don't need the heat. What's that?" He pointed at the screen.

Drew, Mason, and Jensen were each looking at a different camera's feed record. Drew had the back of the house. David didn't really need to be looking over anyone's shoulder, but it was the only thing keeping him from interrupting the women's conversation. Again.

"Are we considering that this might not have anything to do with Cassidy?" Mason asked without looking up from his screen.

"What else could it be?" Jensen asked.

"Well, she's not the only one living at that house. There's also you and Mick."

Mick was back at the house right now, with Harris' team, looking through Cassidy's things to see if there was anything suspicious among them. David hated the invasion of privacy, but it was necessary. That was part of why he'd insisted on moving Cassidy immediately. That way, at least she didn't have to watch all of her stuff being examined by a team.

"Mick did go on a date recently, but as far as I know, it went well," Jensen admitted. "He said he's going to be seeing her again soon. I can't imagine why she would have sent him unsigned black roses."

"They do seem like a threat," Claudia agreed, coming up on the other side of the table where Jensen was sitting. She'd left Ashley and Cassidy on the couch. When David glanced over, he saw that Ashley was pulling out the clothing she'd brought for Cassidy to borrow, showing her the selection. "Red roses? Romantic, for the most part, especially in modern terms. For us, black roses rarely mean anything good."

"Rarely?" David asked, looking up with a frown. "Not always?"

"Sometimes, they mean mystery or rebirth. In Greek mythology, they were created from the blood of Aphrodite and Adonis after their tragic love affair, so they symbolize love and despair. They can mean eternal love, too."

"Or?" Mason prompted, also looking up from his screen with an interested expression. He and Claudia would often get into discussions about mythology, though Claudia was more interested in the stories themselves, and Mason was more interested in what the myths said about the people who told them.

"It can also mean death or farewell, a symbol of the final act of saying goodbye forever."

"As in, he's given up on getting her back, and now he's saying his final goodbye because he's going to kill her," Drew muttered. David elbowed him sharply, glancing over to where Ashley and Cassidy were still talking. Thankfully, they didn't seem to have heard him. Drew looked up with a sheepish expression. "Sorry. I'm just... I'm still kicking myself over the flat tire."

"I know." David put his hand on Drew's shoulder to reassure him. "You did exactly what you were supposed to do. More than." Drew hadn't waited until Monday to type up the report. He'd assumed he would have a chance to talk to David on Friday night, and when he hadn't, he'd typed up the report this morning and sent it.

"It was still too late," Drew muttered. Enough of his reflection was visible on the screen for David to see that he was scowling.

"It wasn't." David squeezed the other man's shoulder. "Even if you'd told me about it the second it happened, we wouldn't have moved her. It didn't happen at Jensen's. It could have been coincidence. Hell, it still could be."

Did he believe it was? No. But it could be.

Just like the tailgating.

That was the shitty thing about stalkers. They didn't even have to be doing everything to instill fear and anxiety. Doing one or two things was enough to make a person look at *everything* askance.

"The roses are the first clear sign we've gotten that he knows where she is," Mason agreed, obviously having listened. David knew he would probably make a point to talk to Drew about it later. "If it's him."

"Who else?" Jensen muttered, even though Mason sounded doubtful. It was more like he was playing devil's advocate just to keep them on their toes. Mason shrugged, and Jensen sighed. "I'll talk to Mick, just in case. It would be just like him to pick up some whacked-out chick at the worst time possible."

He wasn't wrong, but David couldn't shake the feeling that the flowers weren't some new girlfriend gone wrong.

Regardless, he was going to keep Cassidy safe from any threat. He almost hoped her ex would show up to claim responsibility. David would be very happy to explain to Don the Douchebag why he needed to leave Cassidy, and every other woman on the planet, alone.

33

CASSIDY

By the late afternoon, when nothing else had happened, and they hadn't found anything, everyone else cleared out from the apartment, leaving her alone with David. She kind of missed Jensen's house and how comfortable and unique it was, but she had to admit, having David there helped make up for a lot of that.

Though, at the moment, he was going over the security footage again rather than talking to her. Which was fine. She was sitting on one of his armchairs, earbuds in, listening to the latest upload from her favorite true crime podcast and pretending she wasn't watching him. Truthfully, she was only half-listening because her brain was going a mile a minute.

Mostly, she was worried about Brenda, and she wasn't sure she was going to be able to go to work on Monday. David hadn't said anything about it yet, but she figured they'd talk about it this evening. They still had Sunday to get through.

Maybe she'd get lucky, and Don would do something monumentally stupid. Like, get pulled over for a traffic ticket and try to run instead of complying. Then he could get arrested for that.

Unlikely. He's a good-looking white guy. He'd probably have to do something a lot stupider to actually get arrested.

It wouldn't solve the long-term problem anyway, though at least she'd be able to sleep a little easier. Plus, just knowing where he was would be a bonus.

The not knowing was driving her crazy.

Part of her wanted to believe Mason that it could be someone else. Don had hardly been the type to buy flowers for any reason. Spending money on her? Absolutely not. Now, if they'd been dead flowers that he'd pulled out of the garbage bin... she could believe he'd send to the house to mess with her.

But the roses had been beautiful in their own way, if terrifying. They'd been fully in bloom, beautifully arranged, and in a vase.

It just didn't feel like Don.

On the other hand, she had no idea what his state of mind was like. She would never have guessed he'd become fixated on her the way he had or that he'd start stalking her or slashing people's tires. Truthfully, she didn't think she'd mattered enough to him for him to care that she was out of his life.

"Hey." David appeared in front of her, frowning down at her. "What are you listening to?"

"Um..." She didn't want to say. It had really weirded Jensen and Mick out when she'd told them she liked to listen to true crime to unwind. Hitting the pause button on her phone, she popped her earbuds out. "I wasn't really listening. Honestly, I was kind of lost in thought."

He looked her over, examining her for a long moment before nodding in acceptance of her answer.

"What do you want to eat for dinner?" he asked.

Holy crap, was it that time already? She glanced at the clock. Apparently, it was.

"Whatever you have. I'm not picky." She was used to eating whatever she was given.

"Come on." David held out his hand to help her up. "You can help me choose."

Well, fine then.

She ended up not just helping him choose, but helping him cook the meal and laughing as he told her stories about his grandmother and sister. Some of them she'd already heard from Brenda's point-of-view, and she took great joy in telling him that his grandmother's perspective was a little different. The mock scowl on his face made her giggle even harder.

They ended up making salmon, asparagus, and roasted potatoes. Easy and delicious.

It was a little weird being in David's apartment, wearing Ashley's clothing and wondering what was going to happen to her life this week, but she had to admit, she felt safe. And she wasn't sure she would have if she'd still been at Jensen and Mick's.

For now, she could at least hope that Don didn't know where she was.

"Do you think I should go to work on Monday?" she asked.

David frowned, scooping up a forkful of salmon.

"We'll cross that bridge when we come to it," he said. "First, we'll see what tomorrow brings. I want to see what your ex does next."

"You think he'll do something?"

"If he realizes you've been moved... or maybe since nothing has happened. He'll have been wanting a reaction. Getting no visible reaction might spur him to do something. Hopefully, make a mistake." David smiled reassuringly at her, and Cassidy realized her anxiety was showing, which wasn't surprising. "Mick and Jensen are on alert. If he does something, we'd rather have you not there."

"I guess." She would never forgive herself if either of them got hurt, though, even though she knew it wasn't really her fault. It would be Don's. But she didn't want them hurt.

"Let's talk about something else because there's nothing we can do about that right now," David said firmly, reaching out across the table to take her hand. Her senses hummed at his touch, perking up with interest. Cassidy let her fingers wind around his, trying not to blush.

It was kind of crazy how such a little touch could make her body go so haywire, but that was the effect he had on her.

"Okay, what do you want to talk about?"

"Well, you brought up your job... is being my grandmother's caretaker really what you want to do? Jensen said you'd wanted to be a nurse." The way he was looking at her, his gaze focused and intent, it seemed like he was really interested in the answer. He also didn't let go of her hand.

"I did. I don't know..." She sighed. "I feel like I'm completely starting my life over, and I'm behind on where I'm supposed to be. I love being your grandmother's companion, but it doesn't come with benefits." She gave him a look when he chuckled. "I'm not talking about *those* kind of benefits."

He winked at her, unperturbed, and she was hard-pressed not to smile back.

"That's mostly because you're being paid under the table," he said.

Cassidy jumped when his foot slid along hers under the table. Cute. She narrowed her eyes at him, and he smiled guilelessly.

"We can change that once you don't have to hide anymore. In the meantime, we've got you on Black Fox's insurance... Lincoln didn't tell you that?"

"Oh..." She cast her mind back, trying to remember. "He might have said something about it. I'm not sure. I don't have a card, though."

"I'll find out what happened to it," he promised, which made her feel a little better. "It has been a little crazy."

"Just a bit." She smiled. "It's not just that, though; it's trying to figure out everything. Right now, I'm in limbo, but I feel like there's so much I haven't done to prepare for my life. Like, I feel like I wasted my twenties on a shitty relationship that prevented me from doing the things I need to do."

"Like what?"

"Like starting something for retirement. Or a savings account. Or something. Even once I'm able to work a real job with benefits, I'm *behind.* And one emergency away from being homeless because I have no safety net." Don was supposed to have been her safety net. Except he hadn't been safe at all.

David blinked as if that wasn't what he'd been expecting her to say. But Cassidy had had a lot of time to think and realize how precarious her situation was over the past year. Though her friends in Maryland had helped her get a job once she'd gotten away from Don, she'd needed all of that money. She hadn't been able to put anything toward savings or the future. Something she was acutely aware of.

She was behind in every sense of the word.

"You need to talk to Yasmine," David said. It was his turn to surprise her. Since she'd just taken a bite of food, Cassidy tilted her head at him in question. "Yasmine didn't tell you what she does?"

Cassidy shook her head. They'd talked about a lot of things at game nights, but Yasmine's job hadn't been one of them.

"She's a financial advisor, one who specializes in advising women."

She was? Why hadn't she said anything? Then again, it wasn't like Cassidy had said anything about her own financial situation. If she had, Yasmine would probably have told her. Swallowing, Cassidy nodded her head.

"I'll talk to Yasmine." She smiled at David, who appeared happy to have been able to give her a good direction to go in.

Cassidy was happy, too. She'd feel a lot more comfortable talking to Yasmine than she would to a stranger. Yasmine already knew what she'd been through, and she wouldn't judge.

Other than the flowers being sent today, things were mostly looking up. Though, even if the flowers meant that Don had her in his sights again, in some ways it had backfired. They were on alert now, expecting him. And it meant she'd ended up in David's apartment with him.

Kind of ironic that Don could have sent her into another man's bed just by trying to scare her with a flower delivery. It would have made him absolutely furious to know that. Not that she would have slept with David just for that reason, but since she already wanted to be with David, knowing it would outrage Don if he knew... well, it made her feel a little smug. As though she'd gotten one over on him, even though he was doing his best to make her life miserable.

Cassidy wasn't sure how things would work when she and David actually went to bed, but it was nearly as awkward as it had been in the club. Apparently, having her in his house made David a lot more open to just kissing her and maneuvering her into the bedroom, much to her delight.

She wasn't sure how she would feel, being alone with a man in a house with no Dungeon Monitors listening in, no one outside the door... but when David pinned her down to the bed with his head between her legs to devour her, she definitely wasn't panicking or thinking about getting away. By the third orgasm, all she could do was whimper when he finally lifted his head so he could turn her over, propping a pillow under her hips so he could fuck her from behind.

With his hands moving over her breasts, his lips kissing the back of her shoulder, teeth lightly dragging over her skin, he drove her to a fourth, gasping climax despite her declarations that she couldn't bear it.

Turned out, she could.

Though she was pretty sure the man was trying to kill her with ecstasy.

What a way to go, she thought as she snuggled into his hard, warm body.

It was the fastest she'd ever fallen asleep, without a single worry or thought of what terrible thing could happen while she was unconscious. Because David was there and she was safe.

D_{AVID}

Waking up with Cassidy next to him was a hell of a lot nicer than he'd have ever thought. It had been a long time since he'd woken up with a woman in *his* bed. But it didn't feel like she'd invaded his space. It felt like she belonged there.

Which was a sentiment he didn't want to examine too closely. It was far too early in the morning—and the relationship—to be thinking that way.

Turning his head to look at the clock, he was surprised to find that it wasn't as early as he'd thought. In fact, it was pretty late. He'd slept in. He couldn't remember the last time he'd done that.

Hazard of being too comfortable.

He'd slept hard.

And he still didn't want to get up.

He was too comfortable, wrapped around Cassidy's back, the curves of her ass snuggled up against his erection. One hand cupped her ribs, just below her breast, and he could feel the soft underside against his thumb and forefinger.

Damn. She smelled good.

Running his nose along the back of her neck, he shifted when she did, enjoying the way her warmth shivered against him.

"Mmm..."

Her soft little sigh urged him on, and he rocked his hips against her, rubbing his cock along the cleft between her cheeks. David moved his hand from under her breast to slide up around it. Then she stirred and froze, groaning. Immediately, David froze as well, hand still on her breast, cock wedged along the crease of her ass, waiting to make sure this was what she wanted.

Cassidy groaned.

"I cannot have another orgasm. You have wrecked my vagina. It needs at least a day of recovery." The chiding way she said it was both stern and hilarious, and David couldn't help but laugh.

Wriggling around, she turned to face him, putting her hand on his chest. Her hazel eyes danced with mirth.

"You are insatiable," she accused.

David shrugged his shoulder and leaned forward to give her a brief kiss on the lips.

"I'm not going to apologize. Unless you want me to kiss and make it all better..." He quickly glanced down toward her pussy, and she gave his chest a little smack.

"Like you did last night? I don't think I can come again. My clit is on strike."

He snorted with laughter at the unexpected statement. About to pull away, he was surprised when she pushed with the hand on his chest, rolling him onto his back. Amused, he let her have her way, wanting to see what she was going to do.

The hand on his chest slid down to his dick, wrapping around it. The long fall of her hair brushed against his body as she shifted her position, her upper body moving toward his lower.

"What are you doing?" he asked curiously. Cassidy peeked at him over her shoulder.

"Well, just because my clit is on strike doesn't mean your dick has to suffer," she responded teasingly before bending down to take his cock between her lips.

David groaned, his hips jolting upward at the wet heat that suddenly surrounded him. Fuck, that felt good. Sliding his hands over her, he plunged his fingers into her hair, pulling it back away from her face so he could watch as she slid her mouth down the length of his cock and bobbed back up again.

There was no way he was going to argue with a surprise morning blow job.

Wrapping her long hair around his fist, he let her take the lead. She held his cock in one hand and his balls in her other, gently tugging and rolling them between her fingers, adding to the pleasurable stimulation.

"Fuck, sweetheart..." He groaned with pleasure. "Your mouth is killing me."

She slid her lips up and down his shaft, her tongue teasing the head every time she drew back. It felt fucking phenomenal.

Then his phone rang.

Cassidy paused.

David tightened the fist in her hair, using it to leverage her mouth back down his cock as he reached for his phone with his free hand.

"No one told you to stop," he growled, picking up the phone.

An unholy light sparked in her eyes. Damn. He might regret this. But probably not.

The caller ID said it was Lincoln calling. Swiping to answer, David put the phone next to his ear as Cassidy increased the suction on his cock.

"Morning."

"Good morning." Lincoln's voice was serious but not overly concerned, which held David to relax a little. Well, as much as he could be with Cassidy now doing her best to distract him from the call. She was doing a damn good job, too. "I've got some updates I wanted you to know about right away."

Tension immediately knotted again.

Cassidy's tongue flicked over the head of his dick, and he felt his jaw tighten.

"What's up?"

"First, the team looking through Cassidy's things didn't initially find anything, but when Jaxon decided to use a scanner, they discovered that some of her shoes had trackers in them. Jensen is going to bring over the ones that didn't and her clothes since all of those checked out. The good news is that she didn't wear shoes when she went to your house yesterday, so if that's how he's been following her, he'll hopefully have no idea where she is now."

"Fuck." David said it as much for Lincoln's words as for the fact that Cassidy had just released his cock from her hand and decided to take him all the way down her throat. His mind fuzzed for a moment.

This was not the conversation to be having while she gave him head, yet he couldn't bring himself to have her stop.

"Pretty much," Lincoln agreed. "But, like I said, now that we know, we can cut off his access."

"What's the second thing?" David tightened his grip on Cassidy's hair again, pulling her up so her lips were no longer touching the root of his cock. He only managed to pull her off for a moment before she plunged right back down again.

Fine, fuck it. Let her do what she wanted.

"That's a little more confusing," Lincoln said, sounding mystified.

"Mason just called me. He received a delivery of black roses this morning."

"Mason did?" David's confusion matched Lincoln's.

Why the hell would Mason be getting flowers from Cassidy's ex?

She'd never been to Mason's home. In fact, of the team who had been guarding her, he'd been the least on-site.

Drew and Naomi had driven Cassidy around. She spent all day at David's grandmother's. Claudia might have made sense since she was over there every Thursday for game night.

But Mason?

"Mason thinks this might be an indication that the flowers really weren't from Don, but considering the trackers that Jaxon found, we're not going to be taking any chances."

"Yeah, definitely not." Though he was confused about the flowers, David didn't believe Mason was right about them being from someone else. Who else could they be from?

"That's it for now. I'll let you get back to Cassidy." There was something in Lincoln's voice that made David think his boss knew exactly what was going on with Cassidy right now, though he wasn't sure how Lincoln had picked up on it. "See you in the office tomorrow."

"See you tomorrow."

Hanging up the phone, David looked down the length of his body at Cassidy, who was still eagerly trying to make him come. She wasn't far off from it.

"Do you want to wait to hear the news, or do you want it now?" he asked.

Despite her mouth being wrapped around his dick, Cassidy managed to shake her head. Then she redoubled her efforts to make him come.

Rather than trying to fight it, David gave in and let her do what she wanted. The bad news could wait since that's what she wanted. It wasn't going to change anything about their day today.

Groaning, he shuddered as she worked her mouth up and down his cock, her tongue slipping against the sensitive skin. He gripped her hair tighter as the ecstasy wound around him, shuddering as the pulses of cum jetted down her throat. She didn't stop sucking until she'd swallowed every last drop.

Only then did he tell her what Lincoln said, holding her in his arms as he did.

She took it philosophically, seeming both relieved and concerned that the flowers might not have anything to do with her. Then, she seemed to deliberately set the question aside so they could enjoy their day together... which they did.

After breakfast, David worked on self-defense with her, pleased with how far she'd come along. Then she watched him work out while she made them lunch. In the afternoon she read a book while he played a video game, and then they made dinner together.

It was surprisingly homey. Comfortable.

Then, after watching a movie, she let him hold her down in his bed and pound her into a screaming orgasm.

The perfect Sunday.

34

Rather than going to Brenda's on Monday morning, David's grandmother came to his apartment. He ran out to get her first thing, so she could come over and they could explain to her what was going on and what the new safety precautions were going to be.

Cassidy tried not to feel awkward when Brenda sat down at his kitchen table, right where he'd bent Cassidy over it the night before. He'd figured twenty-four hours was enough of a strike for her clit, though he'd kept things to one orgasm last night instead of sending her into overload. She was mostly grateful and just a little disappointed.

"He put trackers in your shoes?" Brenda asked in amazement as David bustled around them, getting breakfast ready.

"Yes." Cassidy couldn't help but shiver. That was a step farther than she would have ever expected from Don. Where had he even gotten the things? Her hand went up the necklace that she was wearing, which was what Black Fox was using to track her. It made sense that *they* had such equipment. Don, not so much.

"Not all of them," David interjected as he plated the eggs and pancakes. The green pancakes. He put spinach in them. Cassidy didn't protest because she could barely taste the spinach this way, thankfully.

"Just my favorite ones." Cassidy scowled. He'd ruined her favorite pair of club shoes. She didn't think she was ever going to be able to look at them the same way again.

It really was amazing what a difference feeling safe made to her mental state. Back in Maryland, she was pretty sure she could have been freaking out. She would have been terrified by how obsessed he was with her, to the point of tracking her like that. Part of her was still freaking out, but her overwhelming emotion was anger.

How dare he?

For the first time, she was more pissed than scared, and in some ways, that felt really good.

"I take it that's why we're here right now instead of my house," Brenda asked, smiling up at David as he slid a plate in front of her. "Thank you."

Cassidy repeated the sentiment as David put a plate in front of her before going back to get his own. Don would have never.

"You're welcome. And yes, that's why you're here. Cassidy's shoes have never been here before, but they have been to your house. This way, Cassidy can still keep you company and take you to your usual haunts. We're hoping Don doesn't realize Cassidy has moved locations since her shoes haven't and thinks that she's under lockdown after the flower delivery."

"So, we can still go out?" Brenda asked as David sat down beside her, sounding both relieved and a little trepidatious. "We don't have to. I want Cassidy safe more than anything else. We can just stay here and watch movies."

"No, you should be able to go out. We're changing what car Cassidy will be driving you around in, and she has a couple pairs of shoes that didn't have trackers in them. Don should think that she's still at Jensen's, but keep your eyes peeled just in case."

"Maybe you should use me as bait," Cassidy suggested, then immediately shrank back in her seat as two pairs of eyes pinned her in place. "Okay, maybe not."

"Definitely not." Brenda gave her a look.

"No, we don't need you, just your shoes." David also gave her a look, the kind that said he was going to spank her later for even thinking he'd put her in danger.

Well, that might not be so bad.

If her poor clit had recovered by then.

The good news was he wasn't going to spank her with his grandmother there.

"Good point. I don't know why I didn't think of that," Cassidy said with very real relief. "I don't actually want to be bait, I just... I just want it to be over with."

"Of course, you do, dear," Brenda said sympathetically, reaching over to pat Cassidy's hand. "Don't worry, David will take care of it."

Rather than protesting that he might not be able to or that it was more complicated than that, David just nodded. Cassidy wished she had his self-assurance. She still wasn't sure what Black Fox was going to be able to do unless Don did something to get himself arrested.

Unless they were going to put the shoes somewhere, rig them with explosives, then blow Don sky high when he came looking for her. Though, if he lived through it, he'd probably be angrier than ever, and he could spend the rest of his life with a vendetta, hunting them all down one by one, saving David and Cassidy for last so he could slit David's throat in front of her.

Oh. My. God. Why is my brain like this?

Apparently, it was back to her normal level of paranoia this morning.

Then again, could it really be called paranoia when someone was actually out to get her? Mistress Julie said it was her anxiety. The important thing was to remember that it hadn't happened, it wasn't necessarily going to happen, and it was actually highly unlikely to happen. No matter how her nervous system reacted to the thoughts.

She wondered if David's brain ever did this to him.

Probably not. She knew it wasn't 'normal.' But it was her normal. Unfortunately.

On the other hand, she'd rather be anxious and paranoid and

therefore on guard rather than assuming everything would be fine and ending up with a bad case of the dead.

"So, where are you staying now?" Brenda asked, jerking Cassidy out of her maudlin thoughts.

"Oh, um..." Cassidy looked at David.

David looked back at her.

Brenda smiled gleefully.

<hr>

DAVID

Did David feel bad about rushing out the door and leaving Cassidy to deal with his grandmother?

Maybe just a little. Not bad enough to stay, though. Especially once his grandmother started talking about his 'butt stick' again. Cassidy found it hilarious. So, the two of them could talk about his butt stick while he wasn't there. And he did have the excuse that there was a lot to do at work, including figuring out what they were going to do about Don.

Cassidy had a panic button, a tracker, and his grandmother. They didn't need him right now. They could have a fun day all by themselves, and hopefully, he would be able to take care of Don for her.

He hadn't told Cassidy, but it wasn't just the shoes that were going to be used as bait. She hadn't met everyone from the other side of the office, which was run by Lincoln's brother Harris. Harris' team, which was led by Grant Sexton, aka Sexy, had a woman on it, and she happened to be about Cassidy's height and have long brown hair just like Cassidy's.

Darcie Maverick had already agreed to be their bait.

The only reason he hadn't told Cassidy was because he didn't want her to feel like she was putting someone else in danger. She wasn't. He was.

But he knew Darcie could handle it.

Walking into the office, he was surprised to see Mason hanging out by the front desk, leaning on it with his elbows and talking to

Jennifer. Mason was dressed in his usual suit, today paired with a grey patterned tie. Jennifer had opted for a colorful spring dress with pink, orange, and red flowers on it, and she'd pulled her hair half-back with some kind of matching clip.

They both looked up as he entered.

"Morning," he said to both Jennifer and Mason.

"Good morning." Jennifer smiled up at him, but there was worry in her eyes. "I heard about the flowers. Is Cassidy okay? I wasn't sure if I should text and bother her or not."

"Text," David said immediately. "She's fine, but she'll appreciate you checking in."

"We're not sure the flowers have anything to do with her at this point," Mason reminded both of them. "The fact that I received some makes me think that they maybe really aren't."

"Well, shit. Then she had to move for nothing?" Jennifer asked, frowning.

"Not for nothing. That's how we found the trackers in her shoes," Mason pointed out. "So, now we know that he was tracking her while they were together, which points to his obsession with her. It also means it's likely that he is still pursuing her. Jaxon is working on reversing the signal to see if we can track him. Even if that doesn't work, we can use the trackers to hopefully trap him. So, it wasn't for nothing."

"There is that." Jennifer sighed and turned to look at David. "She's living with you now? Is she still going to be able to come to game night?"

"Yes, she's there with my grandmother now. I don't know about game night." He glanced at Mason. "It might depend on what else happens this week. We know she had the trackers in her shoes, so if that's the only way Don was keeping tabs on her, it might be safe. On the other hand, he'll also know that it's her normal routine to go there. So, if we haven't found him by then, it might not be safe for her."

Jennifer scowled.

"That sucks. She shouldn't have to miss out on game night. Maybe we can do it at your house?"

"Maybe." David was not the type of person who liked a bunch of people in his space. On Saturday, it had been necessary and protection related. Having a bunch of people over playing games and eating and talking...

But it would also make Cassidy happy, and that would be worth the invasion and the cleanup. Jennifer was right. Cassidy shouldn't have to miss out on something she enjoyed. David wasn't going to let Douchebag take that away from her if he could help it.

"If we're lucky, we'll find him in the next few days, and you'll be able to gather at Claudia's like normal," he said fervently. Fingers crossed. He'd tolerate it if he had to, but he could still hope it wouldn't be necessary.

"Find him and bury him," Jennifer muttered.

"Inside thought, Jennifer," Mason said immediately. "Or at least, don't say it in front of witnesses."

Jennifer just snorted.

"Please, you won't testify against me. You'd be the one helping me bury the body." She tossed her hair, raising an eyebrow at them, daring either of them to disagree. Mason and David exchanged a glance. She wasn't wrong. "Anyway. You two, shoo. I'm going to text Cassidy, and I have work I need to get done."

"I need to talk to you, anyway," Mason said, straightening up and focusing his attention on David. They walked away from Jennifer before she could shoo them again.

"What's going on?" David asked, immediately on high alert. It felt like his nervous system was constantly tense ever since the flower delivery on Saturday, as if he couldn't entirely relax. It didn't take much for him to go from zero to sixty.

"Don't worry, it's nothing to do with Cassidy. It's personal to me." Mason hesitated.

Even as David relaxed again, he frowned.

"What do you need?" He couldn't imagine what Mason would want to talk to him about that was so important. That must have been why Mason had been hanging out at the front desk instead of being back in his office. He definitely had work to do, just like David.

"Remember how I said my parents want to arrange my marriage?" Mason kept his voice low, as if he wanted to ensure no one else over-heard them, even though from what David could see, no one else was in the office yet. Maybe he was just worried his voice would carry back to Jennifer, even though they were walking away from her.

"Yes... wait, is that actually happening?"

"Well, they found someone that they want me to meet."

David stopped in his tracks, turning to look at Mason, who also stopped but kept his gaze averted from David's. Something was going on. David put his hands on his hips.

"If you don't want to meet her, you don't have to. You can back out now. The sooner you do it, the easier it will be on them, so they don't get their hopes up."

"That's the thing, I've already met her," Mason said carefully, like he was measuring out his words.

Impatience made David tap his foot, and he frowned at Mason. It wasn't like the other man to draw things out like this.

"Just say it, man. You're not announcing a beauty pageant winner."

"It's Yasmine." The words came out in a rush, and David's jaw dropped as Mason hurried to continue. "You know her better than me, so I was wondering, before I meet her to talk about us getting married, what your opinion is... if you think we'd be a good match."

"I mean... I don't really *know* know her," David said slowly. "I've spent some time with her. I've seen her in the club. So you guys have that going for you. You're both kinky."

"I had that thought, too, even though we've never scened together. She's a beautiful woman, very attractive, that part's all there... but what would you think of us as a couple?" Mason was obviously uncomfortable, but he was pushing himself to ask, which meant that David could only give him a serious answer.

Which was probably why Mason had come to him in the first

place since any of the rest of their team would probably give him a hard time. Including Claudia, who obviously knew Yasmine the best.

"From what I know of her, you're both smart people who enjoy good food and are kinky… so you have some things in common." David shrugged. Unfortunately, his knowledge of Yasmine was mostly surface-level. "I can picture you together, if that helps. You two look like you'd fit. Why haven't you ever scened with her?"

Mason shrugged.

"I don't know, it just never came up." But his gaze flickered away again. David frowned.

"You don't actually believe she's cursed and that if you scened with her, you'd have ended up marrying the next person you scened with, do you?" David asked, unable to hide his amusement.

"Logically, no, but it is weird that it's happened so many times." Mason's smile was rueful. Reaching up behind his head, he rubbed the back of it sheepishly. "And I wasn't ready to be in anything serious yet, so it didn't seem wise to tempt fate. Especially since the other superstition is that you always find your person when you're not looking for them."

"I guess you're safe there since it was your parents who looked for and found her." David chuckled. "I'm guessing she's doing the same in order to avoid the curse herself. It makes sense. If she goes straight to the marriage, she doesn't have to worry about dating and breaking up and her ex immediately finding the woman he's going to marry."

"Makes sense." Mason sighed. "Can you not tell anyone yet? I want to get through our first meeting without the whole team knowing what's going on."

"I won't, but if Yasmine tells Claudia…" He left the words hanging. Mason made a face.

"Hopefully, she'll feel the same way. If not, maybe that's a sign that she's not the one for me." Clearly, he wasn't convinced that Yasmine was going to be the one for him, anyway, even though he'd decided to let his parents arrange his marriage. Maybe it would have been easier for him if they'd picked a complete stranger.

"Maybe." David wasn't sure what else to say. "How many times do you meet before you decide to get married?"

"I'm not sure. I guess we'll talk about that this weekend, too. Maybe a few times, just to make sure we want the same things out of life. Where we'll live, kids, that kind of thing." He rubbed the back of his head again. "Though my parents supposedly talked to her parents about that already, I feel like we should as well, just to make sure neither was misrepresented."

"Hey, her being local is another plus," David said. "Unless you wanted to move."

"I don't. That's a good point. I feel like, on paper, we're a pretty good match." Mason was starting to look more heartened, as if he was talking himself into the marriage. "So, yeah. I guess we'll see."

Voices came down the hall—Jennifer greeting someone else at the front desk. Far enough away to not be able to make out the words but enough to hear that someone had come in. Mason stiffened, then dropped his hand down from his head, tugging on his suit jacket.

"Anyway, thanks. And, ah, I'll let you know how it goes and if you can tell anyone afterward."

"Great. Um, good luck." Because what else was he supposed to say?

Mason gave him a wan smile, as if he knew exactly what David was thinking.

"Thanks."

Time to get back to work. Mason might be getting married soon, but David had his own woman he needed to focus on—if he wanted to have any kind of future with her, they needed to take care of her stalker first.

35

CASSIDY

Saturday, the flowers had been sent to Jensen's house. Sunday was Mason's. Monday wasn't even their team's; the black roses were delivered to Seth, a member of the other BFS team Cassidy hadn't met yet, and Tuesday was Jaxon, the tech guy on the other team.

Today, Wednesday, they'd been delivered to Claudia's house, which was how Cassidy found out that today was Claudia's birthday. Apparently, she hadn't been planning on celebrating.

The security camera caught every delivery. It was always by a different courier or messenger service. All of them had been paid in either cash or with a gift card. None of them knew who the sender was. Even the ones that required a name and address—they didn't ask for ID, and all the listed names and addresses belonged to someone at Black Fox.

It was utterly baffling and frustrating, though not as frustrating as waiting for Don to show up. David had reassured her that they were using her shoes to try to draw Don out of hiding, but so far, he hadn't fallen for the bait. The prevailing theory was that it was out of her normal pattern, though it could also be something else. Anything else. They just couldn't know for sure.

Which made her want to bury her face in a pillow and scream—and not at all in the same way that David made her do that.

She also wasn't entirely sure how to feel.

The flowers didn't seem to have anything to do with her. But Don had put trackers in her shoes. Had he used them to follow her? Had he been tailgating her? Had he put the nail in her tire?

Or, like the flowers, were those just things happening around her that she attributed to him?

She hated not knowing.

"You're tensing up again, dear," Brenda said, reaching out to pat Cassidy's hand. Sympathy showed in her eyes, and she cast a worried glance up at Cassidy. "We can go if you'll be more comfortable."

"No, I'm fine. You wanted to get yarn. This is out of our normal pattern of behavior. We've never been here before. I'm just jumpy." She also felt incredibly guilty because they'd spent the past two days at David's apartment.

Brenda said she didn't mind at all. In fact, she'd been the one to insist on staying in, but Cassidy could tell she missed seeing her friends. They'd missed two days of afternoon activities at the retirement center. The whole point of Cassidy being her companion was to make sure she could do the things she wanted to do, not prevent her from doing them.

The very least she could do was take Brenda out to a store. They should be safe here. It met all the parameters David had given her. The likelihood of Don knowing she was here was incredibly low, especially since her shoes were elsewhere.

Unfortunately, being out in the store meant her brain wouldn't shut up and wouldn't stop running through the possibilities, no matter how ludicrous they were. In fact, the more ridiculous, the more her mind seemed to latch onto them.

What if the flowers were a distraction?

What if Don knew everything about Black Fox and where she was?

What if he'd put trackers in other places? Some kind of special tracker that the Black Fox tech hadn't been able to pick up?

What if he'd put a tracker *inside* her? Obviously, it couldn't have been while she was awake because she would know. She hadn't usually slept soundly enough for him to do it then. But there had been a few times when he'd gotten her drunk, or she'd been sick and taken medicine... He could have drugged her to make her sleep really soundly, then injected it into her.

Who's crazier... Don for possibly doing it or me for coming up with these scenarios?

While Brenda looked at yarn, Cassidy's brain was on overdrive. It was like having double vision. She could see Brenda looking at the yarn, knew that's what was actually happening, but her brain was playing out different scenarios that felt so real that tears sprang to her eyes.

Don appearing at the end of the aisle, and Brenda putting herself between Cassidy and Don, and Don realizing that he could use her to keep Cassidy under control... and taking both of them.

Don appearing at the end of the aisle with a knife, and when Brenda tries to stop him from taking Cassidy, he stabs her, and she falls to the floor. Cassidy dragged away, not knowing if Brenda's dead or alive.

Don appearing at the end of the aisle and shooting Brenda, and Cassidy not running because she was trying to help, then Don dragging her away while her hands were covered with Brenda's blood. Brenda's dead eyes staring up at the ceiling.

Cassidy's breath caught in her throat, and she turned away from Brenda, blinking rapidly, trying to get the tears out of her eyes and the images out of her head. It was so much worse today than usual. She took in a deep breath and lifted her fingers up to her forehead, tapping the tips of them against her skin.

That's what Mistress Julie had recommended during their last appointment. Grounding exercises. She had to work on calming her nervous system.

I can't always control what's happening around me, but I can control how I react to it.

She knew the imaginings of her brain weren't real. She knew Don wasn't about to pop out at the end of the aisle like some kind of cartoon villain. She knew Brenda was aware of the drill.

She also knew she was a lot stronger and more capable than she had been before. If Don tried to drag her away now, she wouldn't just put up a fight, she knew *how* to fight, thanks to all the self-defense classes.

If I don't freeze.

She wouldn't freeze. She wouldn't let him take her to a second location. If she was going down, she was going down here, in the yarn aisle of a superstore.

Never let someone take you to a second location.

There were things worse than death.

Was it strange that these were the thoughts that made her feel stronger? Her biggest fear wasn't for herself; it was for Brenda. But if she could fight back against Don, Brenda could run for help.

That's what she would do.

"What do you think of this one?" Brenda asked.

Cassidy turned back to face her, quickly swiping away the lingering tears and hoping the older woman didn't notice. Thankfully, Brenda's attention was focused on the yarn she was holding, which was beautiful. Multihued green that made it look like an ombre and speckled with other colors.

"It's beautiful," Cassidy replied honestly. "It reminds me of a meadow."

"Me, too." Brenda inspected it carefully, then put it in her basket, adding a second one right after that. "Plus, it will look nice with Audrey's hair. I want to make her a scarf and hat for the winter."

Her excitement about her granddaughter moving to the area made Cassidy smile. She was both nervous and looking forward to meeting Audrey.

Brenda said they would get along like a house on fire, but it was different meeting someone as a potential friend than it was as an undefined sexual partner's sibling. What she and David were, she wasn't sure, other than living together for the foreseeable future.

She'd like more—a lot more—but she wasn't sure how he felt about her.

"Do you think I should make one for David, too? He probably doesn't need it, but I don't want him to feel left out." Brenda hummed under her breath. "All he ever wears is black. He needs some color in his life. Maybe a nice blue to match his eyes. I'm glad he has you around. Maybe you can get his buttstick out permanently."

Cassidy pressed her lips together.

She was pretty sure the reason Brenda kept saying 'buttstick' was because she found everyone's reactions hilarious. The first time Cassidy had heard her say it this morning, she'd nearly choked. David had made a strategic retreat almost immediately afterward. Something that she fully planned on teasing him about later.

"I will do my best to keep his buttstick out of his butt," she replied solemnly, making Brenda cackle.

"See that you do."

Brenda moved down the aisle, inspecting the array of blue yarn.

A little tingle on the back of Cassidy's neck made her turn around. *Paranoia'r'Us.* Nothing was there. She was just letting her brain get the best of her.

Again.

But as she was turning away, someone walked across the aisle fast enough—and it was out of the corner of her eye—she couldn't see exactly what they looked like. Her head whipped around so fast, her neck cracked, and she put her hand up to the side of it where the sudden ache was. Her pulse fluttered against her fingers as her breath caught in her throat.

A man. Tall. Blond.

There were a lot of tall blond men out in the world. Seeing one out of the corner of her eye didn't mean it was Don.

She was just worked up.

'Don't ignore your instincts.' Claudia's voice echoed in her head. *'They're there for a reason.'*

Cassidy shifted uncomfortably because she didn't trust her instincts. She didn't trust her brain. The most likely scenario was that it was just a tall blond man walking through the store who was not Don and had nothing to do with her, and she was freaking out over nothing.

Knowing that didn't stop her heart from racing, her breath from coming faster, or her hands from going clammy.

"Okay. That's everything I need," Brenda said cheerfully.

Cassidy relaxed as she turned to look at Brenda. As much as she didn't want to hold Brenda back, she also was going to be relieved to get back to David's apartment. She felt safe there, despite everything that was going on.

DAVID

When his phone rang with his grandmother's ringtone, David frowned and immediately reached into his pocket, effectively cutting off the conversation he and Lincoln were having about a potential new hire. He held up his left hand with one finger up, indicating he needed Lincoln to give him a minute while he answered the phone.

"Hello?"

Hearing a man's voice on the other end of his grandmother's phone gave him a shock.

"David?" The thick Scottish brogue should have been a clue, but the surprise had him so off-center that he didn't place the voice immediately.

"Yes."

"It's Gavin." A distressed Gavin, going by his accent having deepened. "I'm with your grandmother and Cassidy at the store. Cassidy seems to be having a panic attack. She's also insisting that she can't go to the hospital, and your grandmother is backing her up. I tried calling you on my phone, but when you didn't pick up, your grandmother gave me hers."

"Shit. Yes." David lifted his hand to rub his forehead, doing his best to remain in place instead of pacing the way his body was suddenly urging him to. "I have it on Do Not Disturb except for specific phone numbers... not important. Is Cassidy okay, other than the panic attack?"

"She doesn't seem to be injured." Gavin's voice got quieter, as though he'd turned his head away from the phone as he asked if Cassidy was hurt. A feminine voice, calm and controlled, answered him, then he responded back into the phone. "Leah says she's not hurt, just freaked out. She saw someone who she thought could be her ex as she and your grandmother were checking out. They got a few steps outside the store when she collapsed. Leah and I were on our way in, and we actually saw her go down and came running."

Leah, Gavin's wife, was exactly the kind of person Cassidy needed now. David blew out a long breath, trying to get his roiling emotions under control. She wasn't in any danger.

But she was in distress.

"Can you bring her to the Black Fox office?" he asked. "Her and my grandmother?"

"Of course. We'll be there as soon as we can."

Hanging up the phone, David tightly relayed the situation to Lincoln, who nodded somberly.

"Poor Cassidy. The toll this shit takes on a person..." Lincoln shook his head grimly. "She doesn't deserve this. Hopefully, that asshole takes the bait soon, and we can finish this."

David didn't bother to question how Lincoln expected to finish it. One way or another, Don wasn't going to bother Cassidy anymore. He was going to make sure of that.

"I need to tell Jennifer to call down and give security Gavin, Leah, and my grandmother's names." His grandmother was already on the approved list, but it didn't hurt to give them a heads-up, especially since she was technically on the 'approved but call first' list. Once they arrived, he wanted them to be able to come up straight away, and Cassidy was the only one on *that* list.

Lincoln nodded. "We'll talk about Zeus later."

Yes, yes, they would. David was not convinced hiring one of Marshall's team was a good idea, even if the man had quit not long after Marshall was ousted from the firm.

His priority right now was Cassidy.

Getting up from the chair across from Lincoln, David stalked out of the office and down the hall. It might have been the fastest he'd ever walked, even though he knew it was going to take some time for Gavin to arrive. He wanted everything ready for them, so Cassidy didn't have to wait even a second to feel safe.

36

―――――――

More embarrassed than anything else, Cassidy followed Master Gavin and his wife into Black Fox Security. Brenda was right by her side, her arm looped through Cassidy's and her hand gently patting her in understanding. Didn't make it less embarrassing, though.

She'd had a freaking panic attack over a guy that hadn't even been Don.

He'd just been a tall blond, probably the same one she'd seen in the store, and when she'd seen the back of him in the parking lot next to a grey car, her body had reacted. There hadn't been anything she could do. One minute, she'd been okay; the next, she'd been falling apart at the seams.

The poor guy hadn't even known that he was the cause of her distress. He was a perfectly nice guy who'd heard the commotion and come over to check to make sure she was okay before driving away.

Knowing that she'd disrupted literally everyone's day, she couldn't help but feel weak.

"Would you get out?" Claudia snapped as Cassidy walked through the door, and Cassidy's head jerked up. It took her a moment to realize Claudia wasn't talking to her. The Domme was standing beside Jennifer's desk with an annoyed expression, but it was directed to the two men standing in front of her. Cassidy couldn't see their faces because their backs were to her, but they were both tall and dark-haired with broad shoulders that filled out their suit jackets nicely. Claudia's gaze shifted. "Hey, Cassidy, you okay, hon?"

Both of the men turned to see who Claudia was talking to. They were both handsome with dark eyes. One of them had a beard, the other was clean-shaven, and they sported matching grins.

"I'm okay. What's going on?" Not sure how she felt about the men's scrutiny, she wedged herself slightly behind Master Gavin, with Brenda on her other side. Brenda, unlike Cassidy, wasn't nervous at all. She was very obviously checking both of the men out.

"This is my pain-in-the-ass brother, Manuel, and his pain-in-the-ass best friend, Ian. And they are leaving." She glared at them. They each waved at the mention of their name. The clean-shaven one was Manuel, and the bearded one was Ian. Manuel winked at her, but Ian turned his attention back to Claudia almost immediately.

"We'll leave as soon as you agree to let us take you out for your birthday tonight," Ian said, his voice simultaneously teasing and coaxing. "You know you want to. I'll even pay for your drinks."

"I don't need you to pay for my drinks, Mr. Richey-rich. I can afford my own drinks."

"A beautiful lady shouldn't have to buy her own drinks, especially on her birthday."

Claudia made a gagging noise, rolling her eyes before looking over at Cassidy, who was watching with fascination.

"If Mr. Smooth here tries any of his lines on you, just ignore him. He spreads his charm around like herpes." She turned her attention back to Ian. "I can buy my own drinks, thanks. And who says I'm a lady?"

"I definitely don't," her brother joked. "But Ian's right, it's your birthday. We should go out and celebrate the day you blessed the world with your glorious presence."

"If it makes you feel better, *no one* should have to buy their own drinks on their birthday, not even you," Ian quipped. He turned toward Jennifer at her desk. "Don't you agree?"

"He's not wrong," Jennifer said, looking at Claudia, who scowled at her.

"Traitor."

"Hey, don't blame me just because I also want an excuse to go out with my friends and celebrate one of them..." Jennifer looked over at Cassidy, smiling encouragingly. Her gaze was soft. "You look like you could use a night out, too."

"A night out where?" David asked as he walked into the increasingly crowded lobby. The moment she heard his voice, something inside Cassidy relaxed. He really did represent safety to her.

In fact, it was all she could do not to throw herself into his arms, knowing that's where she would feel the safest. She managed to contain the urge but barely. If his grandmother hadn't been there, she wasn't sure she would have been able to resist.

"Wherever the birthday girl wants to go," Ian said, grinning and reaching out toward David. Their hands slapped together in a greeting, and they pulled each other in for one of those brief, one-armed guy hugs. He then did the same with Manuel, but his gaze kept flitting over to Cassidy. She did her best to smile at him.

Please don't make a fuss in front of everyone.

She'd already endured enough humiliation for the day.

---

*D*AVID

Even though he wanted to gather Cassidy in his arms, David resisted the impulse. There was something about her stance that made him think she was holding back. She was also hovering very close to both his grandmother and Gavin, and he wasn't going to push them out of the way just to get to her.

Maybe once Manuel and Ian were gone, though he had a lot more trouble shifting them out the door than he did Gavin and Leah. The latter were happy to accept his reassurances, both of them giving

Cassidy a hug and an admonishment to take care of herself before they left. His grandmother patted Cassidy's arm. They all tried to ignore Manuel, Ian, and Claudia's conversation, which was mostly Ian flirting with Claudia and her sniping back at him, the way they always did.

Ian flirted the same way he breathed air, and for some reason, it really got under Claudia's skin, which just made him flirt with her even harder. Not that it stopped him from flirting with every other woman who came within ten feet of him.

Not exactly relaxing to David, but it seemed to be amusing Cassidy, and *she* was slowly relaxing and smiling, which was the only reason he didn't kick the duo out. Surprisingly, Claudia didn't either, and she normally lost patience with them before David did, so she must have also noticed the effect on Cassidy.

Once Gavin and Leah were gone, he was about ready to say goodbye to Ian and Manuel when Jensen sauntered in from the hallway. He must have been in the breakroom because he had a bowl of popcorn in hand.

"Ooh, that smells good," Ian said, stepping sideways around an exasperated Claudia to see what Jensen was holding. "Can I have some?"

"You like spicy stuff, right?" Jensen asked.

"Yeah."

"Then you're fine." Jensen held the bowl out.

Claudia's eyes widened, and she tried to reach for Ian's hand to stop him.

"Wait!"

Seeming to realize that she was going to deprive him of his desired treat, Ian used his arm to block her, quickly grabbing a handful and stuffing it in his mouth before anyone could stop him.

Shit.

"He likes mild to moderate spicy," Claudia admonished Jensen, hands on her hips as she glared at him. Ian was already starting to choke, his eyes bulging as sweat beaded on the edges of his forehead. "He's not going to be fine."

"Oh. My. God. It's like getting pepper-sprayed in my mouth." Ian gasped for air, looking wildly around like he was searching for something to help. "I can't breathe. Everything burns."

Manuel slapped him on the back, which obviously wasn't going to help at all. Not that Ian was in a position to protest. He was now bent over, hands just above his knees, bracing himself to keep from falling over while he shuddered and tried not to die.

"He said he liked spicy!"

"You know your level of spicy and everyone else's level of spicy is completely different," Claudia snapped. She shook her head, waving her hand at Manuel. "Come on, let's get him to the break room. We have some milk and bread in there."

"Please..." Ian gasped, straightening up.

Cassidy had her hands over her mouth, and she was laughing so hard, she had tears running down her face. Kind of like Ian, but for a completely different reason.

Normally, Jennifer would have found the whole situation hilarious, but today, she glared at Jensen as Claudia, Ian, and Manuel disappeared down the hall.

"That wasn't nice," she scolded.

The smirk on Jensen's face faded immediately, and he frowned back at her.

"It was hilarious, and Ian will be fine. You know, the last time he was here he convinced me to try that awful canned fish thing he brought."

"That doesn't mean you have to lower yourself to his level." Jennifer sniffed and turned her attention back to her computer. "Besides, that just tasted terrible. Yours caused him actual pain. You should apologize."

"I'll take that under consideration." Now scowling, Jensen turned on his heel, only to realize he had an audience. Immediately, his expression changed and softened. "Hey Cassidy, what are you doing here?"

"I had a panic attack," she said sheepishly.

Now that the room was a little emptier, and she was talking about it, David didn't hesitate to move closer, slinging his arm over her shoulder. He did his best to ignore his grandmother's beaming nod of approval. Although he liked that she approved, he also didn't want her meddling in his relationship.

Cassidy leaned into him, reaching up to rub her forehead, her voice a mixture of shame and regret. "I just... I don't know. I was getting in my head at the store, then I saw a blond man who could have vaguely resembled Don in the parking lot, and I just lost it. It was ridiculous."

David tightened his hold on her.

"It's not ridiculous. You're going through a lot, and we don't know where he is or why he hasn't popped up yet," he consoled her.

"I shouldn't have made us go to the store," his grandmother said, coming in from the other side to hold Cassidy's hand.

"You didn't. I made us because I'm supposed to be helping you get out and around, not being the reason you have to sit at home," Cassidy replied, obviously frustrated. "I know I need to be safe, I want to be safe, but I also don't want to spend my whole life hiding. I just... I need to get out of my head."

"Hey, you're going through a big thing," David said gently. "Something you don't have much control over, if any. That's going to make everything harder. You need to be easier on yourself."

Out of the corner of his eye, he saw Jennifer nod approvingly behind her desk. Yeah, a very different conversation than the first time she'd seen him in here with Cassidy.

"I just want it to be over with." She sighed. "My brain just latches onto something and spirals, then all I can think about is how everyone around me is going to die a horrible death while I'm either dragged away or dying with them. And it'll be all my fault."

"Well, that sounds... unpleasant," Grandma said, making David snort. "But sweetie, I could die tomorrow from a heart attack or old age—"

"No, you can't," David interjected, scowling at her. He was also completely unsurprised when she ignored him and kept talking as if he hadn't said a thing.

"That wouldn't be your fault any more than some if some asshole takes me out. And believe me, I'd rather go down defending you than end up rotting in a hospital bed someday."

David face-palmed, sighing.

"You could just work on *not dying,* you know," he said.

"Oh, I don't have any plans to at the moment, but if it happens, it happens. And I would love to have a badass epilogue, like 'went down defending her friend and taking out a dickhead at the same time.'" Grandma grinned, and Cassidy burst out laughing.

He wondered if she would keep laughing when she realized his grandmother was completely serious.

"Come on," he said, gesturing toward the door. "Let's get you two home."

37

———

CASSIDY

Claudia's impromptu birthday party was held at her favorite restaurant, the House of Starrett. It was a pretty standard restaurant with a fairly ornate wooden bar, which was where everyone had gathered to celebrate Claudia. The carpet was blue and green, and the walls were wood until about halfway up where they met the wainscoting, then there was blue wallpaper on the upper half, which matched the blue in the carpet. The servers wore green shirts with black pants.

It was a normal restaurant.

But the bartender was completely weirding her out.

He looked *exactly* like Shane, the bartender from Marquis.

Same height, same build, and same face. Same bald head, same salt and pepper goatee. Same neutral expression and brisk efficiency as he served people.

David brought her up to the bar to order her drink, and she couldn't help it.

"Shane?" she asked when he looked up at them.

He blinked.

"No, I'm Seamus." Different name but the same voice, though the inflection was a little different. Which was also freaky.

"Oh... sorry. You look exactly like someone I know."

"Shane's my twin. What do you want to drink?"

"Um, whiskey sour, please," she said.

"Blue Moon," David replied right after her, his hand still resting protectively on the small of her back. Seamus nodded and immediately turned away to get to work.

Apparently, Shane was chattier than Seamus, which Cassidy would not have thought possible. She hadn't even known Shane had a twin. Then again, Shane was known for not talking very much about himself, though he was a good listener. Part of her wondered if Shane had actually been sent up from Marquis to keep an eye on her in the city, like maybe he was some kind of secret assassin now masquerading as his twin, but then he reached into a glass on his side of the bar and picked something up, popping it into his mouth.

It only took a quick glance for her to see that the little bowl he'd just reached into was full of candy corn.

That clinched it.

Definitely not Shane. Everyone knew Shane hated candy corn.

Unless this was part of his ruse to make it seem like he *wasn't* actually Shane.

Oh my God, Cassidy, stop.

Though it was kind of nice to know her brain could spiral about things other than fatal threats and death.

They got their drinks and walked away. She was just going to keep her back to Seamus for the night. Seeing a Shane doppelganger was just too weird. Weren't identical twins supposed to still have some physical differences? Because if that really was Shane's twin and not Shane himself, they looked more like clones.

And why had Shane never mentioned a twin?

David led her over to rejoin the group. Claudia was dressed up in a little black dress, her hair completely down for once, so Cassidy could see it nearly reached her waist. She'd even put on a little makeup. For someone who had insisted she didn't want to come out and make her birthday a big deal, she looked like she'd put some effort into it.

"It's still weird seeing you in a dress," David said as he sat Cassidy down at the table next to Claudia, shaking his head. He stood behind Cassidy. They almost had enough chairs for everyone, but not quite, so several of the men were standing. Mostly the Black Fox men. Ian was seated on the other side of Claudia, Manuel next to him. On Cassidy's other side was Naomi, with Drew standing behind her, talking to Mason, who was standing next to him. Jennifer and Yasmine were at the end of the table, with an empty chair between Jennifer and Manuel, which Cassidy could only assume was for Ashley, though she hadn't seen her yet.

"Great, weird is exactly what I was going for," Claudia said dryly.

"You look beautiful," Ian chimed in immediately. "David is just so besotted with Cassidy, he's blind to all other's beauty."

"You, shut up. You're making me want to drink more." As if to prove her point, Claudia lifted her glass to her lips, taking a long sip... but Cassidy felt almost sure that she saw the ends of Claudia's lips curl up in a smile before she covered her mouth.

Maybe Claudia wasn't as immune to Ian's compliments as she wanted everyone to think. Or maybe Cassidy was imagining things.

"Why don't you like your birthday?" she asked Claudia. Some women didn't like being reminded that they were getting older— Cassidy had a feeling she was going to celebrate every year she was still alive after this one fervently—but Claudia didn't seem the type for that.

Claudia shrugged. "It's not like I did anything. If anyone should be getting presents today, it's my mom for doing all the hard labor to get me here."

"She's got a point," Manuel chimed in. "Mama says Claudia was a much more difficult birth than me. I was nice and easy. Which is why Mama should be celebrated on Claudia's birthday, and I should be celebrated on mine for making it easier on her."

"You were easier because you were the second one out," Claudia retorted. "And 'easier' doesn't mean 'easy.' You did nothing to get here, either."

As the siblings fell to bickering, Cassidy couldn't help but laugh and look around. With the entire Black Fox team here, she was feeling a lot more relaxed than she would have thought possible, being out in a bar. She was surrounded by protectors. It was hard to feel uneasy when there was a literal wall of highly trained muscle on every side of her.

Jennifer and Yasmine had their heads together, and they kept looking over at the bar. Cassidy followed their gazes and spotted Jensen there with Mick, talking to two women. Very attractive women who were obviously hanging out together and were dressed to impress.

No, not talking.

Flirting. Definitely flirting.

As she watched, Jensen turned slightly toward the pair and flexed his bicep. They both touched it and reacted. Cassidy didn't need to be within earshot to know they were squealing.

She glanced back at Jennifer, who was now scowling and staring down at her phone.

Yikes.

Poor Jennifer. And Jensen.

Poor Jens.

Now, it was her turn to use her glass to cover her mouth so no one could see her laughing. She didn't want to have to explain why. They didn't need any more scrutiny.

An arm slid around her waist, David pressing up against her from behind. He was turned sideways from where she was, his palm splayed out across her ribs while he chatted with Drew. It felt both protective and like a claiming. She liked it. A lot.

D*AVID*

Celebrating Claudia with his whole team and his girl felt better than he could have ever imagined. Cassidy fit right in. With his team. With his life. With him. It was the last thing he'd expected when she'd come to Pittsburgh, but he had decided to be grateful for it.

She leaned back against him as she laughed at something Claudia said, and he stroked his thumb over her ribs.

Fully relaxed, fully in the moment, and enjoying herself, this was the life she was supposed to be living. He was going to do whatever he had to do in order to preserve that for her. In this case, the right thing didn't coincide with the lawful thing, but he wasn't going to let her end up like Tasha or worse.

The back of his jeans buzzed, his phone vibrating from a call. Letting go of Cassidy, he reached back to pull it out and check to see who was calling, fully intending to let it go to voicemail, but it was Audrey.

Leaning down, he spoke in Cassidy's ear.

"My sister is calling; I'm going to step outside to see what she needs. Drew will keep an eye on you."

Beaming, Cassidy turned her head to him, her drink in one hand, her fingers of the other holding her straw in place.

"Okay. I'll be here." She giggled. Yeah, she might be a little tipsy. Smiling, David gave her a quick kiss before straightening up.

"I'm going outside to take this," he told Drew. "Keep an eye on Cassidy for me."

"Can do, boss." Drew gave him an abbreviated salute, grinning widely. Since David was leaving, he immediately leaned over to hear what the women in front of them were talking about.

Even though he knew his team would take care of Cassidy, he couldn't help but scan the bar for threats as he made his way to the front door of the restaurant. Nothing stood out to him, and no one even seemed to be watching the group except the odd bartender Cassidy had questioned, who glanced over at them now and then, which didn't mean anything.

David wasn't sure if he'd met the man before. He didn't usually pay too much attention to who was behind the bar unless it was someone he already knew. They didn't come here often enough for him to feel like he knew who all the bartenders were. They tended to gather at the Outlands instead. Obviously, Claudia hadn't wanted to do that tonight with her brother and Ian.

He couldn't blame her.

Stepping out into the evening air, which was sultry and warm, David quickly called Audrey back. He'd taken long enough that it had gone to voicemail while he'd been making his way out. She picked up immediately.

"What's up?" he asked.

"Well, hello to you, too."

David sighed. He knew she was fucking with him, but she would just take it even further if he didn't respond correctly. Siblings.

"Hello, Audrey, how are you?"

"I'm great! Things are moving forward with the bakery, but I have a favor to ask."

"Anything," he said immediately, making her laugh.

"You shouldn't speak so soon, you might regret it," she teased. "I'm going to be coming to Pittsburgh in two weeks to check out some of the apartment buildings I've been looking at online and also to oversee a few things with the renovation for the bakery. The contractor has been sending me updates, but I want to see it in person before making final decisions."

"That sounds smart. So what do you need from me?" He wasn't going to be any help when it came to making décor decisions, as she knew. She always teased him about how utilitarian his apartment was.

"A place to stay while I'm here. I was going to do a hotel, but I'm trying to budget wisely. I'd ask Grandma, but I think Mom would blow a gasket. Though she is my backup choice because I do need to come." Though still cheerful, there was more than a little strain in her voice.

Normally, when Audrey visited, she stayed in a hotel. It had been one of the ways she'd been able to visit without their parents throwing a fit. She was always trying to keep the peace, and that way, their parents could pretend she was just visiting Pittsburgh, the city, not the son or the stepmother they hadn't acknowledged in years.

"Budget wisely? Mom and Dad aren't willing to pay for the hotel even though it's for your business?" He didn't say it aloud, but normally, they were controlling enough that they liked to pay for everything. It was their way of making sure Audrey and David felt like they 'owed' them.

David had gotten out of that trap, but it was a tactic that had always worked really well on Audrey. That and the fact she didn't like disappointing them, whereas David had eventually realized he couldn't live up to what they wanted without losing everything about himself. Audrey had managed to live in the middle space for so long, he had started to assume it would always be that way.

"Ah, yeah, well. It turns out, they thought I was going to fail long before this point." She hummed, a little noise that she did when she was holding back her emotions. Their parents didn't believe in their children expressing themselves, especially when they were upset. "For some reason, they didn't think I was serious."

That tracked. They'd done the exact same thing when he'd decided to join the army, all the way up until when he'd actually left. It didn't matter that he'd signed a contract, they'd been sure they could buy him out of it when he changed his mind—not if, when.

You'd think they would have learned their lesson, but apparently not.

"Of course, you can stay with me," he said immediately. "Though I can put you up in a hotel if you prefer. I um... I kind of have someone staying with me at the moment."

"I can take the couch. It's no big deal. Unless you think it'll be too crowded... or if you'd rather not introduce me to your guest."

The hesitation in her voice had him hurrying to reassure her.

"No, no, it's not that at all. In fact, I very much want you to meet her." He cleared his throat, shifting out of the way of a couple who passed him on his way into the restaurant. Moving farther from the doorway, he settled beside one of the large potted plants beside the entrance. "And there won't be any need for you to sleep on the couch. The guest room is still open."

Pure silence.

He waited.

"Oh... *oh*. So, it's like that, is it?" Audrey sounded gleeful. "When I talked to Grandma last week, she mentioned something, but I thought she was exaggerating. Cassidy, right?"

"Yes. And she might have been exaggerating. Cassidy moved in with me for her own protection. She's got an obsessive, abusive ex who's been stalking her."

"Okay, well, that sucks. But she's staying in your room? Is that for her own protection, too?" There was real concern in Audrey's voice. Though she kept her tone light, it was still more strained than it had been. She would remember what had happened to Tasha, too.

"No, that's for my enjoyment."

Audrey made a gagging noise, and he grinned. She should know better than to prod at him; she was always going to regret it. That's what older brothers were for.

"All gross innuendoes aside, I can't wait to meet her. Just try to keep it down while I'm there, okay?"

"Sure, we'll break out the ball gag just for you."

She made a groaning noise.

"I'm starting to think I should call Grandma instead."

David chuckled.

"Alright, alright, I'll stop. Seriously, I'm looking forward to you meeting her. I think you'll like her. And the whole team should be in town for once, so we should all get together at some point. The ones who haven't met you yet are excited to."

"I'm excited to meet them! I'm sure we can find a time that works. It's not like I'll be able to do any apartment shopping or work in the evenings."

"Great. I've gotta get back. We're celebrating Claudia's birthday right now, but text me tomorrow with all the details of when you'll be coming in and whatnot."

"Oh, tell her happy birthday for me! And say hi to everyone!"

"I will."

"See you next week, big brother!"

"See you then. Stay safe, and don't let the parentals get you down."

"I won't," she promised, but they both knew she was lying. Still, there wasn't much he could do. He was just glad she was finally getting out of Philly and coming to Pittsburgh to be closer to him. Farther from them.

If she was ever going to get their hooks out of her, distance could only help.

For now, he set his thoughts of his sister aside. He wanted to get back to his girl.

38

CASSIDY

There was only a tiny moment of feeling bereft when the comforting warmth of David's presence moved away from her. She was surrounded by friends and the wall'o'muscle, which was very comforting. Jensen and Mick had come back from the bar, though she was pretty sure she'd seen them putting the women's numbers into their phones. They'd both been grinning until Jennifer started talking very loudly about her recent date with Richard.

Jensen wasn't smiling quite so widely anymore.

"Isn't 'Dick' a nickname for Richard?" he asked, snickering.

Jennifer glared at him before remembering that she was ignoring him and turning her gaze away to refocus on Ashley, who appeared highly amused by the entire situation.

"Anyway," Jennifer drawled, leaning forward so she could ignore Jensen better. "It was amazing. He's incredibly smart. And insightful. And a really good kisser."

Yup, now Jensen was scowling. If these two wanted everyone to stay out of their business, they were doing a remarkably bad job of it.

Cassidy's straw ran out of drink. Frowning, she looked into the glass, angling it to catch the last little bit that was in there.

"Oof, I don't feel so good all of the sudden," Naomi said. Bending forward in her seat, she held her hand to her stomach.

"Hey babygirl, what's wrong?" Drew asked, leaning forward with her, his hand on her lower back, automatically rubbing.

"I don't know... just nauseous. I don't think I'm gonna throw up or anything, but it just hit me all of the sudden." Naomi wrinkled her nose, shaking her head. "I think I need some water."

"Yeah, of course, I'll be right back. Don't move." Drew was already moving like the wind, heading for the bar to get her some water. Cassidy took his place, rubbing Naomi's back just where he had been.

"Does this help at all?" she asked. "Or do you want me to stop?"

"I'm honestly not sure. I don't think it makes it worse or better," Naomi said, making a face. "Ugh, I don't know where this came from. I'd better not have food poisoning or something. I do not want to spend the night praying to the porcelain gods."

"Should we go to the bathroom?" Jennifer asked. Everyone had pretty much stopped what they were doing to pay attention to Naomi. Well, everyone except Yasmine and Mason who had already moved further away from the group and seemed to be engaged in some kind of very serious conversation. "Can you walk?"

Naomi shot her a dark look.

"I could walk if I needed to, but I don't think I need to go to the bathroom."

"I'm just asking because I need to go to the bathroom," Jennifer said. "So if you did need to go... you could go with me."

"I don't need to go. I just need some water." Naomi was still scowling, but maybe a little less than she had been a minute ago. "Honestly, I don't really want to get up and walk. I just want to sit here and wait for Da— ah, Drew to get back with my water."

Cassidy wasn't sure what Naomi had been about to say before she switched to Drew's name, but she had a suspicion she'd been about to call him 'Daddy.'

"I need to go," Ashley offered up.

"So do I," Cassidy said, though she didn't stop rubbing Naomi's back. She wasn't sure if she should leave the other woman. "I can wait, though."

"No, go," Claudia said, shifting closer. "I've got her."

Nodding, relieved, Cassidy slid off her barstool. Ashley and Jennifer were already on the other side of the table, waiting for her. They grinned as she approached. Ashley turned away, then squeaked as Lincoln leaned over to swat her backside. She shot him a look over her shoulder as Cassidy joined them, giggling and taking Jennifer's other arm.

None of them were drunk enough that they were swaying or anything; it was just for companionship.

"So, really, how was your date with Richard?" Ashley asked as soon as they were out of earshot of the tables. "How much of that was made up?"

"Not much," Jennifer admitted, sounding conflicted and also a little frustrated. "It really was an amazing date. I like him a lot. I'm just..."

"Still lusting after Jensen?"

"Yeah, but what's the point if he's never going to make a move and shuts me down every time I start to? I'm tired of being rejected. It's nice to have a guy actually want to be with me." Jennifer sighed. "Richard doesn't think I'm too young, too inexperienced, or too innocent."

"Is he kinky?" Cassidy asked.

"Yes, but he's not a member of the Outlands, which is good because that means Uncle Gavin isn't going to be able to intimidate him. He does house parties. Like me. That's how I met him, actually. We've scened together a few times, platonically, then he asked me out on a date."

"Well, then either Jensen will come around or he won't, but you've got options." Ashley bumped Jennifer with her hip, causing her to bump Cassidy, making all three of them giggle just as they reached the bathroom. Two of the stalls were full, and somehow, Cassidy ended up taking the third.

By the time she finished and washed her hands, a few more

women had come in, and it was a little crowded. Rather than making the situation worse, Cassidy quickly called out that she would meet Jennifer and Ashley in the hallway and scooted out the door.

The hallway had four doors—the two restrooms, a door to the kitchen, and the emergency exit. A man was standing next to the emergency exit, head bent over his phone. Uneasiness skittered up Cassidy's spine. He was wearing a hat, and she couldn't see his hair or his face, but she tried to shake it off.

There was no reason to let her paranoia freak her out.

She shifted over to the side, so she wasn't blocking the door to the ladies' room for the next person who would need to exit. Her heart started beating a little faster when she saw the man's head tilt toward her, though he didn't look up from his phone.

It's nothing. Stop freaking out.

Noise to her left made her turn her head. Another man was coming down the hall, headed toward the bathroom, though he stopped when he saw her there.

"Hey, pretty lady. Waiting for me?" The man winked at her. He was good-looking, maybe an inch or two taller than her, very cute in a boyish way, and if she wasn't already involved with David, she might have been attracted.

She laughed, only a little nervous. The flirting seemed ingrained in him—see woman, flirt—just like Ian. It wasn't personal or threatening, though that didn't mean she fully relaxed, either.

"Sorry, no, just waiting for my fri—"

Her words were cut off as someone grabbed her from behind, yanking her back. Fingers dug into her arm hard enough to bruise, and her mouth opened to cry out, but not a sound emerged.

"Stay away from my girlfriend, asshole!"

Her breath caught in her throat, choking on her scream.

NO.

But it didn't come out.

The other man stepped back, holding his hands up and shaking his head as Don dragged her down the hall toward the door he'd been standing next to. It was him. It had been him. She wasn't paranoid; she'd been right, and she could weep for it.

"Hey, man, sorry, I didn't know."

"No." She managed to whisper the word, but it was drowned out by Don's retort.

"Well, now you do, so fucking back off." He was dragging her back, past the other doors, to the exit.

Never let them take you to a second location.

"No!" She heard Don hit the door, and she tried to kick him, hitting, struggling. Twisting in his grip, she saw the flirtatious man still watching. "Help me!"

"Hey, lady, this looks like a domestic thing. I don't wanna get involved." He still had his hands up in the air, like he was surrendering, shaking his head and backing away toward the restaurant.

"Please!" She started to scream, but it was cut off when Don pulled her back hard, slamming her head into the doorway.

"Hey, man, you don't have to be so rough with her—"

"Fuck off!" Don pulled her outside, and she stumbled, dizzy, as the pain throbbed through her head. She tried to kick him again, tears momentarily blinding her, and it pulled her off balance. Thankfully, it pulled him off balance, too, and she tumbled to the ground. "Fucking bitch! Fucking hold still before I fucking shoot you!"

Terror seized her as she looked up at him, elbows digging into the hard ground. The alleyway was well lit from light bulbs along the side of the building, so there was no missing the gun Don pulled out of the waistband of his pants. His blue eyes were cold, hard, as he glared down at her, and her mouth went utterly dry.

***

D*avid*

Walking back into the restaurant, David frowned when he saw the smaller group at the tables without Cassidy among them. They were all focused on Naomi, who had Drew beside her in the chair Cassidy had previously occupied, his hand on her back. Ashley and Jennifer were also missing from the table.

Ladies' trip to the bathroom.

Movement out of the corner of his eye caught his attention, something in his brain signaling a kind of warning. He turned to see Ashley and Jennifer emerging from the hallway without Cassidy. Neither of them looked to be in any distress; they had their arms linked together and were laughing about something, but... where was Cassidy?

Striding over to them, he met them on their way back to the table.

"Hey, David!" Ashley said, giggling. "Fancy meeting you here."

The edges of a smile tugged at the corner of his mouth, but the little alarm in his head was too strong to allow for a full grin, despite how cute she was.

"Hey, is Cassidy still in the bathroom?"

They both looked at him, smiles fading to be replaced by confused—and, in Jennifer's case, concerned—frowns.

"No, she left before us," Jennifer said, twisting to look back around at the hall. "When we came out, she wasn't there, and we assumed she headed back to the table."

Except she wasn't at the table.

Instinct had David darting around them, running for the exit at the end of the hall. A sixth sense knew they were following behind him, but the alarm bells ringing in his head meant he didn't look back to make sure.

Something was very, very wrong.

He plowed through the exit and into the alley beside the restaurant, pulling up when he saw the pair tussling about fifteen feet away. His brain took in the full scene, all at once, the way it had done so many times when he'd been on a mission.

Metal dumpsters to the left, two of them in a row. A stack of wooden crates on the right, stacked to about knee height, more of a tripping hazard than something that would offer any coverage. The target was fifteen feet away and about twenty feet from the end of the alley, where it emptied out onto the street.

Target was tall, muscular, and armed. He was also currently hindered by the fact the client had gone limp-legged, and he was trying to bodily drag her along the ground while she was fighting all the way. David's heart leapt into his throat as Don lifted the gun—but he was pointing it at David, not Cassidy, thank God.

David put his hands up in front of him even as he reached out to kick the door shut behind him. He caught a glimpse of Jennifer and Ashley's horrified faces before it slammed closed.

They would go get help.

"He has a gun!" Cassidy shrieked, twisting in Don's grip, her foot lashing out and catching the man in the meaty chunk of his thigh.

"And I will fucking shoot you!" Don started to lower the gun to point it at her.

"Hey," David said, raising his voice and taking a step forward, drawing the other man's attention. "Let's talk about this."

Lip curled in a sneer, eyes wild with hate, Don lifted his head and the gun back to David.

"No."

Pain blossomed as the bullet sliced through David's body, and Cassidy's screams rang in his ears.

39

It was her literal worst nightmare.

Don, in the flesh, and he'd gotten her alone. Vulnerable.

Except she wasn't listening to him anymore. And she'd been training. She couldn't punch him or kick him the way she'd done in training. He was too close. Not just standing there waiting for it or dancing around her. No, he was holding on to her, and she was shaking so badly, it was a wonder she could move at all.

But she hadn't panicked and lost her head.

And she wasn't letting him take her to a second location.

I'd rather die right here in this alley.

Part of her hoped that useless flirt had gone to get someone who would actually help, but she didn't hold out a whole lot of hope.

Part of her realized Ashley and Jennifer would get out of the bathroom and realize she was missing. But she was also afraid someone would come to help and end up getting shot.

Exactly what she thought was going to happen when David burst through the door.

Her heart dropped into her stomach, but seeing him gave her a second wind on struggling against Don's hold. She lashed out, kicking Don in the thigh, feeling savage satisfaction when he flinched and aimed the gun back at her.

"Hey, let's talk about this," David said, his voice filling the alley. Cassidy didn't have time to react, didn't have time to do *anything*.

"No," Don said, pointing the gun at David and pulling the trigger. Cassidy screamed, lurching up toward Don's arm, hands outstretched, but it was too late. Don cursed, trying to pull away from her, but her arms were around his wrist, aiming the gun toward the sky.

Cassidy screamed again, right in his face this time, and saw the shock that flitted across his expression.

He couldn't believe she was fighting back.

The surge of adrenaline allowed her to push him back, and for a moment, she felt triumph, but then he seemed to come back to himself.

"Stupid bitch!" He turned them, slamming her against the brick wall of the alley, and her head snapped back. Pain exploded from the back of her skull, disorienting her. She could hear things, shouting, but she wasn't sure if it was real or not, it sounded so far away.

Don wrapped his hand around her throat, stepping back as he squeezed with his fingers, but his full attention wasn't on her, so she could still breathe somewhat. Then he outstretched his arm, pointing the gun at someone or something down the alley. Cassidy couldn't see anyone or anything but him, but it didn't matter.

It didn't matter what happened to her. She just needed whoever it was to save David.

Because he was still alive.

She had to believe he was still alive.

Digging her fingernails into Don's wrist, she lashed out with her foot again, hoping she was aiming for his balls. He yelled, jerking, his hand tightening on her throat, shooting again.

Had he hit someone?

She didn't know.

Couldn't tell.

She tried to kick him again, and this time, he yelled even louder, pulling her toward him, then slamming her back against the wall. It didn't hurt as much this time, but she also couldn't seem to stand anymore. Her legs were sinking, and she was going down with them.

Don dragged her forward, away from the wall, and she stumbled, falling, but he was holding her up.

Something appeared in his throat.

Black and silver and sticking out of his neck.

Oh God.

There was a knife in his neck.

Don's gaze met hers, and he blinked as if confused. His grip relaxed, and he let her go. Cassidy sank down to her knees, staring in utter disbelief as Don groped at his throat, then pulled the knife out. Blood sprayed across her, around her, but she couldn't find her voice to scream.

David

Disbelief poured through David as he watched the absolute dumbass pull David's knife from his throat. If he hadn't done that, if he'd waited till an ambulance arrived, he might have had a chance.

A small chance.

But a chance.

Cursing as blood spattered over Cassidy, David pushed himself up to his feet and stumbled forward. Don hit the ground in the alley with a sickening thud. He would be dead in moments, David knew, bleeding out from the wound because he'd been dumb enough to pull out the knife.

On the other hand, it was a quicker death, and David sure as hell couldn't regret it.

At the other end of the alley, Mason and Jensen were already running toward them. He heard the door he'd come through open, but he was already moving toward Cassidy, not waiting to see who else was joining them.

"I've got you," he murmured as he hit his knees beside her, using his right arm to pull her back against him. She turned into his shoulder, shock written all over her face. Don's blood decorated her pale skin, standing out stark and red. Fuck. He hadn't meant for that to happen to her.

It wasn't like she'd needed to be more traumatized.

She burrowed into him, obviously wanting his comfort, despite the fact he'd literally just killed a man in front of her. Drew jumped down from the roof of the building, rolling as he hit the ground and bouncing to his feet right next to Don's body, just as Mason and Jensen pulled up beside him.

"Dammit. I wanted to beat the shit out of this asshole," Jensen complained, kicking the corpse's leg. Mason and Drew shook their heads at him, Drew lifting up his hand to run it over his dreads and giving them a hard tug.

Behind David, Lincoln coughed. He must have been the one coming out the door.

"There are security cameras in this alley, Jensen," Lincoln said, though his tone was only mildly reproving. They'd all been thinking the same thing.

David at least got some satisfaction from knowing it was his knife that was buried in Don's throat. No, he didn't feel bad about it at all. It had been clear self-defense on his part, not to mention defending Cassidy. Who knows what Don would have done with her if he'd managed to kidnap her?

Tightening his grip on her, David twisted, pulling her farther away from Don's body and obscuring her view.

Sirens were already wailing in the distance.

"Mason, can you come check Cassidy over? And where's Claudia?" he asked, looking around. She was the only one missing, which wasn't like her.

"Keeping watch over the others, just in case," Lincoln said. He put his hand on David's shoulder. His right one, thankfully. "We weren't entirely sure what the threat was and what was going on when Ashley and Jennifer came running back in."

"That and she was the drunkest," Jensen added. "Since it's her birthday."

"Dammit. You know she's going to be even more of a pain in the ass about celebrating her birthday next year," Mason muttered, narrowing his eyes at David. "You've been shot. You dumbass, why didn't you say anything?" He dropped down to his knees on David's left, reaching to unbutton David's shirt.

"Well, if you wanted to get me naked, you could have just said so," he quipped. "I'll be fine, though. It's just a flesh wound. Check Cassidy." He was starting to get really worried about the fact that she hadn't said a single word.

Police cars came to a screeching halt at the end of the alley, along with an ambulance, which was good. David and Cassidy would need them, but he still wanted Mason's opinion of how she was. Thankfully, his teammate was already quickly checking her over.

David felt himself slowly relax.

Everything was going to be okay.

<u>*Cassidy*</u>

"I can't believe you killed him," Claudia complained. "It's *my* birthday. I should have gotten to kill him."

That couldn't be right. Either Cassidy had misheard, she was hallucinating, or...

"You were drunk," Lincoln said sternly. "Besides, a dead body is not an appropriate birthday present."

"Says you," Claudia grumbled. "I'm never drinking on my birthday ever again. I didn't get anything I wanted for my birthday."

Cassidy opened her eyes and saw nothing but white. It took her a moment to realize she was staring up at a ceiling.

"Hey, Cassidy's awake!" Jennifer's face blocked out the ceiling, pure relief covering her expression. "Oh my God, I'm so glad you're okay."

"I'm okay?" It came out as a question, even though, technically, she did feel mostly okay. Her head was a little woozy, but nothing hurt. She tried to lift her head to see who else was in the room, but she couldn't.

"Hey, don't try to move around too much," Jennifer said, putting her hand on Cassidy's shoulder to keep her pinned to the bed. "You fainted when the EMTs were checking you over and one of them touched the back of your head. You got really banged up there."

As she was talking, more people appeared around Cassidy's bed. Claudia, Ashley, Lincoln, Yasmine, Naomi, Drew, Jensen, Mason...

"Where's David?" Fear suffused her. The last thing she remembered was seeing him on the ground.

No... wait... he'd been holding her.

No, he'd been shot. She must have imagined him holding her.

Oh God, had she imagined him holding her because he was dead? Had it been some metaphysical—

"David's fine. He's in surgery to get the bullet out of his shoulder," Mason said soothingly, patting near the foot of the bed and managing to catch her ankle.

He was alive.

Cassidy burst into tears.

"Okay, okay, let's clear the room and give her some space," Claudia ordered. "Everybody out."

'Everybody' didn't really mean everybody, it turned out. It meant everyone except Claudia and Naomi, who both stayed to provide a supportive shoulder and give her a rundown on what had been happening while she was out. Cassidy did her best to pay attention, though whatever painkillers they'd put her on was making it difficult, and it became even more so when the nurses came in to check on her now that she was awake.

She got the general gist of everything, though.

David had been shot, but he was going to be okay. The bullet hadn't hit anything vital. He was going to need some physical therapy to help him with movement after he healed, but nothing too terrible. Cassidy still felt horribly guilty, but she was also relieved it wasn't anything worse.

The biggest relief came from hearing that Don was dead.

Which made her feel like a bad person.

She felt worse about feeling relief than she did about him being dead.

She was going to have plenty to talk about at her next therapy appointment.

Once the nurses were done checking her over, they told her the doctor would be by to see her shortly and started to leave. The door was still open when they came to a halt, blocking entry to someone out in the hall.

"That is my granddaughter in there, and I am going in to see her!" Brenda's voice came through loud and shrill.

"That's Brenda," Cassidy said, blinking in surprise because she was pretty sure Brenda was trying to get into *her* room, but obviously, Brenda wasn't her grandmother. She was David's grandmother.

"Let her in, please," Naomi called out, getting to her feet, but it ended up being unnecessary because once she called out her approval, the nurses parted, and Brenda came bustling in.

There were tears in her eyes as she hurried over to Cassidy's side, pure worry etched across her features that only lessened a tiny bit when she met Cassidy's gaze.

"My goodness, you and David. Getting attacked, getting shot, and all without me there! What were you thinking?" She bent over to very gently kiss Cassidy's forehead. "I didn't even get to kick the fucker."

"Don't worry, Jensen handled that apparently, though Don had already caught a bad case of the dead before he did it, so it's not like he could feel it," Jennifer reassured her.

Brenda sniffed derisively. "Yeah, but I wanted to. Is he in the morgue here? Do you think they'd let me in?"

Cassidy couldn't help it; she started laughing.

40

———

DAVID

For the first time, David didn't mind having to stay in the hospital while he recovered from surgery, in large part because Lincoln had pulled some strings and made sure he and Cassidy could have a room together. They had to sleep in their separate beds, but it meant David could truly relax because he knew she was okay.

The physical threat from Don was gone, but he needed to know she was okay in other ways, too.

From what she said, she didn't remember Don's actual death or being sprayed with his blood. She'd woken up in the hospital all cleaned up. Still, he knew from being in the same room with her that she was having some nightmares. She didn't seem to remember those either when she woke up.

He was worried it was all going to start coming back to her, and he wanted to be there to help if it did.

They also had constant visitors. Not just the team but also people from the Outlands, and—of course—his grandmother was there every day. Apparently, Cassidy was now claimed as her granddaughter. Cassidy had admitted to him that when she'd first woken up and she'd been a little out of it, she'd been wildly confused about that until she'd realized Brenda had just said it to try to get into her room.

Thanks to Lincoln, they were also getting released on the same day.

Dr. Grande, David's surgeon, had come to take a final look before signing him out. Or maybe he'd stopped by because Jennifer was there.

As fate would have it, the Dr. Richard Grande who'd operated on David's shoulder was the same Richard who had recently asked Jennifer out on a date. Jensen was already calling him 'Dr. Dick' when the man wasn't around. Unfortunately for Jensen, Dr. Grande was a good-looking guy. There were some similarities between the two of them in looks—tall, brown-haired, and dark-eyed with a lean build. Jennifer definitely had a type.

"Everything looks good," Dr. Grande said, putting the bandage back in place. He was saying the words to David, but he was looking at Jennifer, who was sitting and waiting in the nearby chair, smiling widely at her. She was smiling back at him, and she kept brushing invisible hair off of her shoulder. Thankfully, Jensen wasn't there to see it since the chemistry between the two was just as strong as it was between Jennifer and Jensen. If he'd been hoping she was dating someone else just to get to him... well, it was very clear right now that was not the case.

"Great, thank you, Doc." David was ready to get out of there.

"Is there anything special I need to do to take care of him?" Cassidy asked anxiously, putting her hand on David's thigh to keep him from actually getting off the edge of the bed where he was sitting. She'd been hovering at his side while Dr. Grande examined him.

David had been shot before, so he knew what to do, but he waited patiently while Cassidy listened very seriously to the same rundown the nurses had already given her. If she wanted to take care of him and play nurse, he wasn't going to stop her, especially if it meant some of her anxiety relaxed. Jennifer was also paying close attention, though he was pretty sure it was for a slightly different reason. Dr. Grande kept glancing at her.

Smitten was the word that came to mind.

They finally got out of there. Jennifer had offered to drive them. Cassidy was doing well, but she was nervous about driving after a head injury, and everyone seemed to think it would be better if a third party was there to take him home. David hadn't bothered to argue.

"So, what's been going on?" he asked once they got in the car. Everyone had refused to update him while he was in the hospital, insisting he focus on healing. In some ways, it had been infuriating; in others, it had been a nice break to not be able to think about work at all.

"We finally found out where Don had been holed up. His aunt rented a house for him here using his parents' money, so his family definitely knew where he was," Jennifer said, shaking her head.

Cassidy snuggled up to David in the backseat. He'd made sure they'd gotten in so he would be able to put his good arm around her once they were seated. There was going to be a lot more physical therapy before he could use his left arm in all the ways he wanted to.

"Assholes," he muttered. Cassidy didn't say anything, but he felt her nod.

Seriously, they should be charged with aiding and abetting. On the other hand, they'd lost their son because of it, so hopefully, they'd learned their lesson.

"No charges filed; it was clear self-defense. Saul handed over the tapes from the alley to the police when they arrived on the scene to make sure you didn't get into any trouble. There was also a witness who confirmed that Cassidy didn't want to go with Don," Jennifer continued.

Beside him, Cassidy stirred, then subsided.

"A witness?"

"Yeah, some douchebag who didn't want to get involved when Don was actually abducting her but heroically stepped up to talk to the cops." Jennifer snorted.

"He didn't want to get involved in a 'domestic thing'," Cassidy confirmed in a low voice.

David flexed his hand, closing it into a fist and reopening his fingers. It was probably a good thing Jennifer hadn't mentioned the man's name. In fact, he had a feeling she'd done that deliberately.

Paying a visit to the coward wouldn't be self-defense.

"Lincoln said Don's parents might try to sue, but there's no way they'd win, especially with the camera footage," Cassidy said in a low voice. There was anger thrumming through her tone but also some regret.

David tightened his grip on her. He had *not* been privy to the sessions Cassidy had with her therapist the past few days; she'd gone to a different room for those video chats. He imagined she was feeling guilty, though she didn't say that to him. She did tell him that she hadn't had a single nightmare since Don's death. That didn't do anything for her guilt, though.

The injury he'd received was part of her guilt, but it wasn't her fault. It was Douchebag Don's and no one else's, except maybe his family. Parents who had raised him into an entitled little shit, then continued to support his sketchy behavior.

"They can certainly try." He wouldn't cause them any grief unprovoked since they'd just lost their son, but if they came after Cassidy in any way, he would fucking bury them. He had very little patience for people who weren't willing to take accountability for their actions. If they were smart, they'd leave Cassidy the fuck alone. "What about at work?"

"Claudia's taken on your role for now, of course," Jennifer said. Claudia was his number two. "Lincoln says he wants to talk to you about the new hire he's decided on once you're back, but not yet. And Drew, Darcie, Miguel, Grant, Harrison, and Lincoln have all received black roses at home now. Lincoln got his this morning. We thought there was a missed day between Grant and Harris, but then we realized you weren't home, so Mason ran by your apartment and found that you'd gotten a delivery as well."

"Interesting," David murmured. Obviously, they weren't from Don. Whoever was sending them was aware of where the two Black

Fox teams lived, but they either hadn't known he was in the hospital or they hadn't cared, which was interesting.

He wondered if the order was significant. They'd been sent two per team, alternating, all the way up to him and Grant as the team leaders, then to Harrison and Lincoln as the owners.

"I didn't get one," Jennifer concluded. "No one knows what it means, and they're still having trouble figuring out who is sending them. Lincoln and Harris are waiting to see what happens next now that they're out of people to send them to."

David blew out a long, slow breath. "Well... great." It wasn't great, but there wasn't anything they could do. Sometimes, the only option was waiting. "Anything else?"

"I talked to Kincaid," Cassidy piped in. "He was worried about me, even after Don died. I told him I'm doing okay."

Sudden fear stabbed through David as he realized that the reason Cassidy had come to Pittsburgh in the first place no longer existed. She'd been hiding out from Don.

The rest of her life was back in Maryland, along with a whole group of friends she hadn't been able to see or talk to for weeks. They'd probably expect her to move back now that she could.

He'd thought they would have a lot more time together before she had to make that decision...

Now that it was here, he knew he didn't want her to go.

———

Cassidy

David had gotten very quiet in the car, but he perked up again when they got to his apartment and found his grandmother there waiting for him. Brenda had busied herself with 'cleaning up the place' and 'getting it ready' for his return. Also, getting the guest bedroom ready for Audrey to stay in.

His sister was arriving next Friday, and Cassidy was even more nervous about meeting Audrey after getting her brother shot, but she wasn't going to abandon David while he needed her. Audrey had wanted to come sooner when she'd heard David had been injured, but he'd told her not to, and something had come up at home that she'd had to tend to before she could leave, anyway.

There had been a part of Cassidy that wanted to take the cowardly way out and return to Jensen and Mick's, just for the weekend Audrey would be here, so she could avoid the other woman, but... that wasn't going to leave any better of an impression.

She tried to take heart from the fact that Brenda didn't blame her.

Logically, she knew it wasn't her fault. Still, she couldn't help but wince every time she looked at David and the sling on his left arm. The injury that he'd gotten because of her.

She'd left the bathroom instead of staying with the group. She should have known better.

No, Don should have known better than to stalk me and try to abduct me.

Sometimes, she got mad at Robert Johnson, the man who hadn't helped her in the hallway. If he'd just *done something.*

But then he might have been shot in the hall, and Don would have still dragged her out the door. Sighing inwardly, Cassidy pushed the thoughts from her mind. As Mistress Julie said—what happened, happened. There was no point in going over what might have happened because it hadn't.

"I changed and washed your sheets and Audrey's sheets, and you've got food in the fridge," Brenda said, walking David through everything she'd done. He had his arm around her while she stood in the kitchen, ticking points off her fingers.

Cassidy had quietly removed herself to the living room with Jennifer to give them a little space. She could tell the older woman was full of anxious energy, probably at almost losing her grandson.

Brenda had come to the hospital as often as she could to visit them, and she treated Cassidy like a granddaughter rather than her employee, but she wasn't, really. So, she wanted to give them some privacy to just be in each other's company and reassure Brenda that David was going to be okay.

Because he was.

Thank goodness.

"Thanks for volunteering to drive us around today... and Brenda," Cassidy said quietly to Jennifer, not wanting to be too loud. Brenda was busy showing David where she'd put all the groceries away and the casseroles she'd put in both the fridge and the freezer.

They weren't going to have to cook for weeks with all the things Brenda had stocked them up on.

"Of course, no problem," Jennifer said immediately, glancing over her shoulder at David and Brenda before leaning into Cassidy and lowering her voice. "So... what's next for you?"

Cassidy stared at her, blinking, trying to figure out what she meant. Her brain might still be fuzzy from the injury because she couldn't figure out what Jennifer was talking about or why she suddenly looked so serious.

"Next for me? You mean, like meeting Audrey?" She kept her voice low, too, since she didn't want Audrey's name to draw Brenda or David's attention, though she wasn't sure why they were whispering other than that.

Now, it was Jennifer's turn to stare at her in confusion, though she quickly recovered.

"No, I mean, like... what's next? Are you leaving us? Because you don't have to, you know. Jensen and Mick would totally be willing to let you move back in with them if you don't want to stay here. Yasmine told me to tell you that you can come be her housemate if you don't want to live with boys."

Oh.

Oh.

Because Don was dead.

She didn't need to be protected anymore.

Her friends here were worried that she was going to want to go back home.

But was it home?

Cassidy hadn't even thought about it. She'd been so focused on what David was going to need during his recovery... and he hadn't said anything about her moving back out... But she hadn't even been living here a full week before they'd ended up sleeping in the hospital...

She didn't know what he wanted.

Did she know what she wanted?

Why hadn't this come up in therapy?

Had Mistress Julie just assumed she'd be coming back home now that it was all over? Or had she assumed Cassidy would be staying here?

"I don't know," she said slowly. "I haven't thought past a day at a time... and I said I would take care of David during his recovery... although I guess he doesn't really need me."

"Don't rush to decide," Jennifer said quickly, reaching out to take Cassidy's hand. "Just know that, even though you haven't been here that long in the grand scheme of things, we all consider you one of ours, and we're all hoping you stay. If you want to. We want you to have what you want, more than anything else, but we're hoping that maybe what you'll want is to stay."

"Thank you," Cassidy whispered, squeezing Jennifer's hand. Jennifer squeezed back.

Cassidy wanted to stay, too.

Would she want to stay even if David didn't want to be with her? But he had said that he'd want to date her after the danger had passed.

That was before she'd gotten him shot, though.

She also shouldn't stay just for a man. She should stay because she wanted to for herself. That's what Mistress Julie would tell her.

And it was definitely, probably, too soon to move in with him if there wasn't a real need. He couldn't have planned for that to happen. Without needing protection from Don, she probably should stay somewhere else.

Find a real job.

Pay rent.

Make a life.

Or go back to her old life. Go back to Stronghold and Marquis. Go back to the people who had saved her, who had been there for her, and who had let her go to keep her safe.

It all came down to one big question—what did she want?

41

———————

Cassidy

"Alone at last." David sighed with relief as the sound of Jennifer and Brenda's conversation cut off with the closing of his apartment door. Turning to Cassidy, who had been standing with him to say goodbye, he reached out with his right arm and pulled her against him, burying his nose in her hair. She wrapped her arms around him, hugging him tightly. She couldn't press herself against his chest; it was more of a side hug because of his sling, but it was as close as she could get.

Jennifer's questions had brought up all sorts of thoughts in her head, and she wasn't sure what she should do. She didn't want to disappoint anyone, but it seemed unavoidable.

How strange was it to think that people would be disappointed if she wasn't there, no matter which she chose? She wasn't used to having people care about her.

Once Kincaid had given the go-ahead, her phone had flooded with texts from the other submissives from Stronghold, all of them checking in, most of them complaining that they hadn't been able to talk to her. Every single one of them either offered to come up or asked what they could do to help. They were a community.

But she'd found a community here, too, and not just in David's arms.

"I can practically hear you thinking from here," he said, resting his chin on top of her head. "Is it about anything specific?"

She sighed again. It was probably better to talk about it than to keep it in. Besides, she wanted to know what he thought. Not just because his opinion mattered to her, though it did, but because he would actually have some say in the options since she was currently living in his apartment.

"Jennifer asked me what's next, as in what am I going to do now that I don't have to worry about Don anymore," she said and felt David stiffen slightly against her. Not his dick; his whole body. "She said I could move in with Jensen and Mick again, or Yasmine asked her to offer to be housemates."

"Or you could stay here."

The words were said flatly, and she couldn't tell what he was thinking, so she pulled back so she could see his face. His expression was carved from stone, but his blue eyes were steady, intent on her.

"Do you want me to stay here?"

"If you want to stay here. I don't want to push you."

"Well, I don't want to push you." She sighed, exasperated. "Is it really that hard to just tell me what you want?"

A glimmer of a smile curved his lips.

"I don't know, why don't you tell me? You're doing the same thing."

Scowling at him, she released his waist so she could reach up and lightly slap his chest right above where his left hand was resting against it.

"You know what I mean. You're the Dom. Aren't you supposed to be bossing me around or something?" She said it jokingly. She had actually been in that kind of relationship, and she didn't want it, and she knew he knew that.

He laughed, tightening his one-armed grip around her waist.

"I do like bossing you around, but I'm also not going to make major decisions for you. I don't want to push you, either, especially because of what you've been through. If you choose to live here with me, I want it to be because you want to, not because you're doing what you think I want."

Cassidy huffed because, well, same.

As she did so, David's hand left her side and started traveling further south, off the back of her shirt and down to her jeans. She stared at him as his palm slid over her butt.

"Really? You're injured."

"My shoulder is injured; my dick is just fine." He glanced down to prove his point. He'd now stiffened *everywhere*. The bulge at the front of his jeans was very obvious. "This is the first time we've been alone in days. Besides, a few orgasms might make you relaxed enough to just tell me what you want... and they might help you want to stay with me." He winked at her.

"I still think it would be easier if you just told me what you want. I can't just move in here because I want to. It's *your* apartment."

"If I didn't want you to move in here, you wouldn't." He squeezed her butt, curving his fingers under the cheek and hitching her up closer to him. "If that's what you're worried about."

She scowled at him.

"Why couldn't you just say that from the beginning?"

"Because this is how we communicate." His grin was entirely unrepentant. "It works for us. We get there eventually."

"So, I'm staying here?" She just wanted to make sure she was understanding him correctly.

"Do you want to stay here?"

"I *want* to strangle you." Cassidy glared at him, making him chuckle, but his expression had turned more serious.

"I meant here in Pittsburgh," he explained. "Long term. While you're here, yes, I want you to stay with me... if that's what you want." He ignored the exasperated noise she made. "But I was wondering if you were thinking about going back to Maryland, eventually. I just want to know if I should prepare myself to get my heart broken."

Oh. Warmth and happiness surged inside her. He wasn't just

saying that, and he wasn't teasing. Every word dripped with complete sincerity.

"Your heart would be broken?"

"My heart broke when I thought I'd already lost you," he said, shaking his head. "There's nothing quite like seeing the woman you're falling for being dragged away by her stalker to really narrow your perspective. As much as we dance around things, I don't want to dance around this. You mean more to me than any woman I've ever been in a relationship with, even though we haven't been together very long. I'm also older now than I was in my previous relationships and know what I want and what I don't want, so maybe it's just not taking me as much time to realize it. But yeah, I know if you stay even just a few more weeks, I'd be heartbroken if you leave."

Every part of her wanted to melt.

Before she could answer him, his lips came down on hers, claiming hers with a kiss, and she kissed him back with all the feeling that she hadn't gotten to express. Careful not to jostle his arm, she went up on her tiptoes, wrapping her arms around his neck as they deepened the kiss. Heat pulsed through her.

When they broke apart, she stared at him, her arms still holding on tight.

"What if I want to live with someone else? Because this feels like too soon to live together?" she asked.

"I would argue that we've already been doing it, and it's working out great, but if that's what you want, then, of course. I'll just be happy if I get to keep taking you out."

"I do want to live here, but it feels like it's too soon."

"Is there anything I can do to convince you otherwise?"

"I don't know. I have to think about it."

He nodded.

"Then let me know when you decide. In the meantime..." Despite only being one-armed, when he tightened his grip on her, he was able to lift her up and swing her around, so they were facing the hallway where the bedroom was.

Cassidy laughed, shaking her head.

"We are *not* having sex. It'll hurt your arm!"

"Trust me, little spark, we'll find a way."

It took a bit of maneuvering with the pillows to prop him up, and Cassidy couldn't rest her hands on his shoulders or his chest, but she ended up on top of him, riding him for all she was worth. Maybe it was because they'd almost lost each other, maybe it was because they both knew she was staying in Pittsburgh and they were starting a future together, but it was the most intensely intimate orgasm she'd experienced.

---

*D*AVID

Waking up next to Cassidy, David reached for her since his arm wasn't already around her, then immediately groaned in pain.

Oh, yeah. I got shot.

In the haze of coming awake and being back in his own bed, he'd forgotten for just a moment.

The moment he groaned, Cassidy jerked beside him, sitting up to reveal her delightful breasts as the sheet slipped down. Her head was definitely not in a sexy space as she turned frantically to him, unfortunately, pulling down the covers on him as well as her gaze roved over him.

"Are you okay? What hurts? Did you tear your stitches?"

"Yes, my shoulder, and no, I'm *fine*," he said, turning onto his back so he could reach out with his uninjured arm and pull her down beside him. She only resisted for a moment before conceding and coming down to rest her head on his right shoulder. "I just forgot I was injured for a moment and tried to use my left arm. I'm okay."

"Oh, shoot, what if you pulled your stitches?" She was already trying to push up again, reaching for his bandaged shoulder. "I should look."

"You should relax and cuddle with me. Now." He infused his voice with a little Dom bossiness and felt her immediately subside, settling into his good shoulder. Her hair tickled his bicep as her hand came to rest on his chest, and she muttered something that was probably extremely uncomplimentary under her breath. Since he couldn't make out exactly what she said, he ignored it.

Turning his head, he nuzzled his nose in her hair.

"This is nice. I hope you know that I'm going to want you to come over for lots of sleepovers if you're not living here."

"What, you won't come to me?" she asked, teasing.

"I can, but if you're living with housemates, I'd choose some that you're okay with them hearing you scream." He chuckled as she slapped his chest.

The ringing of his phone interrupted them. Before he could even try to reach for it, Cassidy was up and scrambling to get it for him. Sighing inwardly, he let her. She frowned when she looked down at the display.

"It's Black Fox," she said, handing the phone to him. David frowned, too. He was off all this week. Normally, he'd be chafing at the bit to go back, but it was Friday after all, so he could excuse it as a three-day weekend... a three-day weekend with his girl, who he was trying to convince to move in with him.

He hadn't expected to hear from them until Monday at the earliest, which meant something had happened.

"Hello?" He pressed the phone to his ear.

"You need to come into the office." Lincoln's voice was tense, tight. "We got a bouquet of roses here with a note that says 11 o'clock and has a TV channel on it. I want you here for whatever is about to happen."

"Shit. Yes. I'll be there." David glanced at Cassidy. "Can Cassidy come?"

"I assumed she would. You shouldn't be driving yet. Get here as soon as you can."

Half an hour later, David and Cassidy walked through the office doors. David frowned when he saw Zeus Apuzzio sitting with the rest of Black Fox in the lobby. Well, not exactly with them. He wasn't the only one frowning at the tall, bald man. No one was sitting in the chair next to him or standing anywhere near him, setting him slightly apart. Wearing a tailor-made suit, his dark beard neatly trimmed, he looked like he should have fit in, but he didn't.

"David," Lincoln said in greeting, looking up as soon as they walked in. He was standing with Harris and Grant, both of who kept looking at the television even though it wasn't time yet. Lincoln's gaze swept over him and briefly landed on where his and Cassidy's hands were clasped together. "Thanks for coming in. Sorry we had to interrupt your day."

"It's okay. Obviously, this is going to be important," David said as he led Cassidy over to where Lincoln was standing. He wanted to know what was going on, and he wanted Cassidy there with him in case whatever was going on affected her, too. He glanced over at Zeus again, who was steadily ignoring all the glares and suspicious looks he was getting, keeping his focus on the television. David lowered his voice. "I take it you decided to hire Zeus."

"I did." Lincoln nodded firmly, glancing at Harris, who also nodded in confirmation. Grant's expression was studiously blank. David didn't need to be able to read minds that, while the owners were willing to give Zeus a chance, neither he nor Grant were going to fall right into trusting someone who had been on Marshall's team. He was surprised Lincoln and Harris were. "He left Marshall very soon after the split, and Marshall has blackballed him."

Which would indicate that either the fallout was real, or Marshall wanted them to think the fallout was real.

"What's wrong with him?" Cassidy whispered, sidling closer to David.

"I'll explain later," he murmured. Later, when Zeus wasn't there within earshot. He sighed. They did need a tech person, and Zeus had been a damn good one for Marshall's team. It wasn't that he didn't like the guy; he just didn't trust him because of who he'd been working with before. Which might not be entirely fair, but there it was.

"It's starting," Claudia said, drawing all of their attention to the television. The air in the room seemed to hum as they all focused, waiting to see what was going to happen. The words *Special Report* swirled around the screen before settling at the bottom, beneath the reporter and a tall, broad-shouldered white man with dark hair. He was dressed in a dark grey suit with a long red tie, the tip of which went down past his overly large belt buckle. The man looked vaguely familiar, though David couldn't place him immediately.

"Isn't that the guy who cheated on his wife with a stripper, then married the stripper, and then divorced her so he could marry his son's girlfriend, who he knocked up?" Jennifer asked.

"It's Royce MacLeod," Zeus said, staring at the screen. "He's one of Marshall's clients. And yes."

But what the fuck did this have to do with the roses?

Unless...

"Hello, I'm Lesley Johnson, and this is a special news report coming to you live from the steps of Royce MacLeod's headquarters, which is about to turn into a headquarters of a new kind. Mr. MacLeod, thank you for taking the time to speak with me today."

"Call me Royce, please, Lesley." He smiled genially, not seeming to notice when her own smile froze in place at her first name... which she had not invited him to call her by. "Thank you for coming out to speak with me, as I have a very exciting announcement to make. I'm running for governor!"

Pitting him against the senator.

"Does he even have any experience in politics?" Jensen asked in disbelief.

"No, just business, which he's very mediocre at... and he does a lot of shady shit with it," Zeus replied. He was scowling.

Claudia scowled back at him. "Is he still one of Marshall's clients?"

"How should I know? I have no idea what their client list looks like now, but I wouldn't be surprised. The two of them are two peas in a shady pod."

"He's one of the clients Marshall and I argued about the most," Lincoln chimed in.

With all the conversation in the room going on, it was impossible to hear the conversation on the television until Harris snapped out the word "Hush."

Quiet fell again as Lesley asked him a few more questions, like why he wanted to run—'to serve my state'—and what he was planning to run on—'we'll be rolling that information out over the coming weeks.'

"So, this is just an announcement without saying what he's standing for?" Darcie murmured, wrinkling her nose. She was sitting in one of the chairs across from Zeus, arms crossed over her chest.

No one replied because of what happened next on screen.

"Let me introduce you to my team. My head of security and my right-hand man, Marshall Devlin."

The room erupted with noise as the former third partner of Black Fox Security stepped up beside MacLeod, grinning widely and reaching up to brush his fingers against the black rose he was wearing in his lapel. The threat was finally becoming clear. Devlin was still intent on taking down Lincoln, Harris, and the rest of the firm, and if he managed to get MacLeod elected, he might just be able to do it.

42

CASSIDY

"Do you want to live with David?" Mistress Julie asked, tilting her head as though she could see into Cassidy's soul through the computer screen.

"Yes. But it's too soon."

"By whose timeline?"

Dammit. This was why she'd decided to bring it up in therapy. She'd wanted to talk through the possibility with a completely neutral third party. Especially since most of her friends up here were currently completely invested in the ramifications of knowing Black Fox had an enemy, and he was gunning for them with a bigger force than expected.

She hadn't wanted to bother her friends with her 'should I live with David' problem, which seemed pretty miniscule by comparison.

"I don't know," she admitted and waved her hand. "People. I mean, the last man I lived with was Don. Shouldn't I be more cautious? I mean, what do you think everyone at Stronghold would think if I told them I was moving in with the first guy I've dated since Don."

Mistress Julie's eyebrow rose.

"Why would their opinion about your decisions matter?"

Cassidy's mouth opened.

Closed.

"Well... I guess I don't want them to judge me."

"And that's a good enough reason to keep you from doing what you want to do?"

No.

But she didn't want to say it out loud. She scowled at the keyboard because she was too chicken to scowl at Mistress Julie herself.

"I thought you were going to tell me it's too soon," she grumbled.

"That's because you still don't trust yourself to make good decisions for yourself. You're hoping to find certainty in what other people think rather than in what you think and what you want for yourself. But the fact that you're willing to admit to yourself what you want, even though you're struggling to act on it, really shows how far you've come." Mistress Julie's tone was gentle, despite the way the words hit like blows to Cassidy's chest.

She lifted her hand to the center, right between her breasts, and rubbed where the ache had appeared.

"Ouch. That was a direct hit."

Mistress Julie smiled at her.

"You're doing great, Cassidy. It's a long, slow road. I suggest doing some journaling about what it is you really want. And remember, you don't have to make a decision right away. You also aren't trapped in whatever decision you make; you can always change your mind. If you move out, it sounds like David would be happy to have you move back in when you're ready. If you stay, he'll understand if you change your mind in the future and realize you need more space... and if he doesn't understand, then he's probably not the right man for you."

"He would understand," Cassidy said immediately. She had no doubt about that. David had been nothing but supportive. He didn't push her to make a decision, though he also didn't hesitate to make her feel welcome or to let her know that he wanted her there.

Even though they had a tendency to go back and forth on making decisions, she trusted him not to… well, not to be anything like Don if she changed her mind.

"I think I want to stay here." She sighed. "I just want someone to tell me it's okay to."

"It is okay to." Mistress Julie chuckled. "Whatever you choose is okay."

"Ugh, I hate that. I want there to be a right choice." A right choice would mean she wouldn't get trapped in a bad situation again. Not that she thought being with David was ever going to be a bad situation. Mistress Julie was right. She needed to start trusting herself more. She'd made the wrong choice in the past and suffered the consequences, but that didn't mean every choice she made would be the wrong one.

"Is there anything else going on that you want to talk about?"

"You mean other than getting my Dom shot and him wanting me to move in with him?" She giggled when Mistress Julie gave her a stern look. They'd already had plenty of long talks about her blaming herself, but sometimes, a little dark humor made her feel better. "It's a little crazy. I told you about the governor's race and Marshall Devlin and all that."

"Yes." Mistress Julie made a face. "I will say, I don't love the idea of you getting caught in the crosshairs of someone's vendetta that has nothing to do with you."

"So far, there's no reason to think he's doing anything but trying to take down the company," Cassidy said. "He seems like a pretty awful guy, but not like, take out innocent bystanders awful."

"Mmm." Clearly, the therapist wasn't convinced.

Cassidy's stomach did a little flip. She knew all too well how someone who felt entitled could react when denied what they wanted. But she wasn't leaving Pittsburgh, regardless. So far, there was definitely no reason to.

"Anyway, they've offered their services at a discount to Senator Marlin if she needs them. David's been going into the office. I'm back being his grandmother's companion for now. And I'm meeting his sister this weekend." The last words came out in a rush.

"Nervous?"

"Very. I got her brother shot." This time, she wasn't joking around when she said it, and Mistress Julie gave her another look. "I know, I know, but what if she sees it that way?"

"Do you know if she does?"

Cassidy shook her head sheepishly.

"I might have been purposefully avoiding being around David whenever he's on the phone with her. He hasn't said that she blames me, but I also don't know if he would tell me that. Or if she would tell him that she blames me."

"Okay, she blames you. What's the worst thing that happens?"

"David realizes she's right and dumps me." The pang in her chest was a lot harder than the one she'd had earlier. She didn't want to lose David.

"Do you think he would actually do that?"

Cassidy took in a long, deep breath, and let it out slowly, the way Mistress Julie had taught her. Some of the tension in her body leaked out with the air.

"No, he wouldn't." David did what he wanted to do. He'd become estranged from his parents over it. And he didn't blame her. The likelihood of his sister being able to convince him… "But that could cause a rift with his sister if she blames me, then he'd lose another family member, and it would be my fault."

"Would it? Or would it be her fault for blaming you?"

"Well, if you're going to make me be reasonable about it," Cassidy muttered, huffing and making Mistress Julie laugh. She scrubbed her hands over her face. "I just want her to like me. I don't want David to lose another family member."

"Both of which are very reasonable desires, but they're also not under your control. You'll do the best you can. You are a very likeable person, Cassidy. And David likes you, which is the most important thing."

David said he was falling for her. She was falling for him, too.

If it wasn't too soon to move in together, did that mean it wasn't too soon to use the word 'love', either?

<u>D</u><u>AVID</u>

Back at work and trying to grapple with the new dynamics of the team was interesting. They were all working out together as a team-building exercise. David couldn't do everything, but it was a good time to work in some of his physical therapy exercises. It also allowed him to step back and watch the shifting group dynamics now that Zeus was with them.

He was impressive, David had to admit.

The cohesion of the team could be a lot better, though. They made it through the workout and to the cooldown without any major snafus, so David had to be happy with that for now.

"What do we even call you?" Jensen asked, frowning.

"Zeus."

The man didn't crack a smile. He wasn't joking; he was being serious. Jensen rolled his eyes.

"I meant as a call sign."

Shrugging one shoulder, Zeus kept stretching.

"What about Rosemary?" Mason asked cheekily. Everyone except Zeus looked at him in confusion. "Because it's a spice."

And they were the Spice Doms. Different kind of spice, though.

"I'll answer to whatever," Zeus said indifferently.

He did not seem to be big on showing emotion. Any emotion. David didn't know him well enough to know if it was because he was new to the team and didn't trust them yet, either, or if this was just how he always was. *Or if it's because he's a plant of Marshall's, and he's trying not to get close to us before he betrays us.*

Except if Marshall really had sent in a plant, David would expect the man to be trying to ingratiate himself, working harder to charm everyone.

Cassidy had told him she thought he should be nicer to Zeus. It wasn't his fault he'd joined the team right before Marshall's big announcement. And he hadn't been part of Marshall's team long before that.

"Okay, Fennel," Jensen quipped, making everyone except Zeus and Drew chuckle.

David eyed Drew, who was far more somber than normal. He'd been intense during the training exercises. No matter how many times he'd apologized, no matter how many times David had reassured him that it wasn't his fault Don had gotten to Cassidy, it was clear Drew still blamed himself.

"Alright, everyone, good job today," David said to wrap things up. They had done a good job overall, even if everyone was still leery of Zeus. Eventually, they would start to trust him, or they wouldn't. If he couldn't integrate with the team, eventually, he would be fired. "Who's going to the Outlands tonight?"

Everyone raised their hand, including Zeus, which had everyone looking at him. He shrugged.

"I'm a member, even though I haven't been in a while. But my new girlfriend wants to go, so." He shrugged again, as if it didn't really matter to him, but he was willing to indulge his girlfriend. Which made David think a little better of him. He'd known Zeus was a member, all of Marshall's team had been, but none of them had been back since the firm split apart.

Everyone knew Lincoln and Gavin were friends.

"Great." David nodded firmly, as though saying so could make it so. "We can think of it as another team-building exercise."

"Cool." Jensen got to his feet. "See you tonight, Cinnamon."

"See you tonight, Baby." Zeus' deadpan tone made his response far funnier than if he'd hammed it up, and both Mason and Claudia snickered. Jensen scowled, but the edges of his mouth were twitching. Even Drew managed to crack a smile.

David had a feeling they'd be trying out different spice names on Zeus until one of them stuck. Thankfully, it seemed like he could take it. That one little response had done more to solidify his position with the team than any of the training exercises they'd done together.

His shoulder ached, but only a little, and he rubbed it as he put his things away.

"How's PT going?" Drew had come up so quietly, David hadn't

even heard him. It was amazing how sneaky Sporty could be when he wanted to.

"It's good. Not my favorite thing, but necessary. And it helps, obviously. The sooner I can get back to normal, the better, so Cassidy doesn't have the constant reminder... Every time she looks at my shoulder, I can see the guilt on her face." The same guilt he saw on Drew's face every time Drew looked at him or Cassidy.

"It wasn't her fault," Drew said immediately, sounding almost indignant.

No, of course not, because Drew wanted to take all the blame. David wasn't having that.

"No, it wasn't anyone's fault except Don's. Or maybe that asshole in the hallway who watched Don drag Cassidy away and did nothing. Though, even if he had tried to intervene, he might have gotten shot, and maybe Don would have had better aim. So, everything worked out the way it was supposed to." David finished tucking his gear into his bag and straightened up, hefting the strap over his right shoulder.

Silently watching him, Drew appeared to be thinking about what he said.

"I just keep thinking I missed things. The flat tire. The tailgating. Then letting Cassidy go to the bathroom by herself." He scrubbed his hand over his face, his overwhelming guilt clear as day. It had its talons in deep.

"She wasn't by herself; she was with Jennifer and Yasmine."

"Neither of who could protect her if Don had come up to all three of them."

"Don't let either of them hear you say that." Jennifer might not train with the team, but she was a black belt at the all-woman karate studio she'd been attending for years, and Yasmine had started Brazilian jujitsu a few years ago. David would bet on either of them over Don in a fair fight.

"He had a gun."

"Which we couldn't have known, just like we couldn't have known he was there. He shouldn't have been. It had to have been pure luck." They still hadn't figured out how Don knew where she was. The only thing that made sense was that he hadn't known, he'd just somehow come across them or been in the same place by chance.

Not knowing got under David's skin a little, but he'd long ago accepted that sometimes there were things that were never explained or that he didn't get to know the answer to. That was just life.

The important thing was that Don was never going to bother Cassidy again.

Drew blew out a long breath. "I'm not going to let you down again," he said heavily.

"You didn't let me down this time," David told him, and Drew nodded, but David could tell he didn't really mean it.

Hopefully, over time, he would start to believe it. Until then, David would drop a word in Mason's ear to make sure to talk to Drew about it.

43

The plug in her ass shifted as she walked through the doors to the Outlands, Master David's hand on the small of her back. It was their first night back at the club since Don's attack. They knew everyone wanted to see them, but they weren't planning on scening there. They were going to hang out, see people, then go home, where he was going to replace the plug with his cock.

She was really looking forward to it.

Especially since his sister was arriving tomorrow, and Cassidy wasn't sure how either she or David would feel about having kinky sex while his sister was in the same apartment. She didn't know if Audrey even knew David was kinky. It wasn't something she imagined siblings would talk about. At Stronghold, Master Patrick's submissive, Lexie, was also the sister of his best friend, and both Jake and Lexie made sure never to see each other naked. They played on separate nights.

With how private David was, she couldn't see him admitting that he was kinky to his sister.

"Oh my gosh! You're back! How are you?" Eben ran around from behind the front desk. She skidded to a halt in front of both of them, beaming widely, hands held up as she hesitated. "Can I hug you? What's safe to touch?"

"Me, yes; him, as long as you're careful with his left shoulder," Cassidy opened her arms, and Eben eagerly stepped in and squeezed tightly.

"I'm so glad you're okay."

"Me, too." Cassidy clung to the hug. It wasn't like she and Eben knew each other that well, but the other woman *cared*. It reminded her of being at Stronghold, where everyone had come to support her without knowing her at all.

She might miss her friends there, but she was stepping into a really similar community here. One where she wouldn't feel any guilt over Don having harassed them. Even though she knew no one at Stronghold or Marquis blamed her for his actions, she still felt the guilt.

This was a fresh start, but it was a fresh start in a place that felt a lot like home.

Finally, Eben let her go, then turned to David and gingerly hugged him, too, making sure to be careful of his shoulder.

"Okay, you two kids go have fun. There's a lot of people waiting to see you and do this," Eben said, grinning.

"Oh, I can only imagine," David said with a sigh, which made both Eben and Cassidy giggle.

Eben was right, of course. They had to pause at the door, where a grinning Master Aiden was waiting to say hello to them as well. He hadn't left his post, watching them with Eben since they had to walk by him, anyway.

After that, almost as soon as they were in the club, they were mobbed. There were some people who hung back or who didn't hug Cassidy but just waited patiently for Master David to introduce her to them so they could welcome her. No one seemed to blame her that he'd been hurt, which was a relief.

As the crowd thinned out, she could see glimpses of the Black Fox Doms and her friends over by the bar. They were hanging back, probably because they knew David and Cassidy would make it over to them eventually—which they did. There was a new addition to the group this evening, and he'd brought his girlfriend, just like David had warned her.

Cassidy had met Zeus very briefly. He was incredibly intimidating, though it didn't seem like he was trying to be; he just had that aura. Tall, broad-shouldered, with a completely smooth head, eyes that were so dark brown they were nearly black, slightly tanned skin from the summer sun, and a full beard, he looked even more intimidating than usual in his leather pants and vest with an earring hanging from his left ear.

He had his arm around a blonde woman, whose back was currently to Cassidy so she couldn't see her face, and the woman was talking animatedly to Claudia, Naomi, and Yasmine. That was good. Maybe if she could make a connection to the other women, everyone would be nicer to Zeus.

She knew David was wary of the other man, but if he was a spy sent by Marshall, he was a terrible choice. It was way too obvious. But maybe he could be turned into one if everyone was mean to him and never accepted him. Cassidy didn't know him well enough to automatically trust him, but she wasn't going to be outwardly skeptical, either.

As she and David approached, everyone perked up, happy to see them coming. Yasmine looked as elegantly gorgeous as always in a navy-blue corset with black lace edging, her hair pulled back into a half-up, half-down style, and her makeup stunningly flawless. Beside her, Naomi was dressed in a cute pink teddy that Cassidy would be willing to bet included a ruffled skirt, hidden under the table at the moment. She'd changed her hairstyle again, and it was now in a puffy braid that wound around her head, impossible to tell where it started and where it ended, with the ends neatly tucked in.

Both of them were obviously in good moods.

Claudia was clearly feeling more suspicious, sitting back in her chair rather than forward, her arms crossed under her breasts. Her black vinyl corset came to two high points above her breasts, dipping into a deep V between them to show off her cleavage. Her dark hair was pulled back in a high bun, and black beads dripped down from her ears. There was something about the ensemble that made Cassidy think of Catwoman.

Zeus' girlfriend was wearing a slinky red dress rather than a corset, something that she would have been able to wear on a date to any restaurant before coming to the club. Her blonde hair waved around her shoulders, curling over her upper back. The red skirt of her dress fluttered around her thighs as both of them turned to see who everyone was looking at.

Cassidy and the blonde's mouths dropped open at the same time.

"Cassidy?" the other woman squealed in apparent delight.

"Noelle?" Cassidy was utterly bewildered, though she didn't have time to do much before Noelle threw herself at Cassidy and hugged her tightly.

"Oh, my goodness, it's so good to see you! I'm so glad you're okay. I didn't realize you were the one everyone was talking about tonight!" Noelle kept hugging her, and Cassidy didn't really feel like she had much of a choice but to hug her back as her mind raced.

She hadn't thought about Noelle since she moved up here. She hadn't gotten to know Noelle at Stronghold, though they'd been introduced. There'd always been some gossip around the other woman, but she'd had a group of friends at the club. One of who she'd been the bridesmaid for before eloping with the groom.

Shouldn't she be married?

Also, Cassidy had thought she'd gotten kicked out of the club for some reason. Maybe she'd been mistaken, though. Maybe Noelle had decided to leave because of all the drama after she'd eloped with Jeremy.

There had been a lot going on in Cassidy's life when that was all happening, and she'd only ever gotten peripheral gossip, although she knew that Amy—the bride—had ended up moving in with Zach and Kincaid. She and Zach were good friends.

"Um, hi," she managed to say finally. "I didn't expect to see you here."

"Oh, my gosh, I know. I've had the most awful time of it," Noelle said, releasing Cassidy and shaking her head. "I got married, which was the worst mistake of my life, and we've already gotten the marriage annulled, but I needed a fresh start, and I asked my job if they could move me to a different office, and then I found out there's a club here and, well... here I am." She opened her arms wide, smiling at Cassidy, but it wasn't entirely genuine. There was something in her eyes.

Fear, maybe? Uncertainty?

Cassidy didn't know the full story of what had gone down at Stronghold, and she'd definitely never heard Noelle's side of it. Granted, marrying her friend's fiancé was a pretty shitty thing to do, but it was even shittier of the fiancé. And it sounded like things hadn't worked out after all, so maybe Noelle had learned her lesson.

Plus, if she was Zeus' girlfriend and Cassidy wanted David to be nicer to Zeus...

She smiled back at her.

"It's good to see you again," she said, even though that was an exaggeration. It wasn't like she and Noelle had ever interacted, and she wasn't sure how she felt about the other woman; on the other hand, she didn't have anything to base her opinion on other than hearsay, which didn't seem fair. The brief statement seemed to be all Noelle had hoped for because that hint of unease disappeared entirely, and Noelle beamed at her.

"I had no idea you would be here," Noelle said. "When did you move up here?"

"Oh, um, a few weeks ago... it feels like a lot longer." A *lot* longer. But she wasn't going to get into all of that right now if Noelle didn't know anything about it.

Cassidy's presence and greeting seemed to make both Yasmine and Naomi feel a little more comfortable with the woman, and even Claudia started to thaw. She wasn't sure how she felt about that, but Noelle seemed perfectly nice. Maybe she had learned her lesson.

Any man who was willing to cheat on his fiancé, then marry another woman on their wedding day must be a terrible person. Cassidy herself was proof of how a woman could get involved with an awful man without realizing it. It seemed Noelle had gotten herself out of it, too, though. Now, she was with Zeus, and she was exerting herself to ingratiate herself with everyone and to make things easier for him, as though she could sense he wasn't entirely welcome, and she wanted to change that for him.

So, they had a goal in common, too.

As things went, it was a pretty enjoyable evening, though the plug in her bottom meant it wasn't an entirely comfortable one.

---

*D*AVID

Being back at the Outlands made David feel more settled. Being there with Cassidy made him feel like everything about his life was coming together.

Zeus was a possible complication, but everyone slowly relaxed around him throughout the evening. The presence of his girlfriend helped. No one on the team was enough of a dick to want to make a man look bad in front of his date. There was something about her that was unsettling Cassidy, though. She hid it well, but David had gotten to know her well enough at this point that he could tell. He waited until they were back in the car to ask.

He'd been hoping for sexier talk before they got home, but he didn't think he was going to be able to move to sexy discussion when he was wondering what was going on with his new teammate's girlfriend.

"So... Noelle. You knew her back in Maryland?"

Cassidy nodded, looking out the window, which was another indication that something about Noelle was bothering her. It was late and dark, so there wasn't much to see other than streetlamps and businesses that had closed up for the night.

"Did you not like her or something?" he asked. That hadn't seemed to be the case, but one thing he'd learned about Cassidy was that she would rather make herself uncomfortable than make anyone else uncomfortable. And he knew she wanted him to be nicer to

Zeus, so she would definitely bend over backward to make him comfortable over herself.

"I didn't really know her. I just knew *of* her and... well... a lot of what I knew wasn't that great. But it was all second-hand and from people who didn't have a lot of reason to like her. I also don't know many details because, well..." She hunched her shoulders. "I kind of had a lot going on at the time. By the time things were going on with her, Don had started showing up around me and around the club, so I'd basically stopped going to Stronghold and Marquis. I don't really know exactly what happened, but I could probably ask and find out."

It didn't sound like she was too keen on doing that, though.

"Some people just don't get along, I guess," he said with a shrug. That was just a fact of life, and not everyone had to get along.

"I do know that she was sleeping with one of her friends fiancé, and that's who she ended up marrying... on the day that he was supposed to marry her friend," Cassidy said. "They eloped to Vegas."

David blinked.

"Well, shit."

"Pretty much. So, yeah, I can understand why some people wouldn't like her, but... he's just as much, if not more, to blame. And she got the marriage annulled. Maybe she's just a woman who made some bad choices." Cassidy was looking out the window so determinedly, it was obvious she wasn't just thinking of Noelle.

Reaching over, David put his hand on her thigh and squeezed. She immediately put her hand over his, curling her fingers around the edges of his palm, and he could feel her relax under his touch.

"You don't have to ask anyone what happened with her if you don't want to," he said. "There's no pressing reason to. People make bad choices all the time, and she did say she was here for a fresh start. It wouldn't be fair to bring all the baggage from other people to her here if she's trying to create a new life for herself."

Letting out a long sigh, Cassidy leaned back in her seat and looked over at him. He glanced back at her, happy to see that she was smiling, and he gave her leg another little squeeze.

Good, they'd gotten what was bothering her out of the way.

"Are you having a good night?" he asked. "It wasn't too over-whelming with everyone wanting to welcome you back?"

"I did," she said immediately, then glanced at him. Her fingers stroked along his. "It wasn't too bad for you with all the hugging? No pain?"

"Nope, everyone was very careful." He chuckled. "Don't worry, little spark, my arm is just fine, and when we get home, I'm going to make your night even better."

He couldn't wait to bury himself in her sweet little ass and claim the final part of her. Neither could she, by the way she started squirming in her seat.

44

CASSIDY

Moaning, Cassidy pushed her bottom back at Master David as much as she could when she was bent over the side of his bed. With a pillow under her hips, it was the exact right height for her to be at a comfortable angle, fully supported, which also meant fully unable to get away from whatever he was doing to her.

Not that she wanted to get away.

"Good thing I got shot in my left shoulder and not my right, huh?" he asked, chuckling, just as his hand came down on her upturned cheek again. Cassidy gasped as the heat from the slap flared through her, then turned her head to shoot him a dirty look over her shoulder.

"That's not funny."

"I was being sincere." He winked at her and brought his hand down again, making her whip her head back around to a more comfortable position as the stinging burn settled into her skin. "Granted, you wouldn't go unspanked either way, but it's definitely easier to still have use of my right hand."

As if to prove his point, his hand came down again, right on the undercurve of her sit spot. Squealing, Cassidy rocked forward, not that there was anywhere she could really go since she was trapped against the bed. Her stiffened nipples rubbed against the sheets, aching little buds eager for stimulation.

Master David had declined to clamp them, saying he didn't want her distracted from the feel of his cock sliding into her ass for the first time. That had made her pussy clench. Though, apparently, he didn't think the throbbing aftermath of a spanking would be distracting.

Or maybe that just didn't count since it was all to do with her ass.

Whatever the reason, Cassidy wasn't going to complain about getting a good girl spanking.

Her bottom was hot and pink, and it made her insides all quivery and needy.

"Such a pretty pink ass," Master David said, rubbing his hand over the sensitized skin, making Cassidy moan and lift her hips again in response. The warmth between his palm and her bottom felt good. Her pussy clenched emptily, her inner muscles squeezing around the plug that was still in place, keeping her ready for him.

"Thank you, Sir. May I have another?" she asked cheekily, shaking her hips at him.

As he laughed, his hand came down on her other sit spot, making her squeal and wriggle again. Apparently, he'd had enough of the spanking now; she felt him tugging at the plug in her bottom. There was still enough lube to make the slide easy, but the thick bulb stretched her entrance wide, making her shudder and gasp as it was forced open for a second time. She let out a long sigh as the tapered toy slid out of her.

The emptiness felt very strange after having it in all evening, though she knew that wasn't going to last very long.

It only took a moment before David's hand ran over her lower back, the thick tip of his cock pressing against her crinkled opening.

"Are you ready for me, little spark?" he asked, rubbing her lower back muscles with his right hand.

"Yes, Sir," she replied eagerly, pushing her hips back at him, feeling the tip of his cock starting to spread her open. He chuckled and pressed his hand down, pinning her to the bed, so she couldn't move back like that again, taking charge of their pace with ease.

And his pace was glacial.

Cassidy moaned, shuddering, squirming, as his cock very, very, very slowly slid into her ass. The tapered plug had been easier in a lot of ways, starting small and working its way up in size to the thick bulb, whereas David's cock was as thick at the tip as it was at the base.

The extended insertion ached uncomfortably even as her pussy spasmed with hot need. She whimpered, writhing under his hand, panting as she was filled up, inch by slow inch. It had been a really long time since she'd had anal sex, and she hadn't realized what a difference that would make, especially since he'd prepared her with the plug.

Now, she could understand why he hadn't wanted to put the clamps on her. There really was nothing for her to focus on except her ass. The lingering throbbing from her spanking even seemed to fade as her attention narrowed to the thick shaft forcing its way into her tight passage. It wasn't comfortable, though it wasn't completely painful, either.

It felt incredibly intimate, even as it made her feel more vulnerable, more submissive.

God, she'd missed this.

Though she also wasn't sure how much more she could take, he kept going.

"That's it, sweetheart," he murmured, rubbing her lower back. "Only a few more inches."

A few more inches?

Cassidy whimpered again, but she knew she would take it. For him. She wanted to be his good girl. The gradual invasion was, in some ways, more difficult than if he'd thrust in more quickly. Her fingers dug into the sheets of the bed as she panted for breath, his cock sliding in deeper and deeper, stretching her open more and more.

When his body finally came to rest against her pinked cheeks, she let out a moan of pure relief, her muscles clenching around the invader buried inside her. He felt huge. Thick. As if he'd stretched her almost to the point of breaking.

And so damn good.

It hurt in all the right ways.

"There we go," he murmured, running his hand over her hot cheeks, then sliding it up her back. "How does that feel, little spark?"

"Hot." She shivered, her muscles clenching. "Full. Good."

Master David chuckled again.

"Glad to hear it."

Then he carefully gripped her hips, using both hands, and Cassidy stilled. The last thing she wanted to do was cause him to move his left shoulder in a manner that would hurt, which meant she had to hold absolutely still. No matter how difficult that was.

He drew back, taking her breath with him as the sensation rippled through her, then she cried out as he thrust in. The movement was firmly controlled, much faster than the initial insertion, much harder, but not so rough she couldn't handle it. His body bounced off her buttocks and immediately pulled back again in retreat, making her toes curl as he began to ride her with long, steady, firm strokes that sent her senses scrambling.

"Fuck, you feel good," he growled as he slammed into her, leaving her utterly breathless as she was impaled over and over.

Every nerve ending felt as though it was awash with sensation, her muscles clenching and gripping him internally but finding no purchase along his lubricated length. Every thrust into her, every withdrawal, rasped across her senses, driving her pleasure higher and higher.

Although she was doing her best, she couldn't hold completely still, and she rocked back against him as the need inside her grew. Her hips rose up to meet his thrusts, rocking herself back against him as her nipples dragged over the sheets beneath her.

"Play with yourself, little spark. Use your fingers on your clit and make yourself come for me while I fuck your tight little ass." His voice was low, dark, and sinfully commanding.

Just his words nearly brought Cassidy off.

Thrusting her hand between her body and the pillow beneath her hips, it wasn't difficult to find her slippery clit, slick with the desire leaking from her pussy. She whimpered as her fingers grazed the little nub, then pressed.

"Oh, fuck," she gasped as the combined sensations pulsed inside her. She could feel him thickening, feeling harder than ever inside her as they raced toward the finish line together.

DAVID

The moment Cassidy's fingers found her clit, the tight squeeze of Cassidy's ass around his cock intensified. He groaned, rocking in deeper, feeling the play of her muscles over his thick length, his pleasure skyrocketing ever higher as he rode her. It was pure erotic heaven being balls deep inside her, knowing that she trusted him this much, that she was willing to be so vulnerable.

"That's it, sweetheart," he murmured, feeling his own desire climbing higher and higher. The ache in his shoulder didn't matter in the least as he tightened his fingers around her hips, drawing her back against him, filling her with his cock. His spine tingled, his ecstasy rising as he heard her cry out.

She bucked against him, her muscles clenching in rippling spasms that pulled at his cock. With a low cry, David buried himself completely inside her, her rapture setting off his own. Rocking against her, feeling the warm heat of her cheeks against his groin, he shuddered as her muscles milked every last drop of cum from his dick, leaving him utterly replete.

With a groan, he let himself slowly collapse on top of her. With both of their feet on the floor, she only had to bear half his body weight.

His dick was still buried inside her as she shuddered with the last remnants of her pleasure. The feel of her soft skin against his made him smile, and he turned his head to give the back of her shoulders a kiss.

"Good girl," he murmured and smiled even wider when he felt her ass clench around him again in response.

It was deserved, though. She was his good girl.

They stayed like that for a few moments, getting their breath back, before he got them both up and into the shower. Cassidy leaned on him as the water slid over their bodies, his cum dripping down her thighs to disappear into the drain along with the bubbles from the soap he was moving in slow circles over her skin. Her arms were bent at the elbow, hands in little fists that were tucked under his chin. His left arm wrapped around her back, though he wasn't holding her up with it at all. It was more like she was supporting his arm.

"Hey, Cassidy."

"Yeah?" She tipped her head back so she could look at him. Her eyes were low-lidded and sleepy, the smile on her face one of utter feminine satisfaction. David couldn't help but give the tip of her nose a little kiss before continuing.

"If it was too soon to ask you to move in with me, does that mean it's too soon for me to tell you that I love you?"

She blinked as she took in his words, then her eyes widened when they registered.

"I... you..." She stumbled over her words, turning her hands so they were palms flat against his chest. "You love me?"

Half of his mouth tipped up into a smile. She sounded so disbelieving, but it was the truth. He'd been falling for her since the moment he'd met her. Sometimes, it didn't take long to know something was true, and this was one of those times.

"Yeah, I love you."

The water slid over them, hot against their skin, and she was warm where she was pressed against him. Droplets clung to her lashes as she stared at him. Then she started to smile.

No, she started to grin.

"I love you, too. So, it must not be too soon."

That made him laugh.

"Good, that's something we can agree on then." And it hadn't taken their usual back and forth. Some things were just too obvious for even them.

Lowering his mouth to hers, he kissed her, claiming her as the water swept over their bodies, washing away all the past and cleansing them to go into the future together.

EPILOGUE

MASON

"I'm getting married." Staring at his reflection in the interior door of the elevator, Mason had to admit that didn't sound so bad. It was time, after all. "I'm getting married to Yasmine Jafari."

That sounded a little odder.

Maybe because of the way everyone at the club joked that she would probably never be able to get married. Not with how all her relationships turned out. Which was why she'd been willing to try letting her parents arrange her marriage. Skip all the pesky dating stuff, which was always where her relationships went wrong, and jump straight to the lifelong commitment.

It made sense.

They made sense.

They both wanted the same things out of life. They'd had long talks about their desires, how they pictured their futures, their financial outlooks, children—not just how many but also their parenting philosophies—pretty much everything a couple should talk about before getting into a marriage but often didn't. Mason might specialize in trauma counseling rather than marriage counseling, but he still knew the basics.

They'd covered all of them.

And she was a beautiful woman.

He would have to be made of stone not to recognize that.

Yet when they'd kissed last night, there had been no spark. No kindling. No excitement.

It had been a nice kiss, but it had been missing something.

Passion.

But he felt like that couldn't be too unusual for an arranged relationship. They'd been pushed together by outside forces, not by mutual chemistry. Surely, that chemistry would come eventually. The passion.

They just needed to get to know each other better. His brain needed to adjust to the idea that she wasn't off limits. They'd never scened together before, even at the club, because Yasmine had been a relationship person—and after her relationships ended, her boyfriend always found 'the one'—and Mason hadn't been looking for commitment.

It was time, though. He was getting older, and he wanted things out of his life he needed a life partner for.

Besides, it had been a long time since he'd felt highly passionate about any of his sexual partners. Maybe that was just part of growing up. The high, the excitement, maybe that was all part of being in your twenties, and now, emotions were steadier because the dips and peaks had already been experienced. He and Yasmine could settle into a very comfortable relationship based on mutual respect and enjoyment of each other's company, and they'd probably have very satisfying sex.

She was a skilled submissive, he was a skilled dominant, and they had a lot of kinks in common.

She was exactly the kind of woman he'd always pictured himself marrying, so it would work out, eventually.

The door to the elevator opened, revealing the glass wall that looked into the lobby of the Black Fox Security main office. Since it was a Saturday morning, Mason wasn't expecting to see anyone there, so he was surprised that a woman was standing inside the doors at the front desk. She had her left arm up, leaning against the desk, her back to the glass, staring at… what? He wasn't sure. The only thing that was on the wall for her to stare at was the firm's sign.

Red hair had been pulled back into a high ponytail, tied with a green and white polka-dot ribbon that matched the green and white collared sleeveless shirt she was wearing. Plentiful curves filled out a pair of jean capris that hugged her legs all the way down to mid-calf, where the straps of her green wedge sandals started, tied in little bows just above her ankles.

Frowning, doing his best not to check out her plumply curved ass and how nicely it filled out her jeans because he was now an affianced man, Mason strode forward and ran his ID badge over the scanner to open the door. It beeped in confirmation, and the door clicked, unlocking.

The woman inside turned as he pulled the door open, finally revealing her front, which was just as attractive as her backside. She was an absolute goddess.

Lush curves packed into the polka-dot top, unbuttoned far enough to show off deep cleavage that invited a man to crawl inside and hibernate for the winter. Beautiful face made up with thick black eyeliner and red lips that denoted the pin-up girl style from the 1950s. She was wearing a green and white necklace of chunky beads around her neck.

Staring at her, Mason was hit with an unexpected—and unwanted—wave of utter lust… the type he hadn't experienced since he was young, dumb, and full of cum. His dick went half-hard immediately as his brain launched straight into fantasies of what her lips would look like wrapped around it. Every cell in his body demanded that he do something, *say* something, to charm her and get her into his bed, then keep her there for the rest of her life.

Her green eyes widened, and her expression lit up with delight.

"Mason? Oh my God, it's so nice to finally meet you!" The vision of his desires jumped toward him, only taking a few quick steps to throw herself into his arms.

Soft curves squished against him in the best way possible, and all the blood drained from the rest of his body straight to his dick, making him dizzy. He swayed slightly, struggling against the shocking assault from his libido, his brain finally catching up to him as he realized who she must be—even though she didn't look anything like the pictures he'd seen in the past.

"Audrey?" Her name came out in a croak as his hands settled around her body. Thankfully, he retained enough brainpower not to let them slide down to her ass, but holy fuck... just holding her was pure torture. She smelled like sugar and cinnamon and freshly baked goods.

The desire to lick her was overwhelming.

She squeezed, then released him and stepped back. Thank God. Maybe he could finally get his bearings if she wasn't touching him, if his nose wasn't full of her delicious scent.

"I didn't know I was going to be seeing you here, or I would have brought your baklava—I made three different kinds so you can tell me which one you like the best," David's little sister said, beaming at him.

Fuck, she wasn't just hot, and he wasn't just attracted to her. She'd made him baklava. Three different varieties. He almost whimpered.

She is David's little sister, he told his dick. It had absolutely no effect. The traitorous body part knew what it wanted, and it didn't care whose sister she was.

"Thank you."

"Sorry," she said, wrinkling her nose and taking another step back. Her head tilted to the side as she reached up to tug on the end of her ponytail. "I know I come on kind of strong. I'm trying to get better about it."

"I like how you come on," he said before he could think about what he was saying. "I didn't mind." He wanted to reassure her, then hunt down anyone who had ever made her feel less than perfect for being so warm and inviting and punch them in the face.

Fuck. What is happening to me?

This wasn't him. This wasn't who he was. This wasn't how he reacted to women.

"Hey, Audrey, ready to go?" David came around the corner, and Mason had never been simultaneously so glad and so disappointed to see someone. "Oh, hey, Mason. What are you doing here?"

Not perving on your sister, that's for sure.

"Uh, I just had to pick some stuff up."

"Same." David held up the folder in his hand as he slung his other arm around his sister's shoulders. Was he looking at Mason weird? Or was Mason just being paranoid? "Audrey and I are headed over to brunch with our grandmother now. Cassidy is driving her and meeting us there."

"I love Cassidy," Audrey enthused, beaming up at David. "So does Grandma. We stayed up 'til two o'clock last night talking. I adore her."

"She's pretty great," Mason agreed. It seemed polite to agree with her since she was so excited. It wasn't just so she could look at him and smile the way she was smiling at her brother.

Except that when she did, it felt like the sun had just come out from behind the clouds and was shining on him again.

"She's so great. But we do need to go so we can meet her. Will you be at Jensen's tonight?"

That's where they were having the welcome gathering for Audrey so people could see her—or, in Mason's case, meet her. Though obviously, he'd jumped the gun. They were going to Jensen's because his house was a lot better set up for hosting than David's was. A lot of people were going to be there.

Including his new fiancé.

Yasmine.

They were making the announcement tonight.

Fuck.

"Yeah, he's coming," David said, looking at Mason oddly, and he realized he'd been standing in place, not answering Audrey's question because his brain was finally catching up to how truly fucked he was right now.

"Yeah, I'm coming."

"Great." She brightened again, and it hurt to watch because he knew he shouldn't be enjoying that brightness the way he was. "We'll see you there!"

"See you there," he echoed, turning to watch them walk out of the office. Her hips sashayed with every step, her delectable bottom shifting with the movement in a manner that made him feel a little weak. Like falling to his knees so he could bite that round, juicy—

Mason coughed and turned his head away as the elevator doors opened to admit them.

He needed to get his head on straight. Because he'd made an agreement. Because he couldn't derail his life plan for a woman he'd just met. Because instant lust was just a chemical, hormonal reaction, it didn't mean anything.

And because he was getting married to Yasmine Jafari.

*****

Mason's dilemma continues to get worse in Cuffs and Cupcakes.

ACKNOWLEDGMENTS

I have a lot of people to thank for helping me with this book.

My amazing beta readers, who are invaluable in helping me catch mistakes, doing the initial grammar and word checks, identifying continuity issues, and working through problems with me. Marie, Candida, Marta, Rara, and Katherine – you all make these books so much better!

My Patreon readers who not only read ahead but are kind enough to give me invaluable feedback as they're reading.

Another extra special thank you to Katherine, who got me started down this career path and has been by my metaphorical side ever since.

Thank you to my husband for his continued loved and support. I could not do this without you.

And, as always, a big thank you to all of you for buying and reading my work... if you love it, please leave a review!

ABOUT THE AUTHOR

Golden Angel is a USA Today best-selling author of heart and bottom warming romance.

She is happily married, old enough to know better but still too young to care, and a big fan of happily-ever-afters, strong heroes and heroines, and sizzling chemistry.

When she's not writing, she can often be found on the couch reading, in front of her sewing machine making a new cosplay, hanging out with her friends, or wandering the Maryland Renaissance Fair.

www.goldenangelromance.com

BB bookbub.com/authors/golden-angel
g goodreads.com/goldeniangel
f facebook.com/GoldenAngelAuthor
o instagram.com/goldeniangel

OTHER BOOKS BY GOLDEN ANGEL

Contemporary BDSM Romance

Venus Rising Series (MFM Romance)

The Venus School

Venus Aspiring

Venus Desiring

Venus Transcendent

Venus Wedding

Venus Rising Box Set

Stronghold Doms Series

The Sassy Submissive

Taming the Tease

Mastering Lexie

Pieces of Stronghold

Breaking the Chain

Bound to the Past

Stripping the Sub

Tempting the Domme

Hardcore Vanilla

Steamy Stocking Stuffers

A Sassy Christmas

Entering Stronghold Box Set

Nights at Stronghold Box Set

Stronghold: Closing Time Box Set

Masters of Marquis Series

Bondage Buddies

Master Chef

Law & Disorder

Switch Play

Legally Bound

Shallow Submission

Hidden Away

Secret Submission

Third Wheel

Black Fox Security Doms

Danger and Dominance

Cuffs and Cupcakes

Security and Submission

Whips and Weddings

Rescue and Ropes

Bondage and Bad Guys

Dungeons & Doms Series

Dungeon Master

Dungeon Daddy

Dungeon Showdown

Dungeons & Doms Boxset

Daddies Everywhere

Chef Daddy

Foosball Daddies

Taco Daddy

Cheese Daddy

Garden Daddy

Daddies Everywhere Boxset

Cherry Popping Daddies

Emily by Golden Angel

Lottie by Stella Moore

Titania by Raisa Greenwood

Standalone Daddy Dom

Little Villain

Historical Spanking Romance

Domestic Discipline Quartet

Birching His Bride

Dealing With Discipline

Punishing His Ward

Claiming His Wife

The Domestic Discipline Quartet Box Set

Bridal Discipline Series

Philip's Rules

Gabrielle's Discipline

Lydia's Penance

Benedict's Commands

Arabella's Taming

Pride and Punishment Box Set

Commands and Consequences Box Set

Deception and Discipline

A Season for Treason

A Season for Scandal

A Season for Smugglers

A Season for Spies

Desire and Discipline

A Season for Bliss

A Season for Desire

A Season for Christmas.

Indecent Dukes

The Duke's Indecent Scandal

The Duke's Indecent Match

The Duke's Indecent Purchase

The Duke's Indecent Desire

The Duke's Indecent Proposal

The Duke's Indecent Secret

The Duke's Indecent Courtship

Bridgewater Brides

Their Harlot Bride

Standalone

Marriage Training

The Duke's Pursuit

Rogue Booty

Sci-fi Romance

Tsenturion Masters Series with Lee Savino

Alien Captive

Alien Tribute

Alien Abduction

Standalone

Mated on Hades

Shifter Romance

Big Bad Bunnies Series

Chasing His Bunny

Chasing His Squirrel

Chasing His Puma

Chasing His Polar Bear

Chasing His Honey Badger

Chasing Her Lion

Night of the Wild Stags

Chasing Tail Box Set

Chasing Tail... Again Box Set